Bite Me

Bite Me

by A. J. Louise

This book is a work of fiction. All of the characters, organizations, and events portrayed in this novel are either products of the author's imagination or are used fictitiously. Any resemblance to actual events or persons, living or dead, is coincidental.

Copyright © 2026 A.J. Louise.

All rights reserved, including the right to reproduce, distribute, or transmit in any form or by any means, including photocopying, recording, or other electronic or mechanical methods, without the prior written permission of the publisher, except as permitted by U.S. copyright law. For information regarding subsidiary rights, please visit the author's website.

ajlouisebooks.com

ISBN-13: 979-8-9938239-0-4 (ebook)
ISBN-13: 979-8-9938239-1-1 (paperback)
ISBN-13: 979-8-9938239-2-8 (standard hardcover)
ISBN-13: 979-8-9938239-3-5 (hardcover w/ dust jacket and custom case binding)
ISBN-13: 979-8-9938239-4-2 (audiobook)

Library of Congress Control Number: 2025925479
Cover Design: Holly Dunn Design
Interior Formatting: Holly Dunn Design

*For the graceless, unruly, annoyingly precocious.
Never be afraid to bite back.*

Bite Me is a coming-of-age story set within the cinematic landscape of late 20th-century culture. It is a provocative, darkly comedic narrative that contains: Explicit Sexual Content, Religious Trauma, Slut Shaming, Brief Depictions of Violence, References to Child Abuse, References to Domestic Violence, References to Substance Abuse, Homophobia, Homophobic Slurs, Adult Image-Based Abuse, Grooming, Graphic Depictions of Sexual Assault, Victim Blaming, Sexual Manipulation and Pressuring, and Depictions of Post-Traumatic Stress Disorder.

Please consider this advisory before choosing to read.

You are worth it.

Prologue

It is a truth universally acknowledged, that a horny girl in possession of spreadable legs, must be in want of a brutal fucking.

I'm no modern Austen, but if truer words were to ever be spoken, they certainly wouldn't fall from my painted lips. The shade of which matching the red rows of fictitious graduation caps separating me from an imposingly elevated stage. Sinfully enough, the packed gymnasium isn't the least bit to blame for the heat flushing my fair skin a rosy pink. Here we all sit, finally over eighteen, surrounded by blurred faces typewritten into my mind's eye. While the scene before me is nothing but a product of imagination, none of my classmates are the wiser that an obscure girl among them happens to be lost in the throes of her perverse thoughts. While they sit with impeccable posture for the flashing cameras and watchful eyes of the audience, I rest with a slight arch upon crossing my legs. Humming in bliss as the added pressure eases the ache between my thighs. Momentarily, anyway.

I discreetly rock my hips when the need grows like an incipient flame. Attempting—and pitifully failing—to keep focus on the platform to my front. Red and white balloons line the wide backdrop in our school colors, with a hand-painted banner that reads:

PEAKSHIRE HIGH: CLASS OF 1994

In such a desirous state, I wasn't concerned with looking pretty for the packed bleachers framing our student body on both sides. Instead, I tilt my chin high. Trying to get the best view possible of our valedictorian as he gives his congratulatory speech—the most renowned of our entire class, and the subject of my indecent thoughts.

Andrew Roth.

Even adorned in an oversized gown and shimmery white stole, he was the most gorgeous human to ever walk the halls of Peakshire. Sculpted with strong features, dark hair meticulously styled like he wasn't trying, and eyes blue enough to put the Albuquerque sky to shame. His naturally tall, muscular build made him the picturesque athlete in our years at this school. Where he'd commanded the football team as captain in tandem with parading as the auspicious student every teacher dreamed of mentoring. And to top all that perfection? God-given charisma to complement. I was almost certain he had a girlfriend. No doubt one of the bleached blonde cheerleaders or academic beauties that landed Peakshire's hottest guys with nothing but a flick of their bejeweled wrists. But I couldn't put her to a name. And, even if I could, that name had a habit of changing every other week.

He stands before the podium, flashing his sensual smile as the speech drags on and on. I listen to every word, but hear very few. My attention is sooner occupied with the flexes of his jaw, and how his tongue sweeps over his bottom lip in a way that makes me wonder what else it's capable of. I bite hard on my own when a particularly strong wave of arousal pulses through me. All the fantasies of what I wished our valedictorian would do to me were coming to a vicious head during what would undoubtedly be our final hours together in the procession of formally starting our adult lives. I almost forget that I'm attending a graduation ceremony at all as I allow the sensations to overspill. Shutting my eyes to relish the desires before they're tossed away with the wave of our flying caps.

That is, until two unexpected words slip from Andrew Roth's mouth. Traveling through the discount microphone to command the gymnasium. Or rather, me. "Rosie Ginger..."

My glittery lids snap open. It was the first time he'd ever spoken my name. I brush the light-brown fringe from my forehead with a single finger, returning his gaze the instant I realize he's aiming it at me.

"Rosie Ginger," he repeats, voice falling breathy with unkempt emotion. "I can't walk out of this room for the last time without you knowing how I feel."

Suddenly, every capped head in the pool of graduating seniors turns my way. I pay them no mind. If anything, their awareness evokes a dangerous confidence. Andrew Roth is speaking to me, and everyone else is made to witness. Throwing caution out with my dignity, I stand up. Emerging from the ocean of graduates, shameless as can be. Only focusing on the man of my dreams, who draws me forward with the need in his eyes alone.

Andrew grips the edges of the podium tightly as his profession continues, "I was never brave enough to admit it, not even to myself."

My high stilettos clack on the wood floor as I step to the center aisle parting the sea of red. Every student of Peakshire's class of '94, along with every member of the surrounding audience, watches as the most euphoric moment of my life occurs in real time. Longing wells on Andrew's deviously handsome face as I stalk closer and closer to the stage.

"I don't care about being valedictorian, and I don't care about this school." He says, just as murmurs begin to ramify among the crowd. "All I care about is you…"

Finally, I've reached the edge of the dais. Peering up at him through mascaraed lashes, my pigmented lips tilt in a mischievous smile. He mimics the gesture, blue eyes darkening as he caps his speech with an ending the school will never forget.

"Rosie Ginger, I want to fuck you senseless. Right here on this stage."

Stunned gasps and whispers erupt amongst our collage of peers. Keeping focus on our valedictorian, my legs carry me up carpeted stairs until he and I share the wide pedestal. Andrew meets me halfway, *stopping when we're close enough that I can feel his shallow breaths on my skin. Despite my heels supplying a few extra inches, he still towers above me. Forcing me to stare up at him with the wildest combination of feigned innocence and the outward demand that he take exactly what he'd just admitted to craving.*

He takes it. He takes me.

Into his strong, athletically toughened hands before clutching the front of my graduation gown. Unwavering hunger flashes across Andrew's features a blink before he's tossing me onto a nearby table stacked with sealed diplomas. Then, he's on top of me, crushing his lips against mine.

Sheer pandemonium ensues. There's a symphony of sharp inhales, deafening screams, and rushed footsteps scattering the gym floor. Many bleacher-bound audience members shield their eyes from the lewd sight, but more than a few lose the fight to temptation and ogle us through parted fingers. At the same time, a group of Andrew's teammates howl and cheer as if he's back on the field, running to score the game-winning touchdown. Beside them, a mob of his ex-girlfriends form a party of their own. Jealousy twisting their heavily made-up faces as they loudly declare that I'm nothing but a filthy slut.

And they're right. God, are they right.

I savor the thought as I do Andrew's skilled mouth, before it evades my lips and trails reckless kisses down my neck. One of his hands sinks low as he effortlessly lifts my legs over his broad shoulders.

Then, he shows me precisely *what that tongue of his is capable of as it r—*

My finger freezes on the red-marked "R" key. Ascending thumps on the hallway stairs catch me. But by the time I notice, it's far too late to react with civility.

I tear my gaze from the half-completed page stuck in the typewriter, watching as a shadow slips closer and closer through the crack beneath my bedroom door. Frantically, I rip the incomplete document from the machine. Scrambling for its additional pages before tossing them into the only concealment the desk offered: My leather-clad notebook.

I shut the cover in time with a twist of the doorknob. Just for my mother's curious, yet ruthlessly expectant face to appear in the open threshold. From what little of her I can see, her appearance is immaculate. Most notably, the meticulous updo that clasped her gray-blonde hair in even swirls. I open my mouth to compliment her on the style, hoping it would buy me a moment's grace from whatever lashing I was bound to receive. But I'm too slow.

"Why aren't you dressed?" She snaps, somehow phrasing it as both a question *and* a command to do so.

I glance down at my ruffled, oversized pink nightdress, then study the clock. Nine-thirty. As if the angle of sunlight pouring through my semi-translucent curtains didn't indicate that it was still early enough to spend my precious minutes buried in Andrew's story.

Or rather, with *him* buried in *me*.

"I have three hours." I supply the excuse with a shy smile, realizing too late what a mistake it had been.

"*Mary-Rose*." She bites my given name like a snake offering a warning strike. "If we don't leave at least two hours before walk-in, we'll get stuck in the parking lot." Her eyes dart across my desk. "What have you been doing all morning?"

My hand stiffens atop my closed notebook. Within, pages both clean and marked jut out in all directions. I rub the leather exterior, tracing the pressed indentation of the words *Holy Scriptures* beneath my fingertips.

I avoid her intimidating gaze as if returning it would turn me to ice. "Just working on a story."

Nothing but a tense silence follows. Though, when I finally dare a look at my mother, her expression is softer. A slight smile even tugs the corner of her mouth before she enters my bedroom fully, kitten heels clacking on the old wooden floor.

"I wish you would let me read your stories for once." Her modest, impeccably stitched blouson dress flows past me as she moves to open my closet. "If my daughter is going to write the next spiritual fiction bestseller, I'd sure like to say I supported her along the way."

As she pulls out my bagged graduation attire, I take the opportunity to feverishly organize the splayed sheets of paper within the sanctity of my notebook. "I promise I'll show you eventually. Just trying to make them perfect, you know?"

She sucks air in way of a laugh, but it comes out as a scoff, instead. "Well, you'll have plenty of time for that at Trinity Grace." Smoothing out a few red wrinkles, she hangs my uniform gown on the closet door. "And to think, four years from now you'll be ordering one of these in navy blue."

Making use of her turned back, I roll my eyes at the implication. Of course, she couldn't let me savor the departure from one miserable institution before shoving me tits-first into the next.

When Mom faces me again, I feign innocence. My posture goes stiff as she returns to my desk with an outstretched hand. There's something in her palm I'd failed to take note of through my panic.

"I was going to wait until this evening," she explains. "But I want you to wear it to the ceremony."

Taking the small gift box, I gently flip the lid to reveal a pristine silver cross on a sterling chain. Engraved in the center are the letters *M.R.* A personalized depiction that would look lovely around the neck of a comely Christian woman, proud to symbolize the commitment to her faith. Such as my mother, who wears a similar—albeit aged—version of her own. But she fit all those preconditions. And I fit... exactly none.

I stare at the object, stifling any outward reaction aside from surprise with a hint of forced delight. "Thanks, Mom."

"Here, I'll put it on for you." She was snatching the necklace and noosing me with it before I could even blink. Linking the clasp with a tight pull of the chain against my throat. "Have you even brushed your hair yet? I was just outside grabbing the paper and saw the Fennicks loading their car."

"Lewis is only early to stuff because his mom picks his outfits," I grumble, to no avail.

"As if that's an excuse?" Grabbing a strewn brush, she takes a rough handful of my hair. Starting at the knots formed where my ends dip just below my shoulder blades. "You'd think with all that time you two spend together, you'd have picked up a few of his responsible habits by now." She sighs. "But I'd expect the same of their older one, too. And look at how he turned out."

I gag at the mention. Mom's bony fingers pull a collection of stubborn tangles, the move setting me straight with a wince.

"Behave yourself, Mary-Rose." She warns lowly. "You're going to be the bigger person today. Is that clear?"

My brows drop into a scowl aimed at no one. "Henry's here?"

"Drove in before sunrise on that motorcycle." She blows a breath through clenched teeth, scorn heating her tone. "I know, because he stopped in front of our house in his pass, and the ridiculous thing woke me. I swear my life to God; he only did it to be a nuisance."

Our disdain for the eldest Fennick child was one of the only things my mother and I had in common. It graced me with the faintest satisfaction that she allowed her perfect persona to slip on this singular matter—anything to make her seem more like a mom and less like a damn tyrant.

When the knots are gone, she ties my hair into the same ponytail I've sported since grade school. Then she obtains the discarded white ribbon on my desk and wraps it into a bow around the elastic. I'd stopped throwing them out in the hopes that she wouldn't insist I wear them any longer years ago. All it ever took was a pair of scissors and a march into her sewing room before she came back with another strip to replace the old one. After she looks over my hair—evidently deeming it acceptable—her veiny hand slips beneath my chin to tilt it upwards.

For the first time since she entered my room at all, I meet her eyes. Cold, yet focused. In a flash of a moment, I wonder if something within her is wishing she could be staring back into her own. What it might be like if I'd inherited *her* steely blue irises, rather than a chestnut-colored relic symbolizing a decade of grief.

Whatever she's thinking, it pulls the wrinkles framing her mouth with something that looks frighteningly akin to affection. "You're growing up today, aren't you?"

It's a rhetorical question, but the mere suggestion that she might see me as *grown up* renders me incapable of providing an answer.

Despite the sentiment, it doesn't stunt the revival of her stern tone as she releases my chin to make her exit. "Now, get yourself ready."

Her ivory dress breezes past, and the grin of submission plastered across my face drops the instant the door clicks shut in her wake. At the sound of rhythmic thumps descending the staircase, the breath finally returns to my lungs. I open the cover of my notebook to stare at the unfinished story, cut off right before the antithesis of myself, Slutty Rosie, had truly gotten the graduation she deserved. I debate spending another half-hour on finishing her off—in *every* sense—but the last thing I need is another close call with Mom.

So instead, I take the collection of typewritten pages and kneel beside my twin mattress. Pulling up the bed skirt to view the safety-pinned rip in the box spring's fabric. Unclasping the secret little cover, I place the pages inside, careful to keep them from intermixing with dozens of other ribald stories. My hidden reserve marking nearly five years' worth of desires. Some were fully completed with labeled binder clips. Others lay forgotten and unfinished. But all of them had one thing in common: They were as far from spiritual fiction as God himself could fathom.

Pinning the tear back up, I stand with a heavy exhale. Stopping to ogle my wall-mounted mirror and the girl within. In blinding contrast to Slutty Rosie's carnality, *Mary-Rose's* face greets me as bare and innocent as the day she was born. Her large doe eyes are framed by a juvenile fringe, the longest edges stretching past her jaw in frequently snipped light-brown threads. The ponytail isn't so bad. At least it kept everyone from bearing witness to how awfully bushy that hair could get from too much routine brushing, and not a shred of knowledge as to how to style it any other way. Hesitantly, she slides her hands over the swells of her modest breasts, then her slender waist. Cinching the pink nightdress tightly in a manner of proving that she was, in some fashion or another, womanly.

When the assurance fails to deliver, I break from the pitiful view. My focus shifting to the graduation gown hanging on my closet door.

"Time to grow up..." I force the words as if saying them out loud would make me believe it.

But it doesn't. Despite how terribly I wished it did.

That afternoon, I attended my high school graduation wearing proper formal attire beneath my gown, rather than my birthday suit and stilettos. My mother and I got held up in the parking lot, despite leaving two hours in advance. I received my diploma, but only after tripping and falling over a stray microphone cable on my march to the stage—one that just so happened to trail beside Henry Fennick's seat at the base of the packed bleachers. I took obligatory pictures in front of our school's banner with nobody but Lewis, my only friend in the swarm of graduates, to give me a genuine smile.

And when Andrew Roth gave his valedictorian speech, he did *not* profess his undying feelings for me in front of our entire class. Nor did he beckon me on stage, tear off my gown, or fuck me senseless.

Chapter 1

I look up, craning my neck to get a full view of the most terrifying mural I've ever seen in my life.

On the stucco wall of the art department's exterior, a student-painted adaptation of *God the Father* looks over the courtyard linking each faction of Trinity Grace Christian College. His arms are outstretched in a faithful translation, with a gradient white to gray background framing his massive form. Despite impeccable application, the creepiest part isn't the painting's mountainous scale. It's the sporadic silhouettes in the form of praisers along the bottom. The figures stand hollowed by soulless black paint, true to the size of the artists, I presume. The same ones responsible for the chills that are going to terrorize me each time I have to walk past this depiction after dark.

For the next four years of my life.

Footsteps permeate my solitary grievance, and I don't need to shift my gaze to confirm that Lewis has taken his place beside me.

"That's...unsettling." He utters.

Tilting my head a little, I squint to study every detail of the all-mighty being's features. Only now realizing intimidation to be the mural's positional purpose. Something to keep college kids in line while attending a place of assembly rampant with temptation. Admittedly, a genius tactic.

"He looks so disappointed." I sigh theatrically. "Do you think he ever regrets creating us?"

"He makes no mistakes." Lewis shrugs his frail shoulders. "But one thing's for sure. If he exists, and *you* exist, he's gotta have one hell of a sense of humor."

I pin him with a playful glare, then allow it to soften at the sight of his face—already partially burned from our time outdoors. The emerald speckles in his blue eyes reflect brightly in the harsh sunlight, providing a modicum of familiarity in such an unfamiliar location.

"Mary-Rose!" My mother's voice cuts over.

Both of our heads turn in unison to where she stands among the cluster of adults belonging to Crosspoint Fellowship, all gathered in our allotted section of the campus quad. We're only one of a dozen churches convening at Trinity Grace today, handing out pamphlets to every intimidated freshman unfortunate enough to attend orientation. An event our congregation annually takes part in to support first-year believers, and *definitely not* dick-measure Albuquerque's other evangelical units. Mom is partaking in a conversation with several women. I recognize their faces, but couldn't name them if my life depended on it.

"Exhibition awaits," Lewis mutters, giving me a gentle push.

I covertly flip him off as I step away, pulling my lips into a tight smile once I stop at my mother's side, who remains focused on the group as she announces, "This is my daughter, Mary-Rose."

"What a beauty!" Chimes one of the younger ladies. "I worry for you, Christine. Just imagine how quickly she'll get snatched up by a worthy husband in a place like this."

I lower my eyes to keep from rolling them.

"Oh, I'm aware." My mother expels a deceitful laugh. "She'll more than satisfy the right man."

The eldest of them interjects, "It's so wonderful to see a girl dressed properly. Have you taken a look at the young women heading this event? I don't see how those little jean shorts could possibly meet the standards here."

"And they'll run crying when it draws the attention of the wrong man. It's becoming a lost art, keeping your children dignified." Mom remarks, then glances at me. "I was just telling Mrs. Stafford about your major. She's a big reader."

She presses a hand to my back in what I first believe to be pride, before I recognize it as a gesture to straighten my posture. *The higher you are, the closer you are to God.* Or so I've been told.

I comply, looking to the oldest of the women inspecting me. Mrs. Stafford's white hair is pinned in a similar bun to the one Mom wears, allowing an unobstructed view of her cardigan and long dress. I wonder how she isn't baking alive in that thing. The sweat clinging beneath my short-sleeve button-up is certainly seeping through by now. But thankfully, the skirt ending at my mid-thighs offers a little ventilation.

Habitually smoothing my hands over the navy fabric of it, I chuckle timidly. "Big reader? Me, too."

"I'd certainly hope so." Mrs. Stafford gives me a fanciful once-over. "I suppose you must do a lot of reading, scriptural or otherwise, to make it as a Christian author. Best to follow in the footsteps of those who came before you."

"She's following in her *father's* footsteps." My mother amends, and I instantly drop my cheery front. "He was published only months after earning his degree."

"Spiritual?" The woman questions.

Mom gives a curt huff. "Oh, heavens, no. He passed before I ever came to God. Matthew published in all sorts of genres."

"What kind of tales do *you* aim to capture, Mary-Rose?" Mrs. Stafford asks, drawing my gaze from the fractured pavement.

"I like romance," I say quietly. "I'm working on a story of a lost harlot who finds salvation in her love for a preacher."

Her mouth—coated in a layer of horribly applied lipstick—quirks in aversion. "Interesting. Although I must warn you that if you're going to commit to such a topic, it can be quite the slippery slope."

This, I have to hear. "How's that?"

"I feel that modern romance is spiraling into filth. I can't tell you the last time I read one without wanting to toss it into my fireplace. Particularly Christian. Some material out there makes me question if our devout authors consider themselves devout at all." She offers me a tentative look. "And your inclusion of a…*harlot*…worries me. All I can suggest is that you keep your writings tasteful."

It takes everything in me not to grin like an absolute deviant as I counter with, "Don't worry, Mrs. Stafford. I can assure you that my writings are *delicious*."

The absence of pearls leaves her nothing to clutch as shock parts the woman's smudged lips.

"Mary-Rose…" My mother warns, low enough to reach only my ears before her tone perks again. "Well, I tend to think that a tale of a girl on the wrong path finding her way to God is exactly what her generation needs. Now more than ever. And what better way than through the guidance of a preacher?"

"I'd be a fool to disagree."

I stiffen at the familiar masculine voice. As do all the surrounding women as Crosspoint Fellowship's pastor, Morgan Collins, suddenly invades the small grouping. Receiving a wave of nods and agreeable commends from every lady except me. I only acknowledge him when the mention of my name leaves me no other choice.

"Mary-Rose, how does it feel to be back where you belong?" He asks with a little too much enthusiasm.

I search everywhere but his gaze while turning over the question in my head. At his beige dress shirt that complements his strong build. Up to his cleanly trimmed beard and muddy-brown head of combed hair to match. Finally, I reach his dark eyes. Beaming as bright as the eerie smile underneath them. It takes a bullshitter to *know* a bullshitter. And, God, if he didn't give me a run for my money.

Mom's fingernail circles the white fabric against my back in warning.

I offer the coerced answer. "I'm grateful I went to public school. But I think adjusting to an all-Christian college will be nice, too."

It's a bold-faced lie, but it's what he wants to hear.

"No doubt." He says warmly, raising his thick brows. "I bet you'll find that the friends you make here are the kind that will change your life entirely. Think of all you'll have in common. Your career paths *and* your devotion to God."

"I can't tell you how much better I feel knowing she'll be spending her days here." My mother's mouth pulls so widely, her face looks one praise away from being torn in half. "I like to think secular education gave her enough examples of people to steer clear of."

Pastor Morgan nods. "Couldn't agree more. You remember Faye, my niece? She just earned her master's here last spring. She and a group of girls ran a Bible study on Thursday nights in the arts building. Mary-Rose might look into who's in charge of it this year and join in?"

I feel my stomach clench at the suggestion. And while my tone of voice is naturally light—even child-like, embarrassingly enough—I exaggerate it as I reply. "Gosh, I don't know. I think I'll be really busy getting a feel for classes—"

Mom's nail digs painfully into my spine. An instinctive fear pulses through me as one of her favorite verses overrides my judgment. *Obey your leaders and submit to them.*

Leaders in that context were always conveniently obscure. I'd been inundated with the notion regarding everyone from teachers to youth group hosts. But most of all, our pastor. Like most of the complex phrases the church had thrown at me in my childhood, I'd come to interpret the verse in my own right: You *never* tell the man in charge no.

Her sharp claw injects a lethal dose of compliance, and I lower my chin in submission. "But I guess I'll check it out for myself."

Pastor Morgan grins proudly at me before getting snagged into conversation with the other women, giving my mother the go-ahead to drop her knife-like hold on my back. She's so preoccupied with the change in subject that I have little trouble slipping away to find Lewis alongside his own parents. Spotting him isn't hard. He's one of the only boys from Crosspoint scrawnier than I am. That, along with his over-gelled brown hair and slacks pulled a bit too high, makes him easy to pick out in a crowd. They're chatting with a younger couple I recognize as the Acostas, who were newly married last month. I quickly pick up where the conversation is leading as I near.

"Computer science isn't just mechanics. I think web servers are more interesting." Lewis's voice carries.

"All that technology is leaving a lot of people out of their jobs." Mr. Acosta's gaze flickers to his pretty wife's. "And if the world goes to hell? Computers aren't gonna make our problems any easier."

Lewis's head dips a little. "I guess that's—"

"Actually, Lewis thinks the web is gonna make the workforce more efficient than ever." I place my elbow on his shoulder. It takes little effort, given that he's only an inch or so taller than me. Three, if you ask him. "Plus, it's geniuses like him that are gonna single-handedly keep the Y2K bug from turning your fax machine into a flesh-melting killer. So I'd stay on his good side if I were you."

I give Mr. Acosta a smirk as he looks at me like I've sprouted a second head.

"I have no doubts. There's nothing he can't do once he puts his mind to it." Mrs. Fennick enthuses.

I look to her at Mr. Fennick's side, and she returns my warm glance with a maroon-rimmed smile—one that reaches her bulky cat-eye glasses. Unlike my own mother's, however, I knew hers to be genuine. Mrs. Fennick's personality was so welcoming that it often felt like she was the closest thing to a surrogate mom I'd ever have. Always wearing her unreasonably positive attitude on her sleeve. Quite literally, as her choice of apparel was no exception to her merriment. Consisting invariably of pastel dresses akin to the shade of spring green she flaunts today. The vibrance of it contrasts her short brunette hair, styled in curls I can tell she'd nurtured in rollers all night. She never failed to look out of place next to her husband. He typically sulked around like a grumpy, senescent version of the soldiers on those mid-century military recruitment posters. It was a rarity not to see him with a cigar or flask between his fingers, but I have a feeling he's hiding one or the other in the pockets of his pressed trousers.

"It pays to be a realist, Francis." Mr. Fennick grumbles in his wife's direction, robbing the woman of her grin. "Especially when it's coming out of my wallet."

Mrs. Acosta brushes a few strands of wind-blown hair behind her ear. "It might be a good thing. Just imagine all the resources people who haven't heard the word of God will have once the church catches up with the times."

Before Mr. Acosta can open his mouth to argue, Pastor Morgan calls the group to gather for a newsletter photograph. Once bodies around us begin to shift, Lewis shoots me his best attempt at a stern look.

"You don't need to do that." He says softly, referencing my outspoken defense.

"Yes, I do," I whisper back, leading him by the arm to where the congregation gathers in several rows. I quickly find my mother, who motions assertively for me to stand beside her. It's only after we've begun to take our places that a powerful gust of hot wind sweeps past.

"Your bow." My mother snaps.

I turn my head just to feel the damn thing slip from my ponytail to drift across the surface of the pavement behind us. I have every intention of letting it blow away before Mom pushes me to retrieve it. While the photographer readies, I discreetly slip into a crouch behind the backmost row. The shadeless concrete scalds my hands and knees until I successfully palm the ribbon. Letting out a quiet sigh, I look up.

No…fucking…*way*.

Pastor Morgan stands at the far-back center of the group, with his arms behind the two at his sides. One being Mrs. Acosta, and his hand is grabbing her ass so tightly, the fabric of her dress looks as if it might rip. The woman appears complacent, simply smiling with Mr. Acosta on her opposite end. My mouth falls open as I'm left a split-second to determine if I should scream or laugh. Knowing an outburst of any kind would end in catastrophe, I shove a ribbon-clenched fist between my teeth to refrain from either—biting hard as the sight before me burns in.

"*Mary-Rose!*" My mother hushes.

As if I were never there at all, I carefully return to my spot and re-secure the ribbon to my ponytail before I'm noticed. My eyes are still wide from the lecherous display, but I straighten my posture. Running through the same tried-and-true method of faking it that I had perfected since childhood as I show the camera my teeth.

Chin up.

Don't look anyone in the eye; they might see right through you.

Smile like you mean it, or they'll make you do it again.

Pretend.

Endure.

Pretend.

Endure.

FLASH

Light stains my vision for a few blinks, my mantra seeming to have paid off as those around us begin to dissipate. In an instant, I pull Lewis close enough that my quick whispers reach his ears alone. "Please tell me you're up for getting out of here?"

His gaze sweeps over the group, stopping on my mother and his parents, who have since convened on the walkway. "I got this."

We approach the three of them, breaking their short-lived conversation as Lewis places a hand on my shoulder. "Mrs. Ginger, Rosie and I were thinking about going to that devotional on campus this evening. Would you care if we broke off and spent the rest of the afternoon checking out the school?"

Any falsehood in his tone is expertly undetectable. My mother shares a hesitant glance with Mr. and Mrs. Fennick before questioning him. "You'd look after her?"

Look after me. Like I was a child in need of constant supervision. She may as well hook a leash to the necklace she'd gifted me and hand it over to Lewis.

"Of course." He promises. "We'll be on the first bus home when it's over."

After a contemplative pause, my mother sighs. "Alright, then. Have fun. And *behave yourself*, Mary-Rose. First impressions are important around here."

"Yes, Mom," I say with conviction.

"I'll put supper aside for you, sweetie." Mrs. Fennick tugs Lewis by the arm to plant a smushy kiss on his cheek. Her husband gives no sign of approval, as he's preoccupied with uncapping the silver flask he'd pulled from his backmost pocket.

"*Mom!*" Lewis wriggles out of her grasp, but not before she leaves a maroon-tinted print on his pale skin. Which he quickly swipes away.

"You, too, Rosie. I'm making your favorite chicken fettuccine." She says with a gentle squeeze of my bicep, a mark of her affection that always extended to me.

I bid the woman a kind thanks before her son and I leave the congregation of Crosspoint Fellowship, stepping across the oak-littered courtyard with our arms linked. We offer counterfeit smiles to every passerby, including a couple of the orientation directors Mrs. Stafford had so vocally condemned. *Thank God* little jean shorts meet the dressing standard, if it means such an eye-catching break from traditionalism in a place marketed for its adherence to such. I find myself so envious of their liberty that my gaze lingers even after they stride past. Admiring the way denim hugs their curvaceous hips for… probably a beat longer than I should.

"We're not going to that fucking devotional," I say when we're a good distance from anyone who may overhear.

Lewis scoffs, playing like he isn't long accustomed to my vulgar diction. "Shocking."

"You wanna talk about shocking? I just caught Pastor *Madman* over there feeling up Mrs. Acosta during the photo."

His head snaps my direction. "No way. In front of people?"

In hindsight, it wasn't that surprising. Pastor Morgan had been taking a "hands-on" approach with just about every sexually frustrated wife that came to him seeking marital counseling since his appointment as leader. No one at Crosspoint would speak of his adultery out loud, but everyone knew. Though, he typically went after the ones worn thin by a long-stagnant marriage. The Acostas still had wedding cake in their fridge, for Christ's sake.

"He's getting bolder," I say, undoing the clasps of my shirt to air out my sweaty chest. "Pretty soon, he'll be coming after us maidens."

Lewis watches as I pull open the top third of my button-up. "Careful, Rosie. You show any more skin and I might stumble."

We start down a barren walkway to the street as I perk a brow. "I'll worry about that when your balls drop, momma's boy."

"Low blow, you know I drew the short straw... Figuratively speaking." He cringes, then raises his chin. "Besides, at least my mom actually loves me."

"Oh, she loves you, alright." I wind my arm around his neck and tug at the pressed collar of his shirt. Mimicking his mother's coddling tone. "And how brave of her to let a baby like you wander off with a Jezebel like me."

I press a loud kiss to the same spot Mrs. Fennick had on his lightly freckled cheek, just for him to ram a palm into my nose and shove me off balance. My Mary Jane flats offer no traction on the concrete, leaving me zero chance at getting my footing before I fall ass-first into a thick bush parallel to the sidewalk. It's only after my vision becomes obscured by a sea of green leaves that Lewis's gaudy laughter catches me.

"Look who's *stumbling* now!"

"Asshole." I shift through sharp stems to flip over and attempt to stand, only for the chain around my neck to snag on one. I straighten my legs enough to partially make it to my feet, but my upper half stays concealed in the shrub. Bent low at an awkward angle as I work to pull the thing loose. "Fuck! My stupid necklace is caught."

"Well, this is a sight to behold," Lewis remarks smugly. "You might tell Erica to size up your underwear, by the way. Your ass finally came in, and those hipsters aren't covering it."

I roll my eyes, letting out a mindless laugh as I shake my rear. "What? You think I have any shame left?"

"In that case..." Though I can't see an inch of him, I hear his voice amplify like an auctioneer. "Step right up, gentlemen! Today we have a splendid offer: The virginity of one Rosie Ginger!"

Humiliation renders me frantic as I fight harder to free myself. "*Lewis!*"

His cadence remains unfazed. "Don't let her looks deceive you. This chronic masturbator is equipped with a loud mouth and a *louder* moan. The only thing that'll come quicker than her witty remarks is *you*. Need to take a load off? Why not dump it right *here*?"

I yelp as he swats my ass cheek, then clench a fist around the chain as I melodically caution, "I'm warning you..."

"No ring required. Just whip it out and slide it in! Let's start the bidding at a hundred big ones!" He pauses for dramatics. "Nobody? Let's go for fifty...? Ten...? Pocket change...? How about, *she'll* pay *you* to be her first—!"

I extend my leg and land a kick somewhere fleshy, silencing his little stunt as he groans from the impact. A loud collapse later, I successfully untangle the silver cross from the stem it caught on and stand fully. I brush stray leaves from myself as I find Lewis on his knees, clutching his groin in agony.

I place my hands on my hips, looking down my nose at him. "Last I checked, as long as you have your V-card, I have mine. Or did you forget your part in the pact we made?"

Sure, it had mostly been a joke. But there was solace in your best friend vowing to remain as lonely as you were, at least until we both found the right people.

"If my *parts* even work anymore." He makes it to his feet with a wince.

"You deserved it. Cheap shot, pushing a girl."

We stand there, eyes locked as our bodies go rigid. Then, he lunges to push me again. But this time I take him along, and we *both* tumble into the shrub. Splayed out side by side in the thick leaves, we look at each other once more, then absolutely combust with laughter. So loud, there's no chance passerbys from the courtyard aren't staring at us like we're a couple of freaks.

But we don't care. Because *that's* Lewis and me.

As we leave the college behind, our escape from new adult sanctity evokes pained, yet bittersweet memories of the years following my mother's conversion. There was little that I recalled apart from begging her to take me out of the Christian schools she kept tossing me between. Strangely, the Fennicks had been the reason I was ultimately back in public school by my sixth grade year. It was through finding them at Crosspoint Fellowship that Mom discovered they only lived a few houses down the street from ours. And despite being staunch believers, they thought that putting their children through the trials of public education would ultimately benefit them.

That's when I really met Lewis. And the shy, gangly boy always hiding behind his mother's dress at church suddenly became someone I saw every day. We first connected in a small assortment of fellow evangelicals who gathered on the playground for daily group prayers. Afterwards, we would spend our recesses walking together. First, there were a dozen of us. Then, six. And for a while, only three.

Until our third counterpart was shipped away to the very type of institution I'd been spared from. After that, it was just Lewis and me.

But the true moment we became best friends didn't arrive until halfway through that school year. When I'd woken up on a Saturday morning a bit later than usual, just to go downstairs and find my house completely void of occupants. I waited until the panic began to set in, persuading me to wander down the street and knock on the door of the Fennicks' home. Lewis answered, and miraculously, his family had seemed to disappear when he'd woken as well. Both of us came to the only logical conclusion two indoctrinated children could figure in such a scenario: Our families had been raptured, and we had been left behind.

The two of us spent the following hour screaming, gathering weapons, and fortifying his house to prepare for tribulation and the coming of the anti-Christ. Until our families returned from the neighbor they'd collectively decided to visit without waking us, and we realized we hadn't been damned to an eternity of mutilation and torment. Ever since then, Lewis and I have been inseparable.

Because, to us, we'd survived that hour in literal hell. And if we could make it through *hell* together, we could make it through *anything* together.

He stood beside me through all the times I questioned if the things we were being taught were worth believing at all, and even joined me in my spiritual deconstruction. Leaving us both at the conclusion that we couldn't know if there was actually a God. Maybe there was. But, shit, I don't even know what I'm having for lunch most days, and I'm supposed to know the answer to a question that's plagued mankind since the dawn of humanity?

Beyond that, Lewis was the only person on the planet I felt safe enough to share my perverse hobby with. He knew of my hidden stories and supported my work fully. Even if he does relentlessly tease me for being a virginal erotica writer, I can't say I wouldn't make fun of me if I were in his shoes.

An hour after leaving Trinity Grace, he and I have successfully traveled downtown to the decrepit strip mall housing our go-to hangout, *Marcy's Bookstore*. I tuck my bus pass back into the white fabric of my knee sock as I open the door, cursing the fact that my only selection of wardrobe had no pockets to offer.

"Hi, Rosie!" Marcy calls from checkout as Lewis and I step into the air-conditioned shop, sparing us from the August heat.

"Hey, Marcy!" I scan the modest store's shelves. "Restock lately?"

"This morning, actually." Her words are cut by a firm *clank* of the card imprinter as she supplies a customer with their receipt. "Go wild."

"You should know better than to tempt me like that." I wink, drawing a smile and a shake of the elderly woman's head. Lewis and I wander until we reach the adult section. Which hilariously sits right across the aisle from spiritual fiction.

"You make any progress on your 'harlot saved by a preacher' story?" He asks, ogling the covers printed with crosses and angelically scenic sunsets.

The mention makes me groan. I hadn't lied to Mrs. Stafford earlier. I *was* working on a piece of such fiction. Only, I had no intention of it ever reaching publication—or even completion. It was just to appease my mother, who kept demanding the right to read my material.

"I'm three chapters in and it's the most egregious thing I've ever put to paper." I raise a brow at him. "And that's counting my thirty-page cunnilingus with Gilbert Grape."

Lewis stifles a laugh. "'*What's Eating Rosie Ginger.*'"

My eyes drift over the newly stocked selection of erotic romances, finding…Shirtless hot guy. Shirtless hot guy. Shirtless hot guy.

I yawn. I'm always wishing to find new pornographic fiction aimed at women for inspiration. But the abundance of female-centric smut meant to satisfy sexually repressed, middle-aged moms had long since lost its flair. I didn't want to sit through a hundred pages of monotonous romance to get off. And even when I skipped straight to the sex, it rarely failed to leave me disappointed. The foreplay was too slow. The positions were boring. And you could tell that the author was evading certain terminology to avoid offending readers.

Is "clit" seriously that scary of a word?

I give up surveying the collection and step away to find Lewis beside a magazine rack on the backmost wall of the store. He's fanning through a selection titled *Byte*. A tech-themed publication with a myriad of numbers and codes beneath the headline I can't begin to decipher.

"Didn't you nerd out enough with your 'geeks anonymous' group the past three months?" I jest.

"They aren't anonymous," Lewis shoots me a look. "And you're just jealous that I was off making new friends this summer instead of locking myself away to write porn."

Yeah, I was. But only the *making friends* part. Lewis had offered plenty of times for me to join in on meetings with a group of local web enthusiasts he'd found through online chat rooms over the summer months. But I felt out of place enough parading around my mother. A bunch of geeks in a sweaty gear shop salivating about coding? No thanks.

"That's rich coming from you, hotshot. Maybe you should ask Presley to stop giving you advice on servers and see if he can help you land a girlfriend." I say, referencing his closest friend from the tech-savvy crew. I'd yet to meet him, but I was simply relieved Lewis finally had a fellow guy to talk to after years of me being his only outlet.

"I will when *you* land a boyfriend." He pauses, reaching for a magazine at the peak of the metal display. "Try dressing a little more like her. Might help your chances."

I barely catch the object as he tosses it my way, then study it to find a partially nude cover model beneath bold *Playboy* lettering.

"Not nearly revealing enough," I remark, placing the magazine back in its half-hidden place on the rearmost bracket. I trail my finger across the collection of pornographic publications beside it.

Penthouse. Genesis. Hustler.

All of which house unnaturally positioned, nearly naked women on their covers. I keep skimming until one in particular captures my attention. One woman, that is. My breath actually hitches at the sight of her face peeking from behind the blinder rack. I pull the magazine free, giving her a full look-over.

My jaw absolutely drops. Never in my life have I seen a woman so perfect. So naturally gorgeous. She's Latina, with silky black, collarbone-length hair and warm brown skin that practically glows from the page. And she is showing *a lot* of skin. The only clothing she wears consists of a fuchsia boa looped around her neck and two elongated black gloves that reach her biceps. Velvet-clad hands conceal her bare breasts in a lively manner, the bottom of the cover cutting off at her midsection. But the feature that draws my attention most is her mouth. Perfectly white teeth bordered by full, ruby red lips—completing a smile that reaches her bright hazel eyes. The full sight of her sends a shiver down my spine in an odd, yet not totally undesirable way. I scan the name featured in cursive text beside her. *Valentina Amor*. The title of the magazine hovers above her pretty head in exaggerated lettering.

Wild Thang

At the top of the feature in font almost too small to make out, it reads: *Produced in Albuquerque, New Mexico.*

My heart skips a beat at the prospect that this woman may exist in the same city as me. I attempt to suppress my rouse by studying the coverlines along the edge of the glossy page, then stir when they amplify it.

NEW MEXICO'S HOTTEST SLUTS!
ORDER HARDCORE VIDEOS WITH LOCAL GIRLS!
YOUR EROTIC STORIES COME TO LIFE!

The last line is what does it for me.

Far more intrigued than I'd ever admit, I open the cover and leaf through the pages. All of which display explicit photographs of men and women adorned in everything from BDSM gear to absolutely nothing at all. Some simply model, while others engage in true sexual acts. The positions are pretty creative, I'd *definitely* remember to use them in my own writings. But eventually, I reach a spread that largely consists of wording, apart from a singular photo depiction. The face within the image is familiar, but I manage to pull my attention free from Valentina Amor long enough to realize that the paragraphs beneath are those of a pornographic story. Crowned with a bold blurb at the top.

SEND IN YOUR EROTIC STORY AND WE'LL FEATURE IT RIGHT HERE!

An Albuquerque mailing address is listed beneath.

"Doesn't your sexy boss pay you enough? Put that babysitting money to use and buy it if you're gonna gawk. I don't wanna have to ask Marcy for a mop." Lewis teases, hardly glancing up from his *Byte* magazine. "*Again.*"

I'm too enthralled to counter his jab. But even if I did, there's no way I could sneak this object of my desire past Mom. Instead, I turn away from him and feign a heavy sneeze. Then return Valentina Amor to her spot on the blinder rack.

After discreetly folding and tucking the page I'd torn free into the snug fabric of my knee sock.

Chapter 2

"How was the devotional?" Mom calls.

I close our front door as the outside hues bleed from orange to lavender, home not a minute later than I assumed she would be expecting me. The last thing I wanted was an earful after what ended up being a rather salvageable day—especially one topped with a full belly and lingering taste of Mrs. Fennick's homemade garlic bread.

"It was great!" I answer over the grating yells of her favorite televangelist, stepping from the foyer past the outspread archway of the living room. Quietly bolting for the stairs before she presses for details.

"Mary-Rose?"

Shit. It gags me to keep from vocalizing the word.

Retreating to the threshold, I stand in her line of sight. "Yes, Mom?"

The only light in the space emanates from the television, casting a grim glow on sunken eyes that drink me in. Despite it, I catch the slight tilt of her lips as she says, "I'm proud of you."

For a second, I feel as if my heart just dropped out of my ass. Unable to recall a single instance of her offering such a sentiment before now. I must appear dazed enough that she feels justified in elaborating.

"I know how much you preferred your secular education. Trinity Grace is a big step." She tips forward in her recliner. "But I think you'll realize soon enough how *important* of a step it is. I want you to get involved, go to that Bible study Pastor Morgan suggested."

I lean against the archway, dipping my head so my bangs obscure me. "I will."

"Stepping outside your comfort zone with other believers will do you great." She shrugs. "Who knows? You might find that you make some girl friends for a change. Or meet a nice boy you get along with."

My eyes lift, the implication throwing me even more than her declaration of pride had. "You meant what you said today?"

"You've made it very clear there's no future with Lewis."

The comment evokes a scoff from me, as well as memories chronicling all the early years of Lewis and my friendship. Back when our families enjoyed speaking about us as if I would one day bear the Fennick surname. Which was *never* going to happen, despite how much they wanted to believe it. In reality, I hadn't once felt a shred of romantic attraction toward him. Pulling teeth would've been easier than getting our parents to accept that.

"In that case," my mother continues. "There's no better place to find a respectable future husband. Why else would so many students of God enter college single and end up engaged by the end of their first year?"

Because it's their quickest shot at getting laid, I nearly say out loud.

But I sooner reply with, "Guys aren't looking at me, Mom."

They never have, and I could hardly blame them. If the fact that I looked like a pre-K schoolgirl trapped in the body of a teenager wasn't enough to send them running, the specter of evangelicalism hanging over my head like a neon warning sign was about as solid a fail-safe to exist.

Mom lets out a dramatic sigh. "Well, maybe if you lose that attitude you're always carrying and start smiling a little more, that'll change. God forbid you waste your youth waiting."

I stare at her, my face growing heavy with a frown before I show my teeth. Though, it's less akin to a smile, more like a coyote bearing its fangs right before it bites the head off a jackrabbit.

My mother huffs, fingers finding the crochet hook in her lap to indicate that our conversation is over.

I manage to slip away without further incident, finding relief once I'm upstairs in my room. Pressing my back to the wooden door, I blow an angled puff of air that ruffles my fringe. The subject of our encounter weighing heavily on my already-fatigued mind. It's only worsened when I catch the reflection of my wall-mounted mirror, framing the product of Crosspoint's creation from ribbon-topped ponytail to Mary Jane flats. Resentment heats my flesh beneath the skirt and button-up. I'd be tempted to rip the entire outfit to shreds if I weren't a few paces from a wardrobe filled with identical replacements. The sight is everything my mother had spent her years producing, and yet, her words hang like a vicious taunt.

Lose that attitude you're always carrying.

It wasn't enough that I had to put on an act for everyone, excluding my closest friend, to simply survive. Now, if I ever wanted to find love, I had to forego my real self for them, as well. Should be easy, Lord knows I've had enough practice at it.

Except, my mother, and even I to a degree, was wrong.

My gaze finds the singular anomaly housed on a shelf above my writing desk. Where a tiny, stuffed leopard with shiny plastic bulbs for eyes sits in the center. Between its paws is a linked card dotted in red hearts. I move to retrieve it, flipping open the laminated cover to read the handwritten interior of the note.

To Rosie,

From the moment I first spotted you, I knew we were meant to be.

—Love, your S.A.

Secret admirer.

My pulse quickens as I recall finding the gift in our mailbox over two years ago. Every day that I walked the halls of Peakshire High following the discovery, I waited for the moment my admirer would finally reveal their identity. But sophomore year turned to junior, then to senior, and suddenly I was leaving the school for the final time with as few answers as I'd started with. Even if it had been as simple as a one-off gesture by way of someone too reluctant to approach me, it remained the only confirmation that someone out there looked at me the way I'd always dreamed of being perceived. As somebody *worthy* of being loved just the way I was.

And if nothing else, it was a cute stuffed animal.

I replace the gift before taking a seat at the desk beneath it, unwilling to let myself get too lost in the mystery when there were more pressing matters at hand. I slip the *Wild Thang* magazine page from where it had been hidden between my calf and the tight fabric of my sock. Unfolding it to study the contents more thoroughly. Most notably, the title of the piece consuming the upper-third of the page.

Dick-Sucking Dame Dominates During Date

Beside it is a depiction of a male model in the back of a car, being straddled by the scantily dressed Valentina Amor, who gazes at the reader with a seductive look. The story appears to revolve around a drive-in movie date that turns into an explicit fantasy from the man's perspective. But as I skim the first and only page of the text I'd procured, I'm left wondering what sort of illiterate fool was responsible for such composition. The few paragraphs I can read are abysmal, with phrases like "scalding sperm" and "milk-iful tits" used unironically for the sake of obscene spice. I know I can write better, but all my stories are from a *female's* perspective. Would they even consider such an inclusion if the main character didn't represent their target demographic?

It was certainly worth a try. But which story to choose?

I pull my *Holy Scriptures* notebook from the backpack resting beside my desk and flip it open, breezing past the faux saved harlot novel to skim my more perverse prompts. Sifting through all my strewn works-in-progress proved useless. All of them contained my name, which wouldn't do at all. Even if there were ten thousand Rosies in Albuquerque, I wouldn't underestimate Crosspoint's ability to find my work and sniff out the connection for anything. If I'm going to do this, I need to be anonymous.

Descriptive self-inserts are out, as are pieces including any real people. It's one thing for me to write about my fictional excursions with personal crushes and celebrity heartthrobs in a story only intended for my eyes. But if by some miracle my words come to reach the mass public, I can't in good conscience write about someone who hadn't consented to being named. At least, not without giving them my own unidentifiable spin. Sighing, I lift the torn magazine page, letting my gaze linger on the photographic depiction. Would they shoot one for *my* story if it were to be selected?

The more I stare, the more I consider never looking away. There was something about the woman on this page that absolutely captivated me. Perhaps it was the prospect that she could, potentially, be the very person to act out my salacious fantasies in real life. Perhaps it was the dream that every soul who buys the next issue of *Wild Thang* would get off to my creation, and she could play a part in making it happen.

Perhaps she was simply the most gorgeous fucking woman I've ever laid eyes on.

Whatever the case, the rising heat of my blood becomes too intense to ignore. As does the pulsing of every nerve in my body, supplying a steady hum directed straight between my legs. I slip a hand beneath my flared skirt to skim the silky fabric of my underwear, feeling the wetness already seeping through. Keeping the magazine page in my hand, I make the executive decision to ditch the desk and drop into my far comfier twin bed. Writing could wait. My incessant craving for release couldn't.

Not that I didn't fancy denial now and then. But I'd spent enough time today *edging* the line between actress and despot's daughter. This one wouldn't take long.

Settling on my back with the page above me, I dip fingers beneath the lining of my panties, slipping one inside me to wet it before using the tip to circle my stiff clit. I'm so tightly wound that the little action almost pushes me to the crest far sooner than I'd like. Teasing myself, I fixate on the photo of Valentina Amor alongside her male counterpart, who was grabbing each of her full breasts in his hands—the only concealment offered to her body. With the exception of a black mini skirt hugging her slender waist, leaving little to the imagination. On top of it all, she bears the same ruby-rimmed smile she'd flaunted on the cover. I would say it's her most striking feature, but it would be sinful to choose just one.

Hot, easing waves of euphoria course through me with each stroke of my fingers. I sigh in delight as my deep insides tense and relax with increasingly powerful throbs, pleasure electrifying my every rub. Refusing to tear my eyes from the picture as my efforts grow rapid, I take in every inch of the scene and every ounce of seduction in Valentina's gaze. Consuming it like it's the only cure for this ache, intermixing with the fantasies of myself as a sexually free, promiscuous woman, rather than a virtuous maiden trapped in a body she was taught from childhood to fear.

Me…I imagine it's *me* in that photo.

I can no longer keep proper hold of the page; my fingers falter as it drifts to the floor somewhere out of sight. With a final, hard pinch of my clit between slick fingers, I come undone. It's a nice, strong orgasm. Heightened by a sudden release of stress and a cry of ecstasy

I can't help but expel. One that makes my legs lock and tremble with each wave of pounding, persistent pleasure. The kind that makes me wonder if having a significant other was worth desiring at all—if I'm capable of doing *this* with nothing but my own hand. A fleeting lapse in time where I'm slammed with an addicting surge of undiluted freedom. I'm sexy. I'm happy.

I'm *me*.

Clinging to the final tendrils of release until they inevitably slip free, I'm left a panting mess of a degenerate with a hand down her ruined underwear once it's all over. I hum with closed eyes, pulling it free to trail wet fingers along my sensitive inner thigh as I savor the warm afterglow. It's so welcoming that the lure of sleep tempts me with a provocative embrace, until a slight *creaking* draws me painfully awake. The exact noise I recognize as my bedroom door being opened or closed a little too slowly.

My eyes flare wide not a moment before I shoot upright, staring in the hopes that I *had* fallen asleep post-climax, and this was simply the product of a nightmare. But my mother's petrified face looking back at me isn't something Satan himself would conjure for the sake of a subconscious jest. It's real.

She doesn't even have the decency to avert her gaze as she quietly remarks, "I was just, um…"

If a hushed explanation was offered, it was too faint to make out beyond the swift closing of my bedroom door. Unforgiving time resumes, and I no longer fight the word from greeting my tongue.

"*Shit*."

I would be seeing my mother's horrified face during every orgasm for the rest of my life, wouldn't I?

Which was more than I could say for the day following our encounter, where even she seemed to key in on the fact that we needed a grace period before looking each other in the eyes again. Slipping away to Lewis's house on Saturday hadn't helped. I'd confided in him, thinking he'd have some form of similar experience. Maybe he'd attest that I wasn't the only eighteen-year-old who'd ever been walked in on by their parent while getting off to an imaginary version of themselves getting fucked in a pornographic magazine.

But he'd only laughed at me, attesting that I was the biggest loser he's ever known.

Even so, I happily sit with him during Crosspoint's Sunday service, as I did every week. The Fennicks had enough class to avoid sitting in the first-row pews for the sake of not looking like kiss-asses, unlike my mother. I ignore every word of Pastor Morgan's sermon, staring at the back of Mom's head out of fear that it would, at any moment, spin around like that little girl's from *The Exorcist* and declare in front of everyone that I was destined for hell. She'd stayed entirely silent on the drive this morning, and knowing my mother to be the confrontational type, there's no doubt in my mind she was arranging something horrid in addressing the defilement of my body.

By *my* own hand. What a fucking joke.

Trying to avert my focus elsewhere never worked. The stained-glass windows, the spotless carpeting, the rear of the pew in front of me—none of which offered a shred of solace. Least of all, the ceiling, I *swear* it always reflected the faces of those beneath it as a manner of taunting me. So instead, I deal with the consuming rage the way I typically did when my mother and I weren't getting along, or when Pastor Morgan gave one of his esteemed sermons about a woman's place or sexual deviancy—so, basically, *every* week. And that was by imagining. My go-to was to picture myself in front of the church as they worshiped, only to levitate off the ground like the demonic entity they would see me as if I ever allowed my mask to fall. Fangs would replace my pearly whites, matching the shade of my scleras when they'd wash over my brown eyes, leaving soulless orbs in their wake. The sound of their mortified, illusory screams at such a sight is music to my ears.

But after the service concludes and the congregation disperses among the large hall, I remain with Lewis in our seats. Having lost track of my mother as the two of us converse privately.

"Maybe she'll let it go?" Lewis offers, either to reignite my hope or get me to finally steer the subject away from the wrath of Christine Ginger.

Whatever the reason, I glare at him.

Sighing, his fingers drum rhythmically on his brown slacks. "Or not. But to be fair, you're just as good at holding grudges." He leans closer to provoke me. "*Angel Face.*"

"Not funny." I roll my eyes. "I just wish she would accept that I'm not made of stone. Especially not in the privacy of my own room. How hard can it be to let sleeping dogs lie?"

"Sleeping dogs? Not hard. Acknowledging that her youngest is a fucked up pervert…?" He gives me a once-over. "Still not hard. I did it."

I tilt my head at him. "Do you really think I'm a fucked up pervert?"

"You are *the* fucked up pervert, Rosie Ginger."

Smiling, I rest my head on his shoulder. "I guess that explains my relationship status, doesn't it?"

"Not necessarily." He rubs a palm over my back, settling against me. "Your person's out there, and I bet they're equally crazy."

"Should make the sex interesting." I hum. "Unless, of course, he never shows up."

"Never say never. I have a hunch it won't take much longer. For *either* of us." He remarks, and I swear I feel his cheek heat my scalp.

"Says you. Sorry you got stuck with such an unscrewable best friend."

"You're worth it." He affirms. "Even if I do always make it a point to wash my hands after touching yours."

I jab his bony ribs with my elbow, just as a deep voice beckons me from the aisle to our right. "Mary-Rose?"

Lifting my head, I see our pastor standing a few feet away, flaunting his transparent grin, as to be expected. Anxiously scooting away from Lewis, I return the gesture with the same degree of authenticity. "Hey, Pastor Morgan."

He casually slides his hands into his pockets, nodding my way. "Am I interrupting something? I was hoping to chat with you today. Just to catch up."

My stomach drops, and I reflexively glance across the wide room. Spotting a distant ivory dress among a group gathered at the chancel. Where my mother's expectant gaze lingers on Pastor Morgan, then me.

Son of a *bitch*.

"No, nothing..." I finally respond.

"Perfect. Care to join me in my office?" Pastor Morgan steps away before I can give a proper answer, anticipating compliance rather than demanding it.

Knowing I only have seconds, I fixate on his retreating form while whispering over my shoulder. "Any advice?"

"Whatever you do, don't ask for marriage counseling." Lewis pats my back. "I haven't found my person yet."

Chapter 3

I certainly can't complain about the tranquility of Pastor Morgan's office compared to the rest of the church. If only it wasn't due to the fact that I'm now *alone* with him.

The room itself is inviting. Hexagon-shaped with white walls adorned in everything from framed Bible verses to photos showcasing decades of Crosspoint's history. All windows are concealed behind a veil of finished blinds. Still, the soft lighting therein illuminates his wide wooden desk positioned perfectly in the center of the space, almost akin to a beam from heaven itself—a feature I know to be purposeful. It wasn't enough for people like him to persuade with words alone. Lighting, cadence, even the architecture worked to manipulate worshipers into prioritizing the man in charge. It was as strategic as it was monstrous.

I've had plenty of loathsome meetings sitting in the very chair I am now, staring across Pastor Morgan's desk to where he reigns in his high-backed office chair. Particularly in my pre-teen years. As the fact that I was a young girl growing up without a father supposedly meant that I needed twice the guidance of a regular attendee. He'd always used the analogy that parents were equivalent to the two feet we stood on, and without my father, I was an impressionable child hopping around one-legged in my attempt to navigate the tumultuous world. I'm not sure what that made my mother…except a lousy shoe.

"Mary-Rose," he begins, scooting closer to rest his elbows on the surface between us. "Tell me how you've been. Excited to start classes tomorrow?"

I straighten my posture, hoping to get whatever confrontation he's about to hurl my way over with as quickly as possible. "You bet. I've been looking forward to focusing more on my writing for a long time."

"From what I've heard, you've got everything it takes to be the next big name on the shelf." He remarks with a smile.

I huff a low laugh. "I guess we'll find out."

"Goodness, eighteen years old." He shakes his head, emphatic disbelief in his tone. "Seems like just yesterday you were trying to reach the stage mics to sing *Jem* songs in the middle of worship, and now you're a lovely young woman. Is that little girl still in there?"

"No." My affect remains flat. "She fell down a well."

I'd been aiming for a glare of disapproval, but instead earn a clipped chuckle and swift change of subject. "What about relationships? I know writers are the elusive type, but do you make time for friends? Potential suitors?"

"Just Lewis, since we live so close." My cheeks heat. "And, no. Still no boyfriend."

"That's not a bad thing." He assures softly. "There's nothing wrong with focusing on yourself. Especially in your season of life, when I consider a relationship with God to be as vital as ever. You're at a difficult stage." Pausing, he links his fingers. "I'm gonna be honest with you, Mary-Rose. I called you back here because your mother came to me with some concerns about your behavior lately."

There it is. I squeeze my eyes shut to avoid rolling them.

His justification comes sternly. "Now, don't be upset with her. She only did it because she cares about you."

"She does." It's an effort not to phrase it as a question.

"And she knows good and well that people turn to me during times of need." His lips momentarily purse. "There's no comfortable way to say this, but Christine described something that happened Friday night. Finding you engaged in a...sexual act with yourself?"

The outright question depletes any energy I have to appear heedful. I offer no reply as I sink deep into the cushiony seat—an admittance of guilt in and of itself.

"It's nothing to be embarrassed about." He promises, gesturing around us. "We're all human, which means we're all susceptible to sin nature now and again. But I wouldn't be doing my job if I didn't warn you about how engaging in that kind of behavior can lead you away from God's plan."

God's plan? Or the God of this church's plan? To me, the difference means everything. As one of them is capable of being entirely fictitious, while the other exists squarely before me, ruling the lives of conditioned believers for the sake of autocratic gain. I always found it funny how the business of "saving" people operated as any other monopoly.

My jaw tenses, and I make the risky decision to challenge him. "Pastor Morgan, with all due respect, I've never found anything in the Bible to suggest that the act of masturbation is sinful."

Shit, if they were so concerned with sexual atrocities, maybe they should reconsider their own reading material. It's not as if *Song of Solomon* wasn't just as lewd as my own works—not to mention, responsible for all my earliest stories containing embarrassing comparisons between my tits and fruits.

Pastor Morgan's face tweaks in pity. "Young lady, I don't necessarily see the act itself as the issue. Engaging in it at all suggests a degree of lust, and it's our duty as believers to abstain from sexual immorality. It may not seem important now, but just imagine what it might lead to. Fornication. Strained relationships. Adultery."

I stare at the man before me as the incredulity nesting in my chest turns hot, threatening to ignite. Morgan Collins was a man of no shame; that much was clear. But how could a person look another in the eye and condemn the very thing they themselves were guilty of? My gaze falls to the surface of his desk. Neatly polished, aside from a few dried stains of a particular mystery liquid near the edge. I wonder which of Crosspoint's married women it belonged to, and whether he was keeping it there as some form of grotesque trophy. But, hey, he didn't have a wife. So why *not* have the wives of others when nobody had the balls to tell him not to?

"I'm assuming you have experience with this?" I ask against my better judgment. Mindlessly fingering the *M.R.* engraving on the cross around my neck.

His armor doesn't crack. He doesn't even *flinch* at my veiled accusation. "I've seen a lot in my years of spiritual counseling. And, in extreme cases, the effects can be far more demonic. I've witnessed simple immorality manifest into acts of sexual violence. Or, if it's shared with someone of the same gender, it can even devolve into same-sex attraction. More often than not, it all stems from addictions to masturbation and pornography. I simply won't allow one of our treasured young ladies to stumble down such a dangerous path."

Out of all the nonsense he just spouted, it takes every ounce of my control not to retch at the way he'd so casually condemned gay people—guilty of nothing aside from loving another human being—to the same level as criminals who commit sexual assault. I raise my brows at him. "Dangerous?"

"Absolutely, just look at the times we're living in." A patronizing grimace pulls his features. "This epidemic is no happenstance. Truth be told, it's a wonder something as formidable as AIDS didn't come for them sooner. After all, 'the wages of sin is death, but…?'"

I force myself to swallow the vile taste on my tongue. "'The gift of God is eternal life through Jesus Christ our Lord.'"

"The sexual laws of God's word aren't in place to cage you, Mary-Rose. They're in place to protect you. Your virtue is valued, but once you give it away, there's no getting it back."

Losing patience by the precious second, I try hard to make my false look of astonishment appear genuine. "You know what, Pastor Morgan? You're right. I never thought of it that way."

He smiles again, his trimmed beard obscuring the corners of his lips. "I always return to *1st Corinthians* during discussions of this topic. Your body is a temple of the Holy Spirit within you. A beautiful woman like yourself must refrain from defiling it. Especially while seeking your future husband."

Oh, here we go. The *purity* talk. A sentiment that befell all the girls in church once they reached their developmental years. One that was, coincidentally, hardly imposed on boys—if Lewis's testimony was anything to go by. There were many facets to Christian fundamentalism that I knew I would go my entire life without fully understanding, but the shameless fixation on young girls' sex lives had to be up there with the most perturbing. My earliest memory of such a lesson went back to my sixth grade year, when Mom had enrolled me in a purity camp for girls held here at Crosspoint. The intention was to teach us that abstaining from all types of sexual contact before marriage was expected if we were to be God's faithful children.

The instructor began by handing every girl in the room a plastic spoon. Then held up a silver one of her own and said, *"Imagine you're a spoon, and to be used is to lose your virginity. In the grasp of your future husband, would you rather be a plastic spoon, something to be disposed of? Or would you rather be a silver spoon, meant to be treated with honor and dignity, for only the most special occasion in life?"*

I remember every word of my answer. I'd raised my hand and proclaimed, *"Neither. Because I would never marry some idiot who doesn't know that silver spoons can be washed."*

They told my mother not to bring me back after that. And she gave me her own lesson that night in what happens when I mouth off to authority—one involving a *wooden* spoon.

I often look back at this as the seed that sprouted my desire for sexual liberation, eventually leading to the birth of Slutty Rosie—a proudly provocative version of myself to live vicariously through. Not that I believed in the idea of "sluts" at all, considering there was hardly a term so derogatory for men who slept around. I simply chose that name to flip the stigma, if only in my own head. My fictional self wore the title as a badge of honor. A way to shove a big middle finger in the face of my mother and everyone else who believed promiscuous women were worthy of condemnation.

Although, to their credit, I am still a virgin all these years later. But not out of abstinence. More out of…circumstance.

Ignoring the way my skin prickles at the hypocrisy, I maintain my lively composure to appease the man in front of me. "Pastor Morgan, I can assure you that my body is as holy as it can be. I would *never* want to turn away a good man by virtue of being impure."

How he can't detect the sarcasm that practically stings my every word? I don't know. But regardless, his dark eyes beam in satisfaction. "And who knows who that good man might be? I reckon he's right under your nose and you don't even know it. Lewis, for instance?"

For *fuck's* sake. The more this man speaks, the more I want to smash the desk between us into bits. My fists clench to the point of aching to keep any signs of outrage from tainting my cheery face. "Lewis and I are only friends. But I'm thankful he's always there for me."

"I'm glad to hear it. We all need a little guidance when we find ourselves astray. This is simply a crossroads you've come to, and I have no doubt you'll make the right decision. One that leads to God's purpose for you."

I tilt my chin at him. "Being a writer?"

He huffs a laugh through his nose, leaning closer to look me dead in my eyes. "Being a *faithful* future wife."

Hot, fiery indignation courses through my veins so potent, I briefly wonder if the blur at the corners of my vision is a result of steam puffing from my ears. But I quickly realize it's due to how hard I'm clenching my jaw to keep my tongue from running me to a place that I could never return from. Instead, the words I wish to scream resound thunderously through my mind.

Bite me! You adulterous, hypocritical madman!

Somehow, I find it in me to keep smiling. "Thank you, Pastor Morgan. Is that all you wanted to talk about?"

He offers a single nod. "I'm glad I had this chance to speak with you, Mary-Rose. If you ever need a push in the right direction, you know where to find me." His condescending tone is rampant as ever as I stand to leave on taut legs. "One day you'll see how satisfying a relationship with your future husband can be, knowing you're closer to him than anyone else. Not to mention, closer to God."

I stop with my hand on the door, then glance over my shoulder to shoot him the best shit-eating grin in my arsenal. "And if my relationship with my future husband isn't satisfying, I always have a pastor to turn to in my times of *need*. Don't I?"

After all the bullshit I'd hand-delivered since stepping into his chambers, it's this very remark as I make my exit that succeeds in wiping the counterfeit smile off Pastor Morgan's face.

I march into my room, slamming the door behind me to find the pale pink walls tinted in a distorted shade of red. Grabbing the pillow from the base of my mattress, I smother myself and scream so violently that my vocal cords strain with the effort. I'd banked on the drive after Crosspoint calming me, at least to some degree. But my mother's snide remark before dropping me at home to attend her Sunday brunch had been nothing but an accelerant to the rage.

"Now that you've had some sense talked into you, maybe you'll finally focus on your true purpose."

True purpose? Those two-faced chauvinists wouldn't know the meaning of the word *true* if it manifested as God himself and struck their souls clean out of their bodies!

Throttled by emotion, I let the pillow fall. My chest heaves as I suck vital air in through my nose and out through my mouth. But when I open my eyes, I catch the sight of something protruding beneath the bed's box spring. Kneeling, I grab the strewn *Wild Thang* magazine page I'd abandoned following my encounter with Mom two nights ago. Holding the laminated sheet between my fingers, I scan the header. The text. The photo of Valentina.

The Albuquerque mailing address.

A held breath later, I'm at my writing desk, opening my *Holy Scriptures* notebook to find the bestrewed pages of my spiritual fiction romance within the leather cover. Clenching my jaw, I procure the bundle to flip through its abhorrent beginning chapters, stopping somewhere around my harlot's first encounter with the preacher she'd soon fall for—a scene where she's brought to his chambers for one-on-one repentance.

An idea strikes me like a smoldering bolt of lightning. So hard and so profound, I practically fall into the desk chair as my knees give out. The vehemence for what I'm about to do doesn't snuff out the anger blazing within. But I wouldn't allow myself to sit here and stew in it. I need to sit here and *use it.*

Mom, Pastor Morgan, and all the damn fawners at Crosspoint want me to prove myself by focusing on my true purpose? Enough said. Except, I wasn't going to prove it to them. I was going to prove it to the entire fucking city.

Shoving the notebook aside, I grab a fresh page to load into my typewriter. Find the keys with muscle memory. Then, I write…

"Young lady, do you realize how much trouble you're in?"

His deep voice reverberates with authority off the walls, making the secluded office feel even more inescapable. My focus drifts leisurely over the religious paraphernalia on all sides, until they reach the spacious wooden desk separating me from the heated man across it.

I smile innocently at him. "Pastor Madman, I hardly see how what I did constitutes as 'trouble' in this place of worship."

His gaze narrows at me, accentuating his already magisterial demeanor. He's handsome for a church leader, with a sculpted jaw shrouded in dark stubble matching his neatly gelled head of hair. But I can't keep my greedy eyes from wandering down his form, either. The girthy muscles along his chest and arms are evident even through his apparel.

He clasps his strong hands together, leaning closer with a fixed glare. "I caught you pleasuring yourself on the front-row pew during my sermon this morning. You don't find that to be sinful?"

Funny, coming from a man of God with a habit of fucking every amorous woman who sought him out for guidance. Oh, the stories I've heard. The number of times women would leave this very office bow-legged and stumbling with his seed trickling down their thighs…I'd gotten so aroused imagining such that I simply couldn't control myself through his show of speaking the good word.

"What can I say?" I ask, tugging the chained cross around my neck with playful fingers. "We're all susceptible to sin nature now and again, aren't we?"

He tilts his chin to look down at me. "Seems to me like you need to spend less time making excuses and more time on your knees, young lady."

"I spend plenty of time on my knees, Pastor Madman," I say, weaving the metallic chain between my teeth to bite.

Settling back into his throne-like chair, he shakes his head in disapproval. "An unwed woman like you should have more self-respect. That body of yours is only meant to be touched by the hand of your husband in marriage."

Supplying him with a glare in return, I release my necklace. The cross falls to rest against my pounding heart as I declare, "Bite me."

My comment succeeds in taking him aback as he utters, "Excuse me?"

"I said, bite me! You adulterous whore of a man!" I straighten my posture assertively. "I know exactly what you do to women in this room. What you do to them on this desk." My eyes fall to it, and I can't suppress a chuckle at all the evidentiary stains and scuff marks. "Maybe you aren't the one to be telling horny girls what to do with their bodies."

For a while, he's silent. His strong face unreadable until he finally counters with, "Are you challenging me?"

I quirk a brow, doing exactly so.

He inches forward, resting his elbows on the desk in contemplation. "Well, young lady, looks like you're in need of a more hands-on approach. Why don't you start by showing me exactly what you were doing this morning?"

Offering a devious smirk, I slowly part my legs, drawing the tight skirt hugging my thighs high enough to expose myself. The cool air nips, as I'm void of panties and long since wet for him. Trailing fingers along my inner thigh, I slip them between my folds and part myself for his viewing. He watches with unwavering focus as I dip one into my tight entrance, tilting my head back with a moan as it fills me. I remove it to rub circles against my swollen clit, biting my lip as pleasure pulses in time with my heavy heartbeat. Teasing myself as much as I am him, I busy my other hand with unbuttoning my blouse. Keeping our gazes locked, I slide the limb from between my legs and slowly pull one of my breasts free, trailing a shiny fingertip over my hardened nipple to slicken it with my juices. When it's coated, I bring the digit to my mouth and suck it clean, humming greedily at the taste.

Pastor Madman can no longer mask his ungodly desire. Carefully, he stands from his seat. While his dark eyes consume every inch of me, my own fixate on the long, thick bulge protruding from his pants.

"You think you know what I do in this room?" He asks, rounding the desk, prompting me to match his movements and meet him halfway. "You can't begin to imagine. Maybe I'll show you, if you can prove that you're twisted enough to become one of my harlots."

I look up at his face when the space between us is reduced to inches, gasping as his firm hand catches my exposed breast and squeezes hard.

His low tone carries on, "But one thing's for certain. If you agree, you can kiss the rapture goodbye."

Chuckling, I lace my fingers around his wrist. "I'll show you rapture." Shoving all my weight into his chest, his back hits the surface of the desk behind us. I waste no time climbing atop his virile body, but I don't stop at his groin. I settle my knees on either side of his head, grabbing a handful of his hair. "Now, let's see if you can prove yourself to me, Madman."

Then I lower my hips, closing the distance between my eager cunt and his awaiting tongue...

I go on. And on. And *on*.

Detailing every position. Every climax. Writing each word as if I would be the one personally responsible for delivering this blasphemous fantasy to every *Wild Thang* reader in existence. I don't stop to consider that my story may not be chosen. I don't even stop to rest my rapidly typing fingers. Not until my Slutty Rosie turned *young lady* has fucked Pastor Madman so well, there isn't a shred of doubt that it's the most remarkable sex I've ever put to paper. Call it confidence, or arrogance, or whatever the hell you want.

It was hot. And I knew it.

It's only after I complete the story and give it a final read-through that I realize my rage has transfigured. Now the simmering heat that guides my every move is a delicious cocktail of defiance, with a splash of pride in its most vigorous form. I remove an envelope from the nearest drawer. But before folding the pages to tuck inside, I procure a pen to inscribe one final addendum to the finished piece. On the top corner of the first sheet, I sign:

Written by: M.R.

After finishing the mailing details, it only takes another few minutes before I'm walking with a skip in my step down our street to the nearest postal drop box. And the moment my submission slips through the narrow aperture, any trace of residual fury from my encounter at Crosspoint this morning dissipates.

My satisfaction, however, does not.

Chapter 4

The first week and a half of classes at Trinity Grace taught me one thing: It doesn't matter how often you're forced to act like a fully functional adult in an unfamiliar environment; there are always new ways to prove yourself a complete dumbass.

Classwork had been the least of my worries. Regardless of the subject, almost all of it consisted of written essays, which I found to be a cakewalk. The real challenge came when trying to convince my mother that I was making an effort to be more sociable. "Forgetting" to attend the Bible study Pastor Morgan recommended during my first week had landed me nothing but a ringing in my ear when she was through with her chastising. It was the first time I ever found myself jealous of Lewis's ability to make friends from the convenience of his room with that computer he owned. I would be lying if I said I wasn't pissed at him for denying my request that he join me at the study come the following Thursday in favor of spending his night chatting with Presley over the web. But at the same time, it's not as if I could blame him for refusing something *I* hardly had the stomach to attend.

Walking down the quiet, half-lit hallway of the art department leads me past locked classrooms and cluttered bulletin boards. Desolation persists until I spot a set of double doors to a storage room propped wide open. I round the corner to enter and nearly headbutt a girl striding the opposite way.

"Whoa!" She shrieks. Only to smile widely when she steps back enough to look me over, flashing two rows of shiny braces. "Are you here for the study?"

I blink, my gaze flickering up and down long enough to examine her bulky Trinity Grace sweatshirt in the school's navy and white colors, half-obscured by brunette hair. "Um, yeah. Is this—?"

"You're in the right place!" Her tone is so merry, it echoes loudly down the empty corridor. "I was just getting the doors. Come on in!"

She kicks out the doorstops as I enter the vast storage sector, littered with folded tables and chairs hung on metal racks. In the center, I count ten girls sitting in a wide circle with their attention fixated on me. My cheeks redden with embarrassment as a navy-clad arm links around mine.

"I'm Rebecca, the senior in charge of the study this semester." She explains while tugging me along, stopping to grab a stray chair and motioning for the others to make a spot for me. "What's your name?"

"Rosie," I answer shyly, taking my newly propped seat while Rebecca reclaims her own beside it. "Sorry I wasn't here last week."

"It's no problem, we're always open to new members." She says, never losing her silvery grin. "I take it you're a freshman. What major?"

I nod. "English, creative writing."

"That sounds so fun!" Rebecca presses a finger to the white *TGCC* letters across her chest. "I'm education."

"I like your outfit." The girl sitting opposite her perks up, eyeing my navy skirt and white button-up. "School colors. You didn't get it at the campus store, did you?"

I notice that nearly all the girls are dressed casually in jeans and graphic shirts, which makes me feel even more out of place. I'm certainly no stranger to feeling self-conscious about my appearance. Given that, aside from my physical growth, it had evolved exactly none since I was a child. "No, this is pretty much my whole wardrobe. Even before Trinity Grace."

"It's so cute! Look, we match." Rebecca holds her sleeve to my skirt, then glances around the circle. "We did introductions last week, but I can fill you in before we start."

I pay attention as she gestures to each individual. Introducing their name, year, and major with impressive recollection, keying in to all until one at the furthest point of the circle catches my attention. She's yet to say a word, but something about her tight blonde curls half-up in a bulky barrette draws me to her in a lure of familiarity. She's the only girl in the group, aside from me, dressed somewhat traditionally. Sporting a modest flaxen dress long enough to pile around her chair.

"And that's Lynn," Rebecca points to the blonde. "She's a…a…" The leader fumbles, snapping her fingers as if it will jog her memory.

"Accounting major." Lynn finishes with a polite quirk of her lips.

"Right! Sorry," Rebecca tucks a lock of hair into her zig-zag headband as she addresses me. "Don't know how I forgot, she's our only other freshman. I bet you two will have a lot in common, Rosie!"

I find Lynn's eyes, an unforgettable shade of amber. Recognition hits me like a runaway locomotive. But before I can open my mouth to confirm what I suspect, Rebecca moves on to the next girl, prompting Lynn to avert her gaze and sink timidly into her chair, ushering away any confidence I have to confront the topic before the group.

When introductions conclude, Rebecca enthusiastically claps her hands. "So, Rosie, we were having a little discussion before you showed up. Maybe you can weigh in?"

"Oh, sure." Suppressing my displeasure, I slip the backpack off my shoulders. Unzipping it to retrieve the Bible I'd brought along.

"Does giving a blowjob count as losing your virginity?"

I stop cold, gaping at our leader as giggles chime from around the circle. "What?"

"Tell her, Gracie." Rebecca raises a brow at the member who'd complimented my outfit.

The girl's tan complexion flushes a shade deeper as she shrugs.

"My fiancé wants to put his thingy in my mouth, and I'm thinking about letting him. It doesn't count the same as vaginal."

"It totally does!" Rebecca laughs, receiving several nods of agreement from the group.

"But it's just the mouth," Gracie argues impishly. "He says it's completely different."

"I would *sock* my boyfriend in the mouth if he tried that on me." Rebecca rolls her eyes. "Ugh, Rosie, what do you think?"

Perplexed, my gaze shifts between them before I hesitantly give my honest take on the matter. "I think…if you're still calling it a 'thingy,' you probably aren't ready to have it inside you at all."

There's a single beat of silence before it's completely shattered by roars of laughter from everyone in the circle. Layers of rich echoes reverberate around the storeroom. Even Lynn's tight curls bob in time with her closed-mouth chuckles. For the first time since setting foot on this campus, without Lewis to facilitate it, a genuine smile stretches my lips. Then, I drop the Bible I'd procured back into the deepest pocket of my bag.

Something tells me I won't be needing it.

Turns out, Bible studies among college girls leave very little room for discussion of scripture. The whole hour was spent on boy talk, grievances about classes and professors, and even a few tears. It was absolutely nothing like I'd been expecting. And the most surprising part? By the time it was over, I was looking *forward* to attending again.

Rebecca offered us a cheery goodbye as we parted for the evening. Only holding me back long enough to reiterate for the thousandth time how much I was going to love my years at Trinity Grace, just as she and the other girls had. Her conviction was so admirable, I nearly believed her…Nearly.

By the time I make it outside, the sun is low enough that double-headed streetlamps flanking the walkways cast an orange hue over a shadowy courtyard. The area is desolate, void of sound aside from the distant traffic and footsteps of study members who were given a proper head start. Alone, I release a content breath.

"Long time, no see."

I startle at the voice, turning to spot Lynn leaning against the department's godly mural. Her back is to the chipped paint, propped foot tenting the pale fabric of her dress. She's grasping her cross-body purse strap in one hand and puffing a half-expended cigarette with the other.

Blinking to adjust to the darkness, the stab of familiarity returns. "I wasn't sure you recognized me."

"You haven't changed much." Smoke obscures her face as she exhales, but I see her eyes flicker to my hair. "Jesus, is that the same ribbon from sixth grade?"

I let out a self-deprecating huff. "May as well be."

"I guess that means your mom's still up your ass?" She raises a thin brow at me.

It's an effort not to gape at her. She'd spoken more to me in the past thirty seconds than she had to anyone throughout the duration of the study. Though my recollection of her walks with Lewis and me after group prayers was hazy, I can tell I'm not looking at the same Lynn who'd been mercilessly pulled away to an all-Christian academy years ago.

The prospect gives me courage to say, "My mom's…my mom." I glance over the mural above us, realizing with a shudder how right I'd been about the massive depiction in the dark giving me chills. "As far as she's concerned, I still believe in all this."

Lynn pauses, flicking a few ashes from the bud between her fingers. "I guess Rebecca was right. We do have a lot in common."

I study her face expectantly. "You mean, you don't either?"

She takes a final puff before snuffing out the cigarette on the painted stucco beside her. "No."

"What are you doing here, then?" I ask as she treads my direction.

"Same as you, it seems." Lynn nods down the pathway, signaling for us to walk together. "Trying to appease someone who'll make my life hell, otherwise."

I don't remember many details about her home life, but our talks during recess occasionally turned to how strict her parents were. To the same degree as my mother, if not more. It was one of the reasons I'd been so disheartened when she transferred. Sure, I always had Lewis. But misery prefers *all* the company it can get.

We take slow steps as I press on. "What'd you think?"

"About the study?" The corner of her mouth pulls. "Rebecca's nice, she graduated from the same Christian school I went to. Figured if I were to make any friends, someone like her would do well for me."

"She definitely made an impression." I agree. "But I don't think I'll have her kind of luck fitting in around here."

"I used to hate that I was surrounded by nobody but believers, especially when I started to fall off. But now, I'm kinda grateful for it." She kicks at a stray pebble on the pavement. "At least I know the people around here are decent."

I'm unsure what she means by that, but offer a hesitant nod in reply.

"And you?" She asks, brushing a few tight curls behind her ear to glance at me.

"I thought I was gonna hate tonight, but it was actually pretty fun. I'm not used to being around so many girls."

"Right, you and Lewis still close?"

My shoulders rise with a chuckle. "Oh, yeah. He goes here, too. I just don't see him as often since our classes are so different; he's a computer geek."

"Are you two…?"

"Together?" I roll my eyes. "No, never. He's like my brother."

"Oh. I was only wondering because," she giggles. "This is

embarrassing, but I used to be jealous of how well you two got along. I had a bit of a crush on him."

My head snaps her way. "Really?"

She shrugs. "I thought he was cute."

Before I even consider if it's the right suggestion to make, I nudge her shoulder with my own. "He's *still* cute, if you happen to be as single as he is. I'm sure an accountant and a web genius would have plenty to nerd about."

It was the least I could insinuate. Lewis always made me do the legwork when it came to his potential girlfriends. Despite the countless times I've confided in him about my crushes—often in the most brutally graphic detail I was capable of—he's never once admitted to having one of his own.

Lynn grins, her cheeks flushing in the tinted light. "I wouldn't say I'm much of a nerd. I'm just…good at handling money. I work at a bar uptown."

"Your parents are cool with that?"

She holds an index finger to her lips.

I suck in a breath through my teeth. "Gotcha."

"Do you work?" She asks.

"I babysit most weekends, but no official job."

"I don't suppose something in relation to writing is on the table?"

"That'd be nice," I say, pondering the idea. "But I mainly write on my own. Working on a Christian romance at the moment."

Lynn snorts at that. "The shit we do for our parents."

I marvel at the idea that I'm speaking to someone new who genuinely seems to understand my best-kept struggles. It almost makes me hesitant to know more about the person she's truly become. Anyone who puts on such a sizable front for their own family is bound to store a few masks for everyone else they meet. My *own* slips a little as I agree. "Yeah, the shit we do."

When we reach the edge of campus, Lynn stops before the walkway to student parking. "You need a ride home? I've got my own car."

"Thanks, but I'm good," I reply, nodding over my shoulder as I awkwardly step the other direction. "I've got a few errands to run."

"Alright, then." She doesn't contest, simply giving me a wave and a parting smile that reaches her amber eyes. "I'm glad we got to meet again, Rosie."

"So am I," I say, and mean it.

I watch as she crosses the street, slipping between divided shadows until they envelop her fully. Back in solitary, I make my way to the bus stop marking the northern end of Trinity Grace.

Then pass it entirely.

I don't stop until I reach the nearest convenience store to campus, and upon entering, I go to the same magazine rack I'd been checking every day of the week thus far. Continuously finding the prior *Wild Thang* issue with Valentina's pretty figure. But as much as I enjoyed looking at it—*her*—I feel my heart leap when I notice that the publication in question no longer displays her face on the front. But the face of a pale, curly-haired redhead posing with her legs open, a yellow star concealing her intimates. The newest issue had arrived.

With unsteady fingers, I grab the magazine and slowly flip through the pages. Skimming past naked models, ads for Viagra, and explicit VHS promos until I reach the spread I'm looking for. Long paragraphs of text extend onwards, but the top third of the leftmost page is all I have to read. As it supplies a bold title to the erotic story alongside a singular photographic depiction.

My face splits into the biggest grin of my life when I see Valentina Amor looking back at me, posing with a cross in one hand and the collar of a corrupt clergyman in the other.

Chapter 5

Leaning my lower back against the porcelain sink, I hold the folded magazine in front of my face. Admiring my story and replicated photo for what has to be the millionth time since procuring the object. Although, there is one portion of the sexy confection before me that I don't appreciate.

That being the title. One that had been assigned for me.

Panty-Sniffing Pastor Pounds Deviant Devotee
Written by: M.R.

Jesus. It's been over a week since I purchased the publication from that baffled store clerk to sneak home in my school bag, and my lip still quirks in confusion every time I read it. Slutty Rosie hadn't even worn panties in the piece.

But whatever grabbed the attention of readers…among other things.

Not that Valentina Amor owning her role in the photo recreation couldn't do that all on her own. She's dressed in a low-cut white blouse and a navy skirt that isn't too far off my own, holding a male model portraying Pastor Madman by the neck, pinning him against the desk below. The cross in her other hand is positioned high, like she's about to strike him with it. But the way she eyes the reader, looking straight into the lens with those luminous hazel eyes, makes me think she isn't capable of hurting a fly. The fact that one of my stories was now being read, enjoyed, and likely jacked off to by every subscriber in the city fills me with the most potent satisfaction I've ever experienced. But even *that* pales in comparison to the simple act of admiring Valentina.

Somehow, even in a singular still frame, she'd managed to capture the essence of my own personal character masterfully. Was I really that generic with it? Or was the woman before me so in-tuned with sensuality that she embodied it with seamless perfection? Whatever the case, I can't help but feel a strong desire to see her portray Slutty Rosie again. Imagining her in all the other fantasies I've written makes me bite my lip. My knees press together ever so slightly as I drink in the divine curves of her flawless body...

Until a fierce pounding at the bathroom door nearly sends the booklet flying out of my fingers.

"Rosie! Daniel picked his nose then put his hand in our bag of chips!"

I grab at my chest to ease the panic filtering through my pounding heart, then drop the magazine securely into my backpack. When I open the bathroom door, I'm greeted with the sight of a relentlessly bothered ten-year-old.

"There's another bag in the pantry," I say politely. "I saw it when I made you two lunch."

"That one's barbecue, I only like the sour cream kind." He argues, pushing thick glasses up his nose before bowing his head. "Why did you bring your backpack to the bathroom?"

My pulse jumps uncomfortably, but I quickly conjure an ingenious excuse.

"Well, Nathan," I lean forward, propping my hands on my legs with an innocent smile. "When girls become adults, we have a special time of the month that requires certain tools we keep stored away in—"

"*Ew ew ew ew ew*!" He yells, covering his ears before turning to run away. Socks thumping loudly on the hallway floor as he disappears around the corner.

I laugh, trailing behind until I reach the dining room where Daniel, three years Nathan's junior, sits munching on the sour cream chips in question. His dirty-blonde hair sticks comically in all directions, roughed up from the time we'd spent outside. He and I had battled in a water gun war while Nathan opted to stay in the shade, glaring at us for imposing on the book he was trying to enjoy. The dichotomy between the two brothers never fails to entertain, reminding me somewhat of a different pair I know.

Soft footsteps interrupt my thoughts. Nathan emerges from the kitchen with a bag of barbecue chips that he tears open after finding a seat at the table.

"I thought you only liked sour cream?" I ask, setting my hands on my hips.

He shovels a few into his mouth. "I like barbecue sometimes."

I shake my head while affectionately ruffling his dark hair, which earns me a whine. I'd babysat both of them long enough that Nathan's ambivalence rarely fazed me. The same going for Daniel's unpredictability and brutal candor. Which makes getting struck with a sour cream chip on the side of my head less unexpected than one might think.

"Rosie, your butt's getting bigger," Daniel remarks with a mouthful. "You should stop eating so much candy."

I pick the residual crumbs from my light-brown hair while shooting him a playful scowl, reaching onto the table—cluttered with sweets, board games, and other means of making my job easier—to pick out a heart-shaped lollipop.

"Someday you'll learn that talking to a woman about her weight is a sin." I tease, sticking my tongue out at him as I press the freshly unwrapped treat to it. A gesture Daniel returns as I speak around the sucker. "Besides, the more sugar I eat, the faster my hippo is!"

I lean my chest over the table to start bopping the prepped *Hungry Hungry Hippos* game at the center, getting a head start before Daniel races to join in. Even Nathan jumps to entertain. White marbles scatter noisily about the red base until they're all consumed. My pink hippo claiming the majority.

I twirl the lollipop in my mouth with a winning smile, watching as Daniel's sore-loser pout morphs into a grin when his eyes catch something over my shoulder. "Dad!"

My face slackens, realizing too late that the angle I'm bent leaves very little under my skirt to the imagination. I jump upwards with a twirl, smoothing the fabric to my thighs as Daniel breaks from the corner of my vision.

Mr. Lasker stands in the dining room archway, briefcase long since discarded as he's slammed into by his youngest. He gives a theatrical groan at the impact, patting the little boy's back. "You have a fun day, buddy?"

"Uh-huh," Daniel points at me. "Rosie and I had a water gun fight. I totally soaked her, Dad!"

"Really?" Mr. Lasker's gaze lifts to mine. "Sad I missed it."

My mouth splits wide, the lollipop stick jutting between my teeth before I remove it to address him properly. "My cardigan took the brunt of it. I hung it to dry in the laundry room. Mind if I leave it here until next weekend?"

"Not at all." He says, flashing me a pristine smile before greeting his quieter son. "Nathan, no hug?"

The eldest boy grumbles, ambling out of the chair to welcome his father as I track him with uncertainty. I've been babysitting Nathan and Daniel since I was fifteen, when Mom had arrived home from her shop one day to tell me of a new client. One who'd come in to have his suit tailored for a divorce hearing, which led to venting about finding somebody to look after his sons during visitation on the Saturdays he worked. Mom had volunteered my services the instant she heard that he lived only a neighborhood away. And ever since, I've been the boys' weekend big sister. But despite our lengthy history, I can't pull a single memory of Nathan acting so grumpy at his dad's arrival. And even though my expertise in father figures is nine years past its expiration date, I knew that Ken Lasker was a good one. He was receptive. Always assured that he left his sons plenty to entertain themselves with while they were in my care. I'd never seen him so much as raise his voice at them. He was, in every sense, the perfect dad.

Not that I looked at him that way. No, no, *no*.

I may've had boy crushes throughout my school years, but when Mom first introduced me to the forty-something finance director with enough charm to win *her* seal of approval, there was simply no hope for me. Not when he carried himself like an older, sexier John Stamos fit with tan skin and gorgeous salt-and-pepper hair to top. He might be old enough to be my parent, but the way he made my cheeks flush and lower-belly tingle by simply walking into the room always left me longing for a way to prove myself more mature. The number of times I'd sat before my typewriter attempting to find the courage to put my wistful fantasies of us on paper was simply too many to count. But I always found myself too skittish, knowing I'd have to face him every weekend with that unyielding desire in tow. Maybe one day, that would change.

My eyes consume his debonair form as I lean against the dining table's edge, delicately pulling the lollipop through my puckered lips, savoring the strawberry taste as much as I do the sight of him.

"Whoa, who made that mess?" Mr. Lasker suddenly drops his amiable tone, nodding at a pile of potato chips littering the dining room floor. Both boys point at the other to blame, drawing a sigh from their father. "Broom. Dustpan. Now."

Nathan and Daniel's shoulders drop as they saunter away to do as they're told.

"Sorry," I offer with a wince. "I should've kept a tighter cap on things."

"Don't be, they've gotta learn." He shakes his head, stepping closer—which makes me lift my chin to accommodate his towering height. "You know, if I tried to get away with half the stuff those two pull back when I was a kid, my old man would've swatted my ass black and blue."

"That's horrible," I say, as if I haven't had my own encounters with such measures. Which were, funnily enough, my more customary of childhood memories. Not that I had it nearly as bad as Lewis, as I would often notice the scuff marks left behind on Mr. Fennick's older belts when I hung around their house. It was one of the few things that made me feel the slightest bit grateful for my mother. At least her apparel of choice never offered easy access to such a weapon.

Mr. Lasker shrugs his broad shoulders. "It's how they did things back then. Worked on me."

My gaze sweeps over the pronounced muscles of his biceps, straining against his business casual dress shirt. And I'm *definitely not* imagining what kind of power he'd be able to put into a swing with a particular naughty girl—in need of an old-fashioned punishment—bent over his lap. I glide my tongue methodically over the glaze of the sucker, thankful that the subject of my attention is too focused on his sons reentering with their required cleaning supplies to take notice, only perking when his welcoming gray eyes find mine.

"While they're busy, I can give you a ride home." He insists.

"You sure? I don't mind walking."

"Not a chance. It's scorching out there." He drops a firm hand on Nathan's shoulder. "Nathan can hold things down for ten minutes, right?"

The little boy assertively shrugs away his father's grasp, brushing past me to begin sweeping. I raise my brows at the uncharacteristic act.

Mr. Lasker smiles before smoothing his palm up my spine—a move that wracks it with delicious shivers. "I won't take no for an answer, Rosie."

I submit. Holding his gaze as I dip the candied heart back into my mouth, then crunch it between my teeth.

A few minutes later, I'm watching houses breeze past from the passenger seat of his lavish car, sitting with a *slight* arch in my back in case he glances over while leisurely addressing my forced inquiry about how his day went.

Sadly, he keeps his eyes on the road. "Saturdays are getting tougher. From what Daniel let slip, Charlotte's getting more vocal about how she doesn't like me leaving them with a babysitter on my weekends."

I almost recoil at the mention of his ex-wife, whom he only ever brought up when correspondence regarding their children grew tense. It pushes me to ask, "Is that why Nathan's in such a sour mood all of a sudden?"

"No, I think that's all you."

My gaze narrows. "What did I do?"

He tilts his head in lieu of a shrug. "I'm just speculating. But he's excited when he knows you're coming, then grouchy when you have to leave..." His voice trails off in a suggestion that hits me like a strike to the face.

I gape at him. "No..."

Mr. Lasker tries and fails to stifle a laugh. "Hey, he's at the age."

I scoff, my head falling dramatically against the rest. "He's like my little brother!"

"The heart wants what it wants, Rosie." He says, taking far too much pleasure in my obvious discomfort. "Anyways, you should be used to it by now."

My brows jump at the insinuation, prompting my tone to shift lower. "Used to what?"

He throws me a stern glance. "Oh, come on. Doesn't matter if they're all God-fearing at that college of yours, I know how quick boys are to worship a pretty girl."

A rush flares through my chest at the blatant compliment. Igniting a warmth that courses deep as I delicately cross my legs, allowing my skirt to ride a *bit* higher up my thigh than I usually would. "I wish guys paid that kind of attention to me. But even if it's true, it seems like nobody wants to make a move."

Am I teasing him?

More importantly…is it working?

"Give it time." His smooth, deep voice fans the flame within me. "Just promise me something?"

"Anything."

"When you have all those boys clamoring at your feet and one of them steps out of line," he perks a brow my way. "Let me know. I'll put him in his place."

Heat crawls up my neck and face despite the AC shrouding me in cold gusts. "I may have to take you up on that. Mom keeps insisting I'll find my 'future husband' there."

At that, he sighs heavily. Mr. Lasker was well aware of the disparity between my mother's beliefs and mine. In the years I'd known him, he'd become one of my most trusted outlets for decompressing about her radical behavior. It wasn't uncommon for me to remain at his house hours after he'd returned from work, or for him to take the extra-long route back to my home for the purpose of supplying me ample time to vent. Hell, during my high school years when Lewis and I got into late-night trouble, it was *his* number I punched into the payphone—as he'd promised to keep any clandestine rides I might need a secret from my mother. Despite the disappointment that always came with his leaving, I found solace in the fact that there was at least one fully grown adult who saw Mom's methods of parentship as woefully unjust as I did. And I found even *more* solace in him looking so sexy while doing it.

"I know it can be hard to understand from your perspective, but Christine still sees you as her baby. I'm sure she only wants you to be with someone trustworthy." He explains, then reaches into the passenger seat to set a hand on my leg. "Can't say I blame her, there are a lot of bad people in this world."

My lips part, but not to respond.

In fact, I have to bite the inside of my cheek to keep from audibly gasping as his touch makes my already warm and fluttery insides absolutely *pulsate* with arousal. His large hand consumes my topmost thigh, all but forcing my brain to envision it traveling those few short inches to slip beneath the bunched fabric of my skirt. How the rough callouses of his fingertips would feel toying my clit instead of idly resting. I discreetly study my own fingers for comparison, finding his double, if not triple their size. Just two of them would be thicker than anything I've ever taken—it would take some persuasion to fit them inside, no doubt. I swallow hard as the area in question throbs in a wave of hot tingles, flooding my panties with a slick manifestation of lust. My body prepping for the act as if it wasn't just a cerebral projection of my lewdest fantasy.

"But I also get that you and her don't exactly see eye to eye." He goes on, mercifully holding his gaze forward as I struggle for composure. "It's like I've always said, you're welcome to call if it ever seems like too much. I'm only a drive away."

I keep my breath deceitfully steady as I respond. "Don't tempt me, I'll start camping at your house every time she calls my name."

My subliminal jest produces the exact reply this arousal demands.

"Not a bad idea. The boys would love to have you." His thumb meticulously grazes my skin. "And so would I."

My heart hammers as I fixate from his face to his groin, battling the primordial feminine urge to claw through his pants like an animal and find out just how many inches of his cock I can squeeze down my throat before choking. Surely it won't take much, if it's as big as the rest of him.

"Thanks for watching out for me, Mr. Lasker," I say, despite my mouth watering at the illicit idea.

"It's my pleasure. You aren't just Christine's baby girl, Rosie. You're mine, too."

I lift my eyes from his crotch as, with heartbreaking velocity, the tendrils of my arousal slip. Turning frigid as the cool, harsh breeze from the dashboard vents.

The corner of his mouth pulls into a smile at my silence. "What, you think after all these years I don't see you as the daughter I never had?"

Daughter...He sees me as a *daughter*.

His touch wasn't some coded confirmation of mutual desire, nor was his offer of accommodation an invitation to sneak into his bed and let him do with me what he will. They were nothing but parental gestures from a figure of authority who still sees me as a fucking child. I should probably take it as a blessing. I'd be lucky to have as selfless a man as him—a stellar father to his own children—assuring me he was happy to fulfill a critical role in my life that had been otherwise vacant. But instead, I lose the arch in my back, along with any semblance of hope that he might see me as the mature woman I so desperately desire to be.

The remainder of the short ride is quiet, and I actually feel a hint of salvation when he slows to a stop beside the walkway leading to my house. Securing the bag at my feet, I bid him a friendly farewell until next weekend as I step from the car.

"Forgetting something?" He calls from the driver's seat.

I bend at the waist to see him extending a hand with the money I'm owed. Flustered, I take it. Ignoring the spark between our brushing fingers as I back off with a final thanks. By the time I'm stepping up the cracked concrete to the porch, he's driving away to attend to his sons as if it's just another weekend. And *I'm* cursing myself for being the same stupid girl hopelessly enamored with a man old enough to be her father, as if it's just another weekend.

It might be. Only now, I'm the same stupid girl who's since been published in a pornographic magazine.

The covert thought triggers an involuntary skip in my step, as it had been doing every so often over the past nine days. It only breaks when I stop to procure the short stack of envelopes left outside our front door before entering, catching my mother's voice from her sewing room as I do.

"Mary-Rose?"

"Here, Mom," I call, flipping through the variegated mail.

The distant whir of her sewing machine dims. "How were Ken's boys today?"

"Mischievous," I say, half-grumbling as I sift the final letter to the top. The envelope itself is blood red, but the corner mailing label exhibits three bold words in shimmery black font.

Wild Thang Studios

My eyes bulge. The recipient's information in the center prints as my home address, with the initials *M.R.* listed above it.

"Have children of your own, then talk to me about 'mischievous.'" Footsteps permeate the quiet foyer before Mom rounds the corner, inspecting the stack in my hand. "Mail came?"

Our gazes meet, and I offer a complacent smile along with the bundle. She takes it with a curt sigh that flares some of her loose gray-blonde hair. I pass by, sweeping her ivory skirt with my swift current.

"I have homework to do," I say as my feet pound the stairs.

If she responded, I couldn't hear it over the rapid thumps of my Mary Jane flats on the wood, nor do I stop until I'm shut securely in my room. Recovering my breath, I remove the letter from where I'd expeditiously tucked it between my shirt and backpack. Taking time to look it over, I work to convince myself that it's real at all as I claim a seat at my writing desk.

It's real. But what's it for?

Was this customary for those whose stories were selected? Had I truly been so foolish as to think they wouldn't send some form of courtesy letter to confirm that mine had been chosen? My pulse skitters as I tear open the seal and remove the single document from the red envelope. Unfurling it, the page reads as follows:

To M.R.,

We at Wild Thang Studios wanted to thank you for mailing your erotic excerpt to be included in our latest issue. It is our discretion that the most recent publication, particularly your inclusion, has been marginally well-received. We are writing to initiate contact with you regarding future terms. Given your status as an Albuquerque resident, we request that you visit our studio at your earliest convenience so we may discuss this matter in person.

Yours faithfully,
Ruth Sexton

Below the paragraph is a print of the studio's address alongside their office hours. I reread it several times before the gravity of what's being requested of me begins to settle in. When it does, it nearly pulls me out of my chair.

Well-received?

Future terms?

Visit their studio?

Questions swarm my mind. All of which were fruitless, as they couldn't be answered unless I heeded their request and went there in person to find out for myself. However, something lurches from the mystique to grip me. The same interweave of thrill, desire, and pride I'd come to relish since discovering they chose my story in the first place. But just the slightest hint, and I knew there was only one way for me to experience the full intensity of it again.

Come Monday, I would need to take a little detour on my way to Trinity Grace.

Chapter 6

At first, I thought I'd simply exited at the wrong bus stop. But after checking the map I brought, I conclude that it's more likely I'd slipped into an alternate dimension and was now traveling through a post-apocalyptic wasteland. I have half a mind to find a payphone just to call and congratulate my mother on being right about her doomsday theories.

There isn't a sign of life in any direction, aside from the distant hum of vehicles resounding from a nearby overpass. Nothing about the building in front of me indicates that it's in business at all. It's more akin to a windowless truck stop than a pornographic magazine studio—complete with an inclined, canopied walkway leading to tinted glass doors. It takes craning my neck to check the establishment's sign for a third time before I convince myself that I'm where I should be. On the peeling material, the same *Wild Thang Studios* logo from the letter I'd received stretches wide, almost entirely sun-bleached into the red background from what must be years of exposure.

Hesitation hangs in the dry air as I approach, following the pathway shrouded by a multi-colored sunshade above, casting a prismatic glow on the derelict pavement. When I reach the tinted front doors, I release the strap of my backpack to open one. Once I do, my eyes flare. Not just in surprise, but in natural response to such a consuming shade of red enveloping every inch of my vision. I blink hard, considering the possibility that God had filled my eyes with blood in divine retribution for coming to this licentious place at all. Stepping farther inside the dim lobby does nothing to alleviate the strain, as every wall in sight exhibits the same deep color, including the ceiling tiles. The only exception is the solid black floor, along with a receptionist desk poised before the threshold to a perpendicular-running hallway—the only furniture the entry room offered. The space sits just as vacant as the exterior had been. I stand there for a good while, waiting for some confirmation of the enterprise to make itself known before I go hunting. But when it does, it nearly shakes me out of my skin.

"Eat shit, R.J.!"

The shrill feminine tone comes from somewhere within the obscured corridor. There's a mix of shuffling footsteps before another individual adds to the heated exchange.

It's a man's voice now, accentuated with a thick southern accent. "You're the only one on-site that fits the profile. We make our girl any taller and the whole plot gets thrown!"

"That flighty bitch not showing for call isn't my problem!"

"It is when we need capacity. You're *really* telling me that triple-x Johnson isn't just another Monday for yo—?"

The sound of a hefty slap cuts him off, replacing his solicitation with a guttural yowl.

Moments later, a frail woman dressed in loose-fitting clothing stomps into the hallway's entrance. She could be anything from my age to fifty. It's impossible to tell with the smudged black liner rimming her beady eyes—partially cloaked behind scraggly bangs of the same shade. I go stiff when she spots me, fists clenching the straps of my backpack like a life vest.

She aims a dramatic groan at the red ceiling, then pivots to someone out of view while tossing her arms my way. "She's right here!"

Beside her, a man emerges, rubbing the side of his swollen jaw with a wince. He is *certainly* middle-aged. I can tell from the faint streaks of gray in his otherwise brunette hair. At least, the sides that aren't concealed by the off-white cowboy hat he's wearing. One that matches the scheme of his Western button-up, ducking into blue jeans fit with a bulky leather belt and boots to complement. When his mossy green eyes meet my own, his face slackens. Accent shifting to an accusatory high as he asks, "Where the hell have you been?"

I barely manage a stutter before he's approaching. "I-I'm trying to find—"

"Wait, wait, wait." He cuts me off, looking me over with shrewdness. "You're supposed to be shorter."

"I don't...*Hey!*" I nearly lose my footing as he spins me. A draft sweeps as my flared skirt is lifted.

"You're lucky you've got an ass."

"*Excuse me*—?!"

Before I can be the second woman who strikes this man today, he's pulling me through the lobby and into the hallway beyond. Shaking his head as he remarks, "I hope all that time you took was worth it. If our guy fluffs any longer, that prime cut of his is bound to snap off."

I would've been entirely disoriented had I not been led along. As red indentations in the walls on either side of us gradually register as passing doors, he stops at one to open with his free hand, then shoves me inside with the other.

"Behind the curtain. And get those clothes off." He commands.

I whirl around, but he slams the door in my face before I can convey how mistaken he is. Standing in shock, I slowly inspect the new room. This one is built with a much higher ceiling, trisected with thick black curtains veiling most of the floor. Beneath the closest one, harsh illumination casts shadows in the shape of people moving indiscernibly. Looking for any form of assistance after being so brutally ushered, I approach it to pull aside the heavy fabric.

My ear-splitting scream draws the confused gaze of every individual within. Behind a sea of bulky camera equipment and angled studio lights, a sparse crew of indecorous technicians stands gaping at me. But I'm unable to rip my bulging eyes from the scene at their front, where a staged mattress acts as a plinth for what has to be the most hulking man I've ever seen.

Who also happens to be the most *naked* man I've ever seen.

It might be the first time I've witnessed a penis in the flesh—no, that time Lewis lost his swimming trunks diving at the public pool doesn't count—but something within my native feminine instinct told me that they weren't typically supposed to end between the owner's fucking knees like the one before me. My jaw hangs open as I slowly back away, the expectant crowd tracking me with every inch of my retreat.

"What's wrong with you?" A nasally voice calls from behind.

When I turn, I find a nook of the wide studio fitted with vanities, dressing racks, and metal lockers lining the walls. A curly-haired redhead sits at one of the makeup tables. While her lower half is clothed in shiny black spandex, her upper body is bare as the giant had been. All it takes is a moment of studying the irritated grimace she wears to recognize her as the model from the cover of *Wild Thang*'s latest issue.

"There's been a mistake," I force the words out with a disturbed laugh. "I'm not supposed to be here."

"Aren't any of us?" She quips, her glittery eyes rolling in the reflection of the bulbed mirror.

I approach her on unsteady legs. "No, I mean, I'm not a pornstar like you guys. I'm only here to meet someone named Ru—"

"What did you just call me?" Her head spins my way, made-up features narrowed in rage.

"I-I just meant—" Gasping, I jump on my heels when the sound of a sharp *crack* zips from somewhere out of sight.

"I'm a model, not a video girl. Let's get that clear." The redhead stands. Lengthy heels putting her over a head taller than me, which leaves my face at uniform height with her impressive breasts as she stalks closer. "Only one of us is getting jammed on cam today, and it sure as hell ain't me."

I reverse from her intimidating advance just as my foot catches the edge of another black curtain. Staggering backwards, the cloth divider gives way as I fall on my ass. Bracing myself on the concrete flooring, another loud *crack* echoes off the high walls. Only now, it's much clearer. There's movement in my peripheral vision, drawing my wide eyes to the source of the fierce snaps. The noise hits again, paired with the sight of a woman clad in latex from head to toe, striking a gagged and hog-tied man with a long whip while a photographer snaps pictures of the act. All of their heads—with the exception of the one bound in place—swivel to find me on the ground.

"Are you lost?" The dominatrix asks, voice muffled by her BDSM mask.

The impulse to eject myself from whatever debaucherous domain I quite literally stumbled into seizes me as I jump to my feet with the intent of sprinting straight for the exit. But I nearly run head-first into the still-seething redhead's chest in doing so. Floundering away from her tall stature, I hear the curtain behind me pull as studio lights pour in.

"We shooting or not?"

I spin on my heel and feel my throat burn as another scream tears itself loose. The male performer, awaiting his partner, stands before me, his behemoth body nude as can be.

"Why don't you ask big mouth here?" The redhead shoves my shoulder.

I jump away from them, retreating until my backpack is flush against a metal storage locker at my rear. The two towering figures step closer. Likely awaiting my answer, but looking as if they were ready to grab and toss me in front of the camera themselves if I didn't provide one. My brain swims, and I become too preoccupied with trying not to faint to form any semblance of a coherent response. Certain I'm staring death in the face, I send up a last-ditch prayer to any God foolish enough to grant me, of all people, commiseration for leading such a pathetic existence. Assuming this wasn't always their intended execution for Rosie Ginger.

Death by accidental porn. *Of-fucking-course* that's how I'm destined to go. I screw my eyes shut. Hoping that it—he—comes quickly enough to spare me the misery.

"What the hell is going on in here?!"

The voice belongs to neither of the individuals cornering me, and when I open my eyes again, their heads are turned to the studio entrance. Leaning to peek around their towering forms, I manage to get a look at my savior.

Thank *Christ*, she's clothed.

Rather professionally, in a deep-gray suit fitted to her slim, hourglass-like figure. She looks to be the same age as my mother, even somewhat resembling her. Excluding the fact that there are no traces of gray in the flaxen ponytail she sports, nor the soft tendrils that curtain each side of her face. She stands solidly in the now-open doorway, glaring at us with narrowed, impeccably styled brows.

The redhead lifts her chin. "Either you need to keep a lock on the front doors, or you need to hire stars who don't back out of their roles at the last second. This one's saying she doesn't belong here."

Entering the room fully, the blonde pins me with a brooding look. "If you aren't talent, then what are you here for?"

Her passive tone puts me at ease enough to regain control of my appendages. I cautiously step away from the locker to explain, "I'm here because I sent an erotic story for the last issue, then got a letter in the mail asking me to come. It was from somebody named Ruth."

The woman's eyes widen, flashing steely blue irises for only the slightest moment before her composure takes charge. "Cherie, get Lisa. She'll cover the shoot."

The redhead scoffs. "She already ran. Nearly whipped R.J.'s jaw off his skull just for asking."

"Then find her. And tell her we're offering our no-show's cash advance." Her gaze flickers to the model. "*Now.*"

Letting out a heavy sigh, Cherie steps around the woman and out of the room. At this, the massive nude performer saunters back to his own set. I swallow loudly as I track the casting shadows of his *three* legs before the curtain slices my view.

"Sorry for the confusion." The authoritative blonde approaches, extending an open palm. "I'm Ruth Sexton."

Relief rinses me as I accept the handshake. Though I still have to tilt my head to accommodate the elevation her refined pumps offer—as if I don't feel small enough.

"I'm Rosie Ginger," I say, then elaborate. "Mary-Rose Ginger. But people call me Rosie."

"Mary-Rose…" She thoughtfully tests my name. "M.R."

I nod, and it's only now that she seems to give me a proper look-over. If she's confused by my unforeseen church girl appearance, she refuses to let it show on her face—which is layered in subtle, expertly applied makeup that amplifies her innate beauty.

"Come with me," she says, turning to stride for the door. "Let's talk in our office."

I stand motionless before jumping to follow her tail, matching my steps with the sharp clicks of her heels. "You saved my address?"

"I like to keep tabs on all employees." She takes a right when we reach the fire-engine-red hallway. "Even the potential ones."

Potential employee…The prospect pushes me to ask, "You said in the letter you wanted to discuss future terms?"

"I did."

I feel like a fawn trailing after its speedy mother as she leads me along. "You mean, you want me to write for you again?"

"That's for us to discuss." She shoots a look over her shoulder that I'm hesitant to call a smile. "Any other questions?"

We reach the end of the hall where a singular door stands on the farthest wall. It's the only one that isn't painted a nauseating shade of red, but an inky black.

"Um," I pause. "You said, 'our' office?"

She opens the sable door, motioning me inside the spacious room. While the walls bear the same shade as the rest of the establishment, they're obscured with every variation of decorative memorabilia such a business could possess. Some are body-length frames showcasing years of *Wild Thang* magazine covers—each issue stamped with a bright red tab in the bottom-right corner, marking the copies as official. Others are miscellaneous awards in the form of plaques and trophies housed on shelves. The windowless space offers no natural light, only recessed bulbs circling the ceiling's perimeter. The illumination grows brighter at the center of the room, where a broad wooden desk distinguishes itself.

Poised behind it in a high-backed chair is the man who'd forced me into that obscene studio. His boots are crossed over the table, face obscured by the latest *Wild Thang* issue as he reads. At the sound of our entry, he drops the object. Getting one peek at me before theatrically lolling his head, which houses a vibrant, hand-shaped mark just below his cheek. "Look, if you aren't on the pill, we can't help you. If our suppliers made condoms *that* size, they'd have more inventory than they could ever—"

"Rodney," Ruth silences him with a firm close of the office door. "This is Mary-Rose Ginger. *She's* our M.R."

Every muscle in the man's body goes taut, his mouth falling open as he frantically stands. "Oh! Of course, we were wondering when you were bound to show up." Shaking away obvious panic, his face splits into a smile as he offers a hand across the desk. I reluctantly grab it, wincing as his firm grip tugs my small body with each powerful shake. "Rodney James. The crew here calls me R.J." His southern drawl swells with a slight dip of his cowboy hat. "Don't take my case of mistaken I.D. too personally. You sorta...have that look about you. Go ahead, sit down."

I couldn't begin—and wasn't sure I wanted—to comprehend what that meant. Opting to do as he suggests and claim the threadbare seat behind me. At the same time, Ruth takes a stance beside her colleague, arms tactfully crossed as she watches my every move.

"Me and Rodney are the ones in charge around here." She explains. "I handle the business. He handles the models."

"That, I most certainly do, Baby Ruth." He pats the unflinching woman's ass before clasping hands leisurely behind his head, sinking into the tall leather chair. Pausing, his consuming gaze bleeds to bafflement. As if he finally happened to take note of the fact that I'm dressed like I've just escaped a parochial 1930s orphanage. "So, uh... forgive my ineptitude. But *you're* M.R.?"

My eyes flicker to the splayed magazine, then back to him. "Yeah."

His face tenses in a fearful grimace. "Before we have to get our front doors reinstalled, I need to verify your age."

How courteous of him to consider this *after* throwing me in a room to get hammered by a fourteen-inch nail.

"I'm eighteen," I say, stripping my backpack to pull my I.D. and slide it over.

R.J. visibly relaxes as he views it. "And you wrote the story of the Deviant Devotee?"

I cringe at the title that was definitely not my creation. "Yes."

He perks up, pointing at me with flared eyes. "You know what? I see it now." Chortling, he gestures to my apparel. "You're the 'convert in the streets, cocksucker in the sheets' type, aren't you? Half our models grew up in a church; must be something in the holy water."

I shake my head, disregarding his crude remarks. "I'm sorry, but can we talk about why you contacted me?"

R.J. isn't so quick to respond to this. Instead, he glances up to where Ruth towers.

"It seems your story helped boost our sales with this latest issue." She says, tapping the open page on the desk's surface. "At least, yours has been better received than our previous submissions…If you can call them 'submissions' at all."

"Hey," R.J. holds up a hand in defense. "I may write like a grade-school dropout who caught up on grammar in ABE. But last I checked, that's our target audience."

Ruth glares down at him. "Not anymore, it isn't."

I realize what it is they're implying. The studio hadn't selected my piece from a pool of submissions. They selected it because it had been the *only* submission. The part of me that had spent the past week and a half relishing the idea that I'd earned any form of honor by being the stand-out in something begins to crumble, but I refuse to let it collapse fully. Not when Ruth had just alluded to me being the reason their sales were up.

"How do you know it's because of my story?" I ask.

Ruth and R.J. share another glance, and she gives him some form of silent command with nothing but a pert raise of her brow. In an instant, the man reaches for a clunky telephone and answering machine at the corner of the wide desk, pressing one of the heavy buttons.

BEEP

I jolt at the loud noise, followed by momentary static until a woman's voice cuts through on the recording.

"*H-Hello? Uh…Wild Thing…? Er, Thang…?*" There's muffled chatter with a background individual before the voice returns. "*Hi there, hope this reaches y'all. My friends and I have this little club where we talk about books and magazine columns. One of our members thought it'd give us a hell of a laugh to bring in a dirty mag for our group to read over. But, well, I have to say, we were all real surprised when we did. That story set in church? I didn't know y'all wrote erotica for women. Let alone a story so, uh..."

"*Hot!*" The background voice butts in, just for the main speaker to quietly hush her.

"*Anyway, I just thought you folks would be pleased to know that most of the ladies in our club went out to buy a copy of their own after our read. Can't believe I'm saying it, but if you publish more like this, you have yourselves some loyal new subscribers.*"

The message cuts off, and I feel the unmistakable swell of pride in my chest. *My* story had done that?

BEEP

The deafening tone returns, a different feminine voice taking over.

"*Hey, I know you guys probably get these types of messages a lot. But I just had to call after reading your new issue. I work for the post and couldn't help but peek inside a special delivery I was running. See, I was a Christian girl growing up and... well, you just don't read stuff like that every day. Especially something for women. I liked it, really liked it.*"

BEEP

"*You know, I wasn't gonna bother. But I found your magazine in the backseat of my husband's truck. Planned on rolling it up and beating him in the head with it, but I ended up getting a little curious before I did. That story about the sexy pastor? Never read anything like it. You bring M.R. back, and I might be the one keeping these from him.*"

BEEP

They go on. More and more messages from people who had picked up the newest issue of *Wild Thang* in one way or another. All gushing about how much they loved M.R.'s account of the Deviant Devotee—

alright, it's growing on me—and each and every one of them were women. That is, until the final message. When a younger-sounding male, accompanied by multiple others, resonates over the speaker.

"Hey, Wild Thang! Tell M.R. to stop by our next practice so she can ride us like that pastor of hers!"

An obnoxious wave of laughter and shouting ensues before the line goes dead. I look to Ruth, who offers me an extra courteous perk of her brows.

"Those are just the ones we missed. And they aren't local, either. We distribute to all major cities from Houston to San Diego." R.J. boasts, giving me a suggestive smile. "M.R., you've got every horny woman in the American Southwest lined up for our next issue."

"You have a grasp on appealing to a wide audience," Ruth says with the faintest hint of admiration. "What kind of experience do you have writing this type of material?"

Unprepared for formalities, I simply answer from the heart. "Well, I'd never published anything before sending my story to you. But I've been writing erotica for years. All I did was tweak my usual style. Made the main character obscure, and the porn explicit but easily digestible." I shrug. "In my opinion, getting off shouldn't be a cerebral exercise."

Ruth nods. "And you think you'd be able to deliver this type of content consistently?"

"Oh, definitely," I say, then pause. "Wait, so you *are* wanting me to write for you again?"

"With payment," Ruth affirms. "And also with our approval, any editorial takes, the likes of it. We publish every fourteen days. We'd need your manuscripts at least a week before push out, which'll give us ample time to format and shoot the recreation. I can offer you a flat rate of one-fifty as a start for every issue. Depending on how our sales look over the next period, that may increase."

I almost can't believe what I'm hearing. I'm being offered a job to do what I'd been doing for my own perverted satisfaction since I was thirteen. I should hesitate, take time to think over what sort of consequences awaited me if my mother were to find out about all this. But instead, I jump on it.

"Y-Yes! Of course I'll do it." I enthusiastically stumble through my words, only to retreat after they're out. "I mean, as long as I can just be M.R., I wanna stay anonymous."

R.J. strokes his chin, tone deepening. "With *that* face? And those…" His gaze drops to my chest, then diverts to my I.D. on the polished desk, which he palms to give an affirming read-over. Thankfully, Ruth interrupts before he can finish.

"Anonymity won't be a problem." The corner of her mouth tugs slightly, but the grin appears more contemplative than joyous.

R.J. slaps the card down. "Now, there's one small bump in the road as of right now. Our next issue is pushing out in three days."

Any residual elation plummets into the pit that forms in my stomach. Enough fear must show on my face to be addressed.

"Hey, no reason to panic yet," R.J. says gently. "It's just, we've got a lot of antsy women waiting to get their hands on that issue to see if M.R. will make her return. And, well, if she doesn't—"

"They won't hold out hope for the next one." Ruth finishes.

"Nothing to sweat. All we need is a new story from you by tomorrow, and we'll crunch to prep it just this once." R.J. tilts his cowboy hat at me. "You've gotta have enough experience to grind out some titillating tale in one night, don't you?"

My brows furrow as I find myself unsure if he's referencing my experience in writing or…something else. "What?"

"Oh, come on!" He chuckles, gesturing rashly with his hands. "You rode a *pastor's* face like it was a fucking seesaw. Surely you can jot down some Easter Sunday orgy or Bible study blowjob? We don't judge around here."

Something else. Got it.

"I never had sex with a pastor," I say.

R.J. rolls his eyes. "Alright, so you exaggerated. Maybe it was some half-cocked handjob with your boyfriend in the pews. What else have you done?"

A silence follows. Both of them awaiting affirmation that I'm some harlot mindful enough to make her real-life endeavors sound more appealing than they actually were. Surely I was writing my stories from personal testimony. It's not like I was an inexperienced teenager pulling everything I put to paper directly out of pornography, erotic books, and my ass.

Except, that's exactly what I was doing.

"I haven't done anything," I admit. "I'm a virgin."

Being able to floor two individuals who run a bondage-themed sexploitation business just *has* to come with enough merit to earn a badge of some kind. Ruth and R.J. gape at me, before the seated of the pair breaks into boisterous laughter. I keep my glare fixed on him until he's done heaving, composing himself enough to take notice of the fact that I'm not in on the joke.

R.J. stills, weathered features hardening. "For real?"

All I can offer is a nod.

He leans forward curiously. "You mean, you're one of those *front door* virgins? That's the code all good Catholic girls abide by, isn't it?"

"I'm Protestant. And, no." I release an unsteady breath. "I haven't even had my first kiss. I just write about sex. I've never actually done it."

Bracing the weight of their perplexed stares, I pull my *Holy Scriptures* notebook from my bag and place it on the desk before them. Watching as they open it and sift through pages upon pages of my immodest notes, stories, and God knows what else I've hidden between the lines. And while I feel entirely nude sitting here as they consume my most intimate secret, strangely, I also feel free. If anyone, excluding

Lewis, was to know of my passion, it seemed appropriate that they be the type of people to have unclad women and phallic-shaped awards decorating the walls of their workplace.

R.J. sinks deeply into the leather chair, glancing up at Ruth. Whose face hasn't shifted much, aside from the noticeable incredulity swelling behind her cold eyes.

"And here I was thinking our four-foot-eleven no-show taking a quarter of her height was gonna be the wildest thing I'd see today," R.J. remarks, then raises a brow at me. "What'd you say M.R. stood for?"

"Mary-Rose." I clarify. "But I go by—"

"Virgin Mary!" He points at me with a toothy grin. "See? I knew you'd fit in around here. We already found a name for you."

Ruth releases a curt sigh, disregarding her counterpart. "Look, take the night to work it over. If you can deliver another piece to us by tomorrow, the job is yours. You've already got the formula down. Focus on universal pleasures. A lot of people have been to a church once in their lives; keep that mindset. No real names, no distinguishing features for our lady. Any woman should be able to picture herself in the role. Understand?"

Ignoring the way my heart pounds with the new responsibility, I nod. "I'll try my best."

"Alright, then." She concludes, tracking me as I stand to secure my items. "Remember, this is what you do."

I step awkwardly to the door while bidding them a juvenile wave. All they likely catch is a flash of the ridiculous white bow tied to my ponytail as I hastily exit the office.

"See you in the horny pages, Virgin Mary!" R.J. calls with enthusiasm.

Back in the all-red hallway to hell, I stand stiffly, letting out a slow breath of relief in my newfound solitude. But before I have the chance to move away, the muffled voices of my potential employers find me through the wood.

"Don't give me that look, Baby Ruth."

"Keep it zipped, Rodney." Ruth's tone is as stern as it is vicious. "You may not like our new demographic, but I'll be damned if we don't jump on it. This is the surest bet we've had in years."

R.J. gives an apprehensive reply, "I know you see what I do."

"All I see is someone who might finally dig us out of the fucking hole you put us in."

"*Exactly.*" He hangs on the word with a smugness I can register even from the room over.

There's a pause, before Ruth marks the end of their quarrel in a way that christens the dominant of the two. "Get out of my chair."

I consider listening on, until a figure emerges from one of the hallway's doors with ferocity in her movements. I recognize the smudges around her eyes paired with scraggly black hair, the woman I'd seen first upon my arrival now strides down the corridor. Having since traded her baggy clothes for no clothes at all—except for a complex leather harness that hugs her nude figure. She steals one look at me, then flips me off before disappearing into the stage's entrance.

I can take a hint. I need to get the fuck out of here.

Chapter 7

A story. A story by tomorrow. Surely I'm capable of that?

No pressure. It's only my sole chance of landing a job where I might have the rare luxury of earning money doing what I enjoy. Oh, and even if I do succeed and build a reputable following that would act as my ticket to making writing the career I always dreamed it would be, my mother will disown me and derail my entire life if she were to find out. No pressure at all.

I blink hard to adjust to seeing more than one solid color again as I step into the summer swelter. The outdoors greeting me in tandem with the weight of all I had just agreed to. A damn meteor could fall in this moment, sending the world into ruin and proving Crosspoint correct that all sinners—myself *certainly* included—would be damned to a fate of eternal blaze, and I wouldn't so much as look up. There isn't a single thing that can spare me from the smothering density of what's at stake.

Nothing…except *her*.

The very sight makes me stop cold despite the vigorous heat. Time slows to a commanding halt, and the edges of my vision whirl in a disorienting vertigo that leaves me no choice but to focus on the woman striding like an archangel into my escape from hell.

Her black hair is styled in loose waves that bounce softly in time with her graceful steps, shining with harlequin rays of sunlight filtered from the walkway's canopy. Bulky sunglasses mask a good portion of her upper face, drawing my eyes to her full, ruby red lips. Much of her flawless, warm brown skin shows in her chosen outfit—a cropped halter top woven in a rustic geo-pattern, ending at the peak of her slender waist, stretching bare to ripped Daisy Dukes hugging the prominent curve of her hips. She carries nothing but a beige tote bag over one of her bare, sun-kissed shoulders. Looking down her shapely legs leads to the view of two lustrous stilettos clicking on the pavement beneath. I recognize her stunning physique, her wild hair, even her face, despite the tinted glasses. This is the woman I'd seen on the cover of the first *Wild Thang* issue I ever held—the woman who'd modeled for my story.

Valentina Amor. Who is somehow more bewitching in physical form. I'd bet my life that if she were to part her ruby lips, the prettiest, most pristine smile would greet me. And when she's close enough that ignoring me is no longer possible, she does just that.

She smiles at me. Pretty and pristine.

I melt, and the blazing sun isn't the least bit to blame. Her mouth moves seductively, and it takes me far too long to remember that *words* tend to accompany such an action. Time snaps back. And while my tongue hasn't quite caught up, I manage a primitive response. "Huh?"

She tilts her head like a curious puppy. "Excuse me."

Her voice is akin to the gentle hum of a stream, with a Spanish accent to complement. The smile swelling her cheeks never fades. In fact, it grows in what can only be endearment as I finally realize why she's acknowledging my inferior existence at all.

I'm in her way.

"Oh, sorry!" I quickly sidestep to allow her passage.

She giggles. "¡Gracias!"

I catch the scent of something floral as she breezes by, unable to keep from admiring just how many of my senses she's managed to captivate in such a minuscule interaction. I can't let it end so soon.

"I recognize you!" I blurt.

She stops, turning on her pencil-thin heel to look at me. "What's that?"

My insides flutter, and I consider if this is what it's like to be starstruck. The closest I can place it is the way one's heart beats out of rhythm after a tough run in gym class. You know, when you feel as if you're about to drop dead?

"You were on the cover of the issue before last, weren't you?" I ask.

Her ruby lips press into a thin line, manicured fingertips pushing the sunglasses atop her head. Striking hazel eyes narrow at me. "You tell me."

Fear that I may've just offended her grips me as I stutter, "I-I'm so sorry, I just—"

Her quick movements cut me off. Keeping her feline-esque gaze locked with mine, she reaches into her tote to retrieve the same fuchsia boa she'd worn in the cover photo. Tossing it around her neck, she conceals her breasts in the same pose before topping it with a wink and a smile.

I register that she's playing me when her sweet laughter evokes my own, then force a clumsy response through my relief. "Yeah, it's definitely you."

"Are you the new star for today?" She asks, giving me a polite look-over. "R.J. said you'd be shorter."

"Uh, nope. No." I chuckle nervously as she steps closer. While the stilettos give her a few inches on me, I bet we'd be around the same height without them. "I'm just a writer."

"A writer…?" Her eyes widen, pigmented lips parting in surprise. "Wait, are you the one Ruth was trying to contact? The writer of that church girl story?"

I offer a smile in place of an answer, shrugging innocently.

"¡Dios mío! I was the one who modeled that page!" She exclaims as if it weren't something I was already blissfully aware of. "Did you meet with her?"

I nod. "She offered me a job to write for every issue."

"Well, you have to take it." She says sternly, leaning closer to whisper the rest. "That was the *hottest* erotica I've ever read in a mag."

A shiver strokes my spine. "Thank you. Ruth said that if I can have another piece ready for the next one, the position's mine."

"Oh," her brows draw in discernment. "Can you do that in time? We're only three days to print."

I shove all the panic gouging my insides into an impenetrable box—then sit on it, for good measure—as I give her my best attempt at a confident grin. "Of course. It's what I do."

Her perfect smile returns, charming me to such a degree that I'm unsure how long I'll survive without seeing it again. "I guess that means you'll be around?"

"Tomorrow," I say with twice the certainty I actually feel.

"Sweet!" She holds out a hand for me to shake. "I'm Val, by the way."

I accept the gesture, and the sensation of her skin against mine arrests my focus to the point that I forego my chosen name. Reflexively going with my mother's preferred, "Mary-Rose."

"M.R., that's what it stands for?"

"Yeah. My friends call me Rosie."

"Rosie…" The word lingers on her tongue like she's conjuring a love spell. "I can't wait to see what you've got."

Losing brainpower by the second, I simply reply with, "Me neither."

Val giggles, taking a few more steps toward the studio before halting again. Glancing over her shoulder, her pretty face tweaks into a smirk. "You know, I can see it."

I blink, half expecting her to disappear by way of being a deceitful mirage. "See what?"

"The church girl thing." She nods at me, shifting the soft waves of her hair. "Maybe you should've been the one modeling that page. You would've put me to shame."

Val gifts me a parting wink, mascaraed lashes kissing the top of her cheek for a split-second before the fiery-painted lobby of Wild Thang Studios enfolds her.

I stare at my tinted reflection in the closed double doors. Trying to make myself believe that the past hour of my life had truly occurred, and that I hadn't been struck by a passing car while exiting the bus stop on the trek over. Such an accident and subsequent coma induction would be the only rational explanation for this fever dream fit with long whips, erotic notoriety, and the most unbelievably perfect woman I'd ever laid eyes on complimenting me like she had. But the longer I stand, the more the New Mexico heat flushes my fair skin a deep red, confirming that I'm not in some air-conditioned hospital room clinging to life. And that I'm, instead, just a painfully naïve soul.

A painfully naïve soul…with a job to do.

By the grace of whatever God still had enough faith in me, I managed to make it to my first class by the skin of my teeth. Which are now clamped on the thin wood of my No. 2 pencil as I leisurely hold it by the tip, studying my *Holy Scriptures* notebook splayed on the desk. One day. That's how long I have to prove myself.

I shift awkwardly in the seat, my skin sticky from the sweat I'd accumulated in running to Professor Harrison's anatomy lecture from the campus bus stop. The page before me lies scribbled in various prompts, some of which sit disconnected in strewn scraps of paper I'd had access to in the moment the idea came. There were even a few napkins from Peakshire's cafeteria that I'd marked with on-the-spot sexcapades before shoving into my bra for safekeeping…among other uses. I liked to store all ideas, no matter how absurd. Which had proven a notoriously flawless system. At least, when only I was reading the finished product.

I mean, Jesus Christ.

Aliens invade and stick Slutty Rosie with probes.

Kidnapped by vampires and sucked dry.
Stung by genetically mutated bees that induce arousal.
What the hell is wrong with me?

Something in my gut tells me that alien probes and bloodletting won't pass as universal pleasures. And it's the same voice telling me that a model covered in rashes and red bumps wouldn't exactly be a great look for a porn studio. Another chunk of the pencil dents as I bite harder. There has to be *one* that I can salvage...

"*Ahem.*"

My eyes lift at the noise. Finding Professor Harrison at the front of the classroom, tilting his chin to look over the rows between us with a scowl.

"Miss, are you paying attention?" He asks gruffly.

I blink, smiling widely with the pencil between my teeth as a signal that I am. But when that doesn't suffice, I remove it. "Yes."

His head lowers, supplying me with a glare over the glasses resting on the tip of his bulbous nose. "Yes...?"

It's an effort not to grumble at his inflated superiority complex. "Yes, *sir*."

Professor Harrison continues his disapproving exploit for a few elongated moments to get his point across. Likely thinking he was striking the wrath of God into me by doing so, but it was hard to fear someone so innocuous. Especially a Poindexter with too-tall khakis and enough gel shining his hair to give Lewis a run for his money. But he quickly continues his droning lecture, pointing to the roll-in diagram with colorful illustrations of both male and female reproductive organs.

"Alright, phenotypic sex. We've covered gamete production in the male system. Can anyone tell me what the method of seminal delivery is?"

The class remains quiet following his monotone question, before a hand raises in the front row. "Erection, sir?"

Our teacher uncaps a marker and writes the word on a whiteboard beside the display. "Erection, and?" Another silence follows with no takers. Professor Harrison sighs, writing an additional note beneath the first. "Ejaculation."

A mix of chortles ensues from one section of the group.

Our professor shoots them a humorless glance. "Seriously? You're all adults in this room. There's nothing that compelling about the birds and the bees."

Focusing on the open notebook in front of me, I mutter a quiet dissent, "I beg to differ…"

And then, my eyes flare wide. The pencil between my fingers drops to the page below as I disregard every written prompt in favor of the unforeseen idea now clutching me in its provocative grip. There it is. That rush of inspiration when you no longer fear the blank page before you. But consider it a canvas ready to be filled with the deepest, nastiest desires you'd go to your grave before speaking aloud. I even smile at it.

"Miss."

It wasn't a question anymore, and the voice was considerably closer. I lift my gaze to see Professor Harrison towering over my desk, bringing with him the stare of every student in class. Apparently, my remark had come out louder than intended.

"I won't tolerate the witty comments. From now on, keep them to yourself." He demands.

"Sorry, sir," I mutter—for real, this time.

But my embarrassment is quickly forgone as he steps away, leading the rest of the group back into discussion of human reproduction. I, too, find myself engaged in the topic. But certainly not at the behest of Professor Harrison as I mark the newest prompt onto the page before me.

I have my own lesson to give.

Chapter 8

"Miss?"

A firm voice breaks the silence holding our classroom. I glance up from my notebook, raking over every inch of the sightly man in front of me until my eyes reach his.

"Are you paying attention to the lesson?" Professor Hardon asks, looking down at me through the glasses resting on his nose. A few tendrils of his dark, slicked-back hair falling over his forehead at such an angle.

"Of course, sir." I insist, leaning forward in my seat to gift him a better view down my shirt—buttoned low enough to expose the topmost lace of my brassiere. "I was even taking notes."

He raises a brow, grabbing the booklet from my desk to peer at it. "I see. And what kind of notes would these be?"

He holds up the notebook, showcasing my drawing of Professor Hardon himself. Void of clothing with one impressive seminal delivery device.

"You were talking about human arousal, sir." I bat my lashes. "The transportation of sperm to egg. I was only drawing a visual representation."

"Is that so...?" He drops the marked page. "Well, miss, if you're so informed, why don't you give teaching this lesson a go?"

I smirk at him, then stand to take his wrist. "My pleasure."

I lead him through the rows of desks occupied by watchful students until we reach the front of the class. Their faces are confused, but engrossed, nevertheless.

I project loud enough for the whole group to hear. "Can anyone tell me what the first step of seminal delivery is?"

A hand raises. "Erection?"

Grinning like a fool, I release Professor Hardon's wrist to step behind him, my lips brushing his ear as I unclasp the belt at his waist. "Correct."

The leather slips. Gasps erupt from the class as his khakis and briefs pool around his ankles.

"Miss!" Professor Hardon shouts, but makes no attempt to cover himself as his engorged manhood is suddenly bared for the crowd of students.

I hum deeply in his ear, sliding a palm down the front of his solid abdomen. Peeking over his shoulder, I can see his hard cock standing upright, pulsating lightly in time with the beat of his heart. He lets out a guttural moan as I take it, feeling it twitch beneath my nimble fingers as I start with methodical strokes.

Gradually increasing the intensity of my efforts, I ask, "Now, can anyone tell me what the second step of delivery entails?"

The class watches, transfixed, until another arm extends from the backmost row. "Ejaculation?"

I giggle, pressing my lips to Professor Hardon's neck. Teasing warm flesh with the tip of my tongue, I leave a trail of wet kisses up to his ear as my working hand blurs with speed. "Correct!"

"Oh, miss!" He whines. "You can't, I'm going to—!"

His strong body tenses in my grasp before I hold his thick cock tightly on the downstroke. Watching with a satisfied smile as he expertly demonstrates the method of seminal delivery.

All over the front row.

The females within range holler, many of them laughing and pointing in awe at how far it traveled. The males are simply fixated on me, pressing their anatomy textbooks to their laps in an effort to hide their excitement as I release Professor Hardon and lift my fingers to lick away the milky remains of his display. Its pungent taste swelters my own arousal, making my step around our teacher rather unsteady as he reclaims his breath.

"Perfect demonstration, sir. Unfortunately, for the inferior male specimen, a refractory period is commonly required before a second—"

I'm cut off as hands snare around my waist. The next thing I know, I'm being tossed onto the surface of the nearest lab table by Professor Hardon. Who steps between my open knees, bunching my little skirt high.

"That won't be necessary." He declares, smirking at me before removing his shirt. The muscles of his sculpted torso tense beneath harsh examination lights as he waves the class over. "Everyone, please step closer for the next demonstration."

I hear a symphony of scooting chairs and footsteps before a dozen heads frame the edges of my vision. Professor Hardon fists my low neckline, tearing open my shirt and brassiere for their viewing.

He speaks casually, as if this were any other lesson. "Since this student has proven her knowledge on the topic, I see it only fair that she assists me in illustrating the complete delivery of sperm to egg. Let's prepare her."

I bite my lip in anticipation, squirming as one of his hands disappears between my thighs. Finding me sans underwear and wet from his exhibition.

He grins. "It is imperative that the female maintain a heightened state of arousal throughout the process. Clitoral stimulation is often needed to achieve this. See here," his arm shifts, and my head falls back in a moan as he pulls at my nub's sensitive hood with the pad of his thumb. "Simple rubbing will do, but I find the most effective strategy to be a bit more... primitive."

His head dips only a moment before I feel his tongue give a slow, long drag across my clit. My back arches on reflex, drawing several of the students' gazes to my breasts as they bounce with the quick act.

Professor Hardon speaks between enthused flicks. "Ensuring proper vaginal lubrication is paramount for successful seminal delivery." He slips a finger inside me, tweaking it upwards. "The scientific findings of Ernst

Gräfenberg are key for internal stimulation, considering his discovery of the interior female erogenous zone. Coined as the G-spot."

Deep, encroaching heat pulses through my body as he roughly digs the tip of his inserted finger into something sensitive—curiously prodding the spot a few times before steadily tickling it. I sob in utter bliss, my whines overpowering the noise of onlooking students' pencils scratching notes into their handheld booklets.

"And lest we forget the exterior erogenous zones. While the clitoris is vital, in some females, the nipples can be equally as effective." Professor Hardon sucks my clit tightly between his lips, tugging in a way that makes stars dot my view before he releases it with a firm pop. "However, I'm a bit preoccupied with the former. May I have two volunteers?"

From the group, a man and woman on either side of the table lean in, ducking their heads until two mouths close around the peaks of my breasts. I inhale sharply as their tongues swipe across my stiff nipples.

"A combination of stimuli to this degree is likely to result in a state of delirium," Professor Hardon's breath trickles hotly over my needy slit. "But, in my experience, the effects are worth it."

His mouth is on my clit again, sucking as he strokes it firmly with the tip of his tongue. The male student working my breast mimics the motion while the female traps my nipple between her ruby lips, humming to invoke course vibrations as Professor Hardon fingers my G-spot with stunning accuracy. The union of every sensation becomes too much, too fast. I come in record time. Gripping Professor Hardon's index in tight, rhythmic throbs as my body stiffens with the most consuming orgasm of my life. Darkness raids me as my eyes roll back, riding out the electric waves one, after another, after another. Then, I turn light as a feather beneath the ever-present gazes of my fellow classmates. The two on my breasts step away, leaving me a full view of our teacher between my spread legs.

"Perfect." Professor Hardon removes his finger, holding it up to view my slickness in the light. He presses his digits together and apart, studying *the way it strings in shiny droplets.* "Now that the female is properly lubricated, we can move on to the final demonstration."

Heated eyes lock on mine as he stands, coating his still-stiff cock with the remnants of my climax as he strokes it. The warm head drags teasingly between my folds before a firm pressure at my entrance prods me.

"Everyone, take notes..."

"Mary-Rose?" Mom's muffled voice absolutely wrenches me from the action.

Fingers ceasing, my already-pounding heart lurches as the ascending footsteps grow louder and louder. Luckily, I've done this song and dance a thousand times. Managing to tear the remaining page from the typewriter and hide it with the rest of the story in my *Holy Scriptures* notebook sitting aside. When the door to my room creaks open, I'm admiring my anatomy textbook in an attempt to feign doing homework.

"Hey, Mom." I smile at her, hoping she won't notice that I'm sitting at an otherwise tidy desk with nothing but a diagram of vaginas in front of me.

Thankfully, she doesn't. "Dinner's ready downstairs. I thought we could eat together?"

The high I'd been riding in the midst of my lewd fantasy takes such a nosedive that I actually feel my insides shift, like coming to a gut-wrenching halt at the end of a roller coaster. I close the textbook, forcing an enthused tone. "Sure thing."

Standing leaves me wincing, and attempting to ignore the fact that I'm in desperate need of fresh panties. My own anatomy was easily going to be one of the biggest pitfalls of my new job...

Job. The thought makes it easy to smile as I follow my mother downstairs to the kitchen table. Settling into the meal after her ritualistic prayer, I prepare for whatever mental gymnastics I was about to perform to keep her satisfied.

"Tell me about the Bible study." She inquires when we're a few bites into our pork and green bean casserole. "You did go, didn't you?"

"Yes, Mom. I went." I say flatly, carefully slicing a cut of meat. "It was fun, the girls there are nice. One of them I even knew from public school."

"That's wonderful." Her voice softens, but I notice the tendons in her occupied hand go taut before she continues. "Are there any boys in the study?"

I shake my head. "I'm gonna try to convince Lewis to go. I think he'd like it."

It's impossible to tell if my answer puts her at ease, or if she's actually disappointed that I haven't met any potential suitors through the sanctity of a scriptural gathering. Either way, she keeps her eyes on her plate. "And classes? What are you learning?"

"We're covering human reproduction in anatomy," I jump ahead of the question I know she's conjuring. "But our professor hasn't brought up anything from Genesis."

My mother stills for a few moments, before delicately going back at the dish with her knife. "Well, I suppose when it comes to basic biology, origins are arbitrary in a lesson. It's not like you don't already know how we came to be."

Unable to stop myself, I stab a cut of rib with my fork to hold up. "The pig's name wasn't Adam, was it?"

Her idle look narrows to a glare.

I clear my throat, letting my posture sink. "All my other classes are pretty easy. Most of the assignments are written, so I'm doing well."

She huffs through her nose. "You sound like Matthew when he was in school."

My jaw goes slack at the mention of Dad, but I force myself to keep chewing. "Really?"

"Oh, heavens, yes. The workload wasn't his problem; it was staying focused." Her lengthy cardigan shifts as she sighs affectionately. "There was a part of him that believed he didn't need an education to be a successful writer, but I told him time and time again that it would pay off. And just look what came of it."

I say nothing, keeping my chin lowered until her voice beckons me to raise it.

"Mary-Rose." She speaks gently, looking me in the eye. "I can't tell you how proud he would be knowing you're using what he left you to walk that same path."

My chest tightens, leaving me wordless until the pain mellows. I simply reply with a nod, allowing a prolonged silence to swell between us before pressing the conversation forward. "So, how was the tailor shop today?"

She answers, but I don't listen. Instead, I study her from gray-blonde hair to needle-calloused fingertips. Wondering how the woman a mere arm's length away could be one person when she brought me into this world, then transform into a total stranger at the drop of a tragedy.

If I had a nickel for every time I've wanted to pull out my hair in fury or sheer despair since Mom gave our lives to Crosspoint, I wouldn't need my father's money at all. But strikingly enough, I couldn't pull a single bad memory from my early childhood. It should be illegal to love someone as much as my mother loved my father, or as much as he loved us. The years we'd spent in this very house while Dad shifted from mystery bestseller, to thriller bestseller, to drama bestseller were all happy. He'd encouraged my fascination with storytelling since I was a toddler—when I'd wandered into his office holding a permanent red marker and colored in the "R" key on his typewriter. Instead of getting angry, he showed me how he used it. I would sit in that room for hours watching him type. Loving the sounds it made, the smell of drying ink, and the way he explained the stories he was writing in a manner that my young mind could comprehend. In fact, the only problem I had at all was keeping track of the months until my next birthday. Because the older I got, the closer I was to reading his more mature books…

I was eight years and seven months old when he was diagnosed.

I was eight years and nine months old when he died.

As much as I've tried to, I know I'll never forget that day. Mom was getting us ready to leave home in the early morning, frustrated and panicking that she could only find one of the shoes I was meant to wear. She was crawling under my bed in search of the other when the phone rang downstairs. Half an hour later, I was standing in the doorway of a hospital room, wearing only one shoe. I can still hear the sound of my mother's screams. The strain of being held so tightly, it took all the effort in my small body to even breathe. The way I found it impossible to open my mouth and demand that someone explain why my dad wasn't waking up. I was too young to understand that, seemingly overnight, our family's future had been erased. Leaving Mom with the sole responsibility of filling in the blanks.

She chose to do so with the promise of salvation. Discovering a group of people who sold her the idea that, through God, she would be freed from her burdens. All it would require was submitting herself and her remaining family to a life of devotion, living each and every day to appease the higher power she trusted with her soul, even if it meant running on nothing but blind faith. And for the longest time, I felt that I could understand. Despite how hard it was for me to lean into the things Crosspoint taught us, I gave it my best shot in the beginning. At least, after I realized that the words our pastor had been reading out of that book everyone found so important weren't simple fiction like Dad's stories had been. Not to them, anyway. Maybe I did it because I truly wanted something to believe in. Or maybe I was just a kid with no say. But regardless of making my own sense about church and the concept of God, I couldn't fault my mother for needing all of it to move forward after my father died.

That is, until the day came when I could.

"What about your book?" Mom asks when she's done rambling about her latest client.

I tune back in, scraping my fork lightly over the glass plate. "I'm making progress."

"What you showed me so far is incredible." She says, referencing my abhorrent spiritual fiction manuscript. "Just imagine how many people you're going to touch with a story like that."

If only she knew how true that already was. "With school and all, I'm not feeling so inspired." I shrug. "Not that it really matters."

Her gaze brightens almost imperceptibly, gleaming and fading like a flicker from the centerpiece's candle wicks. "Of course it matters, Mary-Rose. If to nobody else, then to me."

I hold her stare. "You mean that?"

"You're my child." She says firmly. "You matter very much."

At once, everything I'd just eaten churns in my stomach. My mouth goes sour, and I have to avert my eyes to keep her from noticing how foggy they're growing as I'm gouged with lethal recollection.

"I'm finished," I say in a hush.

I manage to put away my plate and bid her a quick goodnight without further questioning. But the moment I'm back in my room, the pressure of keeping every fighting retort to myself is suddenly released. The same dark, consuming emptiness left in the place of my father presents itself at full force—amplified by the sting of my mother's closing remark.

I force myself to take slow, easy breaths as I return to my writing desk. Looking past my illicit work-in-progress to the wall-mounted shelves. On the topmost, positioned above my secret admirer's leopard, was my "safe for mother" collection of literature. Between Jane Austen and Charlotte Brontë, the works of Matthew Ginger occupy the majority of the wooden platform. Books that I'd read so many times,

I could recite many of their chapters without so much as looking. My father left behind so many rich remnants of his mind that it was hard for me to ever choose a favorite.

Hard, but not impossible.

I stand on my toes to peek at the thinnest spine of the collection, marked with bright colors in the shape of musical notes across a blank canvas. Pushing aside the encased cassette tape sitting atop it, I remove the book to study the cover. One that bore a cartoonish drawing of a happy little girl with big brown eyes, sitting before an array of pots and pans that she drums with spatulas. The title arched above her in vivid hues, scuffed from years of sitting idle.

Mary's Music

Written by: Matthew Ginger

Taking a seat at the desk, I open the book to the first spread. The left page shows a group of children playing various instruments in an orderly formation. On the right, the protagonist is depicted just as she was on the cover, banging kitchen utensils together in place of legitimate drums. Along the bottom of both pictures are the beginning words of her story.

Mary didn't like the music others played.

So she made her own.

On the following spread, the other children holding instruments now wear faces of irritation. Some of them hushing Mary where she sat before her kitchenware drum set. Mary, on the other hand, shrugs off their remarks with a carefree smile.

Others told Mary her maturity was delayed.

"No bother," Mary said. "What's the fun in acting grown?"

Turning the page, the same group of children now read from a collection of assorted books. But Mary sits apart from the rest, scribbling intently on a notepad.

Mary didn't like the stories others made.

So she wrote her own.

The next spread shows one of the children from the group—a little boy sporting a hostile expression—standing over Mary's seat like a bully. But the girl simply ignores him.

Some liked to pick on Mary, thinking she'd be dismayed.
But Mary didn't fear walking all alone.

The children's book goes on, showcasing all the ways Mary set herself apart from the crowd, doing so with a determined smile on her face. That is, until a turn in her story where Mary stands along a pristine, populated road. Unable to keep from glancing off to the side—where a dense forest tempts her with adventure and mystery.

Mary didn't like the path before her, neatly paved.
So she strayed away, forging her own.

Mary moves forward to traverse the thick vegetation, trudging along by herself for the first time.

Though the land was scary, and she wouldn't leave unscathed.
Mary continued onward, facing the unknown.

But as the story progresses, Mary loses her unwavering smile. Looking frightened as the dark, lonely woodland offers no sign of salvation.

When she wandered too far to continue being brave.
Mary felt lost, wishing she could find home.

Despite this, the little protagonist pushes through. Suddenly, a reaching hand breaks through the forest. Mary takes it, leading her into a wide meadow illuminated by the painted sky above. In the grassland, a group of other children greet her where she emerges.

But in her sadness, on the path that she had paved.
Other wanderers found her, and she no longer felt alone.

An unsteady smile pulls the corner of my lips as one of the children is revealed to be her former bully. He now wears a remorseful, sullen expression. A look that brightens as a grinning Mary hugs him.

Because through friendship, bond, and forgiveness, far beyond.
They knew that their paths were meant to cross.
And with love at her side, Mary finally realized.
She had never *been lost.*

In the last illustration of the story, Mary and her new collection of offbeat friends sit on the grassy field, joyously admiring the sunset.

So when times get tough, and your story seems done.
Look up, smile, and have fun.
Because, just like Mary, your story has only begun.

Gripping the filmy paper between my fingers, I turn to the end of the thin book. There's no last message, nor notes from the author. There's only a black and white photo of him and his own little Mary sitting atop his shoulders, peering at each other with the purest essence of joy.

Matthew Ginger and his daughter, Mary-Rose "Rosie" Ginger.

I can't remember the last time I looked so effortlessly happy.

My throat tightens at the memory before me, and I'm forced to shut the cover before I stain the photograph with even more tears than it had claimed over the past decade. It was the last book my father wrote before his passing—never reaching publication post-mortem, per the request of my mother. As it stood, the advanced copy in my hands is the only one that remains.

Even though there was so little of me that believed there could be some form of higher power at work, it's the sole idea that my father might still be around in some way that keeps me from ever discarding that last morsel of faith. There was no tangible evidence, but on my worst days, looking up to find an uncharacteristically breathtaking sunset *always* gave me the hint that it was my dad's doing. His own way of telling me that better things were on the horizon. All I had to do was push forward to make it there, just as Mary had done. Either that, or I was making something out of absolutely nothing. But I suppose that's why they're called "signs." It's up to us to follow them or ignore them. And I would be lying if I were to say avoiding all acknowledgement of divine intervention wasn't tempting. If anything, to avoid ending up as fanatical as my mother.

My mother…who had been so determined to run from her grief, she'd left behind the only surviving remnants of her beloved husband without so much as a second look. And all these years later, she has the audacity to tell me that I matter simply because I'm her child?

My head sinks into my hands. Any semblance of comfort *Mary's Music* brought me is swept away by a whole different form of grief. Tears well, then fall as the sting of it seizes my lungs, forcing me to sob in place of breaths. I fight to keep them quiet despite the urge to open my window and scream until everyone in the city understands the cruel injustice I'd been left to drown in since her departure. Injustice for the one who held me the day our father passed. For a girl our mother considered just as buried.

I might be Christine's child. I might matter. But I shouldn't be the only one.

Because Erica mattered.

My *sister* mattered…

Chapter 9

I nervously tap my foot, supplying a beat softened by the ornate rug under my Mary Jane flat. Picking at the worn leather of the chair I'm poised in, I look between the two figures opposite the wide desk.

Today, Ruth is seated in the predominant chair with R.J. peering over her shoulder. Both carefully read each page of the story I'd presented. And while I'm able to gauge R.J.'s pleased reaction with the slight quirks of his brows and huffed laughs every paragraph or two, Ruth isn't so transparent. Her face is set like a stone wall, only offering movement by way of her cold eyes devouring every word.

"This is perfect," R.J. remarks when they reach the final page. "We've got the schoolgirl getup and everything."

His compliment does little to put me at ease. I sooner fixate on the individual whom I assume carries the *actual* weight of the decision.

Fear coils tight around my crossed legs and stiff shoulders when Ruth finally lifts her gaze to ask, "You wrote this in one night?"

My tongue is too busy wetting my dry mouth to affirm, so I give a simple nod. Her chin dips to stare indiscernibly at the piece, a move that stirs my apprehension. As a writer, I've always prided myself on being an observer. But Ruth Sexton is simply unreadable. And I have a sneaking suspicion it isn't by happenstance.

"Rodney," she breaks the silence. "Get Val in costume."

My tense muscles relax, then re-tighten as R.J. claps his hands.

"We're in business!" He declares, rounding the desk to proudly grab my shoulder. "Our saving grace just landed herself the deal of a lifetime. Ain't that right, Virgin Mary?"

I force an awkward smile as his fingers dip unnecessarily low. When he exits, the sound of him yelling for everyone to start prep fades as the office door closes.

Ruth pulls a folder to place my story inside. "We'll have to get this sent off immediately; it still needs formatting and an extra look-over. But given your time constraint, you exceeded my expectations."

"Good to hear," I say, tracking her meticulous movements as she retrieves a metal lockbox from the desk's drawer. When she opens it, I catch a fleeting glimpse of green stacks within.

"I hope you don't mind being paid in cash for now. Until we get your contract processed, you won't be eligible for payroll—"

"Actually," I gently interrupt her. "Is it okay if I get paid in cash every time? I don't have a bank account yet."

And the last thing I need is Mom nosing around my finances if I were to make one. Legal adult or otherwise, she'd find a way.

"If you'd like to be." Ruth slides my earnings across the desktop before storing the lockbox away. "Not sure how I keep forgetting how young you are, you look like you wandered away from a youth group."

A blush colors my cheeks. "Was that a compliment?"

"In twelve years, it will be." She keeps a stiff posture as her styled brows narrow. "Rosie, can I be frank with you?"

I hide my fear behind a forced grin. "Of course."

"I'm having a hard time understanding why a girl like you wants anything to do with this type of career. Your...*lack of experience* aside, it's fairly obvious this is out of your box."

I keep quiet, the initialed cross around my neck growing heavier by the second.

Ruth goes on, "You need to understand what it is you're signing up for. This industry isn't forgiving, and neither am I. Tell me why I should trust that you'll be faithful to us now that you've earned this position."

I consider what she's asking. But in my search for an answer, I have to reconcile the question I'd been suppressing since that devious little urge had possessed me to send in my story to begin with. Why *was* I doing this? The consequences weren't just dire; I had everything to lose. Even if I did survive the impact if this blew up in my face, the fallout would surely finish me off. Why is this worth risking so much…?

I straighten my shoulders, the mask slipping from my face as I fixate on Ruth's with a sureness so foreign, it almost startles me. "Because it feels good."

The woman doesn't even blink. She only waits for me to explain further.

So I do, "When I was growing up, I was taught that we need to live a certain way, make sacrifices, avoid things that make us happy. All for the chance that we might make it somewhere when we die. But I don't want to waste my life convincing myself I'm happy, I want it to be real." I huff an indignant laugh. "I like sex! I always have. I've never done it, but I like thinking about it, I like reading about it, I like watching it in movies, and I *love* to write it. It makes me feel good, and free, and like *me*. For so long, I thought I was alone in that." I shake my head, my focus flickering to the answering machine at the corner of the desk. "Until yesterday."

Ruth follows my gaze, remaining silent.

I look at her with candid eyes. "You can trust me because making your audience feel good makes *me* feel good."

She studies me carefully, tilting her head so the tendrils of blonde hair not tucked into her styled ponytail shift with the motion. "I've been in this business since well before you were born, Rosie. Since before porn was *considered* a business. Whatever you've written in your time, despite how damning you think it may be, I've seen it for real. I've filmed it. I've directed it. I've sold it. I've even…" Her voice trails off, but her professional demeanor carries on. "What I'm trying to say is, the sex industry isn't like other professions. Your job is appealing to a human's most primal urges, laying yourself bare in every sense. There's an…*authenticity* to it that you don't find in other careers." She pauses, blue eyes grazing the desk between us. "At least, that's how it started. Now, it seems like everyone's more interested in staging the best illusion. But I've learned that if you want success, all it takes is recognizing what your audience wants, then giving it to them."

My integrity wavers as I choose to ignore the warning shots hidden within her seemingly generous explanation. Even so, I can't help but sense that she understands this world better than most ever could. It would be foolish of me to distrust her judgment, even if she was only one step above a total stranger.

"I value authenticity above anything else." Ruth carries on. "The people who embody their craft, because they recognize the potential that comes with it. It may be rare, but I have a way of seeing those who can achieve that."

Biting back my fear, I ask, "And, what do you see when you look at me?"

"An amateur…with more potential than she even knows."

Pride flares in my chest so vigorously that it steals the breath from my lungs. Intensifying when I notice the corner of Ruth's glossy lips pull into the surest semblance of a smile I've yet to see from her. But a blink later, it's gone.

She grabs a clipboard and places it in front of me. "Now, your contract."

The stack of pages beneath the metal wedge is so excessive, it looks one additional sheet from snapping entirely. I slowly take it in my hands. The header is marked by the studio's logo, with every page beyond housing indecipherable legal speak. The number of forms and clauses I can't begin to comprehend is almost as daunting as the size of it.

Clearly, Ruth picks up on my discomfort. "Don't let it scare you. To be paid as an official employee, you need to be contracted. Yesterday, I left Rodney to put our legal counsel on drafting something specific to you." Her eyes flutter closed. "Which was my mistake. So you'll be signing our general staff agreement, instead. It's more of a catch-all for our employees who serve odd jobs. You can ignore the payment field since you're taking cash; all we need is a signature on the final page."

A sense of uneasiness comes over me, but I convince myself it's only growing pains as I lift the hefty collection and reach for the pen strung to the top. Aside from my babysitting gig, this would be my first plunge into the work force. Though hesitation lingers, it's overruled by irrepressible ambition. Rosie Ginger. Or rather, M.R., the erotic author.

I sign the dotted line.

Ruth nods my way. "That does it. Now all I need is to get this processed with a copy of your I.D., if you want to hand it over." I do so as I return the clipboard, which she gathers. "You have some breathing room in terms of your next deadline, but I recommend bringing us the finished draft as soon as possible."

"I'll have it ready," I promise her.

"You'll be good to go once I'm done with these." She rounds the desk, stopping beside my chair to extend a free hand. "Welcome to the sex industry, Rosie."

I return the handshake, looking up at my new superior with an artless smile.

When Ruth exits the office, she leaves the door slightly ajar, allowing distant noises from the now-bustling set to leak in. Curiosity pulling me, I stand to follow the sounds down the hallway to hell. Studio lights from the open stage spill harshly across the black floor, broken by shadows as I stop in the threshold to peer inside.

The sight is a far cry from the room I'd been so carelessly shoved into yesterday. All the tall curtains previously dividing the space into thirds are now pulled back. The staff within are preoccupied with constructing the new set as R.J. stands in the center, fluently and quite assertively directing them along. Some are clearing the background of various props, while others position a school desk in the middle of the stage floor, plucked from the pile of other miscellaneous furniture to fit the scene. Beneath the jungle of trained lighting sit more professional photography instruments than I have the patience to count. But it isn't the glamor of what was about to be my fantasy-turned-reality that grips me. It's *her*.

I step inside to get a better look. Sitting at one of the many dressing vanities is Val, her face inches from the mirror as she applies another layer of ruby-red lipstick to her already-pigmented mouth. She's dressed in a sexy school uniform, fitted with a tied-off blouse hugging her bare midsection and a plaid skirt cut short at the tops of her thighs. I hadn't anticipated seeing her in costume. The fact that she modeled my previous story was so unfathomable that I might as well have written it off as a delusion. But here she is, portraying Slutty Rosie in the flesh. And, of course, she looks inhumanly gorgeous doing it.

Lifting her bored gaze to the set's entrance, she spots me. The same reflexive delirium from meeting her returns at full force as her face brightens with a broad, perfectly white smile. I almost lift my hand to return the wave she's sending my way, until I realize she's waving me *over*. Remembering how to move my limbs, I comply as an unusual heat flushes my whole body. But a single stride in, something blocks my path. I nearly run nose-first into the breast pocket of a ridiculous Western button-up as his voice catches up to me.

"Curious about the job?" R.J. asks.

I blink at the obstruction, tilting my chin to see the man flaunting a smirk. "Huh?"

His drawl wears like a purr, "Come on, you're in the business now. Don't you wanna see the side that isn't all grammar checks and contracts?" He doesn't give me the chance to object, opting to grab my arm and drag me along. My face burns even redder when I realize he's pulling me Val's way. "Miss Val, allow me to introduce the masked nympho behind this shoot, the one and only Virgin Mary!" His hand migrates from my arm to my back when we reach the vanity, patting hard enough that I nearly lose my balance. "She's the one who crafted this little excerpt. And lest I forget, Virgin Mary, meet the cover señorita herself. *Valentina Amor*." He accentuates her name with an embarrassing attempt at a Spanish accent. "*Wild Thang*'s signature Mexicana. Ain't she gorgeous?"

"She is," I say to play along, but it's no lie.

"Nice to meet you, *Mary*." Val stands, holding out a hand for me to shake and giving me a discreet wink as I comply. Apparently, explaining that we'd already met wasn't worth interacting with R.J. any longer than she had to.

And here I'd been wondering how I could be any more enamored with this woman.

"Val modeled for your last story, too." R.J. goes on, tipping his hat to her. "No matter the part, she can nail it. Church-dweller, schoolgirl, anything. She's got the uh…got the…" His words trail off as his focus shamelessly drops to the woman's pronounced cleavage.

Val glances at me, rolling her eyes with a piqued pull of her lips. A wordless gesture that implies this happens *a lot*.

R.J. doesn't take notice as he finds his tongue. "Well, you see what I mean."

"Ready to shoot!" A technician calls.

"Oh—!" R.J. presses a hand to my chest, reversing us out of Val's way.

I watch the woman trot over, assuring that her shiny black hair is parted evenly on both shoulders as she leans elegantly against the school desk. Once she's settled, she tips her head low to give the lens a sultry stare. The camera's *FLASH* paints her figure with a momentary strike of light, repeating as she makes minor adjustments to her pose.

"Brilliant, ain't it?" R.J. asks, transfixed on Val's seductive moves.

I don't respond. Instead, I don a grimace while slowly pushing his hand away, which had been planted squarely on my breast, whether he intended so or not.

R.J. doesn't react, preoccupied with whistling at the scene in front of us. "This has always been my favorite part. See the look in her eyes? Not many gals have that…"

He spoke with the same tone my mother used when she was reciting scripture—in awe, as if he wasn't worthy of speaking in such divine tongue. I follow his gaze, spectating as Val is directed by the cameraman to climb atop the desk. She does so with grace, the slightest sway of her hips or bounce of her bust inducing a rush of something that sizzles my veins. I attribute it to satisfaction that my fantasy is, quite literally, coming alive in time with the camera's bright staccato.

FLASH

Val bites her bottom lip. Head tilting as she palms the swells of her breasts.

FLASH

R.J. leans close. Muttering something to the effect of, "If writing doesn't work out, you oughta give this a go."

I ignore him.

FLASH

For a fleeting moment, Val's eyes capture mine from across the set. The corner of her mouth tweaks into a smile I'm not entirely convinced is for the photo. She winks.

Pride pulls my lips into a smirk as I return the gesture.

FLASH

Chapter 10

"'*Sexy Student Makes Science Specialist Spurt.*'" Lewis reads, his reaction shielded behind the open magazine.

I cringe. "Yeah, I really need to negotiate some title input."

I'm seated on his bed, only an arm's reach from the computer desk, where he resides with the latest *Wild Thang* issue in his hands. A copy I was lucky to procure, having traveled to three separate stores before finding a rack that wasn't completely sold out of the publication. Its newest cover depicts a blonde model I don't recognize, peeking over her shoulder as she playfully bares her ass. All with the addition of a freshly added *Women's Erotica* sticker beneath the headlines.

He drops the booklet to his lap, gifting me the sight of his baffled face. "No way you're actually getting paid to write this."

Quirking a brow, I set aside the essay of his I'd been editing to pull my cash earnings from the pocket of my backpack. Flaunting it with a pert grin.

"Jesus H." Lewis stares at it with wide eyes. "You're whoring out your brain for money!"

I fan myself with the bills. "Never thought of it that way, but you're right. Feels pretty nice, too."

He leafs through the remainder of the issue. "Maybe you can spend that cash on some sexy underwear. They seem to have one hell of a supply at that place."

"Actually, I plan on saving it for now. Might be useful if Armageddon ever comes." I tuck my earnings away, side-eyeing him. "Besides, you know I don't need to spend money to have nice underwear."

A smile tilts his mouth as he turns back to the chat room on his monitor. "How *is* Erica?"

My chest aches at the rare mention of her name, making me regret bringing up my sister's business venture altogether. I glance at the calendar pinned to his wall—Saturday, September 3rd. "I can tell you after today."

He follows my line of focus, then nods. "Ah, right. Tell her I said hi."

"I will." I say, a change of subject in order. "Hey, you know that Bible study Pastor Morgan recommended?"

"The one you said you'd rather fall into a lion's den than go to?"

"That one. Turns out, the girls there are pretty cool. We didn't even talk about Bible stuff, just gossip. It was fun." I lean sideways to peek over his shoulder. "Maybe you'd wanna join me there next Thursday?"

"Can't. Pressing matters here." He says as another *ding* indicating an incoming message chimes from the computer's speakers.

I stand to drop my hands heavily on his shoulders. "Do these 'pressing' matters involve a certain 'Presley?'"

"Maybe."

"*Hello*," I rest my chin atop his gelled hair, recoiling at the greasy feel. "I'm inviting you to a room full of college girls, and you couldn't care less."

Lewis replies leisurely as he types. "Did you say something? I can't seem to hear females when they aren't giving me a lap dance."

I scoff, grabbing his chair by the armrests to spin until he's facing me. "Careful what you wish for." Donning a sultry look reminiscent of a certain magazine model, I sway my hips to a noiseless rhythm while running my hands over my breasts. "Do you remember a girl named Lynnette Wilks?"

Lewis can't possibly appear more uninterested as I shimmy in his face. "From?"

"Sixth grade," I explain, turning to grind my ass over his crotch in slow gyrations. "Quiet. Curly blonde hair. She would walk with us after group prayers before her parents moved her to a Christian school."

"Lynn…Yeah, I do remember her."

"She goes to Trinity Grace, too." Bending low at the waist, I shake my rear sprightly enough that my skirt rides high to expose it.

"Still haven't sized up, I see."

"Don't change the subject!" I snap, righting myself. "Lynn's a member of the study, and she was asking about you."

"Asking?"

I shoot him a smirk over my shoulder. "*Asking.*"

"And you're proposing I go there to…?"

"You *know* what I'm proposing." Facing him again, he grunts as I sink my weight onto his lap in a straddle. Wrapping my arms around his shoulders, I plead, "Come on, do it for me?"

Lewis's eyes fill with a recognizable nervousness. I notice his thumb fidgeting with the worn threads of the armrest, interpreting the quirk as reluctance to put himself out there romance-wise. He's always been so shy around people who aren't me. It made me fear that I was scaring him away from finding a relationship with someone who would love him in a way I never could.

Not that I don't love him at all. I love him more than anyone.

"Okay," he relents. "I'll go."

My face splits into a grin.

Which he completely ignores. "Now, will you get off me?"

"What, no tip?"

"You could use some work." He says, pressing the *Wild Thang* issue into my chest. "In the meantime, stick to whoring out your brain."

I snort, lifting myself from his chair to secure my belongings. "I'd better get going."

"See you in the pews, brain whore." He calls as I leave, to which I blow him a goodbye kiss in return.

Upon entering the Fennicks' living room, I have the misfortune of walking in on Lewis's mother and father having one of their hourly disagreements. Though, as usual, it was less of a *disagreement* and more so Mr. Fennick reigning in his throne of a recliner, yelling at his wife for whatever innocuous thing she did to get on his nerves. Meanwhile, she stands with her head low, hands clasped in front of her as she silently takes his vicious insults. As painful as it is to witness, I know interjecting would be a fatal mistake. I opt to leave the house through the garage, instead.

I open the squeaky door and tread down the small wooden steps. Heat spilling in from the driveway hits me instantly, as does the chatter from an FM radio housed on one of the wall-mounted shelves. The announcer gives a prelude to the nation's top charting song before a slow melody begins to hum from the decrepit speaker. But the music, nor the fact that the radio is operating at all, isn't what draws my attention. Typically, Lewis's garage housed his father's janky old Camry. But in its place is a station wagon I've never seen before. It's far more elegant, taking up most of the confined space where it sits propped on several elevated jacks. I'm not the least bit car-literate, but it looks expensive. Antique, even. It bears a red paint job with what might be a very sleek design, if it weren't for the sunbaked grime layering every inch of the exterior. The garage door had been closed when I'd entered the house this morning, and I can't help but wonder how long this has been here without me taking notice.

Intrigued, I discard my backpack on the concrete floor, stepping idly around the side of the vehicle to glimpse inside. Through the screen of dirty, tinted glass, I see an interior the same shade of deep red as the outside. Stepping along, I stop when I reach the door leading to the backseat. Only, from what I can see, there is no backseat. I wipe away dust coating the material and squint. Indeed, the backmost seating is folded into the floor, leaving enough room to fit a body. Or…two.

"*Holy shit!*"

The voice catches me so off guard that I don't even think to scream. My focus snaps to the direction it came from—underneath me. Between my Mary Janes, being gifted a theatric-like view up my skirt, is a human head. I lock on a pair of wide, horridly familiar blue-green eyes staring up at me.

Then, I scream.

And leap backwards so aggressively that the back of my skull cracks against one of the wooden shelves. Pain rattles me, but not nearly as much as the person responsible. My furious gaze finds him lying on a rolling creeper beneath the car, face smudged with oil and God knows what else. If the voice weren't enough of a giveaway, I'd recognize that messy hair and dirty complexion anywhere.

Rubbing the now-aching spot above my ponytail, I plant my foot on the nearest jack. "You know, I could crush your skull for doing that."

"Kinky." He taunts, offering a smug smile. "Nice to see you, too, Angel Face. *All* of you. When did Trinity Grace open a lingerie shop?"

The urge to snap at him grips me, but I know from experience it'll do nothing but spur on his nettling comments. "What are you doing here, Henry?"

He rolls beneath the vehicle to emerge fluidly from the front, sitting upright to wipe excess oil from his stained Henley, pushing it deeper into the fabric. "Well, two decades ago, the geezer running this house did something to his wife." The sarcasm in his tone is so potent, it leaks onto his face as he taps a finger to his head. "Damn, what's it called? Starts with an 'F.'" He glances my way with a quirked brow. "You're the vocabulary buff, what's the term I'm looking for?"

"Forgot to pull out?"

If only. Maybe I'd be spared from this conversation. Not to mention the past six years of him buzzing about my life like a damn hornet.

He huffs at my remark, then stands to grab a stray grease cloth.

I elaborate against my better judgment, "I thought you were gone for that Arizona trade thing?"

"I *graduated* from that Arizona trade thing." He says with a proud smirk. "Can you believe it? Scored a job downtown. I'm living there with some coworkers."

I truly do find myself surprised. The idea of the man in front of me achieving anything of merit is as much of a shock to the system as cracking my head on the shelf.

Henry Fennick. Lewis's older brother by two years. Although, if you didn't know this fact beforehand, one could never guess. Pretty much the only things the two have in common are DNA and their last name. While Lewis had always served as the model child—academic, polite, and at bare minimum willing to put on a performance to please the people he cared about—Henry couldn't be further away if he strapped himself to that stupid Harley Davidson of his and tore down the freeway with no plan for return. During his public school years, I never went a single day in the Fennick household without hearing his parents scold him for missing class, his ever-growing detention record, mouthing off to teachers, the likes of it. He'd stopped attending church altogether when he was a teenager. After he'd been caught screwing Pastor Morgan's niece, Faye Collins, in Crosspoint's custodial closet during service. Barring his permission back…Lucky bastard.

It was no wonder Lewis had kept any mention of his only sibling from me for as long as possible when we became friends. But when I was finally shoehorned into formally meeting Henry at one of Lewis's little league games, Mrs. Fennick had introduced me with her natural enthusiasm.

"*Henry, meet Rosie, Lewis's new friend! Doesn't she have the face of an angel?*"

He hadn't responded, or said a single word to me that whole afternoon. Even as we sat together on the topmost row of bleachers watching the game, a memory that would burn into my brain for the rest of time. It was the fourth inning, Lewis was up to bat, and Mr. and Mrs. Fennick were seated in front of us. The former was snapping at his wife for dragging him out to such a needless event, his tongue-lashing growing loud enough to draw the perturbed looks of surrounding attendees. And in the middle of his father asserting that Mrs. Fennick would hear the worst of it back at home, there was a crack of the bat, cheers broken by rumbling applause, and Henry, without so much as a glance in my direction, shoving me right off the edge of our shared seat. Despite my tears and bruised hip from falling six feet onto sharp gravel, Mrs. Fennick had chalked it up to a teen boy expressing his frustration in an unhealthy manner—or some dumb shit like that. But at the very least, she made him apologize. With a frown and a glare to match, Henry's first words to me had been:

"Sorry...Angel Face."

Ever since then, it's been that fucker's mission in life to make mine as miserable as possible. From his daily insults regarding my appearance or voice. To him pulling borderline-sadistic practical jokes. Even down to his habit of wiping dirt and grime on my nose when he'd come in soiled from working outside. I still don't know what I did to make him hate me so much, but hate me he most certainly does. I'd been spared for a majority of the past couple of years since he'd graduated high school by a hair's breadth, entering an auto-mechanic trade program that put him a good distance from our little street in Albuquerque. But apparently, my luck had run out.

"Like what you see?"

His question draws me from the memories, and I reflexively sharpen my glare. "What?"

He tucks the grease rag into the pocket of his jeans with a nod to the car. "I saw you eyeing it up, among the view you gave me. Sexy, isn't it?"

I entertain him. "I don't even know what *it* is."

He feigns a look of hurt. "*It* is a '76 Pontiac Grand Safari. John Wayne had a few of these. Belonged to my grandfather before he passed, then sat at his old property for a while." Rounding the hood, he moves toward me, dragging a grimy finger along the bumper's edge. "Dad says if I can get it running, it's mine."

My attention is refocused through the back door window. "Why are the seats folded down like that?"

I flinch when I realize how close Henry's gotten. Resting his elbow atop the frame to peer inside, he shoots me a pleased grin. "Room to lie down."

I have no idea what I'd been expecting, but his answer makes me scoff all the same.

"I stocked the door pocket with rubbers, too." He says. Then holds up a dirty hand, derision corrupting his tone. "Oh, right, let me translate that for you. Condoms. Those are for when a guy wants to put his penis inside a girl's—"

"I know what a condom is, smartass." I roll my eyes, pushing him aside to make my exit.

"The plastic wrap that comes on cucumbers you sneak to your bedroom doesn't count."

I stop dead. My ponytail whips as I twist to scowl at him. "You're sick!"

Sure, I had written far worse on paper. But even I have better manners. Besides…cucumbers would never fit.

Henry shrugs as he brushes past me, sending a wave of his all too recognizable scent along with him. Motor oil mixed with that gross citrus-smelling hand degreaser all mechanics use. "I take it you're still high and dry?"

What does he expect me to say to that?

Actually, asshole who makes my life hell, I was recently hired by a porn company to write people fucking at the most ill-fitted opportunities twice a month. What have you been doing with your *dick lately?*

I curtly cross my arms. "Why is that any of your business?"

"Just curious." He digs through a nearby toolbox, clanking wrenches and metal sockets. "You're all grown up now, figured you'd be putting out eventually."

A smirk pulls my features. "Does the lap dance I just gave your brother count?"

Henry fumbles whatever tool he's acquired, snapping his head to look at me with flared eyes. An incredulous once-over later, he expels a short breath. "You two are *so* weird."

"I'm not 'putting out' for anyone." I bite back. "But even if I were, why would I tell you?"

"Because I have a little more experience in that department." He chuckles deeply. "Not like you don't already know that."

Unfortunately, it's something I can't contest. Lewis has been joking for years that out of the two of them, Henry nabbed all the testosterone. He's far taller. Lean in all the places his younger brother is scrawny. I recall thinking he was cute in the first hour we met. My stupid twelve-year-old self may've even fallen for him—*if* he hadn't pushed me to, in the most literal sense possible, speed up that process himself.

Part of me had hoped that puberty would rid him of his boyish charm, but it betrayed me by turning him into a fucking movie star, instead. His athletic stature. His dusty brown hair trimmed in that Hollywood curtain style, with ends lightened to a sun-kissed dirty-blonde from months of working outdoors. Even down to his face, narrow features fixed in a seemingly constant glare that would be incautiously good-looking if it weren't always covered with oil and bruises. Several years ago, I watched the film *Running on Empty* with the Fennicks in their living room, and the following day, my neck was stiff from the number of times I'd glanced from the television to Henry—unconvinced that it wasn't him on the TV screen, swooning Martha Plimpton in some alternate timeline.

The worst part was how grossly aware of it he was. Faye Collins had only been the beginning. I was no stranger to spending my evenings and weekends around the Fennick home back when he still resided here. And by proxy, saw—and *heard*—my own share of Henry's romantic escapades over the years.

"It's not my fault you and your girlfriends only made it to your bedroom *most* of the time." I counter with a huff. "You really think it was fun walking in on you finger-banging some girl on the same couch I nap on every Sunday afternoon?"

A brunette cheerleader I had the misfortune of sharing gym class with. *That* marked the last time she ever made eye contact with me during heel stretches.

"Careful, Angel Face, you're starting to sound a little jealous." He continues to shuffle loudly through the aluminum drawer. "And they were hookups, not girlfriends. Maybe if your tits ever come in, someone'll give you a lesson in the difference."

I glare holes into the backmost layers of his hair. "I think I'd take dating advice from my mother before a smartass like you."

"Sounds like a great idea. When she lets you out of that chastity belt, anyways."

"Sorry, did you see a chastity belt when you peeked up my skirt like a creep?"

"I didn't do it on purpose!" He rounds, eyeing me from head to toe as his lip pulls in disgust. "Like I'd even want to? It'll be a cold day in hell when a man feels sorry enough to put his dick in you."

The insult stings enough to make my jaw clench, but it's nothing he hasn't been hurling at me for years. I straighten my spine. "'What are men to rocks and mountains?'"

His brows narrow at me.

"*Pride and Prejudice*," I explain, then sigh when he stares in confusion. "It's classical literature. *And* my favorite book. You should check it out, might learn something about respecting women."

"You'd have to strap me in handcuffs," Henry mutters, forcibly shutting the toolbox.

"You'd know about that, wouldn't you?"

When he looks at me again, a surge of fear courses from my chest to my outer limbs. I go stiff to mask it, but recollection of the day in question grips me despite my mental protest.

When Henry was sixteen, Lewis and I watched him get arrested after beating a fellow student to the brink of death in Peakshire High's parking lot. Only freshmen at the time, we'd caught the tail end of the brawl. Though, *brawl* implies that both opponents were worthy enough to clash in any sense, it was more of a slaughter. By the time we'd pushed our way to the front of the crowd circling them, Henry's opponent was long out, taking blow after bloody blow to the jaw. As much as I'd hated him up until then, that had been the first moment I ever truly feared Henry. Witnessing firsthand the destruction he was willing to inflict. Seared into my mind was the sight of staff rushing to intervene. Ambulance and police lights blinding the crowd in rhythmic pulses of blue. The look on Henry's face before it was over—unbridled wrath in its purest form. And blood. A *frightening* amount of blood that still stains the concrete to this day. Belonging to a boy who had, surprisingly, been quite larger than Henry. A football player by the name of Will Guerrero. From what I knew, whatever or whomever provoked the fight was never spoken of. Not even by the victim after he'd recovered and had enough teeth replaced to form coherent sentences again.

Henry had been hauled away by police with nothing but a bruised cheek and broken hand, spending four weeks in a juvenile corrections facility before returning to Peakshire and going on like nothing happened. But any chances of fellow students fucking with him were long gone, as were Mr. and Mrs. Fennick's hopes that the trials of public school would benefit their children in the long run.

But regardless of how unbothered Henry presented, it was clear that putting himself in such a position wounded him.

And I'd just reopened that wound.

Fixating on me from across the garage, Henry steps closer. Unsure of what he's scheming, I reverse from his continuous advance until a wooden shelf meets the back of my sore head. I try to keep the anxiety from tainting my expression as he's suddenly face-to-face with me. Well, as face-to-face as you can be with a girl *that* much shorter than you.

A few intolerable moments later, he reaches for something on the shelf, palming a greasy wrench and lifting it to showcase. But then, a pensive look overtakes his features. I close my eyes as he slowly brings the tool forward, wiping its residual oil across the tip of my nose before using a finger to rub it further in little circles. When I open my eyes again, I have to cross them to peer at what he's done, finding my skin stained black with grime. The pungent odor makes my lip twitch as I shift back into focus, blurriness giving way to Henry's shit-eating grin.

He chuckles at my expense, then turns back to the Grand Safari like I'm nothing but a sideshow he's through with entertaining. A growl rattles my throat as I stomp into the sunlight, wiping the gunk from my nose as I welcome its blazing heat over the company of the man at my rear.

"Catch ya later, Angel Face!"

"Not late enough, smartass," I reply, throwing a grease-smudged middle finger back at him.

Chapter 11

Sitting at the island in the center of our kitchen, I leisurely drag my fork across the plate cleared of leftovers. My shoe taps against the wooden stool beneath me as I glance at the wall clock.

Almost noon.

Nerves never fail to corrupt me on days like this. Constantly fearing that each time I get to slip away and remind myself that I still have family elsewhere would be the last. I place my dish in the sink to smooth sweaty palms over my skirt. "Mom, I'm heading out for a while!"

Her chair creaks in the obscured living room. "Where to?"

I offer a partial lie. "Meeting up with some friends to study, then I'm heading to Mr. Lasker's to babysit."

A hazardous silence falls, then breaks with her approval. "Alright. See you tonight."

I suck in a quiet breath of relief as I step to the front door, only to lose it when a loud knocking resounds from the other side of the sturdy wood.

"Is someone there?" Mom calls.

"I'll get it!" I shout back, irritated that my exit's been impeded.

But *irritated* certainly isn't the term for what I feel when I answer. *Disdain* is far more accurate.

"Is this late enough for you?" Henry nods at me, just as oil-covered and uncaring as he'd been an hour prior.

My brows drop into a glare. "What, you think of some new ways to demean me and couldn't wait?"

Lolling his head theatrically to one side, he holds up my discarded backpack. "You left this in our garage."

Jesus, had I really? I snatch it from him.

"Not even a thank you." He remarks, tracking me as I open it. "What are you doing?"

"Checking for snakes." I rummage through the inner pocket, fingering through my cash to assure it's still in place. "And making sure you didn't nab anything."

"Anything, like your porno mag?"

My grip on the backpack nearly falters. My eyes flare as I look up to see him palming my newest issue of *Wild Thang*. A devious smirk twisting his dirty features.

"Who is it, Mary-Rose?" Mom's voice cuts over.

I push Henry backwards with a leap outside, slamming the door behind me for fear of my mother overhearing a single word of his taunting remarks. The moment it's safe, I jump to retrieve what he'd stolen. "Give me—!"

"So much for classical literature." He laughs, dangling the booklet high above my head while opening it to a random page. "I knew you had a potty mouth, but you're into some freaky shit!"

"Henry, I swear to God," I whisper aggressively, leaping into the air to grab for it. "If my mom sees that—!"

"Breath play collars. Triple penetration. Ah, what's this? 'How forced eye contact can make a girl cream.'" He reads from the spread, shoving my face away with a greasy hand. "Gonna be hard with a paper bag over your head, won't it?"

"Give it *back*!" I demand in a furious hush.

Keeping a palm on me, he holds the magazine tauntingly in front of his torso. "Gotta reach it first!"

I struggle against his locked arm, ditching my backpack to go after it without obstruction. Bared ass of the blonde cover model lingering centimeters from my fingertips as I uselessly flail for it. The front door clicks. Our heads snap to the white-painted wood as it swings open. Henry's arm finally relaxes. There's no thought. There's only panic.

I throw myself into his chest, sandwiching the object of my desire tightly enough to be concealed between our bodies. And when my mother stands in the threshold, she doesn't see me fighting someone for dominance over a pornographic magazine. She sees me *hugging* Henry Fennick. Which is, arguably, just as bad.

Hot wind blows a few tendrils of blondish-gray hair from her face. Allowing a better view of two wide, disbelieving eyes.

"Mom," I present her a pageant smile, my arms fixed like a snare around Henry's middle. "I left my bag at Lewis's house and Henry brought it for me! Wasn't that sweet of him?"

Henry's hands find my back, no doubt staining the white fabric concealing it. "Anything for my little bro's friend." He mercifully plays along. Keeping my head nestled snugly against his collarbone, I peer upwards. A noticeable blush reddens oil-smeared cheeks as he offers a curt nod to my mother. "Mrs. Ginger, how's the tailor shop?"

Mom stands tense as barbed wire, providing a not-so-deceiving grin. "Henry…" She begins cautiously, disregarding the question. "Are you home for a visit?"

"Nope. Here to stay." He asserts.

I say nothing, simply glancing between the two throughout their uncomfortable exchange. My chest expands in rapid swells against the sleek magazine as I'm stifled with the scent of oil and citrus.

"Really?" My mother anxiously taps the door frame with her open palm. But the uneasiness doesn't reach her eyes, where a palpable scorn resides. "I don't suppose we'll see you at Crosspoint tomorrow? Maybe it's finally time for you to repent to Pastor Morgan for defiling his niece."

Henry's body stiffens beneath my hold, and I swear I can feel his heartbeat stutter even through the pages between us. I assume her provoking suggestion is the reason for his arms tightening around me ever so noticeably.

"I'll consider it." He says flatly.

Her gaze travels from my face to Henry's, clearly waiting for us to separate. But I don't. I *can't*. She has no idea I'm sparing her from a far worse fate of seeing her innocent little Mary-Rose holding what she considers to be the equivalent of demonic scripture.

"Well, I'd better get back to…" She clears her throat, not bothering to finish the excuse as she keeps her focus narrowed with every inch the closing door allows—a light *click* marking our isolation.

"You can let go now." Henry insists. Though, makes no attempt to pull away himself.

"Shh—" I hush, keeping hold of him until dissipating creaks signal that the coast is fully clear. Then, I forcefully push him away. Rage possessing me to roll the reclaimed magazine and repeatedly strike him before he can lift his arms in defense.

Henry might be intimidating, but there came a point in our lives when I no longer feared chastening him when he crossed my clear-cut lines.

Year after year, I put up with his torment, offering nothing but tears and pouted lips in the way of a reaction. Until the summer before Lewis and my first year of high school, when Henry had passed us in the Fennicks' front yard and pushed me onto the dusty ground for no reason besides cruel amusement—finishing it off with a remark about watching my step. I remember the way his words made all my bottled-up resentment pop like a rattled soda. I lifted myself from the grass and, for the first time ever, hit back. Catching Henry off guard as I pushed him into the side of their house aggressively enough to wind him. Cursing as I declared that he was nothing but a smartass who needed to pick on someone his own size. I'd half expected him to stand up and retaliate after being knocked to the ground. But he just sat there, staring up at me with wide eyes. Unspeaking even after I'd stomped away, leaving him as bewildered as I was furious. As much as I knew that giving him such a response was likely fuel to his fire, I couldn't help myself sometimes.

This is one of those times.

"Fucking! Perverted! *Smartass*!" I bark with each blow, then shove the magazine into my discarded bag to sling over my shoulder.

"Hey!" Henry calls as I step off the porch. "Pervert, me? I'm not the one lugging around porn in my school backpack!"

I say nothing in reply, nor do I give him the satisfaction of another vulgar gesture, despite how badly my middle finger aches to do so.

"Where are you even going?" He asks.

Shaking my head, I answer under my breath. More for myself than for him. "I have someone to meet."

I'm gifted a blissful break from the sun as I make it to Candid Park, only a few short blocks from my mother's house. It was a nice location, one that was particularly shielded from the street, with trees lining the perimeter. Meaning, if Mom happened to be traveling by, she was unlikely to spot us.

I wander toward the sound of laughing children, feeling my heart swell when the sun-bleached, red-and-blue-schemed playground comes into view. I find a familiar form among the chaotic jungle gym, reaching for a little boy's hand to aid him down the stairs of a platform—a little boy that catches sight of me the moment his sneakers hit the woodchips.

"Auntie Rosie!" He screams joyously, releasing Erica's hand to dash my way. I return his smile, lifting him into a tight hug when he closes the distance.

"Hey, Mattie!" I spin my giggling nephew, then press a kiss to his flaxen head—the same shade as his mother's, who flaunts a grin upon stopping at my side.

"Mattie, tell Rosie what you started since we saw her last." She prompts him, crossing proud arms over her pink blouse.

"I started pre-school!" He shouts a bit too enthusiastically in my ear.

"No way you're old enough for school," I say, wincing to recover from his volume. "You have to tell me all about it."

"Play with me first!" He jumps out of my arms and drags me by the hand to the climbing towers. I toss my sister a look as she trails behind us with a smirk.

After a bout of teeter-totters, stick sword fights, and Mattie filling me in on how many smells his schoolmates brought into the classroom when they arrived in the mornings, Erica convinces him to intrude on another group of boys' pseudo-soccer game beside a circle of benches. She and I take our places on one, watching as her son runs back and forth among the scattered kids—feeling included even if the older assortment were most certainly trying to avoid him.

"How you have the energy to even leave your home, I'll never understand," I say, still chasing my breath.

"Shouldn't be that difficult to imagine. All the effort it took to sneak around Mom was great practice." She keeps her eyes on Mattie, a soft smile pulling her lips.

It was weird to hear her mention Mom so casually, but I knew she was likely doing it as a courtesy. After all, I was the only person in the conversation still subjected to her bullshit. Despite Erica being a near carbon-copy of our mother physically—I've always been jealous that she'd inherited Mom's natural blonde hair and striking blue irises, while I'd been dealt our father's mundane brown combo—my sister was nothing like her on the inside.

Erica breaks her focus from the group of children. "Alright, enough kid-talk. Tell me about college."

I lower my gaze, sliding my shoe over grainy dirt as I ponder the best way to go about this. "It's...okay."

She narrows a look at me. "I did not put up with six visits of whining about Trinity Grace for you to say it's just 'okay.'"

I release a curt breath. "It's actually not all bad, if you can believe it. I guess I was expecting everyone there to act just like Mom. But I've met some nice people."

I tell her about the Bible study and meeting Lynn after so many years. She asks about Lewis, of course, and I fill her in on everything that hasn't changed—a ritualistic run-down of how our monthly conversations went. Focusing entirely on all the things I was dealing with has always been Erica's way of avoiding venting her own grievances regarding single motherhood. I suppose that's the shitty thing about being the *younger* sibling. The oldest forever thinks there are things in their life you shouldn't be privy to, even though they press like an iron for all the details about yours.

"Sounds like you're making a name for yourself at school." She says when I conclude.

"You don't know the half of it." I chuckle, but my demeanor lays bare that I'm not feeling too enthused. "I mean, I could always ditch college and work my way to writing away from Mom—"

"Rosie," she gently cuts me off. "Don't start with me."

At once, all the weight I'm used to hauling finally lifts. I feel like crying at the relief, despite knowing it'll be short-lived. "I don't know how much longer I can stand her, Erica. The other night, she told me that I matter to her because I'm her child, like *you* aren't her daughter, too. I was so pissed I nearly broke down right there at the dinner table. What if I can't do this for another four years?"

"You have to," Erica demands. "You're *going* to have a future, Rosie. After you have your degree, you can leave her a cloud of dust for all I care. But right now, you need what Dad left us. And you know damn well she isn't going to give it to you if you step out of line." She sighs deeply, resting against the bench as she rubs her tired eyes. "I love you too much to let you end up like me."

My heart breaks for her, splitting in the same agonizing rift it always did when memories of what drew us apart hammered it a little too forcefully. Erica and I had always bickered the way sisters did. Her being five years older never helped those matters much. But I didn't realize how much I really needed her until she was taken from me, by the very hands of the woman who'd brought her into this world.

After Crosspoint, Mom had both of our futures planned down to the year. Her daughters were to be taken care of, so long as their decisions were godly. And it was all to be funded with the allocations her late husband left for that very purpose. But as grantor of his too-hastily-constructed trust, our mother was in charge of when, or *if* it were to be distributed at all. Meaning, to keep us from acting out, she could dangle what was rightfully ours over our heads like a carrot. All it would take was one slip-up on the part of two adolescent girls to upend any chance of maintaining a secure life.

And Erica getting pregnant her senior year of high school was about the worst slip-up imaginable.

I'd listened the night she admitted it, no doubt hoping our mother would show some scrap of the mercy she claimed God was so full of. But all she received in return was a condescending tirade about irresponsibility and unholiness, topped with a threat to repent for her sins. But when Erica proclaimed she wouldn't be raising her child in the toxic cycle Mom had so heartlessly tossed us into, she was told to leave. Despite what our mother may have thought, Erica never wanted to lose us or her home. But when she'd asked in her final hours of being part of our family if she deserved the punishment of exile for nothing but a difference of beliefs, Mom had responded with a counter I'll go to my grave before forgetting.

"*Whores get what they deserve.*"

Legally, she was allowed to remove her eldest daughter from our lives. Erica had been eighteen at the time. But it didn't make my older sister sneaking into my room that night for the purpose of bawling any easier to witness as a thirteen-year-old. I'd felt just as helpless as she did. Unable to comprehend how a mother could throw away her child for making a simple mistake. Especially one that would, eventually, give her the most perfect grandchild she would never even bother to meet.

That, in retrospect, had been the moment it all began for me. The point when I realized that all the deities my mother lived for—the church, our pastor, God himself—weren't things worth worshiping if they came at the expense of pretending my very alive sister was now dead.

Ever since, Erica has been working odd jobs and living in income-based housing, relying on anonymous donations from gracious strangers to make ends meet. Mattie's father fled shortly after he was born, unable to bear the pressure of a child and opting to leave it all on Erica. How my older sister was still able to move forward with everything behind her, I could never comprehend. She was the strongest person I knew. Always making an effort to continue being my family, even if our mother could never find out.

"What about your writing? Have you finished anything lately?" Erica asks, surely in an attempt to change the painful subject.

Erica didn't know about my dirty stories, and despite her being my sister, our age gap made it a little more than awkward when it came to topics like sex. So she bought the same spiritual fiction claim that Mom did, at least for now. Which also meant that I could, under no circumstance, tell her about my new job. If she knew that I was sneaking around to write professional pornography under our mother's nose, that teenager who used to threaten to skin me for stealing her lip gloss would rise from the grave out of sheer—albeit protective—fury.

"You know me, always working on something," I say sheepishly.

"Well, maybe this will make working a bit comfier?"

I perk up when she reaches into her purse, pulling out a brown paper sack to hand me. Opening it splits my face into a wide smile, finding silky panties interwoven with lace in a bundle. Similar to the ones I'm wearing currently.

"Sized up, just like you asked." She confirms with a glint in her eye. The same one she had last year when I'd filled out to a B-cup.

God, I love her.

A fact I relish as I pull her into a hug. "Thank you."

"You know I don't mind. You're my most valued customer."

"Is the business doing any better?" I ask as I tuck the sack into my backpack. Taking caution so Erica doesn't see the half-nude cover model lounging inside.

"It's slow." She answers delicately. "I'm lucky to get an order a week. The ad I put in the paper didn't do much, but it's all I could afford."

I rarely dared to visit her and Mattie's little apartment. But when I did, it was almost always covered in fabrics, thread holders, and stored packaging for Erica's independent underwear business. "I've been telling you it's the name. *Erica Ginger's Lingerie* is too boring. You need something more eye-catching."

"And I've been telling *you* to come up with a better one." She pins me with a playful glare. "You haven't delivered."

"I'm working on it," I say with a smirk. "Just promise you'll still hook me up with free stuff when you become the top lingerie brand in all New Mexico?"

Erica scoffs. "So long as you put me in the acknowledgements of your bestseller. Deal?"

"Deal."

Chapter 12

Erica insisted on giving me a ride to Mr. Lasker's house after our park date. I was grateful, but more than a little heartbroken to say goodbye to her and Mattie upon arrival. I lean behind the center console to kiss the latter on the forehead, which he adorably tries to squirm away from.

"*Ew, cooties!*" He yells, flailing his arms and legs in distress—despite the smile on his face and surge of giggles that fill the backseat.

"That's right." I melodically tease, giving him a few additional pecks for good measure.

"We'll see you next month," Erica promises as I exit the car. "You know the drill, call me if—"

"Armageddon ensues?" I ask with a raised brow.

She gives me a stern look, which dissolves as quickly as she donned it. "Yeah, if Armageddon ensues."

"I will. I love you both."

"I love you, too." She returns.

"I love you more, Auntie Rosie!"

I blow a kiss to my nephew, then wave as Erica's car backs away, rolling down the street before disappearing behind the row of elegant houses. Entering Mr. Lasker's home offers instant relief from the outdoor heat I'd been subjected to for the better part of two hours. I release a sigh, waiting for Nathan and Daniel to run out from wherever they're hiding to rush me as they always did. But nothing happens. "Hello?"

"In the office!" Mr. Lasker's voice echoes from a few rooms away.

I follow it to the open study, finding his back turned as he writes among a mountain of paperwork. "Am I too early?"

"Not at all," he says. "Charlotte's on her way with the boys."

"Oh…" It wasn't normal that I got here before they did, and I knew that spending time alone with their too-sexy-for-*my*-own-good father would only make me more intolerably awkward than I usually am.

"You can hang out in here if you want. I'm just looking this over before I go in tonight." He nods to the loveseat along the wall behind him. "Best enjoy the peace before they rough you up."

I place my bag on the floor, propping my hands on my hips to stand tall. "You underestimate me. I can handle rough."

Whether the subliminal jest went over his head or not, he turns to look at me with a pleased grin—one that falters almost instantly. "I see that."

His eyes trail up my legs to fixate squarely on my chest, lingering without shame or explanation for a few heavy thumps of my heartbeat before I glance there as well. Spotting a dirty handprint in the center of my button-up, courtesy of Henry's stunt. It, along with my scuffed knees from playing with Mattie, must paint quite the picture.

"Was at the park with…a friend." I force a laugh. "Got a little carried away."

Mr. Lasker crosses one leg over the other before pointing at me. "That reminds me. The cardigan you left here is in my room. I threw it in with the rest of the laundry to take care of those grass stains."

Heat flushes my cheeks for no good reason. "You didn't have to do that."

"Anything for you." He replies with a smirk that's far hotter than he has any right to make it.

"I'll go grab it, then." I gracelessly exit, hoping he doesn't notice the wobble in my step as I do.

I curse myself for being so hopelessly pathetic all the way upstairs to his large bedroom. When I enter, I hum as his undiluted scent fills my nose—a woodsy musk that was most likely an intermix of some fancy cologne or luxury body wash. His extra-wide bed is impeccably made, sitting perpendicular to the left wall. I can't stop the depraved side of my brain that typically only functions when I write from snatching up the intimate setting and running with it. Illustrating a mental picture of myself sprawled out on the surface of that bed, with a ridiculously hot father of two on top of me, expertly stirring around my insides as I absolutely ruin those pristine sheets with—

Cardigan. I'm looking for my cardigan.

A mindless scan of the room proves useless, no piles of clothes or folded stacks to be seen. Only a dresser and a closet. Surely he wouldn't have put it away in a drawer, which leaves me one option. I approach the plantation-style doors and pull them open in a quiet swish. Looking at the closet floor, I expect to see a full hamper. Or at minimum, miscellaneous clutter.

Not…a stack of magazines as high as my knee socks.

Though it's dark in the confined space, the bright colors of the topmost selection are more than visible. As are the half-nude bodies of several women flaunting sexy cover poses. My eyes strain as they nearly pop out of my skull. I instinctively glance over my shoulder to assure there's no sign of Mr. Lasker moving about the house, but there's only stillness. Temptation pulls me like a sinner to my knees. Picking up the first of the collection, I recognize it as a special edition of *Hustler*. The header reading:

Barely Legal: A Celebration of Sexual Debutantes

The next in the stack displays a different issue of the same publication, as do the ones beneath it. One might think that, with myself now *part* of the dirty magazine business, I would be immune to seeing them out in the wild. After all, who's the primary demographic of such? Single men. It shouldn't be a surprise that a divorcée would want to look at naked girls in his off-hours. That's the porn industry's purpose, isn't it?

But being that these belonged to a man that I, on occasion, fantasized about fucking so hard that I'd be incapable of walking in a straight line for days, I'm simply beside myself. I imagine through my mind's default obscenity what it is Mr. Lasker does with these, and exactly how he relieves himself of the desires someone with such an extensive porn collection must have. I set the hefty pile of *Barely Legals* aside, noticing that the bottom of the stack consists of even more salacious booklets.

Good God, I thought I was horny.

Briefly flipping through the covers, however, I see that they're all newer editions of the more popular porno mags. While *Barely Legal* presented itself as his collector's stash, these look to be subscriptions. And all it takes is a bit of sifting to find one that makes my stomach drop straight through my overzealous sex organs.

Wild Thang

Our newest issue with the rear-facing cover model. The one that I, myself, possess in my backpack downstairs. The very location from where I'm suddenly called.

"Find it?" Mr. Lasker's powerful voice compensates for the distance.

Panic seizes me.

"Be right down!" I yell back. Trembling as I arrange the pile of magazines and closet doors as if they'd never been touched. I hastily search the room for the article of clothing I'd yet to locate, releasing a breath of relief as I find it atop a full hamper sitting obscurely beside the bed. Retrieving it in my rush to exit the room, I return to his office with a heavy heartbeat.

At my approach, he turns to face me as he did before. "You were gone a while."

Lord, looking him in the eyes after such a discovery feels so deliciously sinful. I press the bundled fabric closer to my chest, offering a nervous smile. "Sorry, got distracted."

He gives me a nod before leisurely going back to writing. "Now Christine doesn't have to worry about her baby girl getting cold in a hundred-degree weather."

I chuckle as I sit on the loveseat. Only realizing when my underside meets the leather how wet my trip upstairs had left me. "Sure doesn't..." I say, shifting uncomfortably in my ruined underwear as an awkward silence falls over the room, dispersed by the scribbling of Mr. Lasker's pen. "What do they have you working on?"

He sighs. "Just some last-minute edits on this plan for a firm we're overseeing. One of the chairmen wanted us to reevaluate our projections and meet him to go over—"

I don't hear a single fucking word. My focus is instead glued to the small movements of his arm as he writes. He works out, without question. I watch his bicep muscles tense and bulge through his dress shirt, trailing down to the tan skin of his working hand. My mind evokes an image of him using that very appendage to get himself off to a smutty piece about a college girl fucking her professor in front of the class. Never the wiser that precious little Rosie Ginger—who fixes his sons PB&Js and helps them with their weekend homework—was the one who wrote it for that very purpose. An indecent part of myself is disappointed he hadn't walked in on me discovering his secret collection, as I'm unable to keep from envisioning what *else* he can do with that hand, especially in retaliation to a misbehaving young girl.

That's when the idea hits me like a slap to the face—or, someplace lower. Any fear that once governed my inhibitions is now void with the prospect of sharing such a narrative. No specifics. No distinguishing features. No*body* would ever know. Least of all the man who provoked it. The one calling to me from the deepest depths of my sex-deprived mind...

"Rosie?" Mr. Lasker's *actual* voice draws me out of the fantasy.

I blink, realizing he'd resumed peering at me amid my scheming. "Sorry, what did you say?"

His lips pull into a polite grin. "I asked how things were at home, but I guess I got my answer. Have a lot on your mind?"

Be it the completely unjustifiable confidence I have when I'm horny, inspired, or a combination of the two, I decide to respond truthfully.

"Actually, I just got a new idea for a story," I say, pulling the *Holy Scriptures* notebook from my bag.

"Really?" He taps his pen in interest, pale eyes drifting over me. "What kind of story?"

I flip open the book, grabbing the bite-marked No. 2 pencil lodged inside. "A tale of forbidden lovers."

Mr. Lasker gives a slight hum, ditching his utensil to sift through some additional papers as he half-heartedly asks, "Let me guess, sappy? A born-again traveler falls for the preacher's daughter or something?"

A smirk corrupts my innocent face. "Or something…"

Chapter 13

When I step into my boss's living room, I'm expecting to see the kids running amok, as they always do on the weekends I arrive to babysit. But instead, I find their brawny, ruthlessly expectant father standing alone in the center of the den—sporting crossed arms and a stern glare that seizes my body with a rather pleasant rush of chills.

"Where are the boys?" I ask gently, maintaining my professional—albeit falsely innocent—composure as I close the front door. My heels clicking with each careful step that follows.

"It's just you and me." His low voice is heavy with authority. "I have something I want to discuss with you."

I stop a short distance from him, staring up at his tall stature as I finger the buttons of my fitted blouse in a meek play to look nervous. "What's the matter, sir? Did I do something wrong?"

His sleek hair is pushed back enough to display tense features. He lowers his narrow gaze at me before holding up something he'd been keeping tucked beneath his muscular arm. It's a dirty magazine, with scantily dressed young women all over the cover. "You recognize this?"

I gasp, shielding my eyes from the graphic images. "Sir! I shouldn't look at that, it's inappropriate!"

"You should." He insists. "You were snooping around in my bedroom and found the rest of these, didn't you?"

I drop my hands. Thrill and mischief taking hold now that I've been caught. "Sir, I found them by accident. I didn't look through them, I promise!"

"I keep these around for my own pleasure." He says deeply, slowly consuming the distance between us. *"A young woman like you has no business going through my private matters. Even if she does have a little crush on the dad she babysits for."*

My eyes widen, and I fight the urge to smile at the concept, even if my next declaration is nothing but a clean-cut lie. *"Mr. Lasher, I don't have any crush on you. I swear it!"*

"You think I can't tell?" He asks firmly, running a large finger ticklishly along my jawline. *"How you walk in here. Tight shirt. Short little skirt. With no bra..."* He eyes my breasts. As my nipples peak into the fabric of my white blouse, his shameless focus lingers before traveling even lower. *"...And no panties."*

My head snaps downward. Finding myself so wet from his advance that my arousal manifests in a shimmery strand now dangling between my thighs, stretching long before it drips heavily onto the floor beneath. I go bow-legged, pressing hands to my skirt in a meek effort to keep it from cascading. Just for the slickness to coat the insides of my legs, turning soft flesh slippery.

"And to think I saw you as my baby girl." Mr. Lasher's tone shifts threateningly low. He shakes his head as I stir in a forced attempt to look frightened. *"Now, you're nothing but a bad girl. Do you know what bad girls get?"*

I pout at him, expecting my innocent act to deter him while hoping with every tendril of arousal coiling through me that it wouldn't. *"A second chance?"*

He chuckles deeply, tossing the dirty magazine before snatching my arm in his powerful hold. *"They get punished."*

I squeal as he drags me kicking and pleading to the sofa, sinking into a seated position before tossing me headfirst over his lap. He presses a hand to my back, a move that makes my spine arch and my rear perk up.

"Mr. Lasher, please! Don't punish me!" I cry, delicious embarrassment filling me to the brink of implosion as there's suddenly nothing keeping his watchful eyes from witnessing how much I, in actuality, want this.

"You've gotta learn." Mr. Lasher asserts before flipping my flared skirt, leaving my lower half naked for his beating.

SMACK!

I yelp as his large hand comes down hard on my ass. The pain stings, but pierces deep enough to evoke scorching pleasure as his palm assaults my cheeks a second time.

SMACK!

"Ow! Ow! Ow!" I yell, squirming and kicking in his hold. "Please, sir! Not so hard!"

SMACK!

SMACK!

SMACK!

Each blow lands stronger than the last. Wriggling like a scruffed kitten against his legs, I feel a distinct hardness press into my side closest to his strong body. The thickness strains against its cloth barrier, throbbing powerfully each time my plump ass bounces with his brute slaps.

He growls at me between hits. "How am I supposed to enjoy those magazines now that I know you saw them?!" SMACK! "I can't look at them ever again without thinking of you!" SMACK! "How am I supposed to relieve myself now?!" SMACK! SMACK! SMACK!

"I can relieve you, sir!" I shout without thought.

Only then does he halt, leaving my cheeks stamped with bright red handprints after so many strikes. "Can you?"

"Oh, yes." I tremble in his grasp, desperate for relief from my own desires. "I'm so wet for you, sir. You can use me."

"Hm…" He hums lowly, rubbing his palm over my raw flesh before dipping it low to the mess beneath. "Maybe I should. My baby girl deserves it for acting out."

I gasp sharply as he slips two rough fingers into my hot entrance, stretching it as he shoves them deep to feel out my tight insides.

"Your cunt's nice." He praises. "Let's see if it works properly."

He begins slipping in and out of me so hard and fast, my body reacts before I can protest...Not that I was going to.

"Sir—!" I drag with a long whine, screaming in bliss as he puts every ounce of his force into fingering me. Wound up from years of yearning, it only takes seconds before I come harder than ever before. Juices spill from my pulsating slit down his large hand, but that doesn't stop him. His digits hook into my deepest spot, refusing to let up until my orgasmic throbs slow from powerful grips to gentle sucks—a mark of my anatomy trying to pull him as deep as possible even as my climax fizzles out. He removes himself when I go limp. But I jolt as he gives my hyper-sensitive clit a painful flick for good measure.

Chuckling, he rubs a large, come-slickened hand over my tender ass in a counterfeit gesture of care. "So, now that I know it works, tell me. Do you want me to make it mine?"

I struggle to reclaim my breath, already aching for another orgasm at his command. "Yes…"

"Yes, what?"

My wide, innocent eyes peer up at him. "Yes, sir."

I smile gleefully as he suddenly lifts me. The next thing I know, I'm face down on the couch beneath a sturdy weight. The clinks of an unclasping belt give way to a hard, hot mass settling heavily in the cleft of my ass. He grips my reddened cheeks in his hands, squeezing them around his thick cock to give a few experimental thrusts. I whimper at the ridges of his defined length rubbing teasingly against my asshole. The feel of his pre-come trickling over my skin. The primal lust possessing his every move.

"Fuck me, sir…" I beg, biting the cushion beneath me in anticipation.

Mr. Lasher growls as his protruding head slips to my awaiting entrance. "That's my baby girl."

Air breaks with the swift rise of his hand.
SMACK!
SMACK!
SMACK!

SMACK!

R.J. slamming his palm on the wooden desk makes me jump so violently, my hips slip from the seat I'm poised in. I anchor myself to the armrests to hang on, fixating on the man with wide eyes that demand to know what could've provoked such an outburst after ten minutes of intensive proofreading.

"I've got it!" He points at me, elation crossing his face like he's had a stroke of genius. "'*Bubble-Butt Babysitter Buys a Brutal Beating*!'"

Even if he's technically my employer, I was quickly losing any fear of speaking unfiltered around him. Correctly seating myself, I rub the side of my face with a sigh. "Are misleading, alliterated titles your kink or something?"

He flashes me a toothy smile. "One of many, Virgin Mary." Laughing, he stands from the prominent chair to run a slow hand up Ruth's back, who continues to read the last of my piece unfazed. "Well, Baby Ruth, what do we think?"

Rather than continue to stew in the anxiousness that came with awaiting Ruth's decision, I opt to study her. She's wearing a dark blue variation of her typical suits, with a blouse unbuttoned lower than I've yet to see. The sleek material rests stiffly against the exposed upper portion of her chest, but I notice an anomaly among the canvas of her otherwise light complexion. Just beneath the material, a few inches below her collarbone, a red mark of skin lies partially obscured by the fabric of her dress shirt. Too distinctive to be a bruise or a love bite. Maybe a birthmark? It's only visible from the angle her body is tilted, and the moment she straightens upon reaching a determination, it vanishes.

"I think it's missing something." She finally says, no affect in her tone.

R.J., who dons a similar demeanor—most likely for the sake of pretending he knew what Ruth was getting at—nods his head. "Uh, yeah. I think so, too…Maybe a more *explosive* finish on our baby girl's end?" He raises a brow at me, tongue darting grotesquely over his bared teeth. "You ever see a pro squirt before? Best bring an umbrella, if you're picking up what I'm putting down."

I blink at him. Wondering how I ever so foolishly believed there wasn't a soul in Albuquerque with a more perverted mind than mine.

"It's how she addresses the father." Ruth crosses her arms. "We already did 'sir.' It doesn't fit in this context."

"Oh," I say timidly, a bit embarrassed I hadn't considered that. "Well, what could we change it to?"

She offers a light shrug. "How about, 'Daddy?'"

R.J. bends at the knees like he's been struck over the cowboy hat, then draws his words slowly. "Oh-ho-ho, Baby Ruth! You always got the best ideas!" He wiggles his fingers. "Sprinkle a little something in for the ladies with daddy issues."

I find myself lost in translation between the two. "But she's not his daughter. She's his babysitter."

"Well, obviously," Ruth says. "But he's an authoritative male, a lot of women equate that to a parental figure."

"That, *and* it's the only way to feed the incest quota without getting an uninvited lecture on obscenity from New Mexico's finest," R.J. adds. But when Ruth and I only stare at him in way of any response, he clears his throat. "Just saying."

Ruth shakes her head, addressing me once more. "Look, it's more common than you might think. It doesn't mean anything relationally, it's only a pet name."

I contemplate the request, knowing that I don't have the final say one way or the other, and for good reason. Ruth knew the industry far better than I did. It would be wise for me to avoid questioning her judgment. "Okay. Let's change it."

She gives me a slight smile. "I'll make a note to our editor; shouldn't take any effort on your end."

R.J. removes my earnings from the lockbox, eyes drifting below my face as he hands over the bills. "All in a day's work, Virgin Mary. Wanna swing by for the photoshoot this week? We might swap out Val for a more *loyal* depiction of our 'baby girl' if you're up for a few extra Benjamins?"

I stand to tuck the cash away in my backpack. "Thanks, but I'd rather catch it when it hits the racks."

"You know, employees receive free subscriptions," Ruth informs me. "We can have the newest issues sent straight to your address—"

"*No!*" I shout without consideration, loud enough to make the woman's brows perk in surprise. I reel it back despite panic hammering my chest at the idea of my mother opening our mailbox to get an eyeful of what I do for a living. "I, uh… I like getting mine from stores. Anything to help sales, know what I mean?"

"Virgin Mary gets off on seeing her porn in the wild." R.J. purrs. "I like it."

Ruth purses her glossy lips, then nods once. "Suit yourself."

I bid them a quick goodbye, promising to meet the next two-week deadline before making a hasty escape into the hallway to hell. Hoping to avoid any more unsolicited offers from R.J., no matter how tempting he may've thought they sounded. Just as I leave the office, however, another figure exits the studio a few doors down. And I catch the tail end of what sounds like someone *else's* scandalous proposition.

"You can join in, Val! We got extra room on the couch!" A male voice calls from within the stage.

"Sorry, Cummings! You're not my type." Val replies melodically, closing the red door with a swift *clank*. Upon catching my gaze, she cheerfully perks. "Rosie!"

I find myself stunned at the way that, every time I lay eyes on her, she seems less like a human and more like a goddess in a cropped shirt and Daisy Dukes. The very sound of her voice sends the same shiver down my spine it had during our previous greetings. Three for three now, but who's counting?

"Hey, Val." I manage, stepping closer on unsteady legs.

"You bring in another piece for us?"

"Right on schedule." I nod to the studio. "Did you finish?"

Just then, a wave of feminine moans crests from beyond the sealed threshold. Val raises a suggestive brow as my face turns a shade that rivals the walls around us.

"Not—Not *that* type of finish." I clarify, stuttering like a fool. "I-I meant with work today, not if you'd—"

Thankfully, I'm saved by her bursting into a fit of giggles.

I don't know whether to be relieved or fall over dead. "What's so funny?"

"Nothing," she covers her pretty mouth. "You're just the cutest."

As if I wasn't blushing hard enough. It only worsens as the moaning swells in a lewd crescendo, cutting out any chance of us maintaining a sensible conversation.

"Anyways, I'm not a video girl. Modeling is enough for me." Val remarks with a smirk, surely amused by my embarrassment. "You have anywhere to be?"

"Oh, I was just leaving."

"No," she reaches for my hand, gently clasping it. "I mean, any plans tonight?"

Her touch threatens to send me into the same pathetic spiral it always does. "I'm…done with my classes for the day."

Her face brightens as she begins pulling me down the hallway to hell. "Let's go somewhere, then!"

My mind whirls to compute what's being proposed. Me? Go out? With *Val*?

"But I need to catch the bus home," I say on instinct, then inwardly curse my nerves for attempting to sabotage everything.

"I can drive you after." She insists, shooting me her perfect smile as I'm guided into the lobby. "Besides, I want you to tell me all about your stories! We've barely had time to get to know each other."

Thinking it over in the few short moments I have, I make the overdue decision to put a cap on the relentlessly awkward, socially incompetent side of myself. Over the years, I'd foregone countless chances to step outside of my comfort zone for the sake of preservation, or to avoid potential rejection. But here I am—in a dirty magazine studio being led along by a cover model for an evening out. I might be an idiot, but I'd have to be brain-dead to let such an opportunity pass by.

"Alright." I resign with a shy grin. "Where did you have in mind?"

Val stops with her free hand on the exit. "Some place cozy. You're going to *love* it."

Chapter 14

Loud rock music vibrates the stool beneath me as I drink in every inch of the dimly lit interior. The provocative atmosphere of such an establishment lends itself to make me feel completely out of place, yet right at home, given my own twisted fantasies.

"I'll take a stab in the dark and bet that you've never been to a strip club?" Val asks from the seat beside me, raising her voice over the pulsating beat.

We're stationed at the bar, but I can't tear my eyes off the wide stage at the base of the room. More specifically, the dancer gliding effortlessly around the brass pole in the center. Her cyan-sequined outfit and platform heels glitter in the soft backlight, leaving *very little* of her curvaceous form to the imagination—as per intended.

"She is talented," I say in awe as the performer flips, inverting herself with the grace of a ballerina and the lure of a...well, stripper.

"She's worked here a long time." Val follows my gaze. "Since I used to, anyways."

"You worked here?"

Her hazel eyes shift away. "I had a friend who was a dancer; she got me the job. Waiting tables, that is. Anything to put a dent in college fees." She lifts her styled brows in a quick move. "Until I got the *Wild Thang* gig."

I swear, I'll sit here for hours listening to her speak utter gibberish if it means I can listen to the trill of her voice without interruption.

I'd already prodded about her love life to fill conversation on the drive over. To which she had, astoundingly, told me there was no love life to prod about. I couldn't decide if the revelation had made me feel better or worse about my own relationship status. *If this woman is single, then there's no hope for any of us.*

I brush the hair from my forehead to get a better view. "What are you in college for?"

"I'm in my final year of a bachelor's degree in political science. But I applied to UNM Law last month." She says, twisting a superstitious middle finger over her index.

"Law school?" I marvel at the concept. "I could never pull that off."

"The material isn't as hard as you'd think. I got a 172 LSAT score on my first try. It's more a matter of knowing how the system works." Slipping a compact from the pocket of her Daisy Dukes, she clicks it open to view her reflection. Delicately wiping a smudged edge of her ruby lipstick as she goes on. "It's kind of like modeling. Everyone assumes you have to be drop-dead gorgeous to end up on a cover. But really, it's about getting the people who choose that cover to notice you."

"But you *are* drop-dead gorgeous." The compliment—or, *fact*—leaves my mouth without prior thought.

Her tan cheeks turn a shade deeper in the harlequin hues as she offers me the compact. I take the polite gesture, holding it up to clumsily straighten the tendrils of my fringe. But the small reflection gives me pause, and I'm left staring at a face so unremarkable, I half expect the glass confining it to splinter. Not wishing to look at her a second longer than I have to, I close it.

"So why law?" I ask, sliding the object back to her. "It just seems like a far cry from nude modeling."

Val smiles giddily, lighting up like she's been waiting all her life to answer such a question. "But that's just it! I want to represent people in the industry. Of course, I love what I do, but a bad manager can make or break a performer's career if they aren't careful. It's easy to take advantage of workers whose entire jobs revolve around pleasing people who have power over them." Her gaze falls between us. "I want to look out for them. Make sure that if they're going to choose that life, they get the protection they deserve."

My heart burns in the vicinity of such compassion. "That's incredible."

"That's the long-term goal, at least. For now, I'm trying to focus on networking. And on top of modeling for Ruth, I help oversee our staff's contracts. Just to get some experience."

"Must be a handful," I say, recalling my own in-processing. "She didn't make you take care of mine, did she?"

"Nope. Contractor agreements are pretty cut-and-dry. Ruth handles those on her own." She blows a laborious sigh. "The catch-alls? *They're* the real headache. Our general runs over a hundred pages with all the releases. But Ruth likes to have them at the ready so our models can do other work around the studio. Makeup, styling, we even have a few that act as technicians during shoots."

That term…catch-all. Hadn't that been the way Ruth described my agreement? Not to mention the length of it Val had mentioned in such displeasure.

"Does the studio have its models sign the general contract?" I ask.

Her joyful eyes crinkle in confusion. "Of course. It was made for them." She curiously tilts her head. "Ruth did process you as a contractor, didn't she?"

Before I can begin to ponder a topic that was miles from my expertise, a feminine voice interjects from behind the counter.

"Valerie!" Our heads spin to see a blonde, fifty-something bartender make a cheery approach. "Good to see you back in house. Who's your friend?"

"Hey, Michelle! This is Rosie, a co-worker of mine from the studio." Val replies gleefully, tapping her finger on the wooden surface in front of me. "She'll just have a cola. Rum for me."

"You got it." Michelle chimes, flipping a dirty bar mop over her shoulder.

I watch as she prepares our drinks within moments, sliding the two dark beverages our direction as Val offers her a warm *gracias*. Michelle goes on tending, but something about the interaction catches me.

"Valerie?" I ask, cocking a brow at her.

Val hums. "'Valentina Amor' was R.J.'s idea. Said it sounded more romantic. My real name is Valerie Ramona."

Valerie. Knowing her true name sends the butterflies in my stomach into a frenzy. But they startle even more when Val catches my glass before I can take a sip, shooting a subtle glance over her shoulder as she swaps the two. Replacing my regular with her alcoholic.

"What are you doing?" I ask, as hushed as I can above the music.

"I'm driving, remember?" She brings the stolen drink to her lips with a wink.

I stare at the one in my hand. Apprehension and excitement alike stir as I bring it to my nose to sniff, detecting a chemical odor. Taking the plunge, I ingest a mouthful of the beverage. The familiar taste of cola intermixes with the bite of something that burns my throat as I swallow. Nearly choking on it, I cover my mouth with a palm.

Val's brows knit. "Have you never had it before?"

My face flushes crimson as I give a reluctant shake of my head.

She startles. "¡Ay Dios mío! I didn't think to ask. You don't have to drink it if you aren't—"

"No, no, it's fine. Swear." I grimace as I take another long swig. This one goes down much smoother now that I anticipate the kick.

"Okay, enough about me." She says, sipping from her own drink. "I want to know about you."

"Well," I start, rambling with the aim of amusement. "I was born on the third Thursday of March. I'd sell my soul to marry Zack Morris from *Saved by the Bell*, even though he's a total jerk. Oh! I can do this with my tongue—"

I pluck a maraschino cherry from a jar behind the bar top and toss it into my mouth, swallowing the fruit and twisting the stem into a knot with my tongue before sticking it out to showcase.

"*Noted...*" Val giggles with a raised brow. "But I'm more curious about your work. You don't exactly have the 'I write hardcore erotica' look about you."

I half expect hesitation to rear its ugly head, but find myself startlingly eager to divulge. Maybe my newfound conviction was on account of the alcohol now settling warmly in my stomach, because any reluctance to spill about how I ended up here—a virginal erotica author lounging in a strip club with a porno magazine cover model— had simply gone out the window. I tell her about my ever-growing collection of smut stories, and all the terrible things my hyper-religious mother would do to me if she were to discover them. I explain the details of my father's trust and how it had, consequently, been left in the hands of said mother. Whom I now had to bend to the whims of to have any semblance of a secure future. But I spend most of my spiel talking about Lewis, the only person I trusted enough to know of my endeavors. By the time I'm finished, I'm two more rum and colas down, and feeling *muuuuuuch* less anxious than I'd been upon our arrival.

"He isn't your boyfriend?" Val asks, absent-mindedly smudging the lipstick print on her glass.

"No-ope," I enunciate, trying my damnedest to keep the words from coming out as clumsily as they're being stitched together in my head. "He's like my brother. We do *everything* together. But not like that."

"So…neither of you have ever dated anyone?"

"Not once!" I raise my half-empty cup as if toasting to the statement. "We agreed, if we're both going to be old lonely virgins, then we'll be old lonely virgins together. Ooh—" I gasp. "When you graduate first in class and go to law school, promise you'll invite us to celebrate? Nobody cheers louder than we do!"

I down the last of the drink in a single mouthful. The instant I set it back on the bar, Val places her palm over the rim.

"I think you've had your fill." She says gently, standing to pull me from the stool. "Why don't we put some distance between us and Michelle before she notices?"

"Notices what? I'm perfectly fine." I declare not two seconds before nearly tripping on the incline leading to the smaller assortment of tables circling the stage, where Val now guides me.

She stifles a laugh, but resumes our conversation out of courtesy—likely for my humility's sake. "I was just thinking, are you sure that Lewis likes girls at all?"

The implication takes me aback, even in my less-than-sober state. "Huh?"

"I just can't see a guy being so close to you for so long and never making a move. Not unless girls aren't his thing." She sits me down at a cocktail table set for two, only feet away from the vast platform where a dancer spins seamlessly around the center pole.

Despite my inebriation, I overlook the idea, being that there's no chance Lewis would hide such a thing with all *I've* entrusted him with. Instead, I hone in on her indirect compliment. Chuckling dryly, I cover my flushed cheek with a hand. "What do you mean? Why would anyone wanna make a move on me?"

Mary-Rose Ginger. The hopelessly pathetic observer who would rather write about a fictional version of herself living life to the fullest, instead of having the guts to go out and actually do it.

Val cautiously assures I'm steady enough before taking a seat opposite me, scoffing as she does so. "Because you're fun! You're creative. You're good with your tongue..." She chuckles, propping her elbows on the surface between us to lean closer, pretty face twisting in a smirk. "*And* you're hot."

I figured the hum of alcohol would dull the rush that surges in my chest at that. But if anything, the warm tinge only amplifies it. Igniting the same heat that tempts me to verbalize, "Not as hot as you."

Ah...*that's* why they call it liquid confidence.

Val's hazel irises brighten as she pulls a folded collection of dollars from her back pocket, riffling them as she speaks. "We'll call it a draw. But I'm just saying, if it were you on that stage, I'd go broke."

She twists in her stool to toss the bills, the stack scattering in the corner of my vision as it lands like confetti on the raised floor. But, shit, I can't pull my eyes from Val. The edges of her red lips upturn just enough to flash flawless white teeth. Her gaze fixating on the performer—who is surely approaching to give Val her money's worth. Bluish glimmers from a spinning disco ball make her black hair shimmer with every slight movement. The orange halter crop top she's wearing perfectly complements her brown skin, hugging the prominent curve of her breasts that I, crudely enough, allow my focus to linger on. Is she not wearing a bra?

A tingling warmth flushes my lower belly, one that differs from the unnatural chemicals in my bloodstream. No, *this* heat is one I'm far too intimate with. But that doesn't stop me from pinning my unprompted arousal on the alcohol, either. I'd learned to admire the beauty of other women since my very first encounters with salacious material, having never shied away from portrayals of women-on-women acts. Indulging in that form of reverie as I would any other implausible fantasy of mine. There was hardly a shortage of such, considering porn was typically constructed to appease the male gaze. But the way I always saw it, females have eyes, too.

Thank *God* for my eyes…

It's only the shine of yellow sequins that finally pulls my attention from Val's divine body, figuring it would be rude to ignore the dancer supplying her paid performance. The glint off her reflective two-piece is blinding, forcing me to blink and take in the rest of her as she slowly crawls on hands and knees to the stage's edge. Each move is sultry. Precise. The thin, fair-skinned young woman arches her back when she reaches us, tossing tight blonde curls with the motion. Her smile only lingers on Val for a few swift beats of the song, before a pair of amber eyes rimmed in glittery shadow lock on mine.

The buzz holding me in a near-mindless state lifts so instantaneously that it renders me incapable of breathing. All I can do is stare at the face a mere arm's length away—one that breaks in the paragon of sheer horror at the sight of me.

My jaw falls open, taking one single word with it. "*Lynn?*"

Chapter 15

Sudden sobriety is a bitch.

I rub my aching head, bracing its weight with an elbow on the table in front of me. At least now I'm in the corner of the club furthest from the blaring speakers, in a booth nestled beside the solitary hall to the backstage dressing room. Lynn is sitting across from me. Though, I can't tell if her trembling is due to her state of undress, or if the terror that came with me discovering her "bar" job still wracks her. Given that she's now wrapped in a silk robe concealing her stage attire, I assume it's the latter.

"Relax," I sigh. "You can't seriously think I'd tell anyone."

"Nobody knows. Not my siblings, anyone at school, *definitely* not my parents." She covers her face with shameful hands. "If someone found out, if anyone—!"

"Lynn!" Pain pulsates through my skull with the outburst. "I swear to God I won't say anything."

A fickle statement given our shared beliefs, but the thought is genuine.

She shakes her head, sending the blonde curls that aren't pinned bouncing over her glittery features. "The money I earn here is more than I can make working double the hours anywhere else. And with school and payments…"

"You don't have to explain yourself to me," I say, drawing a surprised glance from her. "Look, you shouldn't feel any more shame working here than I feel coming to this club at all. Which, by the way, is none." I offer a smile. "Besides, you were killing it up there."

My sincerity appears to do the trick. I watch her relax as if she'd sat at this table anticipating a tongue-lashing about morals from a model *Proverbs 31* woman. It takes more effort than it should to keep from laughing.

She pulls the silk robe tighter around her middle. "What *are* you doing here?"

I look over the venue to spot Val in conversation with Michelle at the bar. She'd been gracious enough to give the two of us time alone, even with my lack of explanation as to why.

"That woman I was with brought me. She's my co-worker," I explain, fighting a smirk and losing. "At the dirty magazine studio I write erotica for."

There was no reason to hide it with what I now knew about Lynn's endeavors. If anything, I hope it puts her at ease knowing she isn't the only deviant parading around school behind a veil of counterfeit sanctitude.

It does. As her look of utter shock softens, she hesitantly chuckles. "You aren't kidding, are you?"

I shake my head.

She pauses, looking at me like I'm no longer a stranger. "You mean, I'm not going to hell alone?"

I feel her words as if they were my own. "Fuck, no."

She sucks in air like she wants to laugh again. But it comes out as a slow, easy breath. "So you promise that when we go to the study this week, you won't talk about how we saw each other?"

"Promise. Believe me, I know what it means to keep a secret."

"Good. I just really like the girls there, and I want them to like me, too." Her sparkling eyes graze the table between us. "As cool as they seem, I doubt they'd be so nice to a stripping Christian."

"Really? I can't think of a better type of Christian." I say, and mean it.

She snorts. "Maybe we should get you fitted for heels, then. 'Rosie Ginger' already sounds like a stripper name."

I smile at the compliment, even if it wasn't intended to be one.

When we meet up with Val at the bar, I introduce Lynn as my childhood friend turned college classmate. For the rest of the night, the three of us spend the interludes between Lynn's sets spilling about our lives. Val slips me another rum and cola to ward off the headache, which works. And when the club turns up unusually vacant for the late hour, I take a little trip up the stairs to the wide stage. Just to learn that those spins Lynn had been doing around that brass pole weren't half as difficult as they looked.

Lynn sat to the left of me during Bible study that Thursday, and neither of us could suppress the short, suggestive grins we tossed back and forth at every opportunity.

As Rebecca led the campus gossip into muddy waters for the rest of the captivated group, I'm willing to bet Lynn felt the same deceptive surge in her gut that I did. There was an odd lure to knowing you and another in such a subjugated community held each other's deepest secrets. That being said, I would have to be blind to forego noticing how some of her suggestive looks flew right past me to instead land on Lewis, who sat at my right. He'd gotten along with the girls just as well as I'd predicted, laughing and acting as jovial as he would if it were just the two of us. And following the study's disbanding for the night, Rebecca bids a cheery goodbye to Lynn and me as we step into the darkening courtyard.

"See y'all around!" She calls, her voice resounding off the wide buildings. Both of us wave in return before Lynn's hand catches mine mid-air.

The quick act startles me. "What's wrong?"

"Do you think Lewis would go out with me tonight?" She asks in a hushed tone, desperately searching my eyes.

My jaw slackens. I glance over my shoulder to the entrance of the art department, where Lewis had remained inside to use the restroom. "You wanna go out with Lewis? *Right now?*"

"He's just as funny as I remember. And cute!" She says emphatically, never loosening her grip. "And if he's *your* best friend, then I trust him. Do you think he'd say yes to a drive-in date?"

My head whirls at the idea. But after a few moments of turning it over, a grin splits my face. Lynn jumps when the doors behind us clink open. Lewis begins his stride over as I whisper to her, "Let me handle this."

"You were right, they *were* cool." Lewis stops beside us. "And, Lynn, it was great to see you again after so long. We should all make plans sometime."

"Actually, Lynn just invited us to the drive-in tonight." Placing a hand on my abdomen, I feign a look of discomfort. "But I'm not really feeling up to it, got a serious case of girl flu. Why don't the two of you go without me?"

Lewis looks between Lynn and me with a hesitant smile. "Well, I sorta made plans to meet with Presley over chat."

"Yeah, but you can do that anytime with your computer magic. You should get out for once." My brows quirk in a subtle raise, a mark of insistence in our coded communication.

His pale features tense ever so noticeably. But a few cricket chirps later, his eyes soften, then shift to Lynn's. "Sure. That sounds like a good time."

The girl perks as if she's restraining from bouncing in joy, then nods over her shoulder. "We can take my car."

The three of us walk to the edge of campus together, parting ways upon reaching the dim street-side.

"Have fun, you two!" I melodically call as the pair continues down the pathway to student parking, only for a loud honk to spin our heads toward a stalled vehicle on the opposite side of the road. Despite the minimal illumination provided by sidewalk-lining lamps, I instantly recognize it as Mr. Fennick's Camry.

"Oh shit," Lewis mutters, glancing back at me. "I forgot to tell you we were getting a ride home."

"It's okay," I enthuse, hopping from the curb to the street with a wink. "I'll tell your mom all the gossip on the drive back."

Lewis cringes, his gaze flickering to the waiting car. "It...wasn't my mom who offered."

I stop cold, then twist to *actually* get a look at the driver.

No fucking shot...

Henry is behind the wheel, with his denim-clad arm draped lazily across the open window. When he notices I'm staring, I reflexively brace for whatever night-ruining remark he's about to spear me with. But it doesn't come. He only lifts a couple of his fingers in lieu of a wave, the faintest hint of a smile tugging one corner of his mouth. I slowly turn to shoot Lewis the meanest glare in my arsenal. He knew it, too, offering nothing besides an apologetic shrug before he and Lynn resume their walk in the opposite direction.

Pivoting back to the Camry, I approach it with a wide smile. Then pass right by, gifting Henry a middle finger while doing so.

"Angel Face, the ride is this way." His words grate at my ears despite the distance I'm putting between us.

"And the *bus* is this way." I declare.

I don't let the sound of a door opening, nor the amplification of Henry's voice, persuade me into looking back to where he's undoubtedly standing from the car. "You're really gonna make it so that I came here for nothing?"

"Look at you! Putting that big graduate brain to work." I taunt.

It's silent for a few tolerable moments before Henry remarks, "Maybe I'll pay your mom a visit on the way home. I bet she'd warm up to me a lot more if I fessed about her little girl's porn collection."

My entire body locks, and I give that smug son of a bitch the satisfaction of a scowl. "You wouldn't…"

He leans on the open door frame, challenging me with an expectant raise of a brow.

Pushing down every skin-crawling urge to flee like a cornered animal, I retreat to his opposite and begrudgingly click open the passenger side door. Henry reenters with a heavy exhale, one that's cut short when I forcefully toss my backpack at his head.

"Blackmail, Henry? That's a new low, even for you." I say as I settle into the seat.

He throws my belongings into the back, then starts the engine. "You're welcome."

I cross my arms over my chest and puff an angled breath that ruffles my bangs.

The vehicle shifts into gear before he speaks again. "So, who's the bombshell my little brother's off with?"

I keep my eyes forward as the campus passes in a slow blur. "She's a girl from Bible study and she invited Lewis on a movie date."

I'm surprised when he doesn't give an immediate reaction. Surely Henry the playboy would be proud of his younger brother getting a date. With a stripper, no less. Not that I'd ever give him the thrill of knowing that. I chance a look in his direction to see bafflement on his face, which is, along with the rest of him, void of motor oil or grime for a change.

After a thick pause, disbelief corrupts his tone. "Lewis is going out with a girl?"

"Yep," I sigh. "Higher education does that to a man."

Henry smirks. "Well, if a college boy can score a date, what can a trade graduate score?"

"A wrecked car and broken neck when I push you out that door for being a perv."

"That's funny coming from you, Angel Face." He nods to the backseat. "What are you packing in that bag tonight? A few dildos? BDSM gear?"

A scoff catches in my throat. "I wish. You'd look lovely with a ball gag in your mouth."

"Are you *flirting* with me?"

"In your dreams." I bite the inside of my cheek to keep from running my mouth to a point of no return.

We roll to a halt at a four-way stop, the roads framing us vacant of other vehicles as we sit here. We sit here…and don't move forward. I glance at Henry, puzzled. The car seems to be running fine. But he's simply stalled, staring straight ahead with a contemplative look. An uncomfortably prolonged silence, only stunted by the hum of the engine, overtakes us. Then, he abruptly shifts it to park. Turning my way to rest his arm over the steering wheel like he has no care in the world.

He gives me an inquisitive once-over before remarking, "Let's go somewhere."

I stare at him, my lips parting long before I find my tongue. "What?"

He shrugs, the denim jacket he's sported since high school rising with the act. "Lewis is out having fun, let's do something together. Just you and me."

I would burst out laughing if I weren't too stunned to react at all. I scan his head for injuries, but find nothing except abnormally well-styled hair.

"What do you mean, 'do something?'" I ask cautiously.

His eyes drift across the intersection. "State Fair started yesterday. The Expo's not far. Wanna go?"

Alright, I can't hold it anymore. I release a hollow, *disturbed* laugh. "No," I say, like it's the most obvious answer I can give—which it most certainly is. "Of course I don't."

"Why not?" He asks with unwarranted confidence. "You got anything better to do tonight?"

"I think going home to my mother stabbing me with a kitchen knife and tossing me down our staircase would be a better night."

"I'm not asking you to prom, *Carrie*. I'm asking you to the Fair." Henry entertains, and I'm suddenly pissed that I let myself slip a reference to a movie *he* was responsible for sneaking Lewis and me out to watch a few years past.

A night out turned nightmare when the man seated to my left "accidentally" dumped a full cup of fruit punch over my head during the pig's blood scene.

"And I'm saying no." I assert. Is he seriously going to fight me over this?

Henry clicks his tongue, leaning back into the driver's seat. "Well, I'm not moving this car until you reconsider."

Apparently so.

I go stiff, glaring at him as his devious eyes remain fixed on mine. He keeps one hand on the wheel, his smirk ever-present as a pair of headlights from behind us paint the interior of the Camry with harsh illumination. Neither of us budges. Not even as the horn from the vehicle at our rear blares on. And on. And *on*.

The only anomaly to the deafening noise is my defeated sigh, followed by a single word that I would drop dead before giving Henry Fennick the pleasure of hearing twice.

"Fine…"

Chapter 16

Given the weeknight, the crowd isn't nearly as bad as it could be for a cool September evening. But I still get my share of strange glances as I stand at Henry's side in front of the ticket booth, looking as if I'm two seconds away from biting someone's head off if they so much as breathe in my direction.

Henry thanks the employee and takes my wrist, strapping a red paper band matching his own around it. "After you, Angel Face."

I roll my eyes, turning to saunter like a zombie through the lit-up archway of the fairgrounds. He keeps pace beside me as we step onto the pathway branching off to endless rows of colorful games, stalls glittering with flashing bulbs, and concessions of all kinds. I would be lying if I were to say the scent of fried foods and dings of bells and buzzers doesn't bring me some joy. Lewis and I always made it to the State Fair at least once during its running each year. Just add it to the list of things in my life that Henry goes out of his way to ruin.

"Wanna check out the shooting gallery?" He asks as we walk aimlessly. "Bet I could win something."

My focus remains forward. "No."

"Okay…How about that swinging pendulum ride?"

Oh, sure. So he can unbuckle me at the last second and cackle as I'm flung to my death. "No."

"What about food? I've seen you tear through a funnel cake or two."

My stomach clenches at the mere suggestion. "No."

He exhales impatiently. "Is there anything you *do* want?"

"To be home in my warm bed, pretending you were never born," I say as I rub heat into my bare arms. Continuing my goalless trek until a sensation makes me jump, and I glance down to find Henry's denim jacket now resting over my shoulders. My nose crinkles at the smell. Henry might be oil-free for a change, but no number of washes could save his everyday clothing from the stench. Refusing to don the article fully, I simply hold it as I dare a look at him. "Why'd you give me this?"

He smooths out his dark, long-sleeved shirt with a shrug. "You looked cold." Before I can open my mouth to question him further, he grabs my hand. "Look, Ferris wheel's boarding!"

I struggle to match his stride as he hastily leads us, catching up to the short line just as the last of the free carts slows to a halt. There's no time to protest as the staff member beckons him forward with a wave, urging us to enjoy the ride. I have half a mind to drag my heels on the ground like a child throwing a tantrum as Henry pulls me up the narrow, metallic staircase to the platform. The entry awaits as a different fair employee motions us inside.

Huffing, I oblige. Not saying a single word as I take my place, Henry sitting opposite me. At least it's the free-range, two-seated kind. I can't suppress a shudder at the idea of being strapped down with him at my hip. The heavy frame of the attraction rattles as it comes to life, and after a few moments, the fairgrounds shift as we begin our ascent. I cross my arms tightly over my chest, leaning back to keep my eyes narrowed on the man in front of me. But Henry remains preoccupied with admiring the view as the twinkling lights of the city become our sidelines.

"It's a nice night for this, isn't it?" He asks, his smile faltering the instant he notices my seething face. We stare each other down for a few tense moments until he breaks the silence with a scoff. "*What?*"

"What are you planning?" I demand to know, because I cannot for the life of me figure it out.

"Planning?"

"Will you stop acting confused and just tell me how you're going to fuck with me?!" I raise my voice. "For God's sake, whatever it is, just get it over with."

"I'm not going to fuck with you." He has the audacity to look offended by the accusation. "Why would I?"

"Because it's what you do, Henry!"

"Come on," he leans forward. "So I picked on you when we were kids. I picked on Lewis, too. What older brother doesn't? I was just having fun."

My brows strain as I scowl. "And what part of you pushing me off the top of a set of bleachers was *fun*, exactly?"

Henry supplies me with a conditioned explanation courtesy of his mother. "I was an eighth grade boy taking out my frustration."

"What about you slipping that garter snake into my backpack before school? *Knowing* I was terrified of them."

"I thought bus rides were boring and wanted to see people freak out." He forces a laugh. "That wasn't just aimed at you."

"And the time you laced my eggnog with jalapeño extract?" I grit my teeth.

Henry's head falls. "That…was a long time ago."

"It was last Christmas, you dick!"

Timid eyes snap to mine. "It was?"

"*Yes*." I assert. "You might not care enough about anyone but yourself to remember all the shit you put me through, but I remember! *All* of it. Just because it meant nothing to you, doesn't mean you didn't make my life even more hell than my mother was already making it!" I rip my gaze from him to keep the blood from boiling straight through my skin. The Ferris wheel glides to a halt with our bucket at the top. Sparkling lights of the fair warm my downcast eyes, growing foggy with unshed tears at all the painful memories. My voice is smaller now. "What I'm trying to figure out is why you're going through all this trouble when you *hate* me. If tonight is one of your schemes, then just do it and take me home so I can lock myself away to deal with it."

The cart falls quiet. The scent of grease from his jacket sours my nose as I keep my head turned. Every muscle in my body grows taut, as if to provide a physical defense from whatever brutal retort he's about to hurl my way.

"I don't hate you."

Henry's voice is…soft. Gentle, even. It throws me enough that I look at him again. In all the years we've known each other, I can't pull a single memory of Henry Fennick appearing remorseful for anything he'd done. But here he is, in front of me with drawn brows and slack shoulders.

"There's no scheme. I invited you here because I wanted to spend time with you." His eyes—the same vibrant blue-green as Lewis's—fall between us. "When I was away for school, I missed you."

"You…missed tormenting me?"

He shakes his head. "No, I missed *you*."

I stare at him with absolute incredulity. His words burning a deep, furious pit in my chest. Bullshit. Bullshit to *all* of it. Letting out a disturbed laugh, I stand up. The cart rocks slightly as I step to the overlooking edge. We have to be a hundred feet from the ground.

Henry's voice loses all its tenderness. "What are you doing?"

"Jumping," I say casually.

Actually, I'm leaning over to figure out what the hell is taking this ride so long. I squint to see the same Fair employee who'd guided us on board banging on a heavy metallic box in the control tent.

"Hey, sit down!" Henry demands. "A fall from this high would kill you."

"Don't get my hopes up." I throw a shit-eating grin his way, lifting my knee over the ledge for dramatics.

The operator punches the box again. The Ferris wheel grinds in a quick jolt. I feel my balance give as the heavy mechanics catch, my waist slamming against the lip of the now-swinging bucket before I slip forward. Balance teetering, my feet scramble to find the floor, but catch nothing but air. A scream tears from my throat as, for a flash of a moment, the ground below consumes my vision.

"*ROSIE!*"

Hands snake around my middle. Then, they're pulling me backwards with such force, I'm left winded as my body sinks back into the safety of the swaying cart. Only now, I'm not in my seat. Or *any* seat.

I'm in Henry's lap.

His arms are snared around me to the point that I can't discern which of us the trembling is coming from. Our faces are so close that our heavy breaths intermix, the terror in his wide eyes unmistakable. They dart between my own before his hand cups my cheek, as if the act is all he can do to convince himself I'm truly unharmed. Neither of us says a word, silence binding us in mutual acknowledgement of what almost happened. Instead, I watch Henry's features steadily harden. His emerald-speckled gaze lowers, and it takes me far too long to realize it's now focused on my mouth. The world around us slows as he moves again, his eyes falling shut as he closes the fragile inches between our faces. Realization skewers in the split second before our lips brush.

Henry Fennick is about to *kiss* me...

But not before I raise my hand and slap him across the face.

A deafening *WHACK* rings through the air at the same speed his head twists from the impact. I push myself off him and into the seat at his hip. Too out of balance—not to mention, dumbstruck—to attempt moving back to my own spot.

"What the *hell?*" He has the gall to ask, rubbing his already-swelling cheek.

"What the hell, *me?!*" I shout. "What's wrong with you?!"

Henry gapes at me, brows narrowed like he has any right to be offended.

"You cannot seriously be so horny that you'd try to fuck your little brother's best friend!" I say like I'm trying to make myself believe it, let alone him. "I'm pretty sure there are thousands of girls in this city who would sleep with you before I ever would."

"I don't want to have sex with you!" He argues. Then shakes his head, stuttering like a fool. "I-I mean, *yes*, I want to have sex with you—"

WHACK!

My palm stings with the additional slap to his cheek, silencing the abhorrent declaration as he recovers with a guttural bellow.

"*Ow*—!" He shields his face with one hand and snatches my poised wrist with the other. "Will you stop that?!"

"Gladly," I remark, reclaiming enough of my balance to attempt standing.

But his firm grip yanks me back into place, voice and expression hardening in an emotion I can't quite place as anger—but it's certainly trying to be. "You stay put."

"I'm moving back to my seat," I say, but his free arm winds around my middle. The cart sways as I attempt to fight my way free, just to end up locked beneath sturdy muscles. I expeditiously consider the odds of winning a wrestling match against a robust mechanic, then give up trying just as quickly.

"No, you *aren't*." He asserts in a low tone, mere inches separating his stern face from mine. "I'm not letting you scare me like that again."

"What would it even matter to you?" My lips pull into a snarl. "Or are you so desperate for a lay that you're just afraid to watch your hookup get dragged off in a body bag?"

"You're not a hookup." He counters resolutely. "And don't *ever* say that! It would kill me if anything happened to you."

A vile thought creeps in and claws free of my mouth before I can bite it back. "Oh my God, is this some kind of dig at Lewis? Trying to take the virginity of a girl who's like a sister to him, just so you can say you did?!"

"Of course not!"

It was unimaginable that Henry's insolence could astound me as much as it does now. Heating my already-sweltering scorn as I furiously question, "What are you planning on fucking me with, anyway? A ten-foot pole? Or did you bring a paper bag to cover my head with? Because if anyone felt sorry enough to sleep with me, they'd *never* want to look at my disgusting face while doing it, would they?"

Subtle lines appear between his brows like cracks in his solid exterior. "I never meant any of that."

"Which part?" I ask, ferociously keeping his gaze. "The years you spent telling me I'm ugly, or unfuckable?"

"All of it." His hold on my body tightens in what feels like a reflex. "I only said it because I didn't want you to think you were good enough."

"Good enough for what?"

"Other guys."

"Who the hell cared if I saw other guys?"

"I cared!"

"*Why*?!"

"Because I'm *fucking* in love with you, alright?!"

My mouth opens to strike another venom-tipped retort, but it doesn't come. Leaving me to gawk as I'm stunned by the possibility that I *had* tumbled over the edge of the Ferris wheel bucket and plummeted to my death. The prospect that I'd fallen straight into hell, where Satan had initiated my eternal torment by puppeteering Henry to speak such profanity, is simply the only logical explanation for this.

Except…I'm uncertain that the devil would have enough humility to give me the look Henry does following such a heart-stopping admission.

He expels a winded breath, any trace of his fortified composure dissipating with each flicker of his eyes over my face. "I called you ugly because I thought if you heard it enough, you'd believe it, instead of the truth. That you could pull any guy you want." He explains quietly. "I know, because you pulled *me*."

Somehow, I find it in me to move my tongue. But only to deliver my delayed retaliation. "Fuck you. And whatever sadistic joke you think this is."

I shove his arms away and sink into the seat at his side. A move that he, thankfully, doesn't protest. But it's a courtesy that doesn't extend to my words.

"This isn't a joke." He throws his hands in surrender. "I'm attracted to you. I have *feelings* for you. However you want me to say it."

As if I want him to be saying any of this?

"No, you don't." I bite out, unsure exactly which of us I'm convincing.

"Yes, I do." He huffs a pained laugh. "Why do you think I offered to pick you and Lewis up tonight? Or took you here at all?"

"I don't know, Henry. I don't know *why* you do the shit you do, and I don't care!" Surely the unlucky Fair attendees idling on the wheel around us can hear me just as well as Henry can, but I simply can't hold back. "All I know is that I can't trust you. Not after all the hell you've given me. And now you're saying you have feelings for me?"

"Do…you want me to say it again?"

"*No*, I don't want you to say it again!"

He lets out a frustrated growl, doubling over to bury his face in his hands. "I don't know how the fuck I'm supposed to do this, okay?"

A long, hostile silence envelops us until I feel obligated to destroy it. "Why?"

He eyes me shyly. "Why?"

"You've treated me like shit since the day we met." I glare daggers at him. "*Why* would you like me?"

Henry averts his gaze, and I get the hint he's sorting through an answer that even he has to convince himself isn't fabrication. But when he does speak, his voice is hardly audible over the distant tunes of the fairgrounds. "Because you pushed back…"

I fixate on the Albuquerque skyline. Rhythmic heartbeats rattling my body in muted tremors as the seconds tick on.

"Okay," I test against my better judgment. "Let's say that *hypothetically* you were in love with me—" Stopping to catch a reflexive laugh at the vocalization of such a concept, I ask, "Can you please name one instance before tonight when you were anything besides a complete ass to me?"

He offers no answer. He doesn't even give me the courtesy of a look.

I settle against the lip of the seat, keeping my arms crossed over my chest. Anywhere else. I swear to God, if I could just fall through the bottom of this cart and end up *anywhere* else, I would—

"Valentine's Day."

I glance his way so quickly that the white ribbon tied to the base of my ponytail whips in the elevated wind.

Elbows on his knees, his head hangs with a deep breath. "Back when you were in tenth grade. You were upset because you were the only person in your homeroom that morning who didn't get a card. And the next day, when you checked the mailbox—"

"There was a stuffed leopard," I say with a shrug. Surely he knew that. I'd gone on to Lewis for weeks about how much it meant to me.

"'From the moment I first *spotted* you, I knew we were meant to be.'" He forces a hollow chuckle. "I remember, because I thought it was the dumbest thing I'd ever written."

I stare at him. The weight of the entire blackened sky settling in the form of bewilderment on my shoulders. While Lewis knew of the gift, I hadn't told him, nor a single other person what had been written on that card. Which means…

"That was from you?" I ask, my voice quiet with disbelief. "*You're* my secret admirer?"

A shy smile pulls the corner of his lips. "Actually, the *S.A.* was for smartass."

My heart thrums again. Only now, it's for a whole different reason. Which I ignore as I question, "Why didn't you just give it to me yourself?"

"Would you have accepted it?"

Fair point.

I pause in place of an answer. "But…that was years ago."

"Yeah," he speaks in a hushed, almost somber tone. "I know."

I huff, resting back into the seat. "How am I supposed to take this, Henry? I can't just forgive everything you put me through because you did *one* nice thing."

"I don't expect you to forgive me." He finally raises his chin to give me the closest attempt at a guilty look I've ever seen on him—and I can tell his face isn't only reddened from my strikes. "But if I said I regret treating you like I did more than anything I've ever done, would you believe me?"

I think about what he's asking. Really think. Of all the shit Henry Fennick has gotten into in his life—nearly killing a classmate, going to juvie, becoming the resident delinquent of Crosspoint Fellowship and Peakshire High—bullying *me* is his biggest regret?

"No," I answer softly. Honestly.

He doesn't contest. "What would it take to make you believe it?"

After a long silence, I reply with another question. "Why are you saying all this now?"

"I already said, I missed you when I was away for school." His eyes are long void of their typical mischief, and his tone is gentle enough that I *do* ponder the unorthodox decision to buy what he's selling. "And…we're both grown up now. If there was ever a chance to tell you, this was it."

I can't help but catch a scoff. "You're unbelievable."

He narrows a look my way. "What?"

"Never mind that you're my best friend's older brother, and hot enough to land any girl you want." My focus on the cityscape drops, moving from my knee socks to my modest skirt before settling on my uniform button-up. "You still haven't explained why you're chasing me, of all people."

He blinks at me. "You think I'm hot?"

"I think you're a *jerk*!" I assert, blushing at my own slip-up. "And a complete idiot if you believe I'm stupid enough to take you seriously."

At that, his expression sharpens from amused to resentful. As does his tone as he declares, "Maybe you're right. I'd have to be an idiot to go after Christine Ginger's dutiful daughter. Always sucking up to everyone at Crosspoint like it's your job or something." He huffs a mocking laugh, and I stare at him with fury pooling behind my dark eyes—a dam that splits as he leans in to deliver the final blow. "You act like you can't stand them, but deep down, you're exactly what they want you to be: A pathetic little virgin."

I absolutely break, any trace of fear evading me as I grab a fistful of his Henley to pull him close, all but snarling as I bite out, "You disgusting, unbearable piece of shit! As if *you* have any room to judge me?! You don't know the first fucking thing about who I really am—!"

Henry's arm snares my waist again, cutting me off as he surges forward to press his lips firmly against my cheekbone.

Like an electric current, the kiss renders me paralyzed, his touch warming skin chilled by the night air. His breath trickles across my face as he holds me still—letting it linger like he's been waiting a lifetime to do this and wants to make each and every second of it last. I'm too stunned, too absolutely blindsided to give any reaction. And by the time I remember how, he's pulling away. Blue-green eyes trail slowly over the spot his lips had claimed before meeting mine. Then, any of his lingering ignorance melts away as he smiles at me. Not a taunting or demeaning smile. A genuine smile that I've yet to see from him in all our shared years.

"That..." He whispers. "*That's* why I want you, Rosie. Because you're real."

The warmth in his gaze rivals that of the jacket over my shoulders or his arm around my middle. I fight every instinct to push him away as the heat deepens with every fearless moment that passes.

The desert crosswinds tousle his sun-kissed hair as he goes on, "I know you're not some poster child for Crosspoint; you've always been a different person when it's just you and Lewis. I didn't see it until that day you stood your ground." His voice dims, but the glimmer in his eyes shines brighter than the bulbs circling us. "That's why I treated you the way I did, because it always brought out the real Rosie...The Rosie that's not afraid to bite back."

It takes a moment for my mind to truly process what I'm hearing. Henry was speaking *insightfully*, and admitting he'd seen through my mask. The concept makes my pulse jump like it had when I'd nearly fallen off the side of the cart and plummeted to my death—stealing my breath before I can use it to properly reply.

The radiant fairgrounds beneath us flicker in colorful waves across his face, illuminating features more alluring than I'd like to admit. "Not to mention, you're hilarious. And smart. And..." He expels a short breath. "The prettiest fucking girl I've ever known."

With that, he releases me, and I feel every ounce of the willpower it costs him to do so. He sits straight, and though his eyes evade me entirely, I can see something in them give. As if everything he's been waiting to say was finally said, and whatever the next move was, it was mine to make. But the longer I stare at him, the more I recognize that there's something between us now. Something that clears the vitriol polluting our shared ground since the day he shoved me off those bleachers. It's all I can do to keep the beat of my heart steady when I realize that it's honesty on *his* end. Gravity shifts, and it takes me a few long moments to notice it's on the part of the Ferris wheel—which, evidently, the operator had gotten working again—and not my mind catching up with this new reality.

A reality where I might no longer hate Henry Fennick.

Neither of us says another word before it's our turn to get off. When we level, Henry stands, extending a hand that I take as he guides me off the ride and back onto solid earth.

"Come on," he releases his hold, nodding down the path to the fair's exit. "I'll take you home if that's what you want."

He starts in that direction, passerbys dividing us as he walks. And even though I'm not remotely sold on the idea of a higher power, I swear some divine force keeps my feet rooted to the concrete beneath them. After a short stride, Henry realizes I'm not following and looks back. If he's disappointed, then he's doing a damn good job of hiding it. Although, not quite good enough. I may not know him like I do Lewis, but the Fennick brothers shared the same eyes. I could spot sadness behind them a mile away.

Carefully, I push my arms through the sleeves of his denim jacket, dipping my hands into the pockets like it's now mine. Then, with the same unfounded confidence that led me to a particular porn studio just a week prior, I give him a grin that forms a little too easily. "Well, we're already here, aren't we?"

Henry's falsified toughness gives, and that genuine smile I'd yet to see from him before tonight returns.

Chapter 17

An hour or two later, Henry and I have migrated to a lonely picnic table bordering the parking lot, away from the crowded grounds. I'm sitting on the wide top with my feet propped on the elongated seat, sipping lemonade through a plastic straw while picking the remains of a funnel cake.

"Quit being a loser about it," I say, popping a piece of it into my mouth.

Henry, who's seated at the table the correct way, glares playfully up at me. "It was emasculating."

He's referring to the shooting gallery. One of the final booths we'd entertained before concessions, and one that I had completely annihilated him at. If the oversized plush snake draped over my shoulders was any indication.

"A man feeling emasculated by a woman's toy…? That's never happened before." I bite back a deprecating laugh.

"Very funny. But I won't let a stuffed animal mock me." He pulls the plush from my neck and hides it under the table before pointing an accusatory finger. "And not another word about my aim."

I lean back on my arms with a scoff. "Oh, please. Like men are known for having good aim? I've seen the bathroom you and Lewis used to share. The two of you can't hit the inside of a toilet bowl, let alone a target."

Henry tries to maintain a serious look, but the joyous glint in his eyes is too prevailing to convince me he's even slightly as offended as he's letting on. "Where the hell did that trigger finger of yours come from?"

"Lots of exercise." I hold up my dominant index, wiggling the tip rapidly. He quirks a sharp brow at me, and my face instantly flushes as I clarify, "Typing."

It was...*somewhat* true.

"I wanted to ask you about that." He rests his jaw on the heel of a hand. "According to my mom, yours is always going on about some 'spiritual fiction' book you're writing. But I have a feeling that's not really your style."

His potent sarcasm brings a smile to my face, and for a long moment, I debate telling him how I *actually* use my inherent skill. Every raunchy, unfiltered detail of it. If there's any shred of doubt remaining that this was all a scheme to him—a very elaborate, rather impressive scheme—I can't sense it. Henry had all but poured his heart out to me tonight. I could return the favor at least slightly, couldn't I?

"It's not." I take another sip of lemonade in the hopes its sour taste will keep my mouth from drying as I confess, "I write erotica."

He blinks at me. "Like, romance?"

"Calling my stories romance would be like calling *Casablanca* hardcore porn." I chuckle, leaning closer as I claim a sultry tone. "I write people fucking. No feelings, no morals. Just everything a girl can fantasize, all at the tips of my fingers."

Realization softens his features. "You're serious."

It wasn't a question. But I nod, regardless.

He expels a hollow laugh. "But you've never been with anyone. How do you even know what it's like?"

I flip my ponytail over the shoulder of his jacket with a shrug. "You could say I'm a tremendous researcher. Not that there wasn't a learning curve, but sex doesn't seem nearly as complicated as people make it out to be. I got the hang of it from movies, sneaking steamy novels from the bookstore, even personal testimonies. You know how many conversations I overheard from the *busier* girls in high school?" I shake my head, recalling how their complaints often outweighed their praises. "If anything, it made me realize I wasn't missing out on much. Is the clit seriously that hard to find? It's not like it moves around or anything."

Henry stares like he's never seen me before. "I might regret asking this, but is that why you had that porno magazine? Research?"

Shit. As much as I want to be open with him—to be the honest person he claims he's so attracted to—it would be foolish to go off about my endeavors with *Wild Thang*. Telling Lynn had been different. She was also someone still masked beneath the smothering cloak of evangelicalism, making ends meet by engaging in the very acts she'd been taught to condemn. She understood what that felt like.

Not that I believe Henry of all people would judge. I'm just… not ready.

"Something like that," I say, hiding my apprehension behind a smirk. "And to get off to, obviously."

Henry's head dips, and at first, I fear it's in disappointment. But I quickly realize with the shake of his shoulders that he's laughing.

"What's so funny?" I ask.

"Nothing. It's just, that *real* side of you I was talking about? I've never seen this much of her before. She's…"

"Let me guess," I interject, rattling off a few of my mother's favorite adjectives. "Graceless? Unruly? Annoyingly precocious?"

The variegated lights of the fair brighten his face. "She's perfect."

My pulse jumps at the word. Two hours ago, I would've retched at the simple thought of being within arm's reach of Henry…

Now? He's making me feel weightless.

It's the same feeling I used to cling to when yearning after guys in school I knew would never pay me a passing glance. The same feeling that heats my blood in the most delicious way when watching love stories on the wide screen of the drive-in. Dare I say, the same feeling I get when

I write. Desire. Excitement. *Hope*. So volatile, it had slipped from my fingertips too many times for me to truly believe it was worth relishing at all. But I can't stop it from rinsing over me the longer his gaze lingers.

"Sorry," he says, blushing after the prolonged silence. "I know you don't feel the same."

"Who says I can't feel the same?" I ask with the mere intention of being defiant, before I realize the authenticity of what I'm suggesting.

His brows raise in unmistakable thrill, but he stifles it with a laugh. "Come on, Angel Face, you hardly know me. Name *one* thing you like about me."

I look closer at him than ever before. Allowing myself to appreciate his charm for the first time in years. My gaze trails up his arms resting on the table, the swell of his biceps visible even beneath his dark sleeves. The flashing signs of the fairgrounds highlight his strong jaw and pull my focus to the soft edge of lips that had thrown hundreds of taunts at me over the years. An absolutely stupid rush blesses my veins at the memory of them on my cheek. And his hair…why do I have the sudden urge to touch it? Whatever the reason, I do just that. Starting at his scalp, I rake my fingers from dark roots to dirty-blonde ends, smoothing the longer pieces along the side of his head in their natural wave. It's so soft, I delicately rub a few strands between my thumb and forefinger as an excuse to keep my hand in place a little longer.

"I like your hair," I admit, trying and failing to keep from sounding as captivated as I feel. Even so, it was a lie. Because I fucking *love* his hair.

His eyes hold with the same entrancement I know reflects in mine, sharpened with a noticeable disbelief. It's like I'm looking at a different person than the one who made my life what I can only compare to hell—even after being taught ad nauseam about the hopeless, blazing pits that awaited those damned.

Maybe it's because I *am* looking at a different person. Perhaps there's a real side to Henry, as well.

The fire in his stare only dies when he tears it away, nervously clearing his throat as he suddenly stands to collect trash from the table. "I'm gonna throw this away and hit the bathroom before we leave. You okay to wait here?"

"Yeah, I'm good." I smile at him. "Try to work on your aim while you're in there."

The jab makes him halt, then take on a quizzical look. Every muscle in my body tenses as he leans close, bracing his arms on either side of me until the distance between our faces is reduced to inches.

"To answer your question. I might need some work at the shooting gallery, but when it counts," his seductive eyes flicker between us. "I know my target when I see it."

Heat flares beneath my skin. Starting at my face, then plummeting as low as his gaze…

I flinch when his finger abruptly swipes down the center of my face, inhaling a sweet puff of the powdered sugar he'd scooped from our discarded funnel cake. I go cross-eyed to find the tip of my nose dusted in white, then focus back on Henry's far-too-delighted face. Scowling playfully, I raise him a middle finger before brushing the powder away with it.

Henry can't suppress his affectionate laughter as he steps away, disappearing into the fairgrounds beyond my view.

Letting out a slow breath, I stand. Then stretch my legs and back to soothe the ache from lounging on the hard surface. Catching sight of our toy snake beneath the structure as I twist, I find myself chuckling. Bending at the waist, I reach awkwardly between the table and seat. Fumbling for a while before my grip finds the green fabric.

There's a draft as something drags up the backside of my thigh to slip beneath my skirt. Taking the form of ice-cold fingers that grab a handful of my ass to roughly squeeze. It happens so quickly that I can only choke on a gasp, narrowly avoiding cracking my head against the underside of the table as I forgo the plush to pull myself free. By the time I whirl around, my assaulter is backing away. Holding both hands in the air with the biggest, most smug smile I've ever seen on a man.

"Sorry! I'm sorry! It was on a dare, alright?"

Laughter resounds from a group several yards away, composed entirely of young men. Each of them sporting familiar red and white letterman jackets. But despite the high-fives and shoulder bumps they're exchanging at my expense, my focus is narrowed to their frontman. Air draws from my lungs as recognition rams me like a fucking linebacker. The sky-blue eyes. The tall, muscular frame. The voice that had given our valedictorian speech only a few months prior.

"Andrew?" His name falls breathlessly from my lips.

Andrew Roth stands before me, smile falling at the question. "Uh, yeah...Do I know you?"

Does he know me? No. But the last time I saw him, I had written a whole piece about him calling me onto our graduation stage and fucking me in front of every last one of our peers. The memory colors my cheeks a burning red.

"We graduated together back in May. Peakshire." I explain like he isn't still wearing our school's letterman jacket, as if the article holds any merit outside that place.

Andrew tilts his gorgeous head at me as one of his friends breaks from the still-cackling group. He's not as tall, but equally brawny with spiky strawberry-blonde hair and freckles of the same shade. His steps are uneven, clearly maneuvering through intoxication as he quite literally stumbles into our conversation.

"Hey, I know her!" He says, slapping Andrew's arm. "She was always hanging around that scrawny Jesus-freak from computer lab."

"Lewis." I correct, my grip on Henry's jacket tightening at the mention.

"Oh, yeah!" Andrew laughs. "I remember that kid. Always dressed like he was meeting the president."

The shorter of the two clicks his tongue. "Figured a faggot like him would have better style."

His words strike me like a poison-tipped dagger, only half as sharp as the glare I pin him with in turn. "What did you just say?"

He and some of the others snicker loudly. One of them mocking my question in a high-pitched tone.

"Get to the fucking truck." Andrew pushes him away with one arm. The smaller athlete hunches in laughter as he and the group, counting seven in total, approach a decrepit pickup parked in the first row adjacent to the picnic grounds. Andrew looks down at me—and if he's trying to make me feel smaller than I already am, it's working. "Don't mind Josh, he's had one too many. Thinks he's being funny."

"He isn't," I say flatly. But my heart involuntarily leaps as Andrew's focus travels up and down my body.

Mouth quirking, he asks, "You say what your name was?"

I shake my head. "Rosie."

"Rosie," he tests the word with interest. "Did we ever talk in school? I can't place it."

"We didn't, I would remember," I admit, my next statement slipping fluidly from brain to mouth. "I had a big crush on you."

"You did?" His thick brows shoot up as he raises a hand to contemplatively graze the stubble along his jawline. "Damn, I wish you had told me. I'd bend over backwards for a girl as cute as you."

I blink, unconvinced that doing so wouldn't result in him dissipating into a typewritten page by way of this being some foregone fantasy of mine. But he's still there. All the discreet hours I'd spent writing this moment into reality override my better judgment as I question, "Really?"

"Yeah." He drags the confirmation with an enticing allure, then steps closer. "You know, Josh's parents own some land with an old trailer house out west. Nothing around for miles, just a place for us to shoot shit on nights like this. We're headed there now."

His insinuation steals my breath. "Are you inviting me?"

Andrew shrugs, flashing the same beautiful grin I'd illustrated so accurately in text. "I owe you that much, leaving you hooked like I did."

"You don't have a girlfriend?" I ask.

"I'm fresh on the market." He explains, and I stiffen as he brushes the fringe from my brows, then leisurely diverts to toy with my white bow. "Tell you what, you come with us, and when we get there, you and I can slip off somewhere private and get to know each other." His finger hooks the hemline of Henry's denim jacket, tugging it open to peek beneath. Greedy eyes linger on my chest a beat too long. "The bedroom wouldn't be a bad place."

I stare up at him, compiling every urge I've ever had to jump on such an impossible opportunity. Except, the same conviction I would've had on our graduation day is now replaced with something else. Something I can't name, but whatever it is turns the butterflies in my stomach poisonous.

"Come on," Andrew insists. "We've got room in the truck for one more."

I glance at the single-cab vehicle, where most of the group has loaded into the bed. "Doesn't look like it."

"Don't worry," his arm slithers around me, palm smoothing the curve of my hip far lower than necessary. "You can sit on my lap."

He's close enough that I can smell his breath, and the distinct odor of alcohol along with it. "You guys have been drinking. Are you sure you should be driving like this?"

"I can hold my liquor, I'm a big boy." Chuckling, he leans nearer. "A big boy asking a *girl* to come have some fun."

My head snaps to the pickup at a shrill noise. Josh is standing outside, rocking the entire vehicle back and forth as the others hold on. The strawberry blonde squeaks out a few exaggerated, high-pitched moans as he locks eyes with me. Grotesquely sticking out his tongue to send the rest of the boys into a cacophony of laughter.

"I can't." I clutch Henry's jacket like the genuine excuse it is. "I'm here with somebody."

Andrew casts a theatrical look over the empty picnic tables. "I don't see anyone."

I attempt to step out of his hold. "I swear—"

"Let's go," his arm tightens around my waist, voice deep with persuasion. "You can tell me all about that crush you have. And I can kick myself for not snatching you up sooner."

He starts leading me to the truck, but I plant my feet in the dirt. "I don't know if I want to."

"I think you do, Rosie." Andrew never loses his wry smile, but his brows tense as his grip migrates to my wrist. Pulling gently at first, then hard enough to make me stumble toward him.

I freeze. Staring up at his impossibly large form as I part my lips, any protest lodging in my throat. A reflexive fear gets the better of me as I remain silent, unable to utter the simple word that would spare me from his advance. He gives another tug as I vaguely register the beat of accelerating footsteps. My wrist stings as his fist is suddenly torn away. Andrew catches his footing after being shoved with enough force to knock the wind out of him. Any attempt at leading me along catastrophically derailed by the person now fixed like a barricade between us.

It's Henry, and the look on his face is the same that used to seize my body with chills when I knew he was moments from committing a crime. Lawful *or* moral. "What the hell's going on?"

It's unclear who the question is aimed at, but the hostility in Henry's tone gives me enough of a hint to keep my jaw clenched.

Andrew's features slacken with terrified recognition. He shoots a nervous glance at the pickup where his friends are housed. But they, to include Josh, have all fallen deathly silent. Watching the scene play out as tension thicker than the night sky envelops us.

"Fennick. Long time, no see." Andrew forces an uneasy laugh. "I was just having a chat with Rosie…She yours?"

"No." Henry's mouth denies it, but the way he advances on Andrew without a shred of hesitation threatens otherwise. "What she *is*, is the last girl on the planet you want me catching you touching."

Andrew allows himself one step of retreat before stopping, shaking off enough apprehension to lift his chin. "I was only asking if she wanted to go on a ride with us. Are you her father, or can she decide that herself?"

Henry takes pause, then turns to eye me over his shoulder. "Rosie, you wanna go with these guys?"

Clutching my aching wrist, I fix a glare on Andrew. The seemingly impossible command coming as easily as it had with Henry upon arriving at the fairgrounds. "*No.*"

Henry nods before focusing back on my assaulter. "There's your answer. Now, get fucking lost."

Andrew's eyes narrow in animosity. The former football captain has at least a couple of inches in height and a good thirty pounds on Henry. But I can tell that risking a fight with Peakshire's most notoriously feared hellion is giving him logical pause, even despite the backup he has. "I'm allowed to pick up girls, last I checked. My friends and I wanted to top off the night by having a few turns, so what?"

I feel like gagging. But it comes out as a snarl, instead. "Like I'd go anywhere near your friends after what that asshole called Lewis?!"

Henry's head snaps my way. "What?"

Behind him, I catch Josh ducking beneath the wall of the vehicle's bed.

"*What* did he call my brother?" There's no question who Henry's addressing anymore. As he takes another fearless step toward his opponent, who matches it in the opposite direction.

Andrew's jaw flexes once before he shrugs. "You know what he is, Fennick."

"Right." Henry's low tone makes my hair stand on end. "And you know exactly what I did to the last jackass who had something to say about my little brother." He nods pointedly at Andrew's red and white jacket. "He wore one of those, too. At least, he *did*. My guess is they had trouble getting out all the blood I spilled from his skull. Ruined the look."

The memory flashes in front of me. Will Guerrero. The football player Henry had gone to juvie for beating to a pulp in the school's parking lot. The fight nobody had ever known the real motive behind.

Or...had they?

Andrew rakes his teeth over his tongue. "You should be more careful picking your fights. Especially over a girl who just admitted she has a thing for me." He peers over Henry's shoulder at my small form, seduction reclaiming his tone. "Come on, cutie. Last chance if you wanna get railed by a real—"

He dares a step forward, but Henry doesn't give him an inch—ramming his arms into Andrew's chest and pushing like the six-foot-three athlete weighs nothing.

"You'll shove your dick in a fucking rattlesnake burrow before you put it anywhere near her!" Each word bites like a feral animal as Henry shoves Andrew against the bumper of the pickup forcefully enough to sway it.

Stomps on aluminum echo as the others stand from the bed, their misgivings forgotten as they jump to defend their friend. Fear forces me into action. Henry's reputation might be fortified, but this *isn't* a fight he can win. Not when it's seven against one.

"Henry, stop!" I'm placing myself between him and Andrew so quickly that I nearly trip. I press against his torso in an attempt to draw him back, but it's more akin to a one-sided hug. My voice is hushed as I plead, "Don't do this, *please...*"

His body is rigid like stone, and I feel every bit of the self-containment it costs him to rip his furious eyes from the truck. But when they lower to my face, something gives. The anger behind his impenetrable exterior fades the longer I keep my arms fixed. Until eventually, the tension in his strong form begins to loosen.

"Whatever." Andrew huffs, clearly snared between seething vengeance and self-preservation. But he chooses wisely. After straightening himself and pinning Henry with one final glare, he yells for the group to settle in before claiming the driver's seat of the pickup.

Henry slides protective arms around my waist, unflinching as the truck roars to life. Andrew revs the engine as a baseless threat before pulling away and speeding dangerously off. Josh's extended middle finger cresting the tops of vehicles they pass in their dramatic exit. It's only after they've disappeared—as quickly as they'd spawned into our night at all—that the burn in my lungs reminds me to breathe. I sink heavily into Henry's hold to take weight off my shaky legs.

That's until he snorts, dipping his chin to eye me with an undue grin. "You seriously have a thing for that clown?"

Of all the shit that just almost happened, *that's* what he latches onto?

"Had," I amend, stepping out of his arms. "I *had* a thing for him in school. Now? You wouldn't catch me dead with that jerk."

"From the looks of things, I nearly did." His tone hardens as he follows me back to the picnic table. "Rosie, do you have any idea what those guys would've done to you if you'd gone with them?"

I don't answer. Not because I don't know, but because I already feel faint enough. Leaning against the edge of the tabletop, I hold my wrist close, sensing Andrew's unyielding fingers around it despite his departure.

Henry rubs gentle palms up the familiar denim covering my biceps. "Hey, relax. I knew once they recognized me they weren't gonna try anything."

My head remains low as I dismantle the horrific, nearly realized scenarios. But there's one thing about the whole confrontation I can't shake. Something I have to know.

"Will Guerrero," I begin, his hands halting at the mention. "What did he say about Lewis to make you do that to him?"

A heavy silence falls.

When I finally look up, his eyes are closed in what can only be cruel recollection. Though, something tells me the pain isn't stemming from the memory of how he nearly killed someone. But rather, what made him furious enough to *want* to kill him.

His next quiet, forthcoming statement only proves me right. "He said that if we didn't keep my brother locked at home, he and his teammates were gonna tie him to their hitch and drag him to the cemetery themselves. Before they had to dig graves for every other kid at school when Lewis gave them the hi-five."

Nausea twists my insides into knots.

But despite it, for the first time in all the years since that day, there's an alarming transparency between myself and the man standing before me. The way his jaw flexes, the feel of his unsteady hands on my arms. All of it works to prove that it had never been about status or dominance for Henry, as he allowed everyone to believe.

It had been about Lewis. His little brother. Who he *loved*.

"*My God...*" I say softly. "I never knew."

Henry nods. "I didn't tell Lewis, and I never will. The only reason Guerrero's circle knew was because he told them before coming to me. Afterwards, they were all too scared to talk." The corner of his mouth lifts as he exchanges meekness for wit. "My reputation with the football players never recovered, if tonight was any indication."

I smile sadly. "Like you've ever cared about your reputation?"

He shrugs. "What was I gonna do? Kiss-ass and end up like your once-crush there? I'd sooner keep my hands busy."

"Oh, his hands were busy, alright." My gaze falls between us. "At least, when he slid them up my skirt in lieu of a hello just now."

"He *what?*" Henry's grip locks, his posture straightening to glare over the rows of vehicles. "I shouldn't have let him go so easily."

My cheeks heat, but I keep my gratitude suppressed. "That wasn't a fair fight. And you'd be a fool to take a hit all because some asshole touched me on a dare."

Another silence stretches between us, only punctuated with distant festival melodies, eventually drawing my focus back to his face. I'm only half-convinced carnival lights are responsible for the sparkling gleam in his eyes as they welcome mine.

"I'm not good at much, Angel Face. But I'm great at taking hits." He says with a chuckle, then kneels to reach under the table. My heart swells as he offers our plush snake before sliding a hand into my own. "Come on, let's get you home."

He leads us away, and I can't help but consider the impossibility of my circumstances. At the start of the evening, I couldn't have imagined anything more abhorrent than walking hand-in-hand with Henry Fennick.

And right now? It may be the safest I've ever felt.

Chapter 18

The Fennicks' car rolls to a gentle stop in front of my mother's house. Tranquil in the late hour, dim hues of streetlights paint the inside of the Camry. My nerves spike at what is, essentially, the cap on my first date ever. And I had exactly zero idea what was supposed to happen now that Henry and I were parting ways. What could I even say after such a bizarre evening?

Thanks for taking me out, even though I absolutely hated your guts before tonight?

Sure.

"Thanks for taking me out, even though I absolutely hated your guts before tonight." I pertly declare.

Henry laughs. "You're welcome. And…I'm gonna take that as you *don't* hate my guts anymore?"

I pause, really thinking about my answer. Sure, my perception of Lewis's older brother had pretty much done a one-eighty over the past hours. But that didn't undo the years he made me feel like shit for simply existing.

I respond with another question. "What is it you want out of this, Henry?"

The genuine longing in his tone almost makes me regret asking at all. "You, Rosie. Nothing else, just you." He expels a slow breath. "Is there any part of you that wants me?"

I let my head rest against the seat, feeling the pressure of the moment sink like my clothes are suddenly ten sizes too small. "Maybe there is," I answer truthfully. "But I can't just move past all the years between us. I want an apology for everything. A *real* apology."

He offers a steady nod. "I think I can make that happen."

"I mean it." I assert. "And that doesn't mean I'm gonna move past all the shit you did, either. I just want to believe you when you say you regret it."

"I understand. And for what it's worth, I'm not worried about you moving past it. After all," his cheeks swell with a smile. "'A lady's imagination is very rapid.'"

So said Mr. Darcy.

My heart melts. It takes absolutely everything in me to break from the embrace of his adoring gaze, for fear I'd never want to look away. "I really did have a good time tonight," I admit, then recede with a wince. "Sorry for slapping you, by the way."

"It's okay. I probably deserved it." He rubs contemplative fingers into his palm where it rests over the steering wheel. "But if I were to *hypothetically* kiss you goodbye, you wouldn't slap me again, would you?"

Feeling my pulse jump, I can't bite back a grin. "No, I hypothetically wouldn't."

His eyes light up, and the temperature of the condensed interior heats as he leans into the passenger seat. Pressing gentle lips to my cheekbone, right where they'd been the first time. Only now, I welcome it.

I even enjoy it.

When he pulls away, blue-green irises fall to my lips before backing completely off. He doesn't go for it, but the way his jaw tightens lays bare how terribly he wants to. A gesture of restraint I appreciate more than he'll ever know.

I slip his denim jacket off my shoulders, mourning the warmth it's held me in all night as I set it atop our plush snake in the backseat. "Keep Lucifer. If my mother finds out where I was, she'll drop dead."

"And that would be a bad thing?"

I snicker, securing my bag before exiting the car with a smirk that reads more affection than mischief. "Catch ya soon, smartass."

His features brighten, taking the form of a smile that reaches his eyes. "Not soon enough, Angel Face."

The Camry pulls off when I stride up the driveway, leaving my heart buzzing with each step to the porch and beyond entry to the house. Then, it fucking *stops*.

My mother stands in her nightdress, hands squarely on her hips. She's pinning me with the same fearsome glare that used to make me think the world was coming to an end, and if I didn't drop to my knees and repent right then, I'd be damned to an eternity of torture…Not that living with her was all that different.

"Where in God's name have you been? And *why* did I just watch Henry Fennick bring you home?"

Just my fucking luck.

"Mom," I drag the word like it's twice my weight. "He offered to pick Lewis and me up from Bible study tonight, that's all."

"Bible study ended nearly three hours ago, and Lewis wasn't with you just now." She crosses her arms in a move that looks frighteningly like I had when Henry invited me out.

"Lewis had a date," I explain, rounding her with the intent to make it upstairs before the more intrusive questions began. "Henry wanted to go to the State Fair, so I went with him."

"You *what*?"

I screw my eyes shut to keep from rolling them. "Mom, none of this should matter. You told me I needed to step outside my comfort zone now that I'm in college. Consider it done."

"I meant with the people who *attend* Trinity Grace. The good ones from your Bible study!"

If only Lynn were around to enjoy that.

I stop at the bottom of the staircase. "It was one night. I don't see what the big deal is?"

"The *big deal* is that you've been acting different lately." Her glare cuts me like a knife as she stalks closer. "You're barely around on the days you have fewer classes. You aren't spending nearly as much time at church. You didn't come home until God knows what hour the other night. And now, you're running around with the Fennicks' delinquent son? After whatever it was the two of you were doing on my front porch last week? God help me, Mary-Rose, you even let him put his *mouth* on you?!"

Fuck, she'd seen that? This is going nowhere good.

"Henry's not a delinquent, Mom!" I counter, despite knowing my argument is futile. "And I'm not even dating him. Do you not trust me?"

"I trust you." She says it like someone's holding a gun to her head of tousled hair she'd no doubt been pulling out all night. "It's *him* I don't trust. That boy has no morals. And if he's influencing you, I need to know."

"Influencing?" I question. Her worn features harden even more, and suddenly I understand. "You think I'm having sex with him?"

"What else am I supposed to think?"

"Literally *anything* but that!"

"Come to your senses." Sharp fingernails bite into the fabric of her nightdress. "Do I need to remind you what he did to the niece of our pastor? You're a fool if you think it's beneath him!"

I blow an impatient sigh through my teeth. "I've never slept with Henry. Or anyone, for that matter."

"And you expect me to believe that with how you've been behaving?"

"Yes!" I say louder than intended, having a tougher time putting a cap on my mother-induced rage than usual.

As I begin stomping up the staircase, her voice grates behind me. "Mary-Rose, if I find out you're lying to me—"

"What's it gonna take?" Halting halfway up my ascent, I face her again. "Bring me to a doctor and have me examined for all I care. I'm a virgin!"

Alright...I didn't think she would actually do it.

I really need to stop underestimating Mom's incessant need to control every aspect of my life. Because there's nothing quite like being pulled out of bed and hauled into a doctor's office without so much as a word in what was about to be done to your own body. Much to the chagrin of my mother, however, the OB/GYN receptionist promptly informed her that it was the twentieth century, and testing to ensure women were still virginal wasn't a legitimate practice. And, even if it had been, I was eighteen, and my mom had absolutely zero right to drag me like a toddler by my ponytail and demand I undergo any procedure. But she also informed us that, given my age and lack of record, it would be best to have a standard exam and PAP smear while I was there.

And now I'm lying half-naked on a table with my feet in a pair of stirrups, wondering why the hell they keep these rooms so cold. Stifling silence is fractured when the door opens, and I awkwardly lift my head to find the doctor.

The *male* doctor. Of-fucking-course.

"Mary-Rose Ginger," his deep, warm voice is as welcoming as his smile. "Nice to meet you."

"Hi..." I say shyly, my face flushing a deep shade of red. "Dr. Malik?"

"Yes, ma'am." He looks as professional as a middle-aged physician can be, adjusting his pristine white coat while studying the clipboard in his large hand. Dark brown eyes matching the deep shade of his skin stay averted from my vulnerable body, putting me at ease. "I see we're doing a basic PAP today. Is this your first time?"

You bet your ass it is. "Yes."

He goes on to ask me a slew of questions pertaining to my medical history before delivering the awaited, "Are you sexually active?"

"No. Never have been."

I suppress a grumble over the very matter that provoked Mom to bring me here in the first place. Although, there is some beautiful irony there. My mother, for fear that men were getting between her daughter's legs, brings said daughter to get stripped down and tested for purity, resulting in a man between her daughter's legs. It almost makes me wish that I *had* been born a century earlier. Back when the prospect of women having their own sexual desires was so unfathomable that, if they presented the right combination of symptoms—irritability, emotional outbursts, or erotic fantasies, God forbid—they were often diagnosed with a debilitating case of Hysteria.

The remedy? Doctor-induced orgasms. If only it were that easy nowadays.

"Alright, then the rest of these questions won't be necessary." Dr. Malik finishes marking the clipped page before setting it aside, pulling a wheeled stool to the edge of the table.

Damn, at least being a virgin came with efficiency.

Dr. Malik dons a pair of rubber gloves as he sits, reaching for a tool on the steel plate beside him and prepping it with lubricant before holding it up for me to view. "I'm going to start with inserting the speculum. You may feel a bit of pressure."

I certainly do, wincing as I sense careful fingers part me before I'm speared with the device. My teeth grit uncomfortably as it opens. It isn't shameful, or even weird. If I had to describe the emotion stirring inside me, it would be *disappointment*. This is the first time any hands or fingers not belonging to myself have touched me, and the fact that it's happening in a doctor's office isn't much of a story to tell…

Or is it?

My jaw slackens. I lower my chin to view Dr. Malik, who has since rolled away to gather the necessary materials. I study the room surrounding us. Isolated. Private. And the position I'm in, spread open and bearing all for a dutiful man. Resting my head against the table, my mouth twists into a perverse smile. There it is, that feeling I get when an idea hits. That all-encompassing tingle nestling in my lower belly while my mind projects the most obscene, adulterous amendment to reality one could fathom. A warm flush sweeps over me from head to toe. I close my eyes from the force of it, relishing every warm pulsation. Each nerve sparking to life as the scene in my head unfolds moment by delicious moment, every ounce of the emitting heat pouring between my legs and deeper as my muscles tense in pure—

The pressure inside me slips. A *clatter* rings out in the condensed room. I glance between my legs to find Dr. Malik staring in bewilderment at a spot on the floor, before reaching down to retrieve the speculum. The speculum that I'd...

Oh fuck.

"Huh," he eyes the device with intrigue, dark brows furrowing. "That's a first."

I force a laugh as my face reddens, humiliation holding me in the moment long enough to respond accordingly. "Tell me about it..."

I squirm on the table beneath me, legs parted wide enough for the air to caress my bare underbits. Breathing deeply does nothing to soothe the longing I feel inside, laid spread for a pair of dark, tantalizing eyes.

"Are you ready for your examination, ma'am?" Dr. Magic asks, straightening his white coat to claim the space between my legs.

"Oh, yes. There's a terrible ache. A tingling right in here." I slide my hands over my lower abdomen, stopping just shy of my slit.

"I see." His touch trails my skin, grasping the fabric of the patient gown I'm wearing. "I need to take a closer look. Let's get rid of this excess material, shall we?"

I gasp as he tugs it clean off, leaving my body stark naked at the ready. A thrilled grin graces me as professional hands work to examine my hips, then my waist, then my breasts. They linger deliciously on the latter, thoughtfully grabbing and squeezing.

"Everything is in wonderful shape. Now, let's see about that ache." His arm disappears between us a blink before a gloveless finger prods my entrance. "You may feel a bit of pressure."

I moan as his long digit sinks in. He curls it upwards, fondling me from the inside as my walls clench around him. "Dr. Magic, you've found it!"

His efforts induce waves of vigorous pleasure with each firm stroke to my G-spot. "Well, there's your problem. Hysteria. A terrible case, if I do say so."

"Dr. Magic, you have to help me," I beg, grasping tight handfuls of my hair. "I can't stand another moment of this agony!"

"Not to worry, ma'am. I have a solution at the ready. But it's going to require a much longer instrument to get the job done." Removing himself, his pristine white coat shifts open. My eyes trail down a dark, sculpted torso to find him bare. Length standing hard mere inches from the source of my ailment. "First, it's going to require a proper lubricant."

He rounds the exam table to position his rigid cock before my mouth. I readily take the thick shaft, gliding my tongue methodically over its head. Taking time to tease his slit and lap up leaking pre-come before swallowing him deep, filling my throat with inch after inch to wet him thoroughly. Humming at the impressive size, my hand slides to palm his balls, massaging gently in time with my eager sucks.

"You're doing so well." He praises between pleased grunts. The tool in my mouth throbs, and I feel his heavy sack tense and relax in quick succession as he prompts, "Now, are you ready for a hot dose of—?"

My fingertips lock as I read the line once over.

"Dose?" I say to nobody but myself in the nightly serenity of my room, raking a hand through my scalp with a cringe. *Come on, you can do better than that.*

I tear the page from the typewriter to trash, then finish off my glass of fruit punch with a deep exhale. Not that it was too pressing, I still have plenty of time to give Ruth my next story. Now that I'm ahead, I can devote time to polishing them. A fact that puts me at ease as I head downstairs for a refill.

The house sits calm in the late evening, aside from whatever nonsense Mom's televangelist was yelling on about. I can make out some soliloquy about temptation being of the devil as I step into the kitchen. It provides some amusement as I pour a fresh cup, but when the living room sweeps by in my periphery, my mother's chair sits empty. I'm given no time to ponder before the distinct sound of her voice emanates from our entryway.

"Mary-Rose, come here."

My brows furrow as I approach to see her standing in the open front door.

She shoots me an irritated glance. "Next time, tell me when you're going to have people over. One of your friends from Bible study is here."

I stop in my tracks. *What?*

I hadn't even heard them knock. Which of the girls would show up unannounced like this, anyway? I consider as I lift the glass for a sip. "Who?"

My mother steps aside, and a flawless, ruby-lipped smile awaits me. Val.

Chapter 19

Trying to explain to my mother why I had accidentally snorted fruit punch all over myself *and* the foyer had been difficult enough. But sitting at our kitchen island listening to her get lost in a deep conversation with Val, who rests with her elbows against the immaculate surface, engrossed, or at least pretending to be, in whatever religious bullshit she's rambling about? I feel like my chest is about to explode and paint the room with a whole different red.

Not a single word being spoken registers in my brain. My bulging eyes dart back and forth depending on whose mouth is moving. But even in my panicked state, I can't help but linger on Val's body from where she sits across from me. Dressed in the church girl outfit she'd worn for the photoshoot of my sexy pastor story—albeit with more layers to keep it from looking too slutty…Sadly.

It takes my mother snapping her fingers to draw me out of Val's trance after their conversation wraps. A rather pleasant one, if Mom's unusually content expression is anything to go by. "Mary-Rose, I'm headed to bed. The two of you don't stay up too late, understand?"

"Sure, Mom," I say, keeping my focus on Val, who bids my mother a goodbye wave as she exits the kitchen. Silence holding us until the curt echo of her closing bedroom door.

"She seems nice," Val remarks sweetly, sipping from the glass of punch she'd been offered after my little accident prompted Mom to get us more.

I stand, grabbing her wrist and tugging her toward the stairs. Unwilling to take a single chance of my mother overhearing anything I was about to say. "My room. Right now."

"Good idea." Val agrees.

I drag her along until we're secluded in my personal sanctuary, then reduce my voice to a frantic whisper. "What the hell are you doing here?"

"I wanted to hang out with you again." She says, removing her cardigan to reveal the tight-fitted, low-cut blouse beneath. I force my eyes to remain on her face as she tosses it on my bed. "Things have been stressful lately with classes, and the other night at the club helped take my mind off things." She frowns at me. "But if you really want me to leave, I will."

"No—!" I blurt, stumbling over my words. "I-I mean, I don't mind you being here. But if my mother finds out how we *actually* know each other, I'm as good as fucked."

"That's why I told her I was from your Bible study." She says, taking my hands to pull me closer.

Embarrassment burns my cheeks. "Sorry you had to put up with her preaching just to get in."

"Don't be, I was raised Roman Catholic. I still believe in God. *And* deal with my share of people who don't think I have a right to with my choice of job. But I don't let it get to me. Plus, I snuck this out of the studio to sell the story. What do you think?" Her hips sway as she gestures to her body.

Lord, now she's beckoning me to look at her?

"I think—" I clear my throat, fighting to keep my gaze from wandering too recklessly over her tight curves. "I think you're crazy for chancing this. But…I'm happy to see you."

Her smile returns, melting my apprehension. "Is this where you write?" She asks, turning to the desk where my typewriter is housed alongside the start of my doctor/patient work-in-progress.

"Yep, I usually keep the stories I'm working on in my notebook for safekeeping. When I'm done with them, they go in here." I lift the bed skirt to showcase my safety-pinned tear.

"Devious." She purrs. Then drags the tip of her red-polished nail along the typewriter's keys, stopping on the single letter marked in the same shade. "I've been wondering, where do you come up with your ideas, being this sheltered and all?"

"They just sort of come to me. Normally, in the most inconvenient circumstances." This morning was certainly no exception. "But I take what I can get."

Val hums as she strides to the mirror on my wall, straightening her blouse in the reflection. "I've read the stories you've published more times than I can count. You're really good at describing pleasure."

I approach the desk and sort all the lewd papers into my *Holy Scriptures* notebook in a clumsy attempt to keep her from noticing my furious blush. "Thank you. I must be doing something right."

"I would've never guessed you haven't slept with anyone before. No judgment, obviously, it's just impressive." Her lip twitches in annoyance as she pats down a messy section of her styled hair. Then grabs a stray brush to tease it back into place. "Being a virgin, how do you even know what certain things feel like?"

"It's not really about having experience, just fooling people into thinking you do. I'm certainly not a virgin with *myself*. I make use of what I have." I suck in a breath when I realize exactly which brush she's using. "You should wash your hands after touching that."

Val's gaze drops to the handle she's grasping. The long, *slender* handle.

She lets out a disbelieving laugh, discarding the object before pumping some hand sanitizer from my desktop into her palm. "Well, consider me fooled."

"Besides, I've always been," I choose my words carefully while taking a seat on my twin mattress. "Sexually curious. It didn't matter that I had people telling me left and right that pleasuring myself was evil; I never saw the harm in it. At least, not since my first…"

"Yeah?" Val drags the word, claiming the spot beside me with an expectant smile.

I nervously avert my focus. "You don't wanna hear about it."

"Sure, I do! If there's no shame in doing it, then there shouldn't be any shame in talking about it." She gently bumps her shoulder against mine. "It's not embarrassing, we're both girls here."

The invitation makes me pause. Never in my life had I been able to talk so openly about this stuff with another woman. Mom? Hell, no. Erica? There wasn't the chance. Lewis? Sure. But he could never truly understand. It makes me feel absolutely free. And that's just *one* of the effects Val has on me, but I can't risk putting much thought into the others when she's sitting so close.

I sigh thoughtfully. "When I was little, my mom took us to visit some of her well-off family. They had this big farmhouse and a bunch of ATVs the kids would play with. I was riding one on their gravel road when I started to notice that, when I sat a certain way, things down there started to feel…weird. Good, weird. So I kept at it, and after a while, *boom*!" I mimic an explosion with my fingers.

Val's jaw falls open. "You had your first orgasm riding an ATV? On *accident*?"

Leaning back on my hands, I close my eyes with a fond smile. "It was life-changing."

"¡Dios mío! How old were you?"

"Nine," I answer. "I didn't know *what* it was. All I knew was that it felt amazing, and I wanted to do it over and over again. Pretty soon, I figured out how to make it happen myself, and the rest is history."

"Wow," Val shakes her head, face brightening with intrigue. "When *did* you figure out what it was?"

"A few years after that, I think I was thirteen. One of our cousins was staying with us after he got evicted. Mom was trying to be godly and all." My mouth tweaks in a wince. "I'm pretty sure she booted him out after she caught him with a *lady of the night* on our sofa. But when I went snooping through the stuff he left behind, I found a certain adult movie collection." I chuckle as Val's eyes widen. "I waited for an evening when I was home alone and watched them."

It had been the moment I realized, this thing I was doing to myself, maybe it wasn't just me. Perhaps everyone has desires. Everyone wants to feel good. *Especially* the people who act like they don't.

"Is that when you started writing?" She asks tenderly.

I nod. "I guess it was my way of proving that my feelings were actually worth being felt. If I could type them, hold them in my hands, they became just as real as all the stuff my mother was forcing onto me. They meant something. If not to anyone else, then to me."

Val takes a long pause before speaking softly. "I'm jealous of you."

Her words hit me like a punch to the stomach. Valerie Ramona—inarguably the most perfect human being I've ever laid eyes on—is jealous of *me*?

"What are you talking about?" I ask.

Val's shoulders drop. "I lost my virginity when I was fifteen—high school boyfriend, nothing that lasted. But I didn't have my first orgasm until I was twenty. And even then, it was with someone I barely knew. It just sort of happened, we didn't harp on it."

I can do nothing but stare in disbelief. "Are you serious?"

She nods sadly. "That's why I love your stories so much. I think they help me understand what I'm capable of experiencing. Even if it is just a fantasy."

I didn't think it was possible for me to feel so stupid, so instantaneously. Never once had I stopped to think that the people I envied so much—those who had sex without fear of shame—may not be having the inherent experience I always imagined it would be. Sure, overhearing high school conversations taught me that some people were more skilled than others. But being intimate with people for so many years without having a single climax? I'd rather stay a virgin forever, enjoying the limitless, mind-blowing orgasms I knew I could give myself, than put my faith in other people and constantly walk away disappointed.

But even so, I could never shake the lingering humiliation of being a new adult with no romantic history. Aside from whatever Henry and I have. Which, until I get that apology, is nothing definite.

"I'm flattered." My tone dims. "But I promise, there's nothing to be jealous of. I'm miles behind you in plenty of other ways."

Her eyes crinkle in confusion.

I expel a huff. "Val, do you have any idea what I would give to be like you? And I don't just mean how crazy smart you are. You're the prettiest woman I've ever met."

"Rosie, do *you* not realize how beautiful you are?" She asks with the first hint of irritation I've ever heard in her sweet voice. "Whatever happened to make you think nobody wants you?"

Aside from being single all my life, and Henry's nettling—yet now, baseless—remarks? One instance certainly stood above the rest.

"In tenth grade, there was a day I was sitting in class looking at a pocket mirror. I'd snuck some of my mom's mascara for the first time and thought it looked pretty." My chest tightens with the recollection. "This boy was sitting beside me, Landon Hemmings. When he saw what I was doing, he told me to be careful. Because if I looked at it for too much longer, the glass would shatter to spare itself."

Val's lips part, remorse flooding her hazel eyes.

"Just him saying it would've been bad enough." I go on, the pain simmering beneath my skin just as searing as it had been years ago. "But everyone in the room heard him. They laughed so loud, teachers halfway down the hall complained about the noise."

It was a terrible memory, but one with a strange twist. Because, despite crying in Lewis's bedroom for hours that night with no chance of consolation, Landon would go on to, remarkably, apologize to me the following day. The second I walked into class, he was practically on his knees begging for my forgiveness. Claiming he was sorry he said something so untrue to the prettiest girl in the whole school, and the only reason he'd made fun of me was because he was insecure about his small penis. The class was infinitely more amused by his declaration than by his insult the day prior, resulting in all of us getting detention for the raucousness of their hysterics. But I was left too dumbfounded at Landon's apology to even enjoy it, let alone *believe* it. I did nothing but stare with incredulity at the way he'd been trembling like somebody struck the fear of God into him.

Maybe…because somebody had. Somebody who'd overheard my crying fit at the Fennicks' house that night.

My eyes drift to the stuffed leopard.

"That's horrible, Rosie." Val's styled brows narrow in anger. "That guy is an idiot."

I want more than anything to believe her. But the evidence of my pitifully preserved virtue grounds me. "Maybe. But when you go so long feeling that way, it really gets to you. Hell, I'm in college now, and I haven't even had my first kiss on the lips."

"Really?"

I shake my head. "I don't even care about it being special anymore. I just wanna get it over with and be able to say I've done *something*."

A silence falls over the room, and when I meet Val's gaze again, her features are firm, as if she's deep in thought. Then, the corners of her pigmented lips pull ever so noticeably as she asks, "Do you think your mother's asleep by now?"

I blink, desperate to know what devious ideas are whirling in that beautiful head of hers. "Probably. Why?"

Chapter 20

This had long since become the wildest week of my entire life.

Val taking me to a club to drink for the first time? Finding out my Bible study friend is a stripper? Henry *fucking* Fennick professing his love for me, and me feeling anything for him but complete hatred? Yeah, there's no question. Wild.

But I would be lying if I said the thrill that enlivens my veins as we step through the dark hallway to hell of *Wild Thang Studios* doesn't make me believe that it's, concurrently, the *best* week of my life. Val had informed me that R.J. loaned her a key to the building during one of his drunken escapades after a wrap day for a big issue. Directing her to lock up as he was dragged from the establishment by a group of especially friendly models that she, coincidentally, never saw again. He didn't request it back, so she'd opted to keep it in case there was ever an emergency. And according to her, *this* was an emergency.

She leads me by the wrist into their main studio, turning on the overhead lights to bathe the vast space in harsh illumination. The set to our right consists of a long, velvety red divan with several tripods around it. To the left are the standard vanities and scattered racks of costumes—if that's a term one could even refer to outfits consisting of so little fabric.

I repeat the same question I'd been looping since we left my quiet suburban street. "What exactly are we doing?"

Val finally graces me with the answer while sitting me down at one of the makeup tables. "I'm going to prove to you that you aren't some loser nobody wants, Rosie. You are fun, and gorgeous, and *sexy*. Everybody sees that. And after tonight," she clicks on the vanity, the frame of bulbs flickering like a halo around my reflection. "You're going to see that, too."

My cheeks flush for the millionth time today, and as she tugs the white ribbon free from my hair's elastic, I get the feeling it will be *far* from the last. Val retrieves a large container filled to the brim with compacts, brushes, and hair supplies from beneath the table.

"You aren't the least bit worried Ruth is gonna flip when she finds out we were here after hours?" I ask as she finds a worthy palette of nude colors, twisting my stool to face her.

"Ruth is used to me doing my own thing around here. If anything, she probably thinks I've earned it with all the extra contract work I do." She swipes a brush across pale powder with the most likeness to my skin tone, then brings it to my face to begin applying. "Besides, it's not like she's any stranger to girls having fun for the hell of it."

"Ruth doesn't exactly scream 'fun' to me," I say, keeping my lips tight to avoid a mouthful of product.

But suddenly, Val stops to look at me quizzically. "She hasn't shown you yet, has she?"

"Shown me what?"

Setting down the materials, Val's eyes sweep over the set, then shine with a noticeable glint as she says, "Wait here."

I watch her exit the studio, leaving me in a cold silence until she returns a minute later—a derelict VHS tape in hand. She ventures to the equipment-stocked corner of the set to tug over a standing cart packed with miscellaneous electronics, a heavy monitor sitting atop. After fumbling with the extension cord, she slides the tape into the player and flicks the television to life. Static crackles before the screen gives way to a stylized title card.

Passion of the Scarleteer

It dissolves to a scene in an elegant office space, with a lady seated on the inferior end of a boss's work desk. Slowly, the camera pans over her body, fitted in tight, deep red business attire that accentuates her slim waist and curves that would make even the most impassive woman envious. But when the edges of the grainy picture rise to her made-up face, she robs the breath straight from my lungs.

"Is that…*Ruth*?"

Val, who's reclaimed her place beside me, rests a hand on my shoulder. "A triple-X feature, 1971."

The video plays on as a tall, well-dressed man I assume to be her counterpart enters. The two exchange salacious dialogue as he hands her a golden champagne flute, which she generously sips from. He runs a rough finger from her jaw to her slender chin, a silent show of authority as her blue eyes raise in submission.

"Ruth was a pornstar?" I ask as if the evidence isn't before me on a silver platter. Or rather, silver *screen*.

"The late-sixties equivalent. She did nude modeling, peep shows, hardcore stuff for the time. Videos weren't marketable when she was making her come up. But when the industry got wind it was on the horizon," Val nods to the television. "Ruth jumped on it."

The picture quality, set design, even the camerawork appears revolutionary for the year of its creation. I almost find myself lost in the plot until Val's voice draws me back.

"Surprised?"

I can't look away. "Ruth looks unbelievable."

Not just attractive. Sure, she more than sold the role physically. But it's her on-screen presence that captivates me. The sparkle in her eye. Every sultry twitch of her features as the scene progresses. Ruth *embodied* sex, lure, the prospect of her very being laying siege in your head—so maddening yet so addicting that you can't help but allow her.

Val hums in admiration. "She didn't just star in this. She directed it, called all the shots. Ruth didn't want to meet the standard for porn; she wanted to *make* the standard."

I watch on, enthralled as the intro to the film concludes and the true feature begins. When it cuts to the next scene, the office space is cleared. Desks and chairs are replaced with sexual paraphernalia of every variety. Whips line the gray-washed walls, and the focus shifts over a new environment dotted in furniture linked with handcuffs and leather bases. But at the center of it all, a large wooden "X" stands upright, as fastened to the ground beneath as Ruth is to the structure. Her wrists and ankles are bound to each edge of the shape, showcased as the audience is gifted a slow view up her newly naked form. Inch after flawless inch of her body presents itself as the camera rises, her curvaceous chest bare as can be, with the exception of a tattooed lip-print just above her left breast. An outstanding, furious scarlet among the noisy picture.

That mark I'd noticed beneath her blouse…It's reminding enough of who exactly I'm watching that it pulls me from 1971 back to 1994 so quickly, I nearly go dizzy.

"Should we be watching this?" I ask, just as Ruth's male partner reenters the scene. Still clothed as he palms a leather weapon of choice.

"I'm surprised you haven't already seen it. Ruth showed me only a week after signing on. Said it helps instill in her new hires what she expects of us." Val's mouth curves in a frown. "But if you ask me, I think she just wants people to see it, period. Maybe it makes her feel like all this effort didn't go to waste."

I'm drawn to the monitor again. "You mean this video never sold?"

"She tried. But none of the new studios specializing in widespread releases would distribute it."

"But why not? It's incredible." I say, and *truly* mean it.

"It wasn't the movie the studios wouldn't take, it was Ruth." Val's face softens in remorse. "She was thirty when this was made. To them, there was no longevity to her career on-screen. They didn't want to distribute a tape with a star they couldn't market in the long-term." She says like she's heard Ruth recite the painful story a hundred times. "If she'd been eighteen and fresh-faced when videos had their rise, she would've been the poster girl of the whole golden age. *Eso que ni qué.*"

A well of pity forms in my chest for the woman. Suddenly, I understand why Ruth always presents herself so calloused. I can't imagine having so much passion for a business that tossed you aside when you had everything to offer. "What happened to her after?"

"Pretty much what she does now. She assistant managed odd studios and porn sets before starting *Wild Thang* with R.J. in '82."

I glance thoughtfully around the stage. "I hope it became all she wanted it to."

Val sighs. "*That* she's still working towards. If I know anything about Ruth, she's never satisfied. Always chasing that one hit that'll dominate the industry like she never could." Her hazel irises drift back to the screen. "I think she'll get there; it's only a matter of finding that hit. When she does, she'll strike. Magazine, video, whatever it ends up being, it's going to be huge. Nobody can command this world like her."

I hope Val's right. If only because I aim to do exactly that with my erotica. Reaching people in such a way was a kind of validation I hadn't even begun to internalize. Proof that the one thing I felt I was naturally good at really meant something to people besides myself.

After a few strikes to her exposed body with a leather strap, the actor's hand disappears between Ruth's legs. All the while, the heat in her eyes doesn't dissipate. Owning the scene like she *knows* she can. The only break in her performance comes when Val steps to the device and tastefully kills the power.

"You get the gist." She says, then flicks on an FM radio on the cart's lower shelf. Tuning it to a discernible station before she returns my way. Val recoups the powder, going in with a smaller brush around my cheeks, making my nose crinkle. "I know Ruth wouldn't take nicely to the idea of her story being a cautionary tale. But it's the second-most reason I'm so devoted to school. My looks won't always carry me, but my mind will."

"What's the first-most reason?" I ask with a polite grin.

A gesture she doesn't mirror. In fact, her jovial demeanor falls with the question, as does her working hand. "Do you remember that friend I told you about? The one who got me the job at the club?" She asks, continuing when I nod. "I've known her since we were kids. She had a tough life growing up. Was the hardest worker I ever knew, but her past made her a bad…" She expels a shaky breath. "Judge of character."

I keep silent, the air between us growing heavy.

Val quietly goes on, "She was in a relationship with this guy. He wasn't a good man, but she felt like she couldn't leave him. I knew it was only a matter of time before he hurt her, and I was right." She blinks a little too rapidly, a sign I recognize as suppressing tears. "But he didn't *just* hurt her. He…did other things, too."

Nausea grips me as I mutter, "Oh my God…"

"I was the one who told her to press charges, and she did. But when it went to court, it was devastating." She tilts her head high, but it doesn't stop the shimmer from welling in her eyes even more noticeably now. "It was *inhumane*. The things they did to discredit her. They used that she was a stripper. The fact that they were in a relationship when it happened. It was…" She averts her focus, sniffling to compose herself. "It was all for nothing. When it was over, they let him off."

I can't speak. All I can do is stare, enduring the waves of her heartbreak as if they were my own.

Val's posture straightens, a mark of strength even if it doesn't reach her face. "Nobody deserves what she went through. If I can fight for people in her position, I'm going to. I'll dedicate my whole life to it, if that's what it takes."

I look up at her, smothered by the chilled air. "I can't understand it. Why doesn't the world treat people in this industry like *people*?"

"The world isn't as different from the church you grew up in as you might believe, Rosie. They're just as hypocritical on the outside. Real violence? Death? People actually getting hurt? For some reason, the public doesn't pay mind to those things when they see them in the pages. But if it involves sex? Even if it's just fiction, you're going to be torn apart. Scrutinized for speaking about something that's adult human nature. Especially if you're a woman who takes pride in it." Her made-up features dim with compassion. "You've probably already experienced it and don't even know. A lot of people love your stories, but I hope you never have to hear the things those who disagree with your writings call you. And I don't just mean their baseless lies... They can be *evil*."

Fear rises at the mere prospect. And I can tell without a shred of doubt it's a fear Val is all too familiar with.

She goes on, "Sex work isn't for everyone. But the way I see it, people use their bodies for every job out there." Val takes a necessary pause. "Don't get me wrong, it's not perfect. The bigger studios prioritize wellness, but independent studios like this are the Wild West. When I get into law, I want to push for more protocols to keep performers safe. Mandated STD testing. Funding for advocacy resources. Stuff that's going to change the industry for the better."

I marvel at her, admiration pushing me to ask, "Your friend, what's her name?"

Her jaw tenses at first. But it, along with the rest of her, relaxes as she says, "Star." A hollow chuckle escapes her. "Not her stage name, her real one. Star Marquez."

"If you and Star have been friends all your lives, then I can see where you get your strength, Valerie." The resilience to go through such turmoil is beyond me, but I can see it in the woman before me, clear as the desert day. "I didn't think you could get more beautiful."

She looks at me for a long while, her previously tear-filled eyes now glinting with something else. Huffing a forced laugh through her nose, she timidly dips her chin. "Sorry. I wanted tonight to be fun."

"It still is." I declare, straightening my spine to present her my face at the ready. Moments later, I feel the soft brush of powder against my cheek as, from the nearby radio, Madonna tells us all about the boys who romance and slow dance.

I let Val finish her work without further interruption. After a good while of makeup, she undoes my ponytail. Enough hairspray to desecrate the ozone and a *lot* of teasing later, she places everything on the table and looks me over with a more-than-satisfied smile.

"Ladies and gentlemen, I present to you…" Taking my shoulders in her hands, she spins me to face the mirror. "Rosie Ginger, in all her propriety!"

When I see the reflection, my jaw drops.

It's as if somebody swapped my face with the models on the cover of every teen magazine I'd seen girls clutching back at Peakshire. My dark eyes are sparkling beneath sharp black liner that blends out to a shimmery pink shadow. With long, glued-on lashes—that I had nearly sealed my eyelids shut trying to adjust to—and meticulously styled brows to top. My cheeks are a much more appealing rosy than their typical red, and my lips are painted just a few shades brighter than Val's ruby. My hair, voluminous as it is, looks *purposefully* bushy for a change. Feathered bangs and teased waves bounce with each subtle move of my head as I lean in closer.

The resemblance hits me like a train. This is *exactly* how I'd always envisioned Slutty Rosie.

"Holy shit…" The swear leaves me in a hush.

"That's not all," Val's voice, now farther away, draws my gaze from the mirror. She's raking through a nearby rack of outfits, pulling free a metallic, one-shoulder leotard from the hanger. Shining in a color that's vaguely the same pink of my eye shadow as she holds it up. "This should fit you nicely."

I stand to take the article from her, furrowing my brows at its minuscule size. "You expect me to fit into *this*?"

"It's supposed to hug." She smirks, dropping a matching set of heels into my grasp. "Now, go!"

She shoos me behind one of the tall black curtains to do as instructed. I strip entirely nude, managing to squeeze into the bodysuit after some very creative positioning. Securing the single strap over my shoulder, I run my hands down shiny material reflecting the harsh lights of the ceiling. One side of the waist is cut out, and I'm only half-sure the fabric riding so far up my ass is intended to do so. But the way it clings to the curve of my hips and rides seamlessly up my slender middle gives my body an hourglass feel I never recognized it naturally had. The heels end up being the most difficult to navigate. Despite their near-perfect fit, it's only after I slide them on that I realize I have zero idea how to maneuver in them. But I give it my best go, striding with all the grace of a newborn lamb onto the stage floor.

Val's taken my abandoned spot at the vanity, placing all the materials back in their respective tubs until the clicks of my shoes draw her. When her gaze lifts, she drops the palettes in hand, paying no mind to the clatter they make as her mouth falls open. Wide hazel eyes consume my body from heels to hair. Did she apply more blush while I was away, or is that a natural red now layering the golden tone of her cheeks?

"¡Ay Dios mío! *Qué hermosa te ves…*" She breathes, approaching as she does a full sweep of the getup.

I attempt another step, but my ankle twists as the pencil-thin stilt slips from beneath me. I'm falling only a fraction of a second before Val rushes to aid, holding me upright as I recoup my balance. She laughs, a chirp that escapes lips only inches from my own. Sensing my skin heat beneath the layers of powder, I avert my view to one of the full-length dressing mirrors and instantly share her amazement—the hair, the makeup, the bodysuit that clings just as Val had promised.

I look beautiful.

No, not just look. For the first time in my entire life, I *feel* beautiful. I'm so lost in the impossible sight that I only notice Val return from a prop bin clutching a feathery purple boa when she weaves the article around my neck.

"Do you see it now?" She asks sweetly, stalking behind to look over my shoulder.

I hold her tantalizing stare in the reflection, then twist my head to meet the real thing. Our faces nearly brush as I say, "I do…Thank you, Valerie." My focus travels past her to land on the adjacent set, an idea gripping me tighter than the bodysuit hugging my curves. "Do any of those cameras have film, by chance?"

Val follows my gaze, breath ceasing as she matches my mischievous grin.

Ten minutes later, I'm sprawled on the red cushions of the divan beneath a collage of stage lights narrowed on my form. Val operates one of the studio's cameras, peering through the viewfinder as she snaps photos from all angles. Bathing me in blinding flashes.

"What do you think?" I ask playfully, running my hands up and down my body. "Do I have what it takes?"

"*Oh, Virgin Mary, you were made for this!*" Val mocks R.J.'s southern accent, winking at me as she hunches to my level. "*Now, show me those assets, little lady.*"

Shifting to my knees, the most profound confidence—a confidence I've only ever experienced vicariously through Slutty Rosie—possesses me to reach for the bodysuit strap. "Okay."

Val drops the act, staring at me unreadably. "Rosie, I'm only playing around."

My pigmented lips twist into a smirk. "So am I."

I slide the material down my arm, then my waist. Pure thrill rules every beat of my heart as I flaunt my naked breasts for the lens. Val stiffens in shock. But after a pause, a look I can only discern as pride blossoms over her pretty face. She raises the camera, stunning me with a sinful strike of light.

"I don't mean to *actually* sound like R.J.," she says between another click of the release. "But you have great tits."

Her compliment draws a smile that reaches my eyes, captured in the final flash enveloping my nudity before I reset the leotard to its proper position. Val snaps a myriad of additional photos as she directs me into other positions, but stops upon abruptly going quiet. Lowering the device from her face, she fumbles with the intricate buttons before handing it off to me.

"Here," she instructs. "Put this on one of the tripods."

"What are you doing?" I ask when she strides away to slip behind the nearest black curtain.

"I have an idea!" She calls, foregoing further explanation.

I'm puzzled, but comply. Minutes have passed by the time I figure out how to properly attach the camera to the equally delicate tripod facing the front center of the long sofa. In my attempt to position the lens perfectly, I clumsily tap the release and stun myself in the eyes with a bright flash. Stepping backwards, I blink away the momentary blindness. And when it passes, I realize I've never been more grateful for God's gift of sight.

Val stands at the edge of the plush rug, now dressed in a similar metallic bodysuit. Hers is a royal blue two-strap dipping in a much lower neckline. The getup is topped with familiar black gloves that extend to her biceps and stilettos that rival my own. It takes the forgotten camera striking me with yet another flash to break from her hex.

"I set it to the ten-second timer." She says with a smirk, velvety black hands on her hips as she approaches. "You didn't think I was going to let you have *all* the fun, did you?"

I bite my bottom lip and grab her by the wrists, pulling her with me as we both hit the surface of the couch one on top of the other. Our laughter echoes through the unoccupied studio.

FLASH

We pose together. Val hugs me tightly against her warm body.

FLASH

I flip us, straddling her and shooting the lens a half-serious look. Val's head tilts backwards in an open-mouthed smile.

FLASH

We keep this up. Snapping Lord knows how many photos until we've run out of salacious positions. In a rush, Val stands from the divan and snags my hands to bring me to my feet. Propping us directly before the camera as we stand face to face. She takes the end of my purple boa and gracefully pulls half of it around her own neck.

Her words are soft as the feathers tickling my skin. "Kiss me."

FLASH

Every ounce of our juvenile recklessness drops with my stomach. "What..?"

Val's expression doesn't dim, her perfect lips retaining their curve. "You said you want to get your first kiss over with, just to say you've done something. So, do something." She leans forward a subtle inch. "Kiss me."

Have my first kiss…with another woman?

My lungs burn with the realization that I've stopped breathing. "We shouldn't."

FLASH

"Why not?" The longing in her voice melts me to the core. "Give me one reason. If you do, then we won't. We can act like this never happened."

Act like this never happened? Tonight was something I never wanted to forget for as long as I live. Even so, I stand there and think, *truly* think of some reason why what she's offering is wrong. Any reason outside the prospect of eternal damnation I'd been spoon-fed since I was a child, and had stopped believing years ago.

But it doesn't exist.

FLASH

"I know you said it didn't need to be, but this *is* special. You're safe with me." She promises warmly. "Besides, how many people can say they have a picture of their first kiss?"

Like the beat of a furious drum, my heart thunders as I fixate from her eyes to her mouth.

FLASH

After years of thinking nobody would ever see me the way I longed to be seen, Val is standing right here, vowing that she does. And I believe every word of it.

She's beautiful. She's kind. She's so fucking perfect that it hurts. And right now, she's *mine*.

I lean forward and press my red lips to hers.

FLASH

I half expected the flaming mouth of hell to open right beneath my glitzy heels at the moment of our connection. Or, at the very least, guilt to strike me dead where I stood. Anything to indicate that the hatred spouted by every Crosspoint devotee to ever look down their nose at same-sex love hadn't been as baseless as it seemed.

But there's nothing. Nothing aside from pure bliss.

Every inch of my body prickles with raw passion I'd only ever depicted on paper, having no idea it could exist beyond the scope of the illustrious blank page. It's more intoxicating than the first sip of liquor I'd taken at this woman's request. And her lips are just as smooth, more than gentle as they settle against mine. Our mouths fit like pieces of a puzzle, finally worthy of completion after too long boxed away—too *painfully* long. Despite it being my first kiss, my body conforms to hers on its own accord. Like it knows exactly what to do to make this burning rush linger as long as possible before it extinguishes, leaving me craving more, and more, and *more*.

It could've been minutes, but time only resumes when we collectively pull apart. I meet her sparkling hazel irises, not entirely convinced what just happened wasn't the product of a dream I was seconds from losing. But it—*she*—remains real.

A sharp clicking is all it takes for the two of us to be cruelly dragged from each other's eyes, which snap to the propped camera. The automatic timer still functioning despite the film being entirely spent. Val steps away, carefully opening the device and pulling the full cartridge free to hold it out.

"For your eyes only." She beckons.

I take it, squeezing the warm roll in my palm as the last ounce of thrill driving my promiscuity evaporates. But Val doesn't release my hand as she passes it, stroking her velvety fingers along mine in a threat to reignite that hazardous flame.

"See?" Her smile brightens. "I told you it would be special."

If I weren't too awestruck to speak, there would be nothing stopping me from asking what unforeseen force in this universe could've possibly pitied me enough to bring someone like her into my life.

Or…if she would kiss me again.

Chapter 21

The next day, my eyes are burning from lack of sleep as I make the walk to the Fennicks' open garage. Val and I had returned to my home in the early hours of the morning after our escapade at *Wild Thang Studios*, and despite my exhaustion after the full day and night, my heart was beating too quickly lying beside her to get any rest. Especially with the minimal room my twin bed offered. It shouldn't have been the spike in nerves it was after the two of us had *kissed*—but what's a girl to do?

And now, my body feels heavy for so many reasons I can't even begin to name them all. But I would try once I found Lewis, opting to head straight for his home the moment Val said goodbye to attend her Saturday study groups. Besides, I wanted to know how his date with Lynn went two nights before. With my mother dragging me to *Dr. Magic* and Val showing up unannounced in the time since, I never got the chance to ask. I figure I should also let him in on the fact that his older brother had essentially kidnapped me and, despite years of malice, made me fall for him in our hours away.

This is going to be an interesting morning.

I'm joyously welcomed by Mrs. Fennick at the door, where she tells me that Lewis is laying bricks for her flowerbed in the backyard. When I make it there, I step to the far corner of the fenced-in perimeter partially shrouded in trees. Lewis is facing away from me, kneeling at the patch of soil with a stack of ruddy bricks at his side. He's dressed casually for once, with dark jeans and a polo tee that hangs from his scrawny frame.

"I thought your mom made Henry do the heavy lifting around here?" I ask, my pulse jumping at the mention of the older Fennick.

Lewis stops hammering to raise a brow at me. "Why put one to work when you spat out two?"

I smile at the polarity of Henry taking his joy in stripping engines and Lewis being the type to tend to their mother's garden.

He goes on, "What are you doing out so early, anyway? Thought you had a case of the girl flu."

I suck a breath through my teeth. "Yeah, about that. I kinda made it up to get you and Lynn alone. She really wanted to go out with you."

He scoffs. "Well, I figured that much."

I take a seat beside him, minding my navy skirt on the soil-peppered ground. "You mean I'm not a good liar?"

"Not even remotely. You had the actual girl flu two weeks ago." He gestures to me with his dirty work glove. "At Crosspoint, when you whined all through the service about those bulky pads your mom buys sticking to your pubic hair."

Good to know my mother's holy alternative to tampons gave me away. "I'm gonna take this as a sign that I tell you way too much."

"What do you mean? I love hearing about your pubes." He counters with sarcasm.

I chuff, but divert to the more pressing subject. "God, when you hear all the shit that's gone down since I saw you last. But first, I need details. How did your date go?"

Lewis palms a trowel, scooping a patch of earth to lay the next brick. "Lynn was really fun. Very…enthusiastic."

My eyes brighten. "Really?"

"I was surprised how into me she was. She even kissed me goodbye when it was over."

"You two *kissed*?" Warmth floods my chest in the potent flavor of pride. I sigh to stifle it, but know it leaks onto my face as I say, "I knew you and her would go great together."

"She was really nice, but…" His voice trails off. "I don't think we're doing it again."

"What?" I blink at him. "Did something happen?"

He shakes his head, keeping focus on the bricks. "I had a nice time, but I just didn't feel anything, you know? I don't think it's best I go back to Bible study, either."

"I'm sorry. I didn't mean to make things weird between you guys." My posture slumps. "I just hate for you to be lonely when I can do something about it."

"Don't be sorry, I know you were only trying to help." He says softly. "And you don't have to worry, I'm not lonely."

"Being friends with me doesn't count; I'm talking about romance." I nudge his frail shoulder with my own. "Someone you can be in love with."

A silence falls over us, one I hadn't anticipated with the levity of the gesture I was extending.

"Like I said," Lewis finally speaks. "I'm not lonely."

My lips part, and my brows jump beneath my fringe as the implication hits me. "Wait, are you saying what I *think* you're saying?"

He doesn't respond. He doesn't even look at me. His eyes simply fix on the ground. A red tinge betraying the freckled, pale skin of his cheeks.

My face breaks into a grin. "Lewis, why didn't you tell me you were already dating someone? I wouldn't have tried setting you up with Lynn if I'd known. Who is it?"

Complete silence. The hot wind sweeps over us as I wait, and wait, and wait. Until something ticks in my mind. A memory of what Val had implied when I told her that Lewis and I were only friends, and she'd asked—

My stomach drops. The sunlight, backyard, *everything* surrounding us shifts from crisp and clear to a disorienting blur. I go on slowly. Delicately. "Lewis…why *couldn't* you tell me you were already dating someone?"

His head raises a slight inch, and I finally understand why he'd kept his gaze averted. Tears are welling in the bottom of his blue-green eyes, but he forces a smile in a futile attempt to mask them.

"Um," he swallows thickly, offering a pained chuckle. "Because I'm dating Presley."

The pure fear in his tone breaks my heart in two. Discreetly, I grab a fistful of the soft grass, as if the act could somehow anchor me to the world now that it had been turned upside down.

"Oh," I say as casually as I'm able. Trying my damndest to appear unfazed. Whatever I can do to put him at ease after such a mortified admission. "You mean…you've been getting action all this time and never came gushing about it?" I huff a forced laugh. "We're supposed to be best friends."

The jovial attempt at a response achieves nothing. My body grows twenty times heavier as I watch his head bow again, a few tears successfully falling into the loose soil. The sight is almost enough to kill me.

But I suppress my own pain, speaking softly to allay his. "Hey, what's wrong?"

Tearing off his work gloves to throw forcefully into the dirt, he doubles over with a sob. Covering his face like he'd just confessed the most reprehensible thing a man could.

My mouth opens and shuts several times before I think of the words fit to be heard. "Why did you never tell me? Did you think—" A thought absolutely *sours* my stomach, fogging the view of him with tears of my own. "My God, Lewis, did you think this would make me look at you differently?"

"No—" His voice breaks. Air rattles his lungs as he sets a tear-slickened palm on my leg. "I know you'd never do that."

"Then, why?" I have to know.

His bottom lip quivers. "Because I didn't want to implicate you. I never wanted you to have to carry this, ever."

Implicate me. He says it like he's committing some crime that I'm now just as guilty of for simply knowing about. But all it takes is one frightful glance at the house beside us for me to realize he *was* committing a crime. If people knew, if his parents knew, he would lose them.

He would lose his home.

It all becomes clear. No wonder Lewis had been so ready to join me in my spiritual deconstruction. Because for him, it meant escaping a life where everyone condemned his very existence. Just imagining the lonely ages he's spent at odds with what must've felt like the entire world gouges me from the inside out.

I grab his hand to lace our fingers, looking at him with every ounce of promise six years of friendship can forge. "Nobody will find out."

"Yes, they will." His chin dips. "I don't want to live like this forever, Rosie. I *can't*."

Compassion fills my chest to the brink of implosion. I try to fathom a reality where almost everyone I know and care about would turn their backs on me for simply loving someone. I half-debate telling him that just the night prior, I had been guilty as sin in kissing Val—another woman. But logic grounds me from doing so. I liked Val. *Really* liked her. But she was simply my friend. What we did was nothing more than girls having fun. The sight in front of me lays bare that what Lewis feels is real. It was something he could no longer hide, despite the years he'd spent doing exactly that from me.

"Whatever happens," I say, glancing over the harlequin roses grown from the bed's center. "Whatever you choose, you know I'll stand by you, right?"

"I know." He says without hesitation, the sorrow in his voice giving way to a thick silence. Even so, his tense shoulders relax as the moments breeze on. As if a physical weight had been lifted with his confession.

"So," I say after a much-needed reprieve. "When do I get to meet Presley?"

A smile graces his lips, his ruddy cheeks flushing a shade brighter. "You will, I promise. But for the sake of my own sanity, can we change the subject to whatever's going on with you?"

Oh shit. That's supposed to keep him sane?

I expel a nervous sigh. "When you were out with Lynn, Henry took me on a date. Said he's in love with me. And kissed me… twice."

Lewis's head snaps my way. "*What*?"

The wind ruffles my bangs, making it all the more difficult to conceal my shyness. "Yeah. And the craziest thing? I might actually like him back."

Lewis stiffens, before peering upwards like he was about to condemn the potential heavens for such treason. But he doesn't curse, he *laughs*. "It's about fucking time."

I narrow a look at him. "Wait, did you know that he liked me?"

"He's my brother, Rosie." Lewis quips. "I mean, he's never admitted it. But do you seriously think I couldn't tell?"

"*I* sure as shit couldn't tell!" I say with a playful scowl.

"Because you were too busy hating him, dumbass. You never thought it was weird how he always jumped to sneak us out to movies when you mentioned you wanted to see one?"

Shrugging, I try to keep from sounding as stupid as I feel. "I figured he owed you for something."

"And him only bringing those girls to the house when he knew *you'd* be around?" Lewis's brows quirk. "He only did it to see if you'd get jealous. The second you'd leave, he saw them out without so much as a goodbye kiss."

I blink at him. "He wanted to make me jealous?"

"Shit, all the times he called home from Arizona, the first thing he'd ask about was you." Lewis rolls his eyes in affection. "Specifically, if you had a boyfriend yet."

My jaw slackens. The outdoor heat isn't the least bit responsible for turning my face a light pink. "He really did like me all this time... That's so sweet."

"Says you," Lewis remarks with his first hint of disgust at the prospect. "You didn't have to walk past your brother's bedroom door every night and hear him moan your best friend's name when he jerked off."

So much for pink; my face flushes crimson at that. I slap a palm to it as I mutter, "God, help me."

"Like he's got any faith left in us?" Lewis smirks.

I timidly eye him. "You're not weirded out that I may have feelings for Henry?"

"Rosie, that might be the *least* weird thing I know about you."

I shove his shoulder, the two of us relinquishing our worries with shared laughter. But they cease when I wind my arms around him in a tight hug. "I love you, Lewis."

He returns it. "I love you more, brain whore."

Chapter 22

September turns to October, and with it comes no break in challenges.

I've spent much of my time over the past weeks cramming. Cramming for anatomy. Cramming for devotional hours. Cramming for Biblical "history." Cramming to pack my brain with fruitless knowledge that wouldn't benefit my career in the slightest. I found myself pent up to the point that I often considered dropping to the ground and throwing a temper tantrum until someone with enough compassion insisted on cramming *me*. Surely Henry wouldn't mind, but he'd yet to deliver that apology. Thus, I'm forced to trudge along with a packed mind and empty vagina.

At the very least, such desires made my job at *Wild Thang* far easier when it came to inspiration. Following my revised and very well-received doctor submission, I provided Ruth a cherry-topped tale of a confectioner who gifts one of her patrons a creamy treat on the house. Inspired by a sculpted, half-clothed hottie Lewis and I drooled over while in line at one of our favorite outdoor ice cream parlors. Following *that* publication, I no sooner found myself gaping at a crew of construction workers breaking the concrete road off Candid Park after my monthly meeting with Erica. Prompting me to rush home to my typewriter and offer them something else to jackhammer. Imagining Slutty Rosie wearing nothing but a cropped safety vest and a hard hat was hotter than it should've been. Still, it was absolutely nothing compared to the way Val looked in such apparel during the recreation. Her shoot had even made the cover of the issue—her beauty and my piece earning *Wild Thang* an esteemed indie publication award courtesy of *Adult Video News*. The ceremony had been held for all staff at an upscale event center, where I'd been so crudely enlightened to just how hard R.J. celebrates his victories. I'd foregone the fountains of champagne and mysterious white powders to sip rum and colas with Val, but only after receiving a literal pat on the back from Ruth, which had easily been the most unprecedented, yet fulfilling moment of that entire evening.

It served as the break I needed with midterms arriving. But I managed to score well enough on my exams to enjoy the blissful embrace of November as it came. Along with it, a column in *Garden of Eve*—a national feminist magazine—dedicated to New Mexico's mysterious *M.R.* and how her female-centric erotica was shifting the standard for women's sexual gratification in mass media.

> *"Wild Thang's M.R. continues to enchant the American Southwest with her evocative narratives, sending droves of ladies to the corner market every fortnight for her latest edition. This indecorous storytelling so lewdly, yet so deliciously, provokes the very ache that women have been instructed to suppress for millennia. A seemingly undistinguished Albuquerque publication, one that provides a mark of progressive literature that lends itself to oppose the quotidian benchmark of male-propagated pornography. Instilling the idea that some, if not most, women have long since dismantled their desires for leisurely romance novels when they reach the brink of longing. They simply desire the remedy of a good orgasm. It is a wonder what sort of experiences the elusive M.R. must have weathered to manufacture these lecherous tales.*

> *Perhaps we should all take a page from her book if we are to live our limited days to the sexual fullest, as she so proudly does."*
>
> —Priscilla Herschend, copy editor and reporter for *Garden of Eve*.

The ending line was my favorite. In a sense, it brought me undeniable satisfaction that I was duping the entire nation into believing that I'm some perverse harlot. When in reality, my most riveting sexual experience had been achieving my first G-spot orgasm with a cleverly angled high-pressure shower head, then nearly drowning in the bathtub after losing consciousness from the pleasure. But either way, it was a mark in *Wild Thang*'s favor to have their business praised on such a widespread level. Gifting me far more confidence when presenting my materials to the coxswain of the establishment herself—as I do so now.

Sitting across the desk from where Ruth resides in her high-backed throne, I watch as she finishes proofreading my latest piece, studying her face for any hint of reaction, positive or negative. Finding neither, my gaze drifts downward to her partially unbuttoned blouse, slipped loose enough that the smallest corner of her scarlet lip-print tattoo lies visible. A stigmata of her days on the front lines of the industry. I stare at it long enough for the memory of her illicit video to flash through my mind. But when she raises her head to indicate she's concluded, I perk up as if I know nothing of it.

Her sharp brows narrow at me. "In a library?"

I shrug. "Studying got boring."

Ruth chuckles. But any levity is foregone as she retrieves the lockbox, handing over my earnings, which had recently inflated with sales being at their peak since *Wild Thang*'s induction.

"Everything looks good, I'll send it to the editor to push." She says as I secure the cash in my backpack. "But there's one more thing I wanted to discuss with you. Nothing bad, just a new offer."

I readjust my posture, nerves seizing me at the break from our ritualistic exchange. "What kind of offer?"

Her elbows rest on the sleek desk. "Have you ever considered the option of traditional publishing?"

Had I considered it? My stories being available for people of all walks of life to pick up and enjoy was all I'd ever dreamed of. "Of course. But it was wild enough submitting to you, I wouldn't know where to start."

She hums quietly in what seems to be understanding, then tugs a sheet from a strewn folder to place in front of me. "A few days ago, we received this letter from an agency in Texas." Glancing over the heading, the words *Lone Legacy Press* make up the logo. Ruth continues as I read through it, "You know our issues span most major cities in the Southwest. Apparently, someone's been paying attention to the increase in our sales since we brought M.R. on board."

I gawk at the letter, then her. "You mean, they're noticing my stories?"

"It seems so. And since they have a specialty for collections," Ruth's mouth tilts into a smile I'm nearly convinced is genuine. "They want to take your stories and turn them into a book—an *erotic* collection. Nothing in our general contract holds the rights to your work, so it'd be your decision. Is that something you'd like to pursue?"

Pure thrill pours into my chest and spills into every limb at once. I almost feel the need to stand and start jumping for fear the excitement would smother me if I don't. The simple prospect unfolds into years of a long-awaited career before my very eyes—the opportunity to make a name for myself without the burden of shame or trepidation. But first, I need to say yes.

"Yes!" I assert. But upon completing the letter in my hands, my brow furrows. "They want...a longer piece?"

"From the communication I've had with them, they're looking for you to extend your stories beyond our limited maximum. All you'd have to do is take one you've already written for us and expand it. When you're done, we'll send it to the agency for approval. If they like what they see, they'll make a contractual offer. Which means a publication advance." Her head dips slightly, icy blue eyes tempting me with an odd lure. "Since I'd be acting as the manager, I would take a percentage of the deal. But...you would be a professionally published author, Rosie."

My mind carefully works through what's being asked. Fluffing up a pre-written story would be easy, and Ruth taking a cut would be a small price to pay for all she's done for me. Hell, without the chance she took, I wouldn't have this opportunity to begin with.

"Alright," I breathe. "I'll do it."

"Perfect. Turn in the revised piece the second you have it ready, and I'll take care of the rest." Something swells behind her features as she concludes. An emotion I can't place—nothing out of the ordinary for this woman.

I nearly jump out of my seat as the door to her office is violently kicked open. Hung frames and plaques rattle against the adjacent wall, jostled by the perpetrator's entrance. "Virgin Mary!"

I sigh.

"Did you tell her the good news, Baby Ruth?" R.J. nears with a proud gait in the corner of my vision.

"Actually, I was saving it for you." She tells him, studying me as if this is regarding something entirely separate from our previous conversation.

"Oh, Virgin Mary, wait 'til you hear this. With all the extra green we got coming in since you boarded, we just rented out the *top-rated* sound stage in the whole city for our video shoots. And guess what we're filming first?" He slams an enthusiastic palm on the desk. "The *Deviant Devotee* in live action!"

I reflexively look to Ruth for translation.

"We're using the new and improved location to adapt your pastor story into one of our home video releases. Their increase has reflected our magazine's since more people are picking up the issues." She gives a curt shrug, her dark gray blazer shifting with the motion. "The men get the video. The women get the story. Win-win."

As crude as it is to admit, my heart jumps at the idea of seeing the very fantasy that scored me this job play out in real life.

"Of course, as the commandant of the whole church-girl-gone-wild gig, you're welcome to be at the shoot." R.J. leans casually on the table's edge. "Who knows? If our star is a no-show, you fit the description better than anyone—inside *and* out."

"I'll have to sleep on that one." My sarcasm is thick, but the hopeful flare in his eyes tells me it went right over his head.

"In the meantime, work on what you need to," Ruth instructs, giving me an austere look as I stand to leave.

"I will," I promise, bracing the parting tension that capped our every meeting as I step into the hallway to hell—a stress that slowly fades with each stride I take down the corridor. I'd been looking forward to tonight for weeks now, and I certainly wasn't going to let some irrational fear of authority get in my way.

As if I ever did that, anyway.

Chapter 23

The hum of rushing water almost drowns the knocks on our front door, but I still recognize the coded series from my place at the kitchen sink.

"Come in, Lewis!" I shout, rinsing the last of my dishware as I vaguely register the approved entry. Early-afternoon sunlight spills in and dissipates, a prelude to approaching footsteps. "I thought we weren't supposed to meet for another half-hour?"

I get no response, just a minor heart attack when two hands suddenly cover my eyes from behind. Startling me to the degree that I drop the glass cup, wincing at the sound of it shattering against the metallic base.

"Asshole!" I bite out, still blinded as I hover a palm over the newly formed shards. "You realize you just gave me a weapon to stab you with, right?"

"You really *are* kinky." The perpetrator whispers deeply in my ear before pecking it with a kiss.

My pulse leaps as I push his hands away, whirling around with flared eyes. "Henry?"

Lo and behold, Henry Fennick is standing in my mother's kitchen. Wearing his classic denim jacket, Henley, and the proudest smile I've ever seen.

I scoff. "Lewis showed you our secret knock?"

He shrugs. "I may've bribed him with a top-tier ride tonight."

"And if my mother had been home?"

"I can be persuasive." He slips a hand behind his back. "Not like you don't already know that."

I suck in a sweetened breath as he taps me on the nose with a clipped rose, its white petals lightly crumpled from his handling. Taking it slowly, I huff a laugh to conceal my timidity. "You stole this from your mom's garden, didn't you?"

He offers a chipper hum before snatching it out of my hold. "Fine, I'll go put it back."

"No—!" I jump to chase him as he springs around the center island. "I'll miss it more than she will!"

"Too late!" Henry melodically taunts, stopping on the opposite side of the countertop in a low stance. Faking lunges in both directions to make me stumble in place.

I release an unserious growl, recalling years past and all the times Henry would nab my reading material or homework straight from my fingertips, forcing me to pursue him around the Fennick house just like this to reclaim it. As if we were still in high school, I challenge him with, "Hand it over, smartass."

"Gotta catch me, Angel Face." He implores with a deviously sexy smirk, holding up the flower to mock me.

Our laughter echoes off the walls as we circle the island another few times, which leaves us winded and precisely in the same position, as I'd yet to gain an inch. Now panting, I entertain his little stunt, "So much for your romantic entrance."

"Oh, I forgot, I'm going out with an expert." Henry suddenly discards the rose, striding to my side of the kitchen so quickly that I squeal in equal parts surprise and glee as he lifts me bridal style into his arms. "Is this how your stories typically start?"

The question almost makes me blush as fiercely as being literally swept off my feet. Balancing myself with arms around his neck, I chuckle. "Not exactly. My stories don't have such a *flowery* beginning."

Or middle. Or ending.

Henry hums again, a pensive look seizing his handsome face. Before I can even relish it, he's shifting his hold on me from bridal to full-on straddle, then pinning me against the nearest wall—gently enough as not to be rough, but lasciviously enough to make me wish he would be.

"Like this?" He asks lowly, his nose brushing mine.

In an instant, my mouth becomes too dry to give any semblance of a witty retort. Gulping to wet it, my voice breaks with a nervous, "*Yep.*"

It's Henry's turn to chuckle. He flashes his winning smile, which quickly melts into an adoring grin. I feel no instinct to flinch away as his hand—bearing patchy scars on each of the knuckles—delicately cups my face, tilting it to allow me a better view of his own. The waves of his hair are styled almost exactly the way they looked the night of the State Fair. Unevenly parted and pushed back in gradient dark-to-light swoops, aside from the few tendrils that now fall over his brows by way of our roughhousing. It's all I can do to stop myself from absolutely drinking in the sight of him.

"What?" I ask when I realize he's doing the same.

"Nothing, it's just…" He looks at me like I'm lost treasure he's spent half his life trailing. "I missed you."

My heart aches with alluring ferocity. We'd hardly interacted since our first unofficial date, only catching glimpses of each other when he happened to be at the Fennick residence when I was. Seeming to be in agreement that the last thing we needed was his parents keying my mother in on anything that might be blossoming. Especially after her crusade back in September.

I elect to tease him. "Well, you could've fooled me."

"Oh, yeah?" His voice deepens again, hot breath trickling across my skin as he leans in. "Let me prove it."

My heart blazes as his lips find my cheek, pressing softly at first, then harder as he plants another closer to my jawline. His hold on me tightens, as do the muscles of his abdomen where they sit snugly against my crotch. The unexpected friction makes me gasp, the burn in my chest plummeting so quickly that I feel my insides throb at the foreign contact. Henry must sense it, too, as he expels a needy breath before going in for another kiss just below my ear, hot tongue parting his lips to tease the sensitive skin.

I can't believe it. Henry, whom I vowed to loathe for all my life, is holding me against a wall and treating me with all the passion I've only ever written about receiving. And it feels so good…It feels *too* good. The sensations become so intense that thrill tips painfully into fear—fear of waltzing into territory I wasn't ready to enter.

"Henry," I work out through heavy breaths. "Please, slow down."

In an instant, Henry pulls away. Giving my face a sweeping glance before muttering, "Shit."

He carefully places me back on my feet before retreating a respectable distance. Eyes ghosting the floor between us in avoidance of my own. His face reddens in a shade that seems far more reminiscent of embarrassment than lust. The side of my neck grows cold after being wetted by his kisses, the chill bringing both relief and regret along with it. I part my lips to break the tension, but my inexperience grounds me yet again. What was I supposed to say?

Thankfully, he goes on before I'm forced to. "Sorry. This is new for me, too. I've never been a girl's…first."

I find myself surprised, yet confused by the statement. He's never been a girl's first…date? First boyfriend? First *lover*? The prospect of him claiming any of those titles for me still felt unfathomable, despite him already making it a third of the way.

Reclaiming levity, I grab the discarded rose from the center island and hold it to my chest. "I missed you, too, Henry."

Any trace of guilt lifts from his expression, which softens with the same genuine grin I'm becoming wonderfully intimate with. "I told you I couldn't see you soon enough."

"Huh," I playfully reply. "Is that why you're paying an early visit?"

"That," he smirks, then begins backing away. "*And* I've always wanted to see your bedroom."

"My bedroom?" My mouth falls open as he abruptly turns to rush for the staircase. I dart after him. "Henry!"

He laughs with every loud stomp of his ascent, but by the time I make it to the second story, my door is left ajar. Claiming a stance in the threshold, my face flushes brightly. As I've never cared about the state of my most private quarters when it was Lewis visiting. But now, his older brother stands in the center of the floor, taking in my pink walls, framed paintings of cute animals, and twin mattress. Which wouldn't be so embarrassing, *if* the fluffy lamb I've been cuddling every night since I was a toddler wasn't sitting at the helm. I bite my lip in humiliation, but release it the moment Henry turns my way with a smile.

"It's adorable." He remarks before fixating on my writing desk. Specifically, the shelves above it. I follow him as he nears the structure, his eyes drifting over the stuffed leopard he'd gifted me years ago— along with the myriad of *other* little plushes I'd been finding in our mailbox over the past weeks. "I'm surprised your mom didn't chuck any of these in the garbage."

Sighing, I place the white rose on my desk. "I was quick on my feet every morning."

Partly to keep the woman in question from discovering them first, but mostly because finding his gifts had become so enthralling, I couldn't help but jump out of bed each day to see if he'd left a new one. Each addition was complete with a linked card signed by my S.A. beneath the worst animal puns the English language had to offer.

Among them is a hedgehog, with a card that reads: *You're hedgehogging my heart.*

There's also a fuzzy fawn, captioned with: *You are so deer to me.*

But of all of them, I reach for the three-horned dinosaur plush.

Opening the card to read the note therein: *I'm not horny or anything, but I bet you'd look great on triceratop.*

"This one's my favorite." I declare with a smirk.

"That one?" Henry rubs the back of his head, forcing a nervous laugh. "I was worried you were gonna take it the wrong way."

"Like there's a *right* way to take it?" I tease him, my tone softening as I place it back. "Really, it was so sweet of you to do all this. I love them."

"Good." He looks at me warmly, before something on the tallest shelf catches him. Given his height, he has no issue palming the old cassette tape I always keep atop my copy of *Mary's Music* before inspecting it thoughtfully. "You like Bryan Adams?"

I mask any trace of grief behind a sad smile. "It was my dad's."

"Oh," Henry's shoulders drop, and I can tell he's searching for the right words. "What was it, again?"

"Pancreatic," I answer. "By the time he was diagnosed, there wasn't much they could do besides keep him comfortable."

Thumb brushing the plastic casing, he huffs gently. "You and him were close."

I nod, eyeing the object with a tight jaw. "That record came out a month before he passed. We got it for him so he wouldn't have to listen to monitors all day." The memories flash painfully, yet so beautifully vivid through my mind. "*Heaven* was his favorite. Towards the end, he even got out of bed to slow dance with us."

Henry brightens, emphatically raising the tape. "Do you ever play it?"

"Only when I need to." I know that if this conversation goes on, there wouldn't be anything stopping me from ruining what was supposed to be a happy day with tears. So instead, I raise a suggestive brow. "But I'm more of a *'69* kinda girl."

The remark makes Henry chuff as he replaces the tape, propping his hands on his hips to scan my room. "Alright, where is it?"

"Where's what?"

"Your stash." He says, playful authority etching his features when I don't spill. "What, you're gonna make me sniff it out?"

Deviancy heats my blood as he starts riffling through the closet. "There's nothing in there but my old prom dress. Remember, the one you splattered with leak detector while Lewis and I were taking photos?"

"I was jealous that you were going with him instead of me." He says with the faintest hint of shyness, but it disappears as he moves to the most accessible drawers and cubbies.

I cross my arms, drumming fingers confidently on my bicep. "Have you met my mother? You're not gonna find it."

"Have you met *my* mother? I've picked up a thing or two about hiding porn." He lifts my twin mattress enough to peek beneath, frown deepening when he finds nothing. But then, he stills, face going tense in thought. After a brief silence, he pulls my bed skirt to reveal the safety-pinned tear. "Jackpot."

"Hey!" I leap across the room, but he's far too quick. Managing to undo the clasps and nab a random bundle of pages before I can stop him.

He stands to evade my grabbing hands. "Whoa, whoa, whoa, hold on. I'm not gonna read all of it, I just wanna get a taste." Straightening the collection, he skims it with a pleased grin. "If anything, this is just research. Something to give me an idea of what you're into, considering this one's a sexy wedding night between you and…" His brows furrow. "Prince Eric from *The Little Mermaid*?"

I snatch it from him. "I was thirteen."

Kneeling to place it back in the security of my box spring, I feel a tinge of relief that he hadn't snagged something far worse. Let alone any of the *Wild Thang* issues I'd been storing since becoming gainfully employed. Pretty much every morsel of my indecency existed beyond that rip. *Except* for the explicit photos of Val and my trip to the studio all those weeks ago, which I had developed and opted to store in the backmost pocket of my *Holy Scriptures* notebook for extra safekeeping.

That, and *maybe* I enjoyed peeking at them every now and then.

"What's this?" Henry's voice lifts my chin, and I find him on the opposite side of the mattress holding my decrepit lamb. "You agree to a second date with me, and I walk in to find another boy in your bed?"

I shoot him a playful glare. "I like cuddling something when I fall asleep, alright?"

As I finish the last safety pin, the entire bed shifts with a sudden weight. Henry has since lain atop it, leisurely tucking his hands behind his head. "You want it? You got it."

Standing fully, I look down my nose at him. "You don't leave much room."

"Precisely." He drags, opening his arms.

My stomach flutters. It had been nothing more than a witty jab, but now… "You sure that's okay?"

Henry gapes at me like I have snakes for hair. "Rosie, you could tie me to this bed and use me like a toy, and I'd *thank you* for it."

Heat simmers beneath my skin. Despite how nonplussed I am at what should be the ultimate intrusion, I feel my body pull toward him like a magnet. Swinging my leg over his hips, I settle down in a straddle that I'd depicted countless times in the stories just inches beneath us.

"What do you think?" I ask in a mock-sultry tone, aiming to override my nervous spike at finally being in bed with a man.

"I think I bet right." Henry slides his palms up my thighs, then sits upright, wrapping denim-clad arms tightly around me. His breath tickles my face as he mutters, "But why don't we try this?"

He pulls me until we're both lying flat, my head against his firm chest. The way his arms remain heavily around my middle sends a delirious rush through me, while simultaneously putting my mind at rest.

It's more peculiar than thrilling, as I'd spent so many nights on this very mattress wishing I weren't alone. Picturing suitor after nonexistent suitor beneath the covers with me, easing the ache between my ribs *and* legs. Hell, the two of us are quite literally lying on five years' worth of fantasies conveying exactly that. But regardless of my wild-to-a-fault imagination, I never could've predicted that Henry Fennick would be the one to willfully guide these longings from fiction to reality. I marvel at how I fit so beautifully on top of him. The way he's cradling my waist almost turns my contentment to rage at the fact that he didn't confess his feelings for me years ago. Humming in delight, I close my eyes, permitting the beat of his heart beneath my ear to lull me. Bringing with it a lucid evocation of my early childhood.

While Erica had spent evenings learning to sew from Mom, I had been occupied sneaking into our father's study with my lamb and pacifier for the purpose of crawling into his lap and snuggling against his chest as he read his latest manuscript edits aloud. It didn't matter that I couldn't comprehend his complex tales quite yet; I still loved to listen. It became a ritual that I would fall asleep in his embrace, prompting him to carry me to this very bedroom and tuck me in with a good-night kiss every time. I forgot how much I cherished those days. To the point that Henry's voice draws me from the spiraling descent of sleep.

"I could get used to this."

I lift my head to eye him, ignoring the burn of affection it brings me as I tease, "That would be stupid of you, considering we aren't together."

He lets out a heavy, disappointed exhale. Raking gentle fingers through my ponytail.

I fidget with the unbuttoned clasps of his Henley. "You know what you have to do to change that."

His emerald-speckled eyes glimmer with longing. "Yeah, I know."

God, the look on his face nearly makes me fold. It doesn't help that he's arresting every one of my senses by simply existing so close. The warmth of his body. The sound of his strong heartbeat. The scent of oil and citrus that would no doubt linger on my bedding long after he leaves—hopefully, anyway.

"Sorry, but even if you decide you don't want me like that," Henry continues, his tone seductive. "I'm never going another day without holding you like this."

I can't help but deride the remark. "I think there's a word for people who do that. Like, criminal?"

"I'm not a criminal...anymore." He cringes, then tilts his head in lieu of a shrug. "I'm just persistent. So was Darcy."

The reference makes my cheeks flush. "Darcy was also an oblivious idiot who didn't have his priorities straight."

"And yet, he still got the girl."

My fingers trail down the dip between his pectorals. "That's because he was clever when it counted. Willing to admit his wrongs." The breath catches in my throat as my palm slides from his chest to his equally solid abdomen. I'd seen him shirtless around the Fennick house in years past, but my hatred dissuaded me from ever truly admiring his lean build. Lost chances I *suppose* I could start making up for. "Not to mention, handsome."

Henry's brows shoot up. "I'm at least one of those things, aren't I?"

Smartass.

My face falls into a teasing glare. "Do you seriously think that charming me is going to absolve you of all the payback you're due?"

"That depends. Is it working?"

"Hm, maybe." My voice shifts a gear lower as I put my theory to the test. "Why don't you tell me more about how long you've wanted to hold me like this?"

His jaw goes slack for a moment before the corner of his mouth lifts into a half-smile. "Years. I thought about it every night."

"I'm not convinced." Sarcasm weaves my every word. "I guess you're gonna have to be more specific. Did your thoughts stop at holding me?"

I swear I feel his heart sputter beneath my own as blue-green eyes flicker up and down my face. "I may've wanted to do more than that..."

I draw a fingertip along the collar of his denim jacket, ghosting the skin of his neck. "Not specific enough."

His smile slips, but he forces a deprecating chuckle. "Come on, Angel Face, you're gonna do this *on top* of me?"

"Is there a better place to do it?"

He accepts the challenge with a firm look. "Fine. When I still lived at home, I used to dream about sneaking over after dark, scaling your window, and climbing into this bed to find out how sweet your lips taste. Happy?"

"I would be." My finger reaches his smooth jawline, delicately tracing the sharp edge of it. "But kissing is typically reserved for people in relationships."

A devious smirk pulls his features. "Who said I was talking about your mouth?"

My jaw almost falls open, but I keep it fixed, knowing it would be precisely the feedback he's fishing for. Two can play at this game. "So, you've thought about *touching* me?"

"Of course I have."

My teasing digit stops beneath his chin, raising it to get the best view of his reaction as I counter with, "Then do it."

The sun-kissed skin of his face goes ruddy, and his dark pupils suddenly outweigh the blue-green irises circling them. But he remains completely still.

"It's okay." I enthuse. And though I'm not sure how bedroom eyes are supposed to look, I offer him my best attempt. "Show me where you've wanted to touch me."

Hesitation hangs thickly in the sparse air between us. But after a pause, his arms shift. Hands slide inch by inch down my back, stilling when they're planted firmly on the swell of my rear. I hum at the sensation, but refuse to let arousal resurface too vigorously within me. Not even as they move again, palms shifting lower until they've cleared my skirt. Skin meets feverish skin, only lingering for a heartbeat before slipping beneath the fabric. Henry's gaze is hot, commanding, and focused solely on mine as he trails steadily up the backs of my thighs. The breath draws from his lungs when he reaches the unclad curve of my ass, likely intending to push on to the perimeter of my panties.

But he finds none.

The body beneath me locks. Every one of his limbs goes rigid, including his fingers. I have to bite back a delightful gasp at how they dig sharply into the pillowy flesh of my cheeks. Features going stiff as the rest of him, his mouth falls open ages before he finds his tongue.

When he does, he speaks with caution. "Rosie, are you not wearing any…?"

I savor the state of him for a tantalizing while, then allow my head to loll. "You think I have so little class that I'd actually go on a date with you not wearing underwear?" Gracefully slipping off of him, I walk with a skip in my step to the bedroom door. Stopping when I reach the open threshold to peer over my shoulder. "It's a thong. See?"

I grab the hem of my skirt and lift it. High enough that the lacy white strips crowning my rear are visible, even with their minuscule size. Erica had assured me I would be thanking her later, which I most certainly would. Because the look on Henry's face is one I'll never forget. Now propped on his elbows, his lips are parted. Eyes flared so wide, the whites of them rival his paled skin. So much for ruddy, any trace of the blood responsible for coloring his cheeks has since drained—likely to supply something more *important*.

"Come on," I say perkily, letting the navy fabric flow back into modest place as I enter the hallway. "Don't wanna keep Lewis waiting!"

At the top of the staircase, I halt to listen intently. The most pained, unearthly groan ever to grace my ears echoes from my open bedroom. Followed by the sound of something heavy falling limp against the spring mattress.

I smirk in triumph. Payback is a *bitch*.

Chapter 24

After cleaning the glass remains from the sink and giving Henry ample time to compose himself, the two of us ventured to the Fennick house to meet Lewis. More specifically, to meet Lewis's plus-one, who was waiting for us in the driveway. *Beside* the fully functional Grand Safari, which now sat immaculate and ready for the road after weeks of Henry's efforts paying off. But as good as it looked, the pair standing at its front bumper looked even better.

Presley was even cuter than Lewis had described all these weeks. Even if one didn't consider his tall stature, gorgeous bronze skin, and remarkably put-together style for a young college man, all it took was speaking to him for a few brief minutes to understand how Lewis fell. On top of all that, he'd been more than enthused to meet his boyfriend's overzealous best friend. Even after I'd all but tackled him with a running hug before saying hello.

"Did Lewis tell you about the time he snuck me out of detention by slipping laxative in our P.E. coach's Ultimate Orange?" I ask him after proper introductions, bouncing giddily on the balls of my feet.

A stunning smile breaks out across Presley's face. "He did *what?*"

Lewis, who's standing beside us, rubs his flustered cheek in embarrassment. He's adorably overdressed in a button-up and khakis, contrasting Presley's faded jeans and flannel—opened to showcase a tight-fitted undershirt stretched over lean muscles. If I'd known that the geeks in Lewis's chat group looked a *fraction* as good as the one before me,

I would've leapt to tag along all those times he extended the invitation.

"I'll fill you in," I assure him before grabbing my friend's wrist. "But first, excuse us for a minute?" I drag Lewis to the end of the driveway, out of Presley's earshot, as I whisper authoritatively. "Care to explain yourself?"

Lewis frowns. "Explain what?"

My gaze narrows to a glare. "Presley."

His chest goes tight before he timidly remarks, "You said you wanted to meet him, I just thought—"

I cut him off with an arched brow. "You told me you were dating another computer geek…You didn't tell me he was AC Slater's long-lost twin!" I exclaim in a hush. "How the hell did you pull that off?"

Every ounce of tension drains from him, blue-green eyes lighting up as he glances at his boyfriend, who's now locked in conversation with Henry by the hood of the Grand Safari. "I know, right? I always told you he was better looking than Zack Morris."

"You better not screw this up." I wiggle my finger at him, a smirk pulling my lips. "That pact we made about dying virgins? I'm giving you permission to break it. *Immediately*."

"Same goes for you, *Angel Face*." Lewis mocks. "And for the record, I'll pass on all the gory details when my older brother ends up porking you."

The implication turns my cheeks pink, but I mask it with mischief. "What makes you think he didn't when we were upstairs in my bedroom just now? Oh, and by the way, you were right. You really did draw the *short* straw." I raise a fist to my face, pumping it in time with my tongue protruding the inside of my cheek.

He shoves my shoulder with a disgusted chuff. "Whatever."

"Do you wanna smell my breath to prove it?" I tug the sleeve of his shirt as he starts up the driveway. "I was going to rinse, but I kinda like the way it lingers—"

"*Ahlalalalala!*" He trills with hands over his ears, hardly rivaling my laughter as we rejoin our dates.

Dates. I grin like a fool.

"Your parents didn't press about all of us going out tonight?" I ask Henry, chancing a look at the house's windows.

"They're at a church thing." He says, casually retreating to the open garage as my focus returns to Lewis.

"And they didn't force you along?" I question.

"I just told them that I would be doing some important computer science work with a friend," Lewis nudges Presley, drawing a devious smile from his counterpart. "Which is *almost* the complete truth."

"We do have a few hours to kill before the movie," I prop my hands on my hips. "What's the plan?"

Lewis rubs the back of his gelled hair. "Well, Presley and I were gonna head to a tech fair at one of the downtown shops."

I raise my brows, my tone dry as the desert air. "How…exciting."

"Don't worry." He assures. "You and Preppy over there have other plans."

My head tilts as I watch him pull a set of keys from his khaki pocket, then tap the red hood of the Grand Safari.

"Wait," my eyes flicker between the pair. "If you guys are taking that, how are Henry and I supposed to get anywhere?"

"Heads-up!"

I twist in the direction of Henry's voice a split-second before something black and heavy is tossed my way. Reflexively grabbing it mid-air, the hard material catches stiffly in my hands. The air in my lungs freezes when I discern what it is.

A helmet.

Henry mounts his '81 Harley as he pulls on one of his own. Shaded behind its dark visor, he coaxes me with a nod over his denim-clad shoulder. "Coming?"

A *prior* heads-up would've been preferable, especially with my choice of undergarments.

I must've spent ten minutes trying to tuck my skirt around my thighs in a manner that wouldn't involve public nudity while riding full throttle on the back of Henry's sporty motorcycle. Even so, the rouse I feel as air whips around us and Albuquerque streets pass in kaleidoscopic blurs was worth all the surprise in the world. That, *and* getting to hug Henry so close. Heavy wind pelts us as we navigate from city lanes to the highway leading only he-knows-where—another thing he'd wanted to keep a surprise.

The dry, bush-speckled hills roll on in paralyzed waves, forested crests of the Sandia Mountains grazing the sky beyond them. Existing this raw and liberated is beyond foreign, amplified by the constant roar of the engine. Its sheer power purrs beneath us in a strong vibrato. Realizing my taut hips are growing numb with the pressure, I tighten my hold on Henry's waist to shift my underside against the leather seat—

Oh. *Oh*...

I recognize the sensation instantly. The gentle fizz courses through my groin and lower belly. A feeling I had experienced countless times in my life, and only once in this particular manner.

It's no ATV, but close enough.

Assuring my fingers are laced in a death grip to secure myself, I let my hips rock ever so gently. Quickly discovering an angle that sends my back arching and my eyes shifting out of focus. Incessant vibrations pummel my clit, challenging the beat of my heart and speed of the bike as the surrounding desert continues to blur in a beige vertigo. Resting my helmet against Henry's shoulder blade, I bite my lip as the thrumming inside me crescendos with more intensity than I could ever manage with my own fingers in this little time. Seconds tick by, the pleasure coursing so deep that I can no longer discern where I end and the seat begins. There's no plateau. No slow build. There's only the unrelenting bind of euphoria dragging me higher and higher until it throws me over the edge at a merciless velocity.

I can only pray that Henry is incapable of hearing the moan I expel over the thunderous wind. Everything stacked—the speed, the throbbing that grips my deepest insides in rhythmic pulses, the fact that I'm quite literally holding onto another person for dear life as I come—it all makes for the most heavenly release I think I've ever experienced. Gasping for breath, I smile as my body relaxes against Henry's in the fuzzy afterglow. Soothed by the still-humming vibrations between my thighs. And suddenly, I don't care how long it takes us to arrive where we're going.

In fact, we can't get there slow enough.

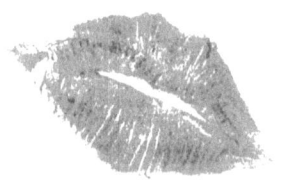

Chapter 25

I manage another three orgasms by the time Henry's motorcycle slows to a stop at a lookout site off the highway. By now, we're elevated enough to see acres beyond the forest. Bordered by steep rock faces and hillsides, the pavement beneath us bleeds to gravel where a small clearing sits lined with decrepit wooden fencing. His mighty engine cuts as he drops the kickstand, the growl giving way to a serene quiet that feels jarring after so long without it. I step off the bike first, my legs wobbling the moment I have my weight on them—making me reach for Henry's shoulder to steady myself.

"Pretty intense, right?" He asks, helping me reclaim my balance before dismounting.

I'm certain he's referring to my first ride on a motorcycle and… *not* the actual reason my knees are weak.

"Yeah, intense." I breathlessly agree. We both remove our helmets before I steal a glance around the barren lookout. "So, care to tell me why you brought us here?"

He grins, leading me by the hand to the chest-level—for me, anyway—wooden barrier on the crest of a steep drop-off. I suck in a breath of thin air when I stop at the perimeter's edge. Tall trees hundreds of feet beneath offer a panoramic view of the hills and desert beyond. Albuquerque sprawls like a map before us, nestled below behind a blue-tinted hue of distance. But greatest of all is the view of the sky. Wide open and clearer than I'd ever seen it within the confines of the bustling city miles below.

"Wow..." I breathe, stepping on the lowest link of the fence to peer farther. "Henry, this is amazing."

"This is my favorite place to be alone." He settles next to me, my elevation putting us at roughly the same height. Focus dropping to where the terrain curves out in a forested pass, he cups his hands to his face before letting out a deafening, joyous scream. The noise echoes in declining layers as he shoots me an enthused look. "Try it. Anything you want."

My smile draws tight in mischief. Bringing my hands to my mouth as he had, I inhale deeply before shouting, "*I'm horny!*"

I giggle as my distant voice loops it back again and again.

Henry lets his head fall. Then, shakes it in disapproval I'm not remotely convinced is genuine. "Rosie..."

"You said *anything*." I tease, stepping down to lean on the wooden barrier beside him. "But, really, how did you ever find this place?"

Despite the revelry, his ardor dims at the question. "It's not exactly a fun story."

I curiously blink to affirm that I want to hear it, regardless.

Henry hesitates, fixating on the view before expelling a defeated sigh. "It was probably three years ago. All of us were home one night. I was in my room, alone."

I tilt my head at him with a smirk. "Thinking of a certain someone up the street?"

"I was..." Affection pulls his mouth, then falters just as quickly. "But I was also trying to avoid my father. He was drinking more than he usually did after a bad day. Eventually, he started yelling at Mom, which wasn't anything out of sorts. But after a while, Lewis joined in, shouting for him to get away from her." His voice lowers. "It wasn't until I ran to the living room that I heard the whips."

Dread clenches my throat, and I have to press my lips tight to keep them from quivering.

Gaze narrowed at the pass below, he continues, "I didn't think to call for help, I just knew I needed to get the belt out of his hand. So I attacked him." His fingers flex against the wooden rail. "I wanted to *kill* him, but Mom was begging me to stop. He got me against a wall, almost strangled me to death. Told me that if I ever touch him again, Mom, me, *and* Lewis were as good as dead."

"Henry…" I place a gentle hand on his arm. Any words of aid coming up short.

He gives an indignant huff. "It wasn't just what he did, Rosie. It was how everyone acted when it was over. He went back to drinking, Mom finished her chores for the night, and Lewis locked himself in his room. It was like nothing happened." His breaths grow labored, but slow when he pauses to compose himself. "I just got on my bike and drove. I didn't care about coming home or where I ended up. All I wanted was to get away from him. Eventually, I ended up here." Vibrant blue-green eyes drift over the miles in front of us. "I just stood here and screamed for hours. I didn't stop until the sun came up. Then, I went home…and pretended nothing happened, just like the rest of them."

My grip tightens around his bicep. "You couldn't have stopped what he did. Some people are just bad, and angry, and there's nothing you can do to help it."

Henry's jaw flexes. "What if I'm one of them?"

I lean closer to peer at his quelled face. "What?"

His brows draw tight, focus flickering everywhere but me. "God, what kind of person almost beats a kid to death because he made some fucked up threat?"

Staying quiet, my gaze falls to the scars marking the protruding knuckles of his right hand.

"I don't like what I did to Will Guerrero, Rosie. But once I started, I couldn't stop. Because every time I thought about letting up, I imagined him and the rest of those assholes doing what he promised they would to Lewis. If what happened kept them from ever *thinking* of touching my brother, then I'd do it again." He swallows hard, then lowers his chin. "Does that make me bad?"

My heart breaks at the pain in his tone. I keep mine soft as I say, "It makes you a good brother."

"What about a good *man*?" He scoffs. "Look at everything I put you through. All because I wanted your attention and was too fucking afraid to say it out loud." A tense silence falls, only broken by the rattle of his shaky breaths. Finally, he looks my way. Rinsing me in absolute sorrow as he takes my hands and declares, "I'm sorry, Rosie. For all of it."

It's as if his touch becomes a relic of sheer contrition. And the longer his skin lingers against my own, the more I realize. Maybe I hadn't been waiting for that sorry. Maybe all I needed was a promise that he wasn't all I believed him to be. Some break in his riveted shield to allow enough room for sincerity, remorse, and above all, honesty. Everything I'd spent my years believing he was incapable of. But perhaps I was wrong. The real *him* had always been there, made to hide, just as I had.

And now, I see him. Clear as the open sky. Sound as a promise.

"I understand if that's not enough," his fingers tighten around mine. "But you need to hear it. I can't go the rest of my life taking the people I love for granted. If I do, I'll end up just like my father."

My response comes with every ounce of certainty I feel. "Henry, you are *nothing* like your father."

I can tell the remark cracks his shield, but his unbelieving face doesn't give. "How can you know?"

Like a woman possessed, I release his hands to slip my palms over his shoulders. "Because I would never do this if you were."

I lift to my toes, then press my lips to his.

And suddenly, this is no longer a salvageable day away from our parents. Nor an afternoon removed from responsibilities, occupational or spiritual. The moment his body connects with mine, it becomes a mark in time. For Henry, the conception of certitude that his chasing had paid off. For me, the cremation of what I'd built him to be in my head. Though, unlike with Val, there's no immediate surge as I initiate the kiss. Not some all-encompassing flame that engulfs me like the desert heat. This, in combination with Henry's lack of reaction, sends a hesitant chill down my spine. But despite it, my lips hold steadfast.

Then, matching our breaths, his hands are slipping around my waist. He dips to accommodate my height and returns the kiss with all the passion an adolescence of yearning can devise.

It's only when he pulls me impossibly closer that I begin to feel it. As if his desires are being poured into me through our connected lips, they no sooner become my own. My skin prickles at the intensity of whatever this intrinsic sensation might be. I foolishly assume it can't get more profound, then relish how every perfect moment beyond doing so proves me wrong. Despite my closed eyes, I swear I can picture us like a spectator from above. The impassioned drive intermixing with an urge that doesn't seem like it entirely belongs to me—the urge to smile, inflamed with the fierce burn of pride.

When we separate, we do it slowly. My cheeks flushing bright red as our gazes meet in consummation after such an act. The familiarity of his emerald-speckled irises evokes memories of the years between us. The nearness of how we'd grown from children to young adults, and the animosity that interposed us all the while.

But I blink, and now we're here.

There's a heavy pause before Henry's face splits into a grin only matched by the one he'd given me that night on the Ferris wheel. Hesitancy forgone, I return the expression. My whole body turns weightless beneath his gaze—a feeling that's made real when his hands abruptly slip beneath my thighs to lift me. I squeal at the sudden motion, wrapping my legs around his hips and laughing like a fool as he spins us, peppering my face with kiss after kiss. Short ones that christen my jaw. My cheeks. Even my nose.

Until he captures my lips again, *that one* he lets linger.

Keeping track of time had been the last thing on my mind. But when I finally remember that we have plans, long shadows are beginning to cast from the surrounding trees.

Henry and I are lounging on one of the horizontal rock faces bordering the lookout's edge, the view below holding us captive. I'm resting with my back to his chest as he holds me, dipping his head to press slow kisses along the side of my face and neck. I'd stopped counting them after the number exceeded the hundreds, but he was yet to be satisfied, having assured me that he needed to catch up on all the time he *should've* been doing this.

"You know we have to leave soon," I say softly, humming when his lips graze a sweet spot on my neck. "Lewis and Presley'll worry."

The huff he expels tickles my skin. "Like they aren't sucking face behind all those nerds' backs as we speak?"

Every muscle in my body stiffens, and I hastily pull away to peer at him. I hadn't questioned Lewis about whether Henry was aware of everything. For no reason other than I felt that it wasn't my place to mention such. Reluctance crawls sharply up my spine as I ask, "You know?"

The question doesn't faze him, save for the incredulous glint in his eyes. "Know what? That Lewis is gay?"

Shock and relief alike rinse me of fear. "When did he tell you?"

Henry laughs. "Shit, if anything, *I* told *him*. He never talked about girls he liked. Never asked me for dating advice." He shakes his head in affection. "You were a pretty good indicator, too. Years of the two of you spending all that time together, and he never tried anything? Yeah, fucking right."

Damn, the sentiment was verbatim what Val had suggested. It almost makes me want to laugh. Was it so unfathomable for a girl and a boy to be friends, and friends only? Or had Lewis simply mastered the art of fooling everyone into thinking otherwise for his own self-preservation? Whatever the case, it makes my heart ache for him all the more, but seeing him as happy as he was this afternoon? I had to believe it was worth the uphill battle—a battle he might never be free of fighting.

"Point is," Henry continues, pulling me closer against him. "Let's enjoy our time while we still have it."

Sorrow gouges me at the idea that, after this evening, we'd have to go back to our routine of avoiding each other at all costs. But I don't let it hover, sooner preoccupying myself with the sight before us.

"I love it up here." I breathe. "If I have a shit day, or if I'm ever acting like...not myself, promise you'll bring me back?"

"I promise." He gently nuzzles my temple. "So long as *you* promise that, if I'm ever not myself, you do this."

He guides my chin toward him with a finger, then kisses me deeply on the lips. My pulse jumps like it's still our first, and I'm left beaming when he pulls away with a smile.

I hum in time with the buzz of my heart. "That's all it takes, huh?"

"It's a step above daydreaming about our future. God knows I've done enough of that."

"Really," I eye him cautiously. "Care to share?"

He twists a gentle finger around the jaw-length strands of my bangs. "When stuff got too heavy, it always helped thinking about us grown up. In a home where I'd run my own garage, and you'd write your books. It'd be just you and me." His mouth quirks. "And our three babies."

"*Babies?*" I startle, unable to hold back a scoff. "Henry, you realize we've been dating for less than an afternoon?"

"Yeah, but I've spent a thousand afternoons planning it out."

I sigh, my uncertainty melting as I entertain the fantasy. "I can barely keep up with my nephew on his own. We're not having three."

"Two, then." He amends, then relents as I pierce him with a hounding glare. "Fine, we can stop at one. But only if it's a girl."

My frown lifts. "You want a little girl?"

He nods, and there's a gleam in his eyes I'm only half-certain the light of the falling sun is responsible for. "Growing up watching what the church fed girls like you made me sick. I wanna have one so I can teach her that it's all bullshit, and she can be anything she wants."

Fuck. It's more effort to keep from lying down on the rocks with my legs open while insisting I give him that child *immediately* than I'd ever admit. But the irony of his unserious proposition grounds me. "That's a little funny, since I've yet to hear what kind of say *I* have in our future. Do I even get one?"

"Of course you do." He exchanges his delighted smile for a mischievous one. "I'll let you name her."

I slap his shoulder with a chuff that reads twice the offence I truly feel, then lace my fingers with his. "How about we stick to right now? Hell, we've been in each other's lives for years, and I feel like I know hardly anything about you."

"What do you wanna know?" He questions warmly.

I blow an angled puff that ruffles my bangs. "I don't know…Do you have any close friends?"

"Close? Not really. A couple of my roommates were in the same program as me, but I mostly keep to myself." He pecks the side of my head. "Used to, anyways."

I grin, but it slips as a more pressing question comes to mind. "How many girls have you been with?"

His gaze falls to our entwined fingers. "Dated, or slept with? Because those are two different numbers."

My chest tightens. "Slept with?"

"Six. And of those, three were girlfriends."

Admittedly, it was less than I had been anticipating. "Even with all your high school hookups?"

He chuckles. "I guess that depends on what you mean by 'slept with.' I never went all the way with most of them. And even with the stuff we did do, I was the one getting them off, not the other way around. Besides, none of the actual relationships lasted longer than a few months."

"Should that worry me?"

His eyes flicker delightfully over my face. "It shouldn't. Considering the reason they all ended is because none of them were you."

I blush in the glow of the setting sun. "What girl gave you your first?"

Half-smirking, he tilts his head in lieu of a shrug. "Phoebe Cates."

My lashes flutter as I narrow a playful look at him. "*I meant*, who did you lose your virginity to?"

For the first time since his apology, I watch the joy dissipate from his features. "Faye Collins."

"Oh, right…" I avert my gaze, apprehension gripping me. "You probably don't wanna talk about it."

"It's okay. It was a long time ago."

The invitation extended, I push myself to ask, "What was it about her that drew you?"

"She was the one who made the first move. And, I was only fourteen." He releases a slow breath. "Faye was really…"

"Persistent?"

He dips his chin. "*Insistent*. And I don't just mean the physical stuff. I thought she actually cared about me."

My brows knit. "And you cared about her?"

"Yeah, I did. I trusted her when she promised it would only stay between us. But when we eventually got caught, she had no problem spilling *everything* we'd done. It felt like everyone in the world was suddenly seeing me naked." Affliction weaves his soft words. "Obviously, everyone wanted to believe the pastor's niece when she said I'd 'influenced' her. Nobody bothered to ask whose idea it had been in the first place."

The scandal resurfaces in my mind. The way he'd been barred from ever returning to Crosspoint after the uproar it created. All this time, everyone had trusted Faye over the real victim in the matter.

Myself, included. "I'm sorry, Henry."

His contentment returns. "Don't be. It's not like I ever complained about never having to go back to that place."

"Is that when you stopped believing?" I ask, then realize I've overstepped. "I mean, *do* you still believe?"

Henry shakes his head, though I get the hint it's not a complete denial. "I don't really think about it, especially after being around my father all those years. Always bitching about people who don't adhere to his values, just to turn around and make our house a warzone every day. After so long, all of it started to seem as fake as he was."

"I get it," I say, timidly peering at him through my fringe. "That's when you started acting out?"

He offers a light shrug. "I think at first, I was just taking out my anger. But after a while, I realized..." His voice dims with his eyes, a sadness shining through them clearer than I've ever seen in our lives. Releasing my hand, his own smooths out the fabric of my skirt, stopping at the curve of my hip. He rubs a tender thumb over the spot before regaining enough conviction to quietly remark, "If he were always focused on me, he wouldn't have the energy for Mom or Lewis."

I stare up at him, the blood beneath his touch cooling with realization.

Every missed class. Every suspension. Every time a police officer dragged him home in the middle of the night. His behavior was never the feat of a rebellious teen with no decency. No, for every one scar Lewis bore from growing up in their household—physical *or* emotional—Henry was marked with a hundred more. Each a sacrifice for the better of his mother and little sibling.

"Even Will Guerrero?" I reluctantly ask.

He nods once. "Like I said, I'm not proud of it. But I didn't care what was waiting for me after the fact."

A desire for clarification pulls at my mind. "Earlier, you said when it was happening, you felt like you couldn't stop. What made you?"

He swallows thickly in what can only be lethal recollection. But despite it, the corner of his lips tugs. "You really wanna know?" He asks, then sighs when I tilt my head in approval. "It was you and Lewis."

I remain silent, but his furious eyes that day stare me down from the depths of my deepest memories.

"Seeing Lewis was bad enough, but I knew he was scared *for* me. You?" Concern notches lines between his brows. "You looked scared *of* me. I knew that look, because I'd seen it on my mom's face a hundred times when my father…"

He doesn't finish, but there's no need to.

Sensing him slipping away, I grab Henry's face with gentle hands and press a soft kiss to his lips. Sanctifying my earlier promise. It works, the light in his eyes returning as I pull back—a subject change in order.

"Lizzy," I say.

He stares in obvious confusion. "What?"

"Our make-believe daughter." I clarify. "Let's name her Lizzy."

His cheeks warm beneath the pads of my thumbs. "Lizzy…I love it."

"And speaking of prejudice, answer me this," I raise my chin at him. "Was it you who made Landon Hemmings apologize for calling me ugly?"

Henry's brows jump, then tweak as he smirks. "Maybe."

I lean into him as he resumes dotting my cheek with slow kisses. "What did you ever do to scare him like that? He looked like he witnessed the coming of the anti-Christ."

"I just pulled him aside before class and told him he messed up. He got the hint and agreed to say sorry on my terms." Henry explains. Then, I feel his mouth tug with a smile. "After changing his pants, anyways."

My eyes roll. "And the part about me being the prettiest girl in school?"

Kisses travel up my jaw. "Well, you were."

"And the part about him being insecure about his small penis?"

Henry snorts against my ear. "Alright, *that* was just for fun."

I can't suppress a laugh. "So you had no issue soliciting other people for apologies, but it took you this long to give me one of your own?"

"The wait was worth it." He declares, giving me a final, firm peck on the cheek. "Okay, Angel Face, my turn for questions."

"Ask away."

He takes a thoughtful pause. "Was today your first kiss?"

A conflicting emotion needles beneath my skin, bringing with it a slight frown. "No."

"Oh..." He remarks flatly. "Who was it with?"

"Nobody you know," I answer, and leave it at that.

"Alright, miss cryptic. What about your stories? I get the hint that erotica isn't just a hobby, you wanna make a career out of it?"

As raw and exposed as Henry had been with me these past hours, there isn't a shred of doubt remaining that I could trust him with my biggest secret. A proud smile splits my face. "Well, I sort of *already* have. That dirty magazine you caught me with? I write for it."

His features slacken like he's been dealt a blow to the chest.

I tell him everything. From stumbling upon that first *Wild Thang* issue on an outing with Lewis, and becoming too intrigued by their request for submissions to resist. To writing my ticket in, inspired by Pastor Morgan's little chat with me in his office. To Ruth calling me to the studio when their new demographic requested that M.R. return and deliver them another lewd fantasy from a female's perspective. I even tell him about Val, and how she'd essentially turned into the closest girl friend I've ever had. Upon concluding, I leave him gaping.

"Hey," I hold up my hands in submission. "You wanted the *real* Rosie. Take her or leave her, she'll be writing porn either way."

He lets out a hollow laugh, bracing an arm on the rock face as if he'd fall over dead without the support. "First off, I'm taking her. And second...*fuck*."

"What? Are you appalled?"

"No." He stares at me, transfixed. "It's just, with your mom and Crosspoint..."

"Yeah, it's a catastrophe in the making. But I'm in it 'til it's over." My gaze wanders away. "Being M.R. is worth it. To the rest of the world, she's more than just a loudmouth who can't hold her tongue to spare her own life."

"Hey, that *loudmouth* is my girlfriend. And I wouldn't take her any other way." There isn't an ounce of sarcasm in his tone.

"Ah," I play along. "So, 'you admire me for my impertinence?'"

"I admire you because you *bite back*." He asserts with the faintest hint of flirtation.

"'You may as well call it impertinence.'"

"I mean it, Rosie. Everyone at that fucking church has been trying to wear you down since day one, but you never let them. Never laid down to take what they say you deserve." His eyes soften. "And despite it, you're still innocent."

An incredulous chuckle escapes me. "Now you're starting to sound like everyone at Crosspoint."

"Not like that. I mean, they haven't broken you." He explains tenderly. "Being around Lewis. Writing your stories. Whatever it is, what they've done hasn't ruined right now. Some of us aren't that lucky."

I study him silently, finding myself drawn to the way the wind sweeps a few tendrils of lightened hair falling over his forehead. But behind his tough exterior, I know he's speaking from grim, unforgiving experience.

"If anyone ever took that from you, it…" His jaw tightens, as does his grip on my waist. "It would destroy me."

I slide fingers into his layered hair, ignoring the rush it sends through me as I speak with absolute certainty. "You don't need to worry. If it's my virtue you're concerned with, the only person I'd let change me is sitting right here."

The look on his face melts my core, intensifying as he gently removes my hand to kiss it. "Just say the word."

My thoughts go ablaze when I realize what he's insinuating. I'd been so fixated on the relational side of things that I barely allowed myself to consider what the future held for us physically. Even with the stunt I'd pulled back in my room, or the years I'd spent writing the idea of it into reality. Now, the real thing is finally in front of me. I never thought it would make me as nervous as it does.

With a careful cadence, I ask, "Are you anticipating anything in that department? Like, off the bat?"

His brows narrow at me. "Of course not. We move at your pace, nothing sooner than you're ready for."

It helps ease the tension, but I still feel a ping of guilt that my fears may come at the expense of his desires. I fixate on the stones around us, forcing an uncomfortable laugh. "I know that's a little unconventional, given my job. But if you say so."

"Look at me." He requests, rubbing gentle circles into the fabric of my white button-up as I comply. "I don't want to be one of your stories, Rosie. I want what we have to be real. Just for us." He tilts his head, donning a smirk that's as handsome as the rest of him. "Even if you are the craziest girl I've ever met."

With the apprehension finally lifted, I rest my head on his shoulder, allowing his citrusy scent to console me. "What can I say? I'm full of surprises."

"Any other confessions?" He asks, tone jovial with a hint of sarcasm. "Dead bodies in your box spring? Telekinetic abilities?"

I grimace slightly, feeling my inner debauchery rise and spill over before I can contain it. "Riding up here on the back of your motorcycle, I came four times."

His body tenses as it had on my twin mattress hours ago. After a long pause, he chuckles deeply. "*Full* of surprises."

"Told you." This time, it's me who peppers his jaw with kisses.

"Damn," he marvels breathlessly. "Four?"

"What kind of prudes have you been with to set your standards so low?" I pull back to quirk a brow at him. "My record is forty. In a *single hour*."

His face pales, and I can't help but notice the way he shifts his groin away from where it had been pressed snug against me.

I don't let him get far, nuzzling his neck with a giggle. "Rethinking your promise that we'll only have sex when we're ready yet?"

"Yep."

Chapter 26

"He's so amazing! And romantic! And sweet! And genuine! And handsome! And he's such a good kisser! And he talks to me like I'm all he's ever wanted! And he holds me like he never wants to let me go! And I can't *believe* I ever hated him!"

I don't take a single breath through my rushed declaration. But when I finally do, it comes out as a blissful sigh. I wrap Henry's jacket tightly around myself before dipping my nose to savor its scent. Who knew that motor oil and citrus would become my favorite combination?

"Settle down, there. You know I came from the same womb as him?" Lewis counters, playfully tugging at the denim collar too big for my neck. Henry had insisted I wear it after night fell, the November dusk arriving with an ungodly chill. I really need to start bringing a jacket of my own. Maybe…

Nah. His is better.

I flutter my lashes like a lovestruck schoolgirl, thinking of nothing better to occupy our wait in line for the drive-in's concessions. "Lewis, if someone had told me three months ago that I'd be falling for Henry, I would've begged God to strike me dead where I stood. But it's really happening."

I can tell he wants to take another jab at my shameless ardency. But instead, he matches my joyous expression. "I know what you mean."

"How was the tech fair?" I ask, despite the incessant urge to keep gushing about my own romance.

Lewis bounces giddily on the balls of his feet before leaning close to whisper the answer. "We were just wandering the aisles at first. But after a while, Presley pulled me into one where there weren't any people. Then kissed me, right there under the ribbon cables!"

"That is so sexy," I say in a hush.

His voice shifts an octave higher as a broad smile splits his face. "*I know!*"

I take a deep breath of the cold night air, my cheeks pink beneath the heated lights. "Lewis, do you realize what's happening here? We both found our people…"

We look at one another, then simultaneously devolve into squeals. Grabbing hold of the other to jump in unison like star-struck fangirls who'd just been pulled backstage at a Bon Jovi concert. Which earns us a few odd looks, but we couldn't care less. We'd been waiting too long to enjoy this feeling. Let alone getting to experience it *together*.

A little over an hour later, we're settled among rows of parked cars as Henry and I sit on one of the elongated wooden seats lining each spot poised for a vehicle. Occasionally passing the popcorn bucket between each other, completely enthralled by the massive screen overlooking the clearing. Nala had just rediscovered Simba after years apart, and neither of us could look away. Parked behind us is the rear-facing Grand Safari, which Lewis and Presley had disappeared inside a good few scenes ago. Luckily, Henry had invested in retractable curtains along the backmost windows, making it the equivalent of a bedroom on wheels. Its red frame rocks slightly in the corner of my vision, pulling Henry and me from the action, or rather, *toward* it.

"I guess you were right about the whole 'room to lie down' perk, weren't you?" I ask.

He grins mischievously. "I guess we'll find out when it's *our* turn for a little privacy."

My tone shifts a gear lower. "Why would we need to wait for privacy?"

He takes the not-so-discreet invitation. Our lips meet, and I waste no time sliding my hand up the soft fabric of his Henley before running it through his gorgeous hair. Something I'd caught myself doing quite often in the hours since our first, as if my body was settling into a language I'd never spoken before—but found myself remarkably versed in.

"Rosie?" A familiar voice draws me from the high.

When I pull away from Henry, I'm met with the view of a smiling pale face framed by curly blonde hair. Stopped like she'd been strolling along before catching sight of our public display.

"Lynn!" I jump to greet her with a hug. Taking note of her modest dress when we part, putting two and two together. "You here with your family?"

She rolls her eyes. "Unfortunately. And my younger siblings won't stop screaming every time the hyenas are on-screen. I needed a smoke break." Her blonde brow raises at the seat behind me. "But whatever I just walked in on is *way* better."

"Oh!" Blushing, I nod over my shoulder. "Lynn, this is Henry. Henry, Lynn. She's a friend from Bible study."

I shoot the girl a coded grin, which she returns.

"You have a friend from Trinity Grace that *isn't* my brother?" Henry teases. "I'm impressed."

I scoff theatrically before elaborating for Lynn. "Henry is Lewis's older brother."

"Well," she muses. "Color me surprised."

"Don't be, I'm only dating him for his car." I tilt my head to the Grand Safari before smirking at Henry.

A look he reflects. "That's okay, I'm only dating you for your ass."

I shrug, twisting to eye the back of my flared skirt. "It is a nice one, isn't it?"

Lynn breaks into giggles, then sighs. "Please, for the love of all things holy, give me a reason not to go back to my family's car. I can bring you guys snacks? Just sit and act like I'm not here?" She pulls at the collar of her flaxen dress. "Or, if you two wanna get back to your porno, I can get a camera."

I hum in mock-debate, raising my chin as I wander back to where Henry sits. "What do you say, babe? Up for a threesome?"

His smirk melts away, voice softening to meet my ears alone. "You just called me 'babe.'"

My pulse jumps as I gently rake fingers through the natural highlights of his hair. "Do you prefer 'smartass?'"

"No," his hand finds my waist. "'Babe' is good."

"You know," Lynn's voice cuts through. "We could probably see the screen better if we sat in the back of this."

A handle clicks.

Panic grips me as I whirl to stop her. "Wait—!"

But I'm too late. The Grand Safari's backseat door is propped open by Lynn, who stands stiffly. Her wide, unblinking eyes are fixed on the interior—where Lewis is lying beneath Presley. From this angle, I can discern that they're still clothed, at the very least. But in the most compromising position imaginable as I hear them break from their heated kiss. Terror slithers up my spine and strikes the base of my neck with sharp, venomous fangs. Smoldering my veins with every thump of my rapid heart. Lynn remains unmoving as she stares for a single beat of it. Then another.

But on the third, I'm lunging for the door to close it with a powerful *slam*, nearly striking her through the haste. My ribs constrict my lungs so tightly, I fear they'll implode if I risk another breath. So I hold it...as I dare a look at Lynn's face.

It's entirely illegible, but her jaw trembles when she catches me staring. Amber irises momentarily dart to Henry at my rear. After a thick swallow, she retreats with uneven steps.

"I need to get back..." The excuse is barely a mutter, but it's all I hear before she's walking away at a brisk, startled pace.

My ponytail whips as I look to Henry. He's standing now, face twisted in the same horror that possesses me to make my next move.

"Lynn!" I take off in a run before I can even consider if it's the right way to handle this. Shuffling through the maze of cars and benches she's putting between us, I sprint to close the distance and snatch her wrist in a vice, yanking her to the perimeter.

"Rosie—!" She pulls against my hold, but I refuse to let go as we make it far enough to speak without someone overhearing.

"You can't tell anyone." I hush. Trying to phrase it as a command, but it comes out as a plea.

"Let *go* of me." She demands, tearing from my grip.

"Swear it." I don't care anymore if it's a beg. "Nobody can find out. Promise me, now!"

"Fuck, he's..." She lets out a disturbed laugh. "He shouldn't be at school. He shouldn't be anywhere near Trinity Grace."

The statement in and of itself isn't wrong, but I know she isn't referring to Lewis's safety. Tears sting my eyes as I open my mouth to respond, but she doesn't allow it.

"Did you know?" She pierces me with an accusatory glare. "When you helped me ask him out?"

"No," I answer honestly. "But I do now, and I don't care. Neither should you."

"You don't *care*?" She looks at me like I've just pleaded guilty to treason.

"As if you and I ever believed what our families preached about right and wrong?" I counter aggressively. "I'm pretty sure writing porn and grinding on a pole for money isn't acceptable by the Bible's standards, either."

"It's not about the Bible, Rosie. It's..." She pauses, eyes flaring as she sucks in a sharp gasp. Her already pale face turns a shade whiter as she steps back, fury morphing to terror as she holds shaky fingers to the edge of her lips. "I kissed him that night. I *kissed* him! Oh my God, does that mean I have it?!"

As if her rage had been syphoned into me, my jaw nearly unhinges at what she's implying. "What the *fuck* is wrong with you?!"

Looking as if she's about to retch, Lynn glares at me with red-hot fury. "Stay away from me. Both of you."

My teeth clench as I grab her wrist again. "You aren't going to say anything."

"You can't just tell me to—!"

"You *aren't* going to ruin his life." My fingers tighten. "Not when I can just as easily ruin yours."

Her narrow eyes widen in vicious understanding. "Like you have any room to threaten me? You filthy bitch."

She rips her arm free, no sooner disappearing into the labyrinth of vehicles. Incapable of thinking through the panic, I saunter back to where the Grand Safari remains parked. When I notice Henry in the driver's seat, I enter the passenger side and close the door tightly behind me, slicing away the cruel outside world.

"She saw us. She fucking saw us." I hear Lewis's stricken voice from the rear, finding him sitting with his head in his hands. His breaths are quick and shaky, despite Presley's hold on him.

"We don't know that she's going to tell anyone," Presley says, glancing hopefully at me.

I push aside any doubt. "She won't."

"How can you know that?" Lewis asks, raising tear-filled eyes.

"I know. She'd be a damn fool if she did." I assure, chancing a look at the eldest Fennick, whose jaw remains fixed. A mark of holding back fright for the sake of putting his brother at ease.

I want nothing more than to do the same.

"We shouldn't stay here." Henry finally declares. "Lewis, are you gonna be okay to take Presley home?"

Lewis sniffles, composing himself enough to nod.

"I'll meet you at the house, alright?" Henry's voice is calm, but the grim silence as he and I exit the car and trek hand-in-hand to his bike lays bare that he's anything but.

The quiet corner from my home is shattered with the roar of the Harley's engine, which Henry promptly cuts as he stops at the edge of the curb.

"Thanks for dropping me off down here," I say while dismounting. It was a solid idea to avoid any lashings from my mother. Figurative *or* literal.

As we remove our helmets, he tilts his head down the street. "I'll wait until you make it inside and drive around the block to my parents' house. Just to be safe."

I slip off his denim jacket to hand over, dread surfacing with the cold its absence leaves me in. "Henry, I'm..."

"Hey," he dons the returned article with a look that presents more hopeful than I suspect he feels. "Don't worry, I'm not leaving Lewis alone tonight. I'll make sure he's okay."

I nod, my lip quivering. "I never should've spoken to her, Henry. I had no idea she was going to..."

Fuck. If terror didn't succeed in drowning me, guilt would surely finish the job.

"It wasn't your fault," Henry promises.

Unable to discuss it further, I offer the closest semblance of a goodbye I can. "Please, just take care of him for me. I'll see you soon."

I try to step away, but his arm slips around my waist, pulling me back to the bike.

"Rosie, wait." The sadness holding his expression melts. "Before what happened...today was the happiest day of my life."

His words warm me so greatly, I almost think they're going to thaw the embalming fear...Almost.

"Mine, too." I lower my head to kiss him, letting this one linger—unsure how long it would be before I'd get to do it again.

And when it's over, I have to practically force my body out of his arms and onto the sidewalk leading home. Keeping a mental hold of his goodbye, only to mourn as it fades with each step I take in the direction of Lewis and my personal prisons. The dark, quiet street feels insubstantial beneath my shoes. As if it were a minefield he and I had been traversing all our lives, surviving without a single misstep after all these years. But something inside me screamed that tonight had been our first.

And, if we survived the fallout at all, it wouldn't be the last.

Chapter 27

I never imagined that watching two people have sex could be so… *unsexy*.

It wasn't as if I hadn't seen porn in my life, but today was most definitely my first time seeing it in live action. And despite the shoot only being half-over, I'm fairly certain I never want to see it again. Although, my contempt likely stems from the fact that the Deviant Devotee and Pastor Madman appeared far different in my head. The woman before me is a petite brunette I'd occasionally seen around *Wild Thang Studios*, going by the name of Roxy Rimmer—a performer bearing a frightening resemblance to me. If I were to get breast implants and obscene tattoos in the most questionable bodily locations, that is. And the actor portraying Pastor Madman—stage name Cummings, I was sure of it with all the times I'd caught him flirting with Val—appears less like a corrupt man of God and more like a college frat boy who tripped and fell into a clerical collar. Not entirely faithful, but I suppose religious accuracies were arbitrary in porn.

Roxy has him laid out on a wide wooden desk in the center of a set designed to look like that of a church's office. Cameras at varied angles fixate on tussling body parts as she violently rides him. Her theatric moans echo around the massive, foreign sound stage the rest of the crew resides in—myself, included. I bite back a wince at the brunette's roughness. Evidently, the two stars had a history, and even got into a full-on yelling match over a disastrous prior shoot before they finished makeup this morning. I had tuned out the argument after Cummings refused to stop throwing the word "klismaphiliac" at her.

R.J. stands beside me, all but purring at the sight. "Now *that* is what I call repentance."

He had pretty much hauled me onto the set over his shoulder when he found out I'd actually shown. Which, to be fair, I was as surprised by my own presence as he was. But Ruth had told me she would be at the new location for meetings regarding updated distribution plans since their video sales had increased, and I wanted to drop off my completed manuscript for the publishing agency as soon as possible. I'd opted to expand the church-dwelling tale that landed me my job in the first place, coincidentally enough. And I would be lying if I said there wasn't a morbidly curious part of me that wanted to see the fantasy that started all this play out in real time. But Ruth had yet to come downstairs, and Cummings wasn't exactly living up to his name.

I guess we're all leaving here dissatisfied, aren't we?

"An hour ago, they were at each other's throats. How can you have sex with someone who just threatened to castrate you with a flat iron?" I ask, my gaze trained on the jostling couple.

"I think you just described most God-fearing marriages, Virgin Mary."

It might be the first accurate statement ever to leave R.J.'s mouth. I even have a momentary urge to agree with him.

His cowboy hat dips as green eyes rake over me. "Not that you believe in waiting 'til marriage, right? Because the offer's still out if our writer wants to make a little actoral cameo for some extra pay."

And the urge is gone. "I like my job now, thanks."

"I never took you for a lady who settles. You know our stars get cash advances the day of the shoot? You could make in one hour what you make in three months writing those pornos of yours." He hums thoughtfully. "Probably more with your niche."

After so many weeks of enduring the man, I can't help but humor him when I get the chance. It makes for good entertainment despite the toll it takes on my faith in mankind. "And what niche do I have to offer?"

His body shifts in that dramatic way it does when he's about to pitch something with far too much passion and not nearly enough decency. "Picture this, Virgin Mary, it's 1850. And that hole between your legs? California!"

I stare at him, incapable of even pretending I've got the slightest clue as to what he's suggesting. "R.J., I'm pretty sure this is why Ruth hired *me* to write the porn. Narratives really aren't your thing."

"No, no, no. It's just a…what do you call it? Anal…orgy…"

"Analogy?"

"Doesn't matter. It means, in *this* world," he gestures wildly to the studio around us. "Virtue equals value. And I happen to know that every red-blooded man with a VHS player would sell his soul to watch a little doe-eyed gal get her cherry popped." He clicks his tongue. "You got all the equipment for the job. If our readers caught sight of you, they'd be ravenous for a peek under that skirt."

My stomach twists at the idea that someone's awkward, clumsy first time is somebody else's wildest fantasy. But I suppose I don't have much room to judge. Considering *my* fantasy is currently lying twenty feet away, verbally and physically beating the orgasm out of her co-star. "That doesn't exactly cater to my area of expertise."

"That's why they call it amateur, little lady. I've run the idea by Baby Ruth on more than a few occasions. Just say the word, and we'll make you a star."

At this point, his exploits are falling on deaf ears as I glance at the digital clock screwed to the high eastern wall. Fixed beneath one of the wide windows leading into what I assume to be the conference room Ruth is housed in. Porn shoots, to my surprise, take place at the same waking hour as any other workday. Meaning, I still have school to get to.

"Sorry, Guccione. I think I'll stick to writing." I drop the bag from my shoulder to remove the clipped collection of typewritten pages. "Listen, I have to get going. I need you to hand this off to the big lady upstairs. She's expecting it, and she'll have your balls if something happens to it."

"That woman's had my balls for the last twelve years." He takes it from me with a grimace. "At least, the one I got left. You'd be amazed how sturdy they make those platform heels. Built like a damn concrete pillar for no good reason."

I roll my eyes, then turn to make my escape.

"Consider the offer, Virgin Mary!" He calls after me. "Your pussy? *Gold!* Just gotta let us go digging!"

I almost growl in response. But the pained grunt that echoes across the set as Roxy Rimmer supplies Cummings his brutal end makes me cringe, instead.

Hours later, I'm finished with my classes and sitting cross-legged in the hall of Trinity Grace's tech department, waiting for Lewis to do the same. I've tried to be around him as much as possible in the week since the drive-in incident, just so he feels less on edge walking the same campus as Lynn. It's not much, but I'm more than happy to do it.

My *Holy Scriptures* notebook lies open in my lap. All the time I'd spent since our previous issue had gone to constructing my expanded pastor story and staying around Lewis at every opportunity, resulting in a complete drought of new prompts. I'd almost be proud of my new record for celibacy if it weren't impeding my responsibility to produce *Wild Thang*'s next piece. The page in front of me remains unmarked by the time the classroom doors start to swing open. But regardless, I jump up when Lewis exits into the now-flooding hallway.

"Hey, how was class?" I ask as he nears.

He doesn't reply. He doesn't even look at me as he passes.

My stomach drops when I notice how red his face is. Pace accelerating down the corridor, he keeps his limbs tucked tightly, as if trying to make himself as small as possible. A few obnoxious chortles pull my focus, coming from a small group of boys leaving the same room in a cluster, all shooting my friend conceited smirks.

No...*Fuck no.*

"Lewis!" I yell after him, practically plowing over the students intercepting us.

He doesn't look back. His quick strides shift into a jog as he dashes inside the nearest men's room, as if that's going to stop me. I push through the crowd and enter the bathroom without hesitation, stopping when I see Lewis bracing his frail weight on one of the sinks. Beside him, a pair of guys drying their hands gawk at me like I've just ascended from hell.

"*Out.*" I point to the door, ignoring their deprecating glances as they comply.

Lewis keeps his chin low as he asserts, "You can't be in here, Rosie."

"Tell me what's going on," I demand, stepping to the edge of the sink in the hopes he'll finally look at me.

He doesn't.

"Lewis..." I beg in a soft hush.

His chest swells heavily for a few long moments before he reaches into the bag at his feet and hands off a textbook. "They asked if they could borrow it."

I stare at the object, then open the cover with a shaky finger. My vision tunnels, peripherals fading to an inky black matched by scribbled marker over the otherwise pristine page.

FAGGOTS BURN IN HELL

"I told you she would say something." Lewis steps away, his back finding the side of a stall before sliding to the ground.

It takes all my effort not to crumble alongside him. "Maybe it was just them? We don't know how many people—"

"It isn't just the textbook, Rosie." He cuts me off. "Everywhere I've gone today, there were people moving seats. Hugging the walls to avoid me. Acting like I have some kind of disease."

That...*that* makes me crumble. I sink to the cold bathroom floor, keeping my jaw fixed until I find the right words. Words that will dull even a fraction of his turmoil. But they don't come.

"I can't stay here." His voice is barely a whimper. "What am I supposed to tell my parents?"

I rub a gentle hand up his arm. "We'll think of something. If anyone can spin a story, it's *me*."

He sniffles. "What happens when someone from Crosspoint hears? They'll tell my mom and dad. You know they will."

My throat tightens, but I force the question through. "Have you considered...telling them yourself?"

He takes a deep, unsteady breath. "I don't know. I *can't* know."

"I get that. Not completely, obviously, but I know how it feels to hide things that could ruin you." I squeeze the flesh beneath my palm. "You're the one who told me you can't live like this forever. Look what it's doing to you, Lewis. I would never tell you to do it if you weren't ready, but is living with this much pain worth it?"

There's a long silence. As if he's really, *truly* hearing me. "I'd lose everything."

"No, you wouldn't," I say firmly. "You'd never lose me. Or Presley, or Henry. We'll do anything for you."

"I know you would." He swallows hard. "That's what I'm most afraid of."

I pretend the statement doesn't shake me the way it does as I carefully pull him to his feet. "Let me worry about me."

We gather our things, and I take his hand, interlacing our fingers as he finally meets my gaze with foggy eyes. I offer a sad semblance of a smile as I lead him out of the restroom and through the halls until we're outside. I don't pay any mind to the people staring at us, challenging anyone who dares to impede our exit with a scowl. I love Lewis. I care about him more than anyone.

And he isn't safe here.

A fact I keep in mind as we step across the courtyard. All I want is to get off this damned campus before the ground opens and sucks us right into hell like everyone presumes it will. But the moment I see a flaxen glint in the corner of my vision, my feet all but scrape to a halt.

It's her. She's standing beside Rebecca and the other Bible study girls beneath one of the tall trees marking the center of the quad. Her back is to me, but the shake of tight blonde curls cascading down her back signals that she's laughing at something. She's fucking *laughing*.

"Rosie." There's fear in Lewis's voice, and I know he sees what I do. I pry my hand from his. "I'll meet you at the bus stop."

"*Rosie!*" Lewis repeats in a firm hush.

It doesn't stop me. Absolutely nothing can.

None of the girls notice my approach. At least, not until I'm grabbing Lynn by the collar to tug her away. Rebecca's confused babbling proves pointless as I drag her friend far enough so she isn't privy to my furious whispers.

"You *monster*." I hiss upon releasing Lynn, who stumbles to catch her footing with a gasp.

Horror flashes across her face for a single satisfactory moment. She opens her mouth, but mine bites faster.

"Why?" I demand a reason. "Why would you talk? You knew what would happen to him if you did."

"I don't know what you're talking about." She's breathless as she speaks. In shock or fear, I can't tell.

"*Lewis*," I say like I'm scolding a petulant child.

The laugh she expels is entirely hollow. "Like I'd have to say anything for people to catch on? Everyone already knows."

She's lying. I see it in the way her gaze darts everywhere but mine, quaking hands balling to fists at her sides.

"You're really brave talking about my friend like you didn't just fuck up his life." I step closer, speaking through gritted teeth. "Like *I* can't fuck up yours just as easily."

Her blonde brows tense. For the first time since I dragged her away, she looks me in my furious eyes. "Nice try. But you have secrets, too." She scoffs. "This shouldn't even be a problem between us! As if the things we hide are *remotely* comparable to what he did."

In a way, she was right. But she had it twisted. She and I chose our jobs. We chose the consequences that went with them. Lewis didn't choose who he loves. It was just him.

"So go ahead," she lifts her chin. "Tell everyone the truth. But you'll go down just as hard."

"Is this about that guy friend of yours, Rosie?" Rebecca calls from where the group remains. "You didn't know about all that when you invited him to our study, right? Because," her nose scrunches, silver braces flashing as her mouth tweaks in disgust. "Just...*ugh*."

I glare at her with a fire that incinerates any lingering respect for the people I'd considered friends. A heat that blazes when my focus shifts back to Lynn, who holds her head high like she has the upper hand. But indissoluble terror is seeping through her mask. She thinks she's calling my bluff. But in reality, she's begging me to stay silent through the dialect of vicious blackmail. I bite my tongue, feeling the weight of every rejective stare at once.

No, fuck this.

"You deserve them," I say, quiet enough so only she can hear. I scan the courtyard speckled with people who would burn Lynn at the stake if they knew the truth. "You deserve all of this."

Something behind her forged exterior gives. Although, I can't decipher if it's relief or a very different kind of fear. I can only hope it's the latter as I stride away, cutting scornfully through the watchful group.

"Careful, girls," Rebecca warns. "She's probably only upset because she's already got it."

I stop cold.

Laughing heartily with the others, she presses on, "Everyone knows you can't be around one of them without running a risk. Don't worry, Rosie. I'll pray for you when you and he are in the hospital knocking on Satan's—"

I turn on my heel, silencing her remark with the crack of my knuckles against wire and brackets.

Chapter 28

Academic suspension.

I had gotten off pretty easy, all things considered. At least Rebecca decided against pressing criminal charges after the incident was documented and supported by more than two dozen witnesses. Lynn had *miraculously* dissuaded her from the option while helping dab away the blood marking her navy sweatshirt, which had been the least surprising turn of the ordeal when all was said and done. The most? I now understand the kind of anger that induced Henry to assault Will Guerrero and get hauled away to juvie.

And there I'd been thinking I couldn't fall for him any more.

The lack of sleep I'd gotten last night leaves my eyes burning as I look down at my typewriter, warm as the early afternoon sun beaming from the window. But despite it, my insides feel frozen. Inspiration for the next issue runs dry in the wake of everything. The ache in my knuckles from striking Rebecca square in her braces doesn't help much, either. I type experimental first sentences, only to trash the page every single time. But I find myself thankful when a knock from the front door echoes up the staircase, breaking my slump as I trudge to answer it. Upon doing so, I instantly perk up.

Henry's hands rest in the pockets of his denim jacket, his mouth lifting in a smile when I appear. "Hi."

"Hi…" I repeat, my surprise must be evident enough to warrant explanation.

"I, uh—" He timidly glances beyond me. "I saw your mom's car was gone. Figured she was at work."

My cheeks flush. "She is."

Henry nods, gaze drifting to my hand. "Lewis filled me in."

Oh, the bruise. I flaunt the purple gash with a half-sorrowful, half-satisfied look.

"Damn." A proud grin splits his face. "I didn't think you had it in you."

"I learned from the best." My eyes rake over him. "I guess now we both know how far we'll go to protect him."

His smile falters, focus falling to the porch. "Yeah, I know that feeling a little too well right now."

Dropping my hand, I take his change in demeanor like the warning sign it is. "What do you mean?"

He doesn't answer.

"Henry," I step from the threshold, forcing myself into his line of sight as I realize, "It's too early in the day, why aren't you at work right now?"

The rise and fall of his chest turns shallow. "There was an emergency."

My stomach knots, and I brush past him to peer down the road at the Fennicks' house. The Grand Safari is parked in the driveway with its rear gate open. A figure travels from the garage to the vehicle with a suitcase over his shoulder.

Lewis.

"Oh *God*." I try to breathe, but the air evades me. "Who told them?"

"Lewis did," Henry says, reclaiming my attention. "First, about school. Then, the rumors. Then...everything else. Dad flipped, obviously. Told him to get his shit and never come back. That's when I got the call."

"He's going with you?" The prospect dulls a fraction of my sorrow.

He gives a nod, then shrugs. "I'm not supposed to have guests, but my roommates can go to hell if they say anything."

I look back at the Fennicks' house. "Is he…?"

"He hasn't broken down yet. If anything, he's acting relieved. Hasn't said a word to Mom or Dad since I showed up."

"And what about you?" I ask delicately.

Henry's jaw tenses, but he forces a sad smile. "It doesn't matter how I feel, Rosie. I'm just worried about him."

"It *does* matter," I say, closing the distance between us. "It's your family. I know all this is hard for you, too."

Something in his expression alters, like he'd been waiting for someone to say that out loud.

"Um…" He looks away, shifting his weight as he lets out a hollow laugh. "It just has me thinking, you know? I've given my parents more hell than anyone should ever have to take. All the shit I've gotten into. The trouble I caused." He purses his lips, tone dimming with his resolve. "I gave them a thousand good reasons to turn their backs on me, but they didn't. They never stopped loving me." My heart aches as his eyes shift to his childhood home, then well with pooling shimmers. "Lewis has never done a damn thing wrong his entire life, Rosie. And they're—"

His voice falters when the tears overspill, running in hot streams down his cheeks. Never in my life have I seen Henry cry. It was no wonder he expected Lewis to break, because *he* already had.

I hug him with every ounce of ferocity such injustice can elicit. He cradles me tightly in return, like the very act provides some fleeting relief from the burden he and his brother were now forced to bear. I can only hope it does as I pull back enough to slide my hands to his wet face, then kiss him deeply on the lips. We only part when the heartsease persuades his body into relaxing. Reddened nose brushing my own for a slow, indiscernible number of breaths.

"You're a good man, Henry," I whisper to him, hoping with everything in me that he believes it as much as I do.

By the time he composes himself, I'm not remotely interested in hearing his reasons for why I should stay home. I walk at his side to the Fennicks' house just as Lewis finishes with the last of what he was able to load. I break from Henry's stride to rush him with a hug that's twice the force of the one I'd given his sibling.

When I have him in my arms, I can't stifle a sob. "I'm so sorry, Lewis."

"It's okay, I promise." He draws away, and I can see the tough exterior he's putting up hold strong. "You were right. It wasn't worth it anymore."

A faint crying catches my ears, and I turn to view Mrs. Fennick in one of the house's windows overlooking the driveway. Her cat-eye glasses are gone, exposing a face that's wet and swollen from crying. It breaks me as I tear away from the sight, focusing all my attention on Lewis as he and Henry enter the Grand Safari.

Stepping to the open passenger window, I place my hands on the lip. "I'll call you every chance I get. Whatever you need, I'm here."

For the first time since approaching him, Lewis's firm expression falters. "Rosie, you know your mom isn't gonna let you—"

"*Fuck* my mom." I cut him off, reaching through the gap to squeeze his hand. "I love you, Lewis."

His fingers tighten over mine. "I love you, too."

"I'll look after him," Henry assures from the driver's seat. Any shred of the emotion he released on my front porch is now gone. Or rather, buried.

"I know you will," I say, letting go of my friend to back away.

My feet remain planted as the car pulls from the driveway and starts down the street. It isn't until they've turned the corner and disappeared entirely that the weight drops squarely on my already-fatigued shoulders.

Lewis is gone. His home—the home I had spent Christmases, birthdays, and graduation parties in—was no longer his. The parents who'd seen me as their own were no longer his. Through everything I'd endured since Erica's departure, I always had the smallest tether of security in that, with a simple walk down the street, my best friend was right there. Ready to make things better, even by simply existing.

But not anymore. He's moving forward. And bound by the chains of a promise, I'm still here. In our little prison. *Alone.*

My knees hit the pavement, and I weep.

"I never want you to see him again."

That was what my mother said, dead to my face, when she was told what happened.

Lewis. Whom she'd known since I was in sixth grade. Who, by all accounts, she'd seen as her own son. A boy she trusted immensely with her daughter, whom she never trusted with any boy. Just like that, years of familial bond and friendship, smothered like a treacherous flame.

She hadn't asked me if I knew of anything beforehand. Though, I couldn't figure out if it was because she already suspected the answer, or if she simply didn't want to know. Nor did she give me any of the hell I'd been anticipating when she'd heard of my state of enrollment at Trinity Grace. I was unsure how she knew of the assault, but it's not as if I could put it beneath Lynn to clue in someone at Crosspoint for the sake of bitter vengeance. I couldn't bring myself to supply a proper reaction, either. Even if there was one enforced with everything I desired to say. I stayed silent. Out of fear. Cowardice. Whatever the fuck you want to call it.

The night she'd gotten the call from Mrs. Fennick, I'd stayed silent.

The following day, when I was forced to face my mother for a meal in our dining room, I'd stayed silent.

The ride to church on Sunday and the slow, painstaking walk inside, I'd stayed silent.

And now I'm sitting in the first-row pew beside my mother, because the person I'd always opted to sit with instead was no longer welcome. I thought my head would be swarming. That I'd want to tear out my hair and scream at the top of my lungs in front of everyone here. But I stay silent.

Emptiness feels so ironically heavy.

If I had been listening to the opening of Pastor Morgan's sermon, I'm sure I would've heard something about valuing the Holy Spirit more than we should our own blood. I know, because I'd heard Mrs. Fennick's sobs echo down every bend of the corridor to our pastor's office before service began. I hadn't attempted eavesdropping, but by the time both she and Mr. Fennick exited, her husband presented disturbingly unbothered in contrast to her tear-streaked face.

Regardless, Pastor Morgan's affect remains enthused as ever as he recites, "'If your brother or sister sins, go and point out their fault, just between the two of you. If they listen to you, you have won them over. But if they will not listen, take one or two others along, so that every matter may be established by the testimony of two or three witnesses. If they still refuse to listen, tell it to the church; and if they refuse to listen even to the church, treat them as you would a pagan or a tax collector.'" He glances up from the scripture. "To put it simply, those who live in sin are bound to remain there without proper accountability. The father who does not discipline his child, *hates* his child. And if that child should remain defiant, it is no longer the responsibility of the father to harbor such evil."

Instead of paying the man before me a shred of my precious attention, I chance yet another look at Mrs. Fennick. Her face reflects the heartbreak of mine from where she sits with her husband, the space opposite her void for the first time in eighteen years. I swear her eyes catch my own for a fraction of a second in silent understanding that our pain is mutual. That her child and my best friend is, in fact, still alive. Undeserving of being erased like he was nothing but a blemish in their family's scrapbook. A fleeting, yet hopeful sentiment that draws me so far from Pastor Morgan's sermon, absolutely nothing can bring me back.

Nothing, except my name. "Mary-Rose?"

The beat of my heart ceases. My head snaps to the chancel, convinced it was my imagination.

Pastor Morgan's fixated gaze supplies me with all the confirmation that it hadn't been. "Mary-Rose, would you please join me?"

My mother's hand finds my back, smoothing it in delicate circles at first. But when I don't move, her nail digs forcefully into my spine. I shoot a silent glance at her. The horror on my face screaming, *what did you do*?!

But she isn't looking at me. She's staring eagerly at our pastor, relinquishing parental responsibility in place of pious submission.

It's the needlestick of her administered compliance that lifts me onto trembling legs. I close the short distance between the front row and Pastor Morgan, who migrates from the lectern to the spacious platform in front of it. Ascending the steps, I stop before him. His touch is ice cold as he gently turns me to face the countless bodies that make up Crosspoint Fellowship's sea of believers. There could be hundreds. There could be thousands. There could be *millions*. It makes no difference in this unescapable moment.

"Mary-Rose," he stops with a palm on my shoulder blade, voice amplified by the lavalier clipped to his collar. "Are there any sins you wish to repent before the church?"

My mouth goes bone dry. Terror smothers me with every watchful set of eyes. I look to the one I know will bring me some semblance of ease in the chaos. But Mrs. Fennick's head has since lowered, disheveled brunette hair masking the face beneath. Condemnatory stares cut into my skin like a thousand little gouges, leaving me stricken with two options to avoid them. Look up, or down. I try the ceiling, but their faces are there, too. Relishing in my torment with satisfaction, like I'm finally being dealt my deserved penance. So instead, my chin dips low.

"Any acts worthy of being rebuked?" Pastor Morgan goes on, tilting his head at me. "Perhaps, an act of violence against another believer?"

While it was one of my lesser offences—if you could call it an offense at all—my voice wavers as I admit, "I hit someone."

He nods in forged understanding. "You assaulted another believer, for…?"

I swallow tightly. "She said something horrible about somebody I love."

Mom shifts uncomfortably in the corner of my drawn vision.

"Despite the remarks," Pastor Morgan leads. "You understand that the thoughts spurring your actions were unjust?"

Never tell the man in charge no.

I squeeze my eyelids shut as the answer comes with deadened, mechanical ease. "Yes."

"Do you wish to seek forgiveness for this act, along with the sinful nature that provoked it?"

My small, child-like voice travels gracelessly through the speakers. "Yes."

Taking my shoulders, he spins me until my back is to the crowd. "Mary-Rose, let us pray on your behalf." His head bows, and the symphony of creaking wood and sweeping hair brings with it assurance that the group behind has followed suit.

I, however, raise mine. As Pastor Morgan leads into a sanctimonious plea for my pardon, I glance above him. Finding the towering cross on the frontmost wall, elevated for all to honor. The one around my neck grows heavy as my mind's eye fills in the gaps. Bringing with it an illusion of their savior nailed to the wood, willingly sacrificed as an act of mercy for the sinful humankind. A declaration of unconditional love so enduring that it was still being repaid with the devout lives of worshipers after all this time.

Where? I think. *Where was that love to be found in this room?*

For the compassionate who do no harm? For the ones who wish to love freely? Is *love* not what these vipers preach? What their God himself lived and perished for? How could so many centuries of everlasting love beget nothing but such vile hatred?

These are the fruitless questions I pose to nobody but myself as Pastor Morgan concludes, guiding me to face the congregation once again. "Your accountability partners care for you, Mary-Rose. This was no act of punishment. This was an act of rescue." His tone amplifies to address the crowd directly. "Brothers and sisters in Christ, allow this young lady to hear your praise for her forgiveness."

Voices break among the endless rows. Some, *amens*. A few, *we love you*s. But most of all, quiet prayers muttered at my expense. All the while, I stand at the helm beneath lights angled like sanctified rays onto my body. The target of their self-indulgent commiseration for a human they believe to be sparing from an eternity of damnation.

Except…I wasn't human. Not an individual worthy of respect, decency, or true compassion. I was nothing but a product of their righteousness. A topic for them to sigh and gossip over coming meals. A spectacle to be molded, observed, used, then pitied. It's what I've always been. And so long as the crowd before me remains, a *product* is all I'll ever be.

Luckily, I know how to be a good one.

I take the cue from my mother. Who pins me with an expectant glare as she raises a stiff finger to the corner of her lips. I hit my mark like a true professional.

Chin up.

Don't look anyone in the eye; they might see right through you.

Smile like you mean it, or they'll make you do it again.

A new one... Use the unshed tears to give your eyes an illusory gleam.

Pretend.

Endure.

Pretend.

Endure.

I show the audience my teeth. As rote and poised a grin there ever was.

"Don't worry about me, Lewis." Despite my isolation, I speak quietly into the receiver. "Just focus on you for now, alright?"

"Rosie, you sound off."

I twist the spiraled cord around my finger, resting with my back against the kitchen wall. It was the first time I'd been able to speak to him in the week since his departure, and I knew it wouldn't be long before our conversation was cut short. Mom had been arriving home earlier than she usually did over the past days. Likely with the intent of assuring I'm not committing the treason I am now. "Of course I'm off, I'm not used to you being gone."

"And church last weekend?"

My jaw clenches, but I force the necessary lie. "It was normal. Nobody talked about what happened."

Thankfully, he doesn't press further. Going on to tell me about his plans now that his future had shifted. There wasn't much I could do aside from express my support for his efforts, then bid him a hopeful goodbye before he turned the phone to Henry.

"Rosie?" The sound of his voice nearly breaks me.

"Hey, Henry." I maintain decorum. "How's he settling in?"

He explains, talking about how their limited space reminds him of the days the brothers used to share a bedroom in their early childhood. All the while, I listen with an unfeigned smile on my face. Allowing his fond recollection to ease my whirring mind, if only for the brief period I get to hear him speak. But, of course, he counters with the inevitable question. "Are you doing okay?"

The same sting that came with lying to his brother pierces my heart. "I'm fine."

There's a long silence before it's broken by, "Rosie, Lewis isn't listening."

The guarantee is all I need to crack. Turning to rest my forehead against the kitchen wall, I release a shaky breath. "It's awful, Henry. They're acting like he's *dead*."

Through horrid memories that coil tightly around my throat, I tell him of Crosspoint. The state of their parents, particularly their distraught mother. And how I'd been so viciously dragged in front of the commune to declare that the action I took to defend someone I considered family was ungodly. When I finish, there's a heavy stillness over the phone.

But it's soon fractured by his long, wounded exhale. Followed swiftly by the words I'd been both anticipating *and* dreading. "I want you out of there, Rosie."

"I can't leave." I close my eyes, brows knitting to the point of fatigue as I bear an explanation. "I promised Erica."

"It's *your* life." His tone weakens. "You can live with me, just like Lewis."

"It can't work," I say as if the option were a possibility at all.

But that doesn't sway him. "Yes, it can. Lewis has the cot, and you can take the bed with me. I'll even clear out some of my stuff to make room for your typewriter. I want you *here*."

I bite back a sob, nearly slipping away into the hazardous idea of such an escape. But the swift opening of the front door makes me whirl around, wiping away the fear and emotion as fluidly as I had at the helm of Crosspoint's chancel.

"Hey, Mom," I say, both casually and loud enough so Henry understands.

When she notices my stance, she pins me with a scowl over the brown paper bags in her arms. "Who are you talking to?"

"Val, from Bible study. I'm trying to see if she'll talk Rebecca into letting me apologize." The lie practically singes my tongue.

But it's sufficient enough to serve its purpose. Mom keeps me affixed beneath her focus, even beyond entry to the kitchen.

I hold her dubious glare, lifting the receiver from my shoulder. "Val, I need to help my mom unload groceries. Let me know what Rebecca says, okay?"

There's nothing but silence in way of response. Until the sound of a voice so pained, so desperate, reaches through the telephone like a vow.

"I love you, Rosie."

My mother would see no change in my front. Not a flinch or a blink. But I can't help but wonder what she would feel if those steely blue eyes could see beneath my poised exterior. Would witnessing her daughter's spirit cracking in two make her rethink a decade of misguided devotion?

Doubtful.

Though my features impassively fix, the corners of my vision grow hazy with tears that surface from the pressure of words I wish to say back. They nestle in my throat, scratching, demanding to be freed. But I keep them contained at the expense of my remaining willpower, before depleting it entirely with a firm *click* of the receiver.

Chapter 29

I stare at my typewriter like it's moments from growing fangs and biting my fingers off. The next piece is due tomorrow, and I've yet to ink a single word.

The nighttime casts deep shadows from every corner of my room, and part of me wishes it would leap out and consume me as an act of mercy. I rest my face in my hands as if doing so would evoke deep thought. But I find myself unable to clear the hurdle of how the hell I'm supposed to write about pleasure, when the previous days have dragged me through nothing but the most all-consuming pain.

"Just write *something*," I whisper to no one. "It's just one story…"

Nothing. Absolutely nothing comes to mind.

I slump in my seat, my eyes drifting from the red-marked "R" key to the white rose at the corner of my desk. Petals wilting and flaking off in tiny specks. My heart beats anew as I take the stem between my fingers, holding the object like it's one breath from breaking. The desire to have its gifter here takes me back to the fateful hours before catastrophe struck. The way Henry had held me on my bed, warm and secure. The feel of our first kiss. Pulling his body close as the two of us rode his motorcycle, sending me into a feverish arousal before I succumbed to…

I shouldn't. I don't even *want* to. But it's the only thing that brings me clarity. It was everything I hadn't known I needed. Setting the rose aside, I place unsteady fingers on the cold typewriter keys.

The thin air swirls my wild hair, tangling long waves in the collar of my fitted denim jacket. Straddling the stationary motorcycle beneath, the view of the mountainous lookout sends a shiver of anticipation down my spine. Being this raw and liberated is startlingly...arousing.

The metal handlebars are smooth, warming under my touch as I grip the throttle and rev the powerful bike. Vibrations hum between my thighs where the soft leather seat presses snugly against my slit, bare beneath the little skirt concealing it. I smile, teasing my clit with quick, fleeting jolts of the engine. The coil of need tightens in my lower belly, wetness turning the material beneath me slippery as a denim-clad arm snares around my waist.

"You're full of surprises. Aren't you, Angel Face?"

I glance over my shoulder to find the bike's owner. His wind-blown hair shines bright in the setting sun, unbound jacket revealing inches upon inches of taut muscle.

"I'm no Angel...Just a horny girl." I tease with a quick pucker of my red lips.

Settling his firm chest against me, he reaches for the throttle himself. "I can help with that."

I moan as he pulls it, a symphony of vibrations rocking my underside as it thunders in loud bursts of power. His free hand snakes around my chest, gripping my breast over my jacket before roughly unbuttoning the article to pull it free.

"Harley—!" I cry out as he catches my nipple between calloused fingers.

Harley's tongue strokes my neck as he gives a final, powerful tug of the throttle. I unravel, the orgasm pulsing through me to draw a scream so euphoric that it challenges the roar of the engine. Pleasure fades to a gentle fizz as he finally lets up on the source of my climax.

He pushes me forward, pinning my chest to the bike before my skirt is torn off with a mindless tug. Bare skin gives way to the sensation of his hard length prodding my entrance after some careful fumbling.

"Just say the word." He prompts as I steady myself.

Losing a chuckle, I bite my lip in the rouse of his dominance. "I'm ready, Harley…"

I write on. Detailing *Angel Face's* experience as she's fucked on the back of a stylish Harley Davidson, at a scenic lookout with a sexy biker that carries a few striking similarities to my Henry. Though I conduct myself to express the fictitious pleasure, a burden of a whole new variety settles in place of the emptiness.

For the first time in my entire life, the work at my fingertips feels sinful.

"It's never been this heavy before, even after Erica left. At least then, I still had Lewis. But now…?" My voice trails off as I rest my chin atop my knees, hugging them tight.

Val's warm hand rubs circles into my back, sitting close enough that I can pick up her floral scent in the confined space. One of the studio's small dressing rooms had been the most private place I could slip away and fill her in on everything that had gone on while Ruth was busy overseeing my latest story.

She shakes her head, shiny black hair ghosting my shoulder. "I can't believe Lynn would do something like that. She seemed so accepting."

"I thought so, too." A stab of betrayal gouges me, but I suppress it for Val's sake.

Sad hazel eyes flicker over me. "Have you spoken to Lewis since he left?"

"I call every chance my mom steps out. Right now, he's focusing on finding a job to pay off what he still owes Trinity Grace for the semester." I give an indignant huff. "His parents were covering it, but clearly that deal's expired."

Her shoulders sag. "And how are you feeling?"

I rest my head against the rack of assorted, musty-smelling clothes behind me. "I'm glad he's finally out of there. It's gonna be hard for him to get his footing, but at least he doesn't have to pretend anymore." Pausing, guilt burrows in my chest before gnawing its way to the surface. "But a very selfish part of me wishes he were still around, so at least I wouldn't have to pretend by myself."

She dons a look that suggests my problem isn't nearly as convoluted as I'm making it. "So then, why are *you* still pretending?"

It's a valid question. One that comes with an answer I'd long conditioned myself to accept. "Erica. Her life went to hell because Mom took away what was rightfully hers. She made me promise I wouldn't let the same happen to me."

"I know," she says delicately. "But do you even need it?"

I don't answer. Instead, I let my head hang in consideration.

Val shrugs. "Look, I'm not in your shoes. My parents have never condemned what I do. I'm just saying, school is important, but it's only one path. You seem to be just fine walking your own." Her ruby lips curve into a sweet smile. "More than fine, actually. *Kicking ass* is a better way to put it."

The compliment ignites a warmth within me, but practicality extinguishes it. "I wish I believed that."

"You should." She assures. "Because everyone else does. Ruth, your readers, me. You wouldn't be here if it weren't true."

I glance around, sarcasm corrupting my tone. "In a muggy porn dressing room that smells like wet underwear?"

Val giggles. Then reaches a hand for mine, her red-polished fingertips curling snugly over my skin. "Exactly."

Her touch hexes me in that odd way it always does. "Thank you, Valerie...This is gonna sound so stupid. But after Lewis, you might be the best friend I've ever had."

"Why would that be stupid? I could say the same about you."

My cheeks flush, and I know it isn't from the confined humidity. "Come on, you've gotta have a hundred friends that are way cooler."

"Not even close. I'm not so great at making female *friends*."

"What about Star?" I ask gently. "I know she's been through a lot, but you stood by her. Aren't you two still close?"

Her grip on me stiffens. The light in her hazel eyes flickering away with her averting gaze. "Yeah, we were."

The remark steals my grin. "You mean, you aren't anymore?"

She takes a few tense moments before elaborating. "Everything that happened changed her. She'd always self-medicated with pills, but she started taking so much that she'd be out of it for days. She wouldn't return my calls. She stopped letting me over. And I was so frustrated. I couldn't understand why she wouldn't let me be there for her. Eventually, I just did as she said and stopped coming around." A shallow breath rattles from her lips. "It was the biggest mistake I've ever made."

Something inside demands that I remain quiet. Giving Val the room to disclose whatever it is that pains her enough to keep her focus on the ground between us.

"If I had only checked in on her, regardless of what she wanted—" Her throat closes tightly, smothering the admission. "Maybe I could've found her before the landlord did."

The air goes from stifling to frigid so quickly, it gives me goosebumps.

"Oh my God," I whisper as if speaking too loudly would break her. "Val…"

"It's okay." A mascara-tinged tear runs down her cheek a blink before she swipes it away. Sniffling, she gathers the strength to attempt a sad smile. "You remind me a lot of her. She was so driven, witty, always stood her ground…I think that's the reason I was so drawn to you when we met." She huffs, her tone softening. "Part of the reason, anyways."

I lose myself in the refuge of her hazel gaze, feeling her hand tighten around mine. And suddenly, I'm questioning if the care pouring through her touch may be enough to remedy my aching heart after all.

The door of the dressing room swings open, startling us as we find Ruth in the threshold. At once, Val and I stand like we've been called to attention.

"There you are," her cold eyes rake over me, then flicker to Val and back. "The piece is good. I'm already late heading out the door, so you'll have to see Rodney for your payment."

"You're leaving?" Val asks in place of my own response.

"I have some old connections in California to meet with. Rodney will be handling next week's issue. It'll be a crunch with the holiday, but I'll be back in the office come Friday."

"What about my book deal?" I butt in. I'd been so desperate to talk to Val after arriving that I hadn't even thought to ask if Ruth had obtained it.

Her expression remains impassive. "What you gave me looked spot-on. If they like what they see, I'd say we'll hear from them within a reasonable time."

Val nudges my shoulder, radiance reclaiming her pretty face. "I helped her send it off. It'll push through, I know it."

I really hope so. If Val was right and I didn't need to endure four years of hell to earn a slip of paper determining my worth, then it would take me proving myself as a competent writer all on my own. I wouldn't be given a better opportunity than this.

"I'll let you know the instant I get word from them. Until then, keep up your work here. And don't let Rodney destroy anything before I get back." Ruth offers us a dubious raise of her brows before stepping from the room, the click of her heels dissipating down the hallway to hell.

Val sets a palm on my waist. "I'd better get back. You okay to take off?"

"Yeah, I'll be fine," I say with twice the assurance I truly feel.

I trail her into the corridor. But before she passes through the set entry, she shoots me an expectant glance. "Remember, I'm here if you need me."

I give a single nod, mourning as the tether of relief she'd extended snaps with the closing door behind her. I trudge to the end of the eerie red hallway, nearly running chest-first into R.J. as he exits the superior office.

"Virgin Mary…" His tone is less brash than usual, substituted with coquetry. "I was just coming to find you." He hands me my bag by the strap, then holds up my leather-clad *Holy Scriptures* notebook with the cash I'm owed folded beneath his fingertips—items I had all but discarded in my haste to speak with Val. "You gave us quite the piece this time around. I have a feeling this issue is gonna be your biggest yet, little lady."

I cautiously take my belongings. "What makes you say that?"

He clicks his tongue. "You could say I have a fruition."

Sighing, I sling my bag over my shoulder. "I think you mean *intuition*?"

"Same difference." He leans an elbow against the door frame, crossing one of his Western boots over the other. "If you have any addenda before our next push, speak now or forever cast your pearls. Come drop day, I'll be at a little congregation in Nevada preaching the good word."

I don't stop to ponder, favoring the urge to escape his company over the urge to know more. "No, nothing."

He hums deeply. "You know, I've poured twelve years of passion into *Wild Thang*. But I can't recall ever being this proud."

My brows furrow. "Of what, me?"

He smirks, tilting his head in a move that tells me I'm right.

Damn, I practically hammered that story out of my skull and onto paper. It wasn't my best work by a long shot. "Um, thanks…I guess?"

He concludes with an emphatically long drawl. "Don't mention it."

I simply turn, striding toward the hallway to hell's exit with absolutely no intention of doing so.

Chapter 30

The day after Thanksgiving, I finally get to see Lewis in person for the first time since he left home. We planned to meet at *Marcy's Bookstore* before his introductory shift at a tech resale shop in the nearby district. One scheduled on the busiest day of the year for shopping, given his luck.

So far, I'd been able to keep what happened at Crosspoint suppressed for his sake. I knew the last thing he needed was to hear about how badly everything had been affecting me. Not when *I* should be the farthest thing on his mind at a time like this. Rather than harp on the negatives, we sat in our usual corner of the store, sifting through a growing pile of potential selections. But all the erotic material in the world couldn't pull my mind from the relentless chase of reality.

"The new job sounds perfect for you," I mention as he flips through a *Macworld* magazine taken from the display Marcy works to restock a few shelves away.

"At least I'll be in my element." He forces a smile. "But I'm still nervous."

"You're gonna do great." I affectionately tap his leg with the toe of my shoe.

He chuckles. "I like the area, too. There's this café across the block with computers inside. They have free dial-up and everything. I've been dying to get back on the Internet."

I shake my head at his enthusiasm. "How's Presley doing?"

"I haven't talked to him much since I left, but I think he's okay," Lewis remarks with fondness. "I don't think I ever told you, but his parents aren't like ours." His features harden at the mention, and I'm certain he's questioning if the people who raised him were still deserving of that title.

"That's a relief." I try and fail to break the tension, opting for a subject change. "And Henry?"

His mouth quirks. "Always asking about you."

A glorious heat reaches my cheeks. By the time Henry was out of the garage every day, my mother was already home from work. Meaning our communication had been reduced to one-off words of affirmation delivered through his little brother. I need to see him again. If not for our relationship, then for my own sanity.

Lewis shuts the magazine to rest in his lap. "The other mechanics aren't too happy with me being there, but I don't think Henry gives a damn."

Sarcasm thickens my tone. "*Henry* not caring what people think?"

"Another day on the job for him."

Marcy procures the cardboard box she'd been restocking from and disappears beyond the rows of bookshelves. I sit tall to peer atop the magazine rack, where the obscene material had been cautiously tucked away.

"Speaking of jobs," I say, standing to riffle through the top row. Finding the newest *Wild Thang* issue in pristine condition. The brunette model who'd played my live action Deviant Devotee, Roxy Rimmer, is on the cover this week. Posing in a skin-tight suit of black latex.

"What, you can't get off to your own manuscript?" Lewis teases.

I roll my eyes, flipping the booklet open. "I like seeing *Val's* photo adaptations."

Quickly enough, I locate the spread in question. Complete with one of R.J.'s awful titles:

Horny Harlot Humps a Harley
Written by: M.R.

Val looks as gorgeous as ever in the themed photo, fitted in denim apparel with a biker's helmet hanging from one of her fingertips. I drink in her captivating form before skimming over the next few pages to see how the rest of the story looks. Text trails on to text until I reach the climactic end, the final paragraph leading on to...

The steady tempo of my heartbeat slows to a deathly stop.

No...It isn't real. It can't be.

I break away, looking up at the surrounding bookstore to take in the sight of the overhead lights. The sound of shuffling boxes. The smell of inked paper. Every sensation that offers itself to prove that I'm actually here and not in some dream.

Not a dream. Some *nightmare*.

I blink, the edges of my vision tunneling in panic. Maybe I was seeing things. There was no feasible chance that what I'd just witnessed wasn't a terrible trick of my own mind. But upon finding the courage to look back at the page to convince myself of that, I'm left with the bitter realization that it hadn't been my imagination.

I look back...at *me*.

Kneeling on a red divan in a metallic pink bodysuit pulled down to my waist, eyeing the camera with a careless smile as I flash my breasts. While the half-naked snapshot of myself is the largest photo on the spread, it isn't alone. Scattered around are the images of Val and me. Including the still of my first kiss we'd shared in the privacy of the studio. Except now, it's only *private* among us and every of-age buyer in the American Southwest.

"Rosie, you okay?"

Lewis's voice is hardly discernible through the ringing in my ears. As I force myself to read, the caption crowning the page quakes with my grip.

Meet the mind behind Wild Thang's erotica: Albuquerque native Mary-Rose (M.R.), pictured below with Valentina Amor!

The bright lettering blurs to an illegible smudge as my wide eyes fill with tears, several running down my cheeks in hot rivulets before slipping into my agape mouth. The rest of my body slowly catches up, every nerve prickling with sharp, lethal terror. A human form now hovers in the corner of my misty peripheral. But by the time I truly notice and dare a look at him, I can already see the shock reigning heavy in his features. Lewis stares at the page as if it has a life of its own, independent from mine.

He's as breathless as I feel upon asking, "What the hell is that?"

I try to find my tongue, but all that comes out are a few choked syllables in a sorry attempt at words.

How the *fuck* could this happen? Those photos were—

My gaze snaps to my discarded backpack. I drop the magazine where I stand, rushing to unzip it and pull out my *Holy Scriptures* notebook. Opening to the back cover, where I knew I'd kept the photos for safekeeping. I reach inside, going stiff when I find it empty. A disturbed, irrational cry rattles my throat as I rip the pocket open to reveal the same voidness I'd felt at my fingertips. It only takes a few seconds before I'm tearing through my backpack like a madwoman, dumping everything onto the floor until it's cleared. But the photos are nowhere to be found.

Because somebody else already found them.

"Rosie...what's going on?" Lewis is behind me now, speaking cautiously as if a single misguided remark would kill me. "Why are those pictures of you—?"

My frantic grabbing to reclaim strewn items stuns his impossible question.

"I have to go." I bite out, ignoring his desperate calls as I bolt out of the bookstore and down the block to the nearest bus stop.

I can only assume Lewis didn't run after me because he was too dazed to react. But I can't stop to find out, or even think. Not until I'm seated in a lonely aisle on public transit, enduring the slow pass of blurring streets beneath the hum of the overhead radio. The ride to *Wild Thang Studios* lasts fifteen songs and four commercial breaks, and I'm just as out of breath stepping off the bus and sprinting up the canopied ramp as I had been when I'd left *Marcy's*. The glass doors rattle loudly as I enter and make a beeline for the hallway to hell. I don't slow my pace until my palm slams open the door to Ruth's office. And for a split second, I fear my drastic actions will be in vain if she hasn't yet returned from California.

But there she is. Sitting at her throne of a desk, gawking at me like I'm an intruder.

"Rosie—" She starts, her voice as firm as her features.

"What the fuck did you guys do?" The demand comes out as a pitiful whimper, my throat bone-dry from an hour's worth of hyperventilating.

Ruth stands from her seat. "What happened?"

"What do you mean, *what happened*?!" I shout as I stomp closer.

She has the audacity to scold me. "Lower your voice! I only just got back. Now use your words and tell me what the hell is wrong with you."

I force a few agonizing breaths before daring an excuse. "The new issue…My story…"

I can't bring myself to say it. And thankfully, I don't have to.

Ruth gives me an enigmatic stare before stepping to one of the storage tables lining the walls. A plastic-wrapped stack of identical magazines stamped with red publisher tabs sits at the center—Roxy on the cover. Tearing the packaging, she opens the first and flips to the spread containing my piece. Her French-tipped nails carefully flicker from page to page until she finds the exact source of my distress. Her reaction is unreadable, and not simply because she's *Ruth*. But because my eyes have grown so full of tears that I can hardly make her out through the fog. They trail to dampen my white button-up as moments pass void of the explanation I'm owed.

It doesn't come. She sooner settles for, "Where are these photos from?"

Decency evades me as terror spirals into rage. "What does it matter *where* they came from?! What the fuck are they doing in your magazine?!" I set a hand to my thundering heart as if the added pressure could pacify it. "They were hidden in my notebook. Somebody had to—" My watery eyes flare. "R.J."

Our odd last interaction comes back to me. His strange behavior. *He'd* been the one to hand over my notebook that day.

"Rosie?" A familiar voice sounds from the doorway. I turn to see Val in the threshold, but her enlivened smile slips at my state of hysteria. "What's wrong?"

Ruth folds the magazine to hold up. "Want to explain this, Val?"

Val's chest ceases expanding as her gaze finds the page, then flickers from Ruth to me. "Rosie…you gave them the pictures?"

"No! R.J. stole them and put them in the issue without telling me." I choke out. "He's been going on for weeks about getting me to act in one of the studio's tapes. He *wanted* the audience to see me."

"This is illegal!" Val storms across the room to rip the magazine from Ruth's hand, glaring down at it with the most aggression I've ever seen from her. "She's contracted to write. She never signed a release!"

"Yes, she did." Ruth blows an exasperated sigh, pacing with a tense posture. "Because she didn't sign on as a contractor. To get her paid, we gave her what was on hand—our catch-all. Which includes releases for employees that model." The woman shakes her head, steely eyes averting. "And R.J. knew that."

It takes all my effort not to collapse.

Looking as gutted as I feel, Val presses further. "Where is he now?"

"He left for an expo in Vegas yesterday. I won't be able to get a hold of him."

A fragile idea strikes. My lip quivers in a juvenile pout as I desperately seek Ruth. "You can recall it, can't you? You can stop it just this once?"

"The copies were sent out yesterday for distribution, they've been stocked in stores all morning. It's too late." Her chin dips in what I might assume to be sympathy, if not for her next admission. "But even if it weren't, I couldn't order a recall for something like this. Missing an issue would pull us under…I'm sorry, Rosie."

Her cruel honesty shatters my will to remain civilized. I grip the strap of my bag with clenched fingers and throw it at the table, pages atop scattering in an explosive burst.

"*Fuck!*" I wail, my knees buckling as I hit the tile floor and devolve into sobs. A warm set of hands clutches my shoulders that I know belong to Val. My voice is hoarse as I attempt to speak, "If my mother finds that…If *anyone* I know finds that…"

Anguish pools heavily in my stomach. Making me wish the ground would open up to spare me from the consequences I'd more than risked with the signing of my soul.

"I'm taking her out of here." Val shoots a bitter glance in Ruth's direction as she pulls me onto unsteady feet. "To *my* home. You shouldn't be around your mother right now."

Our manager must give some gesture of affirmation, because she doesn't protest Val gathering my strewn belongings and leading me out of the office. I swallow back enough sobs to think through precisely where I need to be. Or rather, *who* I need to see. "Can you take me somewhere else first?"

She doesn't question it. She only nods.

Thankfully, I'd stored the address to Henry's garage in my notebook after obtaining it from Lewis. Val waited in the car as I approached a muggy, multi-door garage scattered with grease-covered mechanics who'd informed me that Henry was on break. Then promptly directed me to the adjacent housing complex one driveway over.

The entryway and hall leading to the residential apartments sit eerily silent as I locate the correct number and knock on the frail wood. Heavy moments pass before the sound of footsteps alerts me to his presence, which arrives when the door is swung open. He's as scuffed as the other men had looked, reeking of motor oil that discolors his skin and uniform. But the enlivened flare in his eyes I'd come to expect upon our greetings is just as vacant as the corridor flanking me.

"What are you doing here?" He looks me up and down. "Is Lewis okay?"

"He's fine. I came to see you." I take an apprehensive pause. "I need to talk to you about something."

"Really?" His tone is thick with…what is that? Indignation? And his face is fixed in the way I always remembered it looking in our years of malice.

"Yes." I recoil slightly at his off-putting demeanor. "About my job with the magazine—"

He holds up a stained palm to silence me. "Don't waste your breath. I already saw it."

He may as well have taken that raised hand and ripped my heart out of my chest with it. "*What?*"

He disappears inside the apartment, only to return seconds later. All the despair I'd expelled at the studio threatens to resurface when I see what he's holding. Roxy's cover.

"One of my roommates brought it home this morning. I recognized the name, the same one I found in your bag." Henry leans a shoulder heavily against the door frame. "I wanted to see the kind of stuff you wrote, so I read it."

Fear gouges me at the thought of what he'd seen—me kissing someone else. I frantically shake my head. "Henry, I swear to God, those pictures of Val and me were taken months ago. It was before we—"

"It wasn't the *pictures*, Rosie." He cuts in, voice dimming as pain sours his features. "Harley…That's clever."

Oh God. The story. The one inspired by our evening at the lookout.

I release a rattled breath, shame pulling my head low. "I didn't mean anything by it. It's just what I could think of before the deadline."

The glare he's spearing me with feels like it's moments from fracturing what remains of my soul after the events of today. "You wrote a fucking smut piece about us, then published it for half the country to read, because you couldn't think of anything?"

"It wasn't like that," I say firmly, caught between understanding his anger and growing equally pissed that he's holding something so trivial against me when my entire life is hanging by a thread.

"I told you I didn't want to be one of your stories. I *trusted* you." He bites out. "What we do isn't just yours to take and manipulate. It meant something to me!"

"Henry, I'm sorry!" I raise my voice. "But I have bigger problems right now. They stole those pictures of me and published them without my permission! You know what's going to happen if someone from Crosspoint finds them!"

His furious expression doesn't shift.

"Please," I beg, my tone falling to a desperate hush. "I need you to understand, that story didn't mean anything to me. But *you* do." Tears cloud my vision for the hundredth time today. "It doesn't change what we have."

Wounded blue-green eyes scan the floor between us, then break me in two when they lock on mine. "Had."

The amendment hits me so hard, it takes all my effort not to stagger backwards.

"Henry…" His name comes out in a breathless whisper. Sorrow constricts my throat as I plead, "I need you now more than I've ever needed anyone. Please don't leave me…"

For a fleeting moment, I see something behind his resentful gaze that wants so desperately to do exactly what I'm asking of him. Something that wants to brush aside all the bullshit. Just so he can reach for me, pull me close, and never let me go again.

But whatever it is, it's gone when he reaches for the door, instead.

"You needed space to decide. I gave it to you. Now it's my turn." His jaw tenses as he steps back into the apartment. "Talk to Lewis all you want, but don't ask about me."

Sweeping air hits as the wood swings closed, embalming me with an icy chill as my view of Henry cuts away. Stealing my last, fleeting shred of hope along with it.

Chapter 31

Night has fallen by the time I'm sitting on a plush couch with a warm blanket wrapped over my shoulders. Tissues dampened by my tears litter the coffee table in front of me, marking the center of Val's living area.

I couldn't be more grateful for her inviting me to stay, especially when she offered to call my mom and let her know. Because, to my mother, Val was a good Christian girl from Bible study. Being so, I had to practically tear the phone away and end the conversation myself when she started forcing Val into a talk about their shared *end-time* conspiracies. Needless to say, my sleepover had been approved.

The space is cozy. I'm surrounded by wall art and colorful, meticulously arranged decor. If my nose wasn't so stuffed from crying, I'm sure the floral scent that always clung to her would be deliciously drowning my senses. It feels as if I've stepped into the purest embodiment of Val's personality. Bright, warm and welcoming, a place you go to when all is wrong because you just *know* it will make you feel better.

And it had. Or maybe I had just run out of tears.

Either way, the salty streams down my cheeks dry up by the time Val returns from the kitchen to sit beside me. "You sure you don't want anything to eat?" She asks, handing me a crimson mug of tea she'd prepared. "I don't want you going to bed hungry."

"Thank you," I offer a sad smile, the thought of eating making my already-sensitive stomach clench. "I'm okay, though."

"Well, the kitchen is yours if you change your mind." She props a few pillows at the end of the couch that would act as my bed for the night. Her chest falling with a slow exhale. "Henry will come around, Rosie."

I close my swollen eyes. It was only one of the terrible things that had transpired today, but it easily cut the deepest. There was a *chance* that someone I knew would find my pictures in the magazine, but the damage I had done to Henry's trust in me was certain.

"And what if he doesn't?" I ask, sipping the warm drink.

"He will." Val's gaze momentarily falls. "But if not…then you move forward and learn from it."

"That wouldn't be fair to him. He doesn't deserve to have his heart broken because I made some stupid mistake." I shake my head. "I spent so long writing about sex, I never stopped to think about what it meant to be in an actual relationship. I should've been smarter about it."

Especially after all the supposed years he's been waiting for me. But Val interrupts that thought with a scoff, the corner of her plush lips tilting in an imposing smile.

"You are smart, Rosie. Definitely one of the most creative people I've ever known. But even you aren't attuned enough to avoid the tragedy that comes with love. Nobody is." She rests an elbow over the back of the couch. "Hell, I've been in the game for years, and I'm still learning new things about myself."

I take another sip of the tea before setting it on the coffee table and sinking into the cushions at my back. "It's hard to believe that. Everything about you is perfect."

This draws a laugh from her in lieu of reply.

"It's true," I glance woefully in her direction. "You are the most gorgeous, brilliant, undeniably perfect woman I've ever laid eyes on. And right now, you're the only person keeping me sane."

She stares silently at me before her chin dips, grin falling along with it. "I don't know why you would think that after today."

I narrow a look at her. "What are you talking about?"

"Rosie, if I'd never taken you to the studio that night, those pictures wouldn't exist." She sucks in a short breath, face tensing in a manner that appears frighteningly like guilt. "R.J. wouldn't have taken them, and you wouldn't be in pain like you are now."

I place a hand on her shoulder clad in a tight-fitted long-sleeve. "Val, that's ridiculous. None of this was your fault."

Her focus averts, brows pulling tight in a mark that she doesn't believe me.

I go on, "Even with what happened, I wouldn't take that night back for anything. Our kiss, either." Warmth settles in me, and I know it isn't just the tea. "It was the first time in my life I really felt beautiful. Or even…human."

She huffs, her affectionate grin returning. "Now you're the one being ridiculous."

"I mean it." I assert. "You think I ever would've believed it if you hadn't shown me? I'd spent my entire life convinced nobody would ever want me for who I actually was." Sorrow tugs violently at my heart, my eyes shutting to brace the burden that follows. "And now that Henry's gone, I'm starting to think that might still be true."

"It isn't."

Stewing in the darkness, the question comes weakly. "How can you know?"

A hand takes my own, reclaiming my attention. Val has shifted closer to me. Only inches between us, hazel irises dance across my face like it's a fragile floor of glass.

Her words are barely a whisper, the message taking its first and only breath before dying on her tongue. "Because *I* want you…"

The heat inside me flourishes. In an instant, I recognize the look she takes on—something akin to a mirror. It's the same face of unrelenting desire I knew I had been donning with every stolen glance since meeting her all those months ago. Her evocative gaze falls to my lips. Mine does the same to hers, studying the flawless outline of ruby lipstick. Every bad omen. Every tear I had shed today. After it all, my mind *screams* for reprieve. Just a simple moment of the same fleeting carelessness I'd experienced when she gifted me my first kiss. All at once, I'm tossed into a war of letting my inhibitions win, or leaning forward to get another taste of Valerie Ramona's intoxicating lure that I'd been deprived of since our night at the studio…

Inhibitions lose.

Our mouths meet so quickly, I can't even discern which of us initiated it. But the speed at which she effortlessly finds the best angle to kiss me deeper gives me reason to believe it had been her. The same tinder of passion that had caught flame the night of our photoshoot returns. Only now, there's no hesitation. No anxious predisposition. It's only heat. *A lot* of heat.

I shake the blanket from my shoulders to slip fingers around her slender waist. In tandem, her warm hand slides to cradle the base of my neck. I suck on her plump bottom lip, and she takes it as an invitation to glide her tongue across mine—the bold move making me hum. Her mouth tastes *so* damn good, and her tongue is just as perfect as the rest of her. I mourn its loss when it slips back into her own mouth just long enough to form a word so familiar, yet so foreign in the tone of such carnal desire.

"*Rosie…*"

I can't tell if it's the two of us moving in sync, or simply gravity pulling us downward onto the length of the couch. But either way, I lay there with her on top of me, our mouths fixed as I squeeze her shapely hips between my thighs. *God*, this is exactly what I need. No thoughts. No question of the consequences. No grander picture. The perfect weight of her body atop mine feels as if it could sustain me in place of water, nutrients, even *air*. I slide my palms to her lower back, cresting the hem of her pants as the first blade of fear slices the tendrils of my delirium. Only for Val to quickly vanquish it.

"You can touch me." She laughs against my lips.

Thrill seizes me, and I act.

I slide low to grab the pronounced curve of her ass, cursing the fabric that impedes me from feeling her skin directly. She's dressed in baggy cargo pants, given the colder month, making me long for the warm days when she wore crop tops and shorts. But I wouldn't let something as pesky as a layer of clothing get in the way of feeling every inch of the body she was offering on a silver platter. Her top is fitted enough that I'm blessed with the firm press of her chest against mine, temptation all but forcing my hands to release her rear and take her breasts. My fingers tighten, drawing a moan from Val against our never-ending kiss. The indissoluble ache between my thighs throbs so mercilessly, it robs the breath from my lungs. This isn't just temptation, or even spur-of-the-moment ecstasy. It's the unmistakable burn of arousal that fueled the fantasies responsible for leading me here. I recognize it as I would the sound of Lewis's voice, the feel of typewriter keys beneath my fingertips, and the pain that comes with smiling for a room full of people you despise.

I move on instinct alone, grinding my hips against Val's in an attempt to cure this ailment of feverish lust. It's only moments after I find the *perfect* angle to satiate the burning that I realize she's grinding in turn. Our bodies slide together in unison, speaking a language I never realized I was fluent in until this very moment.

"I've wanted this—" I manage, just as a delicious buck of her hips cuts me off.

"So have I," Val says, breaking from my mouth to trail kisses down the side of my jaw.

I snare my arms around her to pull us closer, as if it were at all possible. Unable to bite back the smile stretching my lips as Val nips at my ear. She mumbles a ciphered declaration in Spanish that sends shivers down my spine. Everything is so hot. So feverish. So untamed. So—

"I'm in love with you, Rosie." Her breathy, desperate confession is whispered gently.

But it rattles around my brain for a good few grinds of our hips before truly sinking in.

In love with you.

Slowly, my body stops moving.

Not, *I love you*. As the closest of friends would say. *In love* with you.

"What?" I ask, utterly winded. Though, I'm unable to tell if it's from our kiss or her words.

"I'm in love with you." She repeats, pulling back to stroke my face with her thumb. Directing that unbelievably perfect smile down at me. "I'm so, *so* in love with you."

Every nerve in my body that had raged in an uncontainable blaze mere moments ago deadens. She…*what?*

There was no way that was true. But the look in her eyes doesn't lie. It's the same look Henry had given me on the Ferris wheel when he'd kissed my cheek for the first time—a state of joy that couldn't be suppressed on the exterior. But this, what Val and I had, was just fun. Simply a friend trying to make me feel good after one of the shittiest days of my entire life.

Wasn't it?

"I thought we were just…" If the correct explanation existed, I couldn't verbalize it. But I quickly learn there's no need to.

Because I lie here, watching Val's radiant face slowly bleed with realization. Her gorgeous smile falters, hazel eyes unmoving. But the horror behind them fills the silent void. Her bottom lip and the now-smudged outline of her deep ruby lipstick tremble slightly—the rest of her soon following. If she weren't already on top of me, I'd think the sight alone would absolutely crush me with the weight of her irrepressible pain.

It dawns on me that I am, in real time, witnessing a person's heart breaking.

She sucks in a quick, shaky breath in one moment. The next, she's off me. Standing beside the couch and making a feeble attempt to sweep her wild hair back to where it had been before our escapade. Her frantic gaze searches everywhere but mine, ultimately landing on the floor.

"I'm sorry." Her voice isn't a whisper anymore. It's a *whimper*.

I prop myself on unsteady arms. "Val—"

"I should go to bed. My room's down the hall if you need anything. Sleep well."

She says it and makes her exit so quickly, I barely have time to turn and watch her disappear down the short hallway. A swift *click* of a distant door gives way to the heaviest silence I've ever had the misfortune of carrying. The only break from the eerie quiet is the hammering beat of my heart, which refuses to slow. I sit here, unmoving, and unable to comprehend a single thing that had just transpired, aside from one lone certainty in this sea of dubiety.

There's no chance I'm getting any sleep tonight.

It wasn't until the predawn hours that I'd managed to calm my mind enough to attempt any sort of rest. But when I wake, I can tell by the harsh light streaming through semi-transparent pink curtains that it's, at the earliest, late morning.

The smell of cooked spices and the faint crackle of a stovetop stir me fully lucid. I pull the blanket from my body to peer over the back of the couch at the kitchen. Val is standing in an oversized sleeping t-shirt, her black hair flaring from the messy bun it's twisted in. When she faces me, transferring the completed meal she'd prepared from pan to plates, I can see her face barren of makeup for the first time—her nose and cheeks spotted with a sea of adorable freckles typically concealed by foundation. When she finally notices I've roused, a smile tugs her lips. Though, it doesn't reach her eyes.

"Morning." She says, setting the pan aside.

"Morning," I repeat, my voice thick with sleep. I stand to stretch my stiff body. "What time is it?"

"After eleven." She picks up one of the plates, placing it before an empty stool at the corner of the island. Her gaze narrows at me. "I'm not letting you leave until you've eaten something."

My stomach growls, clearly angry at my decision to refrain from anything the night prior. I relent, stepping to take a seat at the stool and palm the warm burrito in my hand. "Thank you."

My mouth waters as I bite into it, the taste of spicy eggs and sausage warding off any trace of residual drowsiness.

She takes a bite from her own, humming. "My mom always makes these for me after a long night. Does wonders for a hangover."

If that wasn't the perfect term to describe how I feel, one didn't exist. I manage a few more swallows before the silence between us grows too great to ignore. Resting the meal, I nervously trace my fingertip along the plate's glass edge.

"I'm sorry about what happened." I finally say, forcing myself to look at her.

She doesn't return the sentiment. "You shouldn't be; it wasn't your fault."

I think carefully through my following words. "I didn't realize you liked me that way. Or even, girls at all." It sounds so stupid in hindsight, especially considering our first kiss. "If I had, I wouldn't have…I don't know, *led you on* like I did."

"You didn't lead me on, Rosie." She lets out a hollow chuckle, red-polished fingertips rubbing the side of her neck soothingly. "I wasn't trying to hide that I'm bisexual. I just figured, all those times we spent together, you would look at me like you couldn't believe I was real."

She's right, and it only worsens my lingering guilt knowing that she had recognized it.

Val hesitantly goes on, "And, I get it. Every time I was around you, I just wanted to know you more. I took you to the studio that night because I couldn't dream of a reality where you didn't see the effect you had on people just by walking into a room. The effect you had on me..." She exhales deeply. "I guess I hoped you felt something more. God knows I always did."

A thought forces entry to my mind, making it spin uncontrollably until I vocalize it. "What if I did feel something more?"

I was asking myself more than I was her. But the idea is a revelation I hadn't been prepared for. Every time I'd admired her since that first cover of *Wild Thang*—her beauty, her charm, down to the smallest detail no passerby would take time to notice—I always thought it had been because I wanted to *be* her. But what if that was never wholly true? All this time, had I really wanted *her*?

Not just as a friend, but as something more.

No, I'd never liked girls in that way. Not that I'd recognized, anyway. There's nothing wrong with women who do. Hell, I'd fight for Lewis to love whomever he wanted until my dying breath if that's what it took. But I would know if *I* had those feelings for someone of the same gender... Wouldn't I?

Val's gaze finally lifts, quelling the tension between us. "You'd know. And, even if you don't, that's okay. You'll figure it out. We both will." She pauses, giving me a sad smile. "But there is one thing I know. If you aren't absolutely sure of what it is you want, we have to stop this feeling before it turns into something dangerous."

This feeling. Our attraction to each other.

Despite what I still very much feel for Henry—even if he currently doesn't feel the same—I can't imagine a life where Val doesn't light up my entire world by simply existing in it. Meeting her had been the best thing to come out of all of this. And to lose her just because I can't figure out what the fuck I want?

"What if we don't?" I stand from the stool and round the island, demanding she recognize how fearful I am at the prospect. "We can still try. Maybe if we do, I'll realize what it is I—"

"Rosie," she cuts me off, taking both my hands to look at me sternly. "I wouldn't pull you into something you aren't ready for, even if you begged me to." Her thumb delicately strokes my skin, a visible pain shimmering beneath hazel irises by way of unshed tears. "You weren't raised the same as I was. You grew up around people who fed you lies. Telling you these feelings are evil."

"But I *know* they aren't." I assert. "I've never thought that about others, even before Lewis."

Her brows draw in sympathy. "Others...but not yourself."

My lungs burn for reprieve, but the air evades me. I close my eyes the moment they start to fog, speaking through a despondent hush. "I just feel so stupid."

"You aren't stupid, Rosie. You're just *human*." Val says as if she's somehow aware that it's the first time anyone's ever told me such. "There's nothing wrong with not being ready for something."

My head dips. "There *is* if it means I'm losing you."

Val scoffs, the gesture drawing my attention back to her bewildered face. "You're not going to lose me. I still care about you. This... *misunderstanding* could never change that."

Just as they had last night, my intuitions falter. Only now, I settle for guiding her into a tight hug. One that she graciously returns.

"I love you, Val," I whisper. Just because I can't decide to what extent, doesn't mean it isn't true.

Her body settles gently against my own. "I love you, too, Rosie."

I pull away, and for a slight moment, my gaze falls to her lips. Hers does the same to mine, but this time, she lowers her chin and steps out of my hold. Taking with her any dying hope that the passion of our experience last night could be relived. Even just one final time. It was the smart move, despite how much I hate the fact that she made it.

Over the next few minutes, Val cleans up the remains of breakfast as I finish eating and gather my bag from the living area. Slipping on my shoes, I hear her voice cut through the rushing faucet of the sink.

"You can stay longer if you want. I have no plans." She offers kindly.

"It's Saturday," I give her a shy look. "I have a babysitting job to get to."

"Oh," she replies. "Want me to drive you there?"

I consider it, but shake my head. "I…kinda want to spend some time alone."

Thankfully, she doesn't protest. "Alright, if you're sure."

I stop at the front door of the apartment, clicking it open before giving a final glance over my shoulder. "Thank you, Val. For everything."

She pauses, smiling at me. This time, it reaches her eyes. "I'll see you soon, yeah?"

"Yeah…" I agree before stepping outside into the cool, late-morning air.

The trill of buzzing traffic and distant horns pervades my senses as I begin my cautious trek down the second-story walkway. But with every step I take away from Val, the more it sinks in.

I may've just gained the best friend a girl could ever ask for. And in tandem, lost what could've been the love of my life.

Suddenly, the bag over my shoulders weighs a thousand pounds. I can't ward off the way my chest tightens at the loss I'd just endured—one I hadn't considered alive until it was already snuffed. With every unknown that now faces me, there's one thing I'm sure of. I had just experienced, firsthand, the tragedy that comes with love.

And it fucking sucks.

Chapter 32

The bus ride and subsequent walk to Mr. Lasker's driveway had supplied ample time to shake off the hours behind me. Even so, the tranquility of the house as I enter is nothing if not stifling.

"Hello?" I call, anticipating a pair of hyper little boys to come running. But the home sits entirely vacant. That is, until the quick echo of footsteps on the adjacent staircase proves otherwise.

Mr. Lasker stops at the bottom of the steps, dressed in his business casual attire for an unfavorable Saturday at the office. "Rosie."

I offer him a smile, dropping my backpack on the wooden floor. "Where are the boys?"

"Still with Charlotte." He says, brushing a hand through his dark hair speckled with gray streaks.

"Oh. Well, I don't mind waiting for them if you have to leave." I say politely.

He doesn't respond. His contemplative eyes simply drift over me.

"Is…everything okay?" I ask, smoothing uneasy palms over my skirt.

I expect a quick assurance that it is, but I don't get one. Instead, his features grow tense. "Can we talk for a minute?"

A reflexive pit forms in my stomach. "Sure."

He gives me a nod, then ascends the stairs from which he came. I feel a strange pull inside me, something that tells me I should grab my bag and high-tail it out the front door. But I don't listen. Sooner replacing it with the sound of my Mary Janes thumping up the steps as I follow Mr. Lasker to the second floor. He stands before an open doorway at the base of the hall I know belongs to his bedroom, signaling for me to go first. I momentarily meet his gaze in my pass, finding his expression unreadable. When I enter the expansive room, the first thing I notice is how tidy it is. Everything is tucked neatly away. The large bed is made to perfection, which makes the open magazine sitting on the structure's edge so vibrantly out of place.

I stop dead, terror skewering my heart when I lock eyes with my half-naked self.

Behind, there's a faint *click* of a closing door. The eerie silence I thought had been out of place upon arrival now threatens to smother me entirely. It's only broken by the sound of Mr. Lasker's voice, which abandons any trace of cordiality. "Care to explain?"

In a rush, I flip the magazine closed to keep from exposing myself more than I already have. Forcing air into my pained lungs, I dare a look toward the man behind me. He stands with arms crossed over his broad chest, staring down at me the same way he looks at his sons when they're due for a reprimand. I use the pause he extends to curse myself for not heeding that urge to flee when escape was still an option.

But when I do speak, fear strings each of my words. "Mr. Lasker, I..."

What the hell can I say? I can't vomit months of explanation onto him when I'm too stricken with horror to work out a single sentence.

"M.R.," He goes on when I don't. "Mary-Rose. It's been you all these months, hasn't it?"

Trembling now, shame pulls my head low. "Yes."

Fuck. His subscription. A lethal fact I'd overlooked after the shitstorm the past twenty-four hours has been. Silence swells again, and I only lift my chin when I hear him scoff. His focus averted, the muscles in his arms strain visibly through his shirt.

"The babysitter story…You wrote that." He mutters, shaking his head.

If the bed weren't at my rear, there would be nothing stopping me from collapsing into a heap on the floor. I sit at the edge of the mattress as nausea weaves through my insides. My mouth falls open with the intention to bring a defense along with it, but my throat clenches tight.

He must take the reaction as confirmation enough. Miraculously, though, his tone softens. "Does your mother know about this?"

"No!" The answer comes fluidly. "No, she doesn't. But if she found out, if she even suspects anything…You can't tell her, Mr. Lasker, you just *can't*. She'd take away my home, everything my father left me." I fight the urge to retch at the way I'd so recklessly put my promise to Erica at risk. My watery eyes plead with his as I raise my voice to a desperate beg. "Please, don't tell her! *Please*—!"

"Hey, hey, settle down." He steps close to set large hands on my shoulders, looking down at me sternly. "I'm not gonna tell her."

I want to sigh in relief, but I'm too stunned to breathe. "You're not?"

"Of course not." He says like it should be obvious. "You're eighteen, what you do is none of her business."

He understands. Thank *God* he understands.

I glare at the magazine, an onset of tears wetting my cheeks. "I wanted to stay anonymous. They published that without my permission."

"*What?*" He kneels in front of me. "Rosie, tell me how this happened."

I suck in a quiet sob, then do exactly that. Explaining everything from my entry to the profession, to how those photos were obtained, then so mercilessly stolen by the hands of someone with intentions to pin me in a corner. All the while, Mr. Lasker listens without interruption. Keeping a warm, delicate hand on my leg, he rubs it soothingly each time emotion surfaces to choke me. As petrified as I'd been to admit it all, he was remarkably patient, especially for someone I'd unfairly dragged into this nightmare.

When I conclude, my voice is reduced to a quiet whimper. "I don't know what to do. I'm just so scared."

He expels a long breath, eyeing me sadly. "All that sounds like…a lot. But even if your mother knew, it wouldn't mean she'd disown you."

"Even if she wouldn't, she had our pastor crucify me in front of everyone at Crosspoint, all because I stood up for my friend. If they found out about *this*? I just—" My throat closes again, and I can't stop myself from regressing to a snapshot in time when these fears were no possibility at all. Back when I was protected and loved unconditionally by a person who, if here today, would assure that I'd make it through this. Sobs gouge me as I double over to bury my face in my hands. "I just want my *dad*!"

After a few heavy heaves, I sense calloused, yet gentle hands grab my wrists. Mr. Lasker lowers them, then carefully raises my chin until I'm forced to look at his face. It's firm, but bears a striking solicitude I hadn't counted on. "I know you're feeling helpless right now, but you aren't. I'm right here."

My eyes squeeze shut in guilt. "How can you say that after what I did?"

"Because I care about you."

I choke back another sob. Sucking air through trembling teeth as I feel fingers brush the hair from my forehead, then slide to cup my wet cheek.

"Look at me." He commands softly enough that I comply, a stray tear falling as I do. He swipes it away with his thumb, his deep voice offering me solace. "How long have I known you?"

Sniffling, I answer shakily. "Since I was fifteen."

He nods. "You're like a daughter to me, Rosie. I've been telling you for years that I'd take you in if you needed it."

The declaration is so genuine, it puts a slow end to my periodic sobs. "You mean that?"

"Absolutely. God forbid your mother finds out, you'll always have a home here with me." He stands, pulling me from the bed into a hug.

My face settles against his chest. The warm embrace is enough for my body to finally relax, and I feel safe enough to shed the last of my tears. For the first time in nearly a decade, I consider if this is what having a father is like.

"Thank you…" I whisper against him. "I'm so sorry, Mr. Lasker."

His large hand cradles my head, fingers teasing the white ribbon as he huffs. "For what?"

I swallow hard. "Writing that story inspired by us. I shouldn't have done it. It was just a stupid fantasy."

First Henry, now him. I hadn't begun to figure out what it would take to earn their forgiveness. An apology is all I can offer until I do.

"There's nothing to be sorry about." Nose settling against my hair, he inhales slowly. "If anything, I was flattered."

His words hit me like an electric zap as I look up. "You were?"

"I was." He's smiling now. "I think it's cute that you have a crush on me."

I blink at him, unsure how to respond. "I…was afraid you'd be mad."

"How could I be mad at you?" He asks deeply, eyes narrowing in playful sternness. "You're just a little girl."

I step backwards to end the hug. He steps with me.

"U-Um," I glance at the closed door behind him, my voice hoarse from crying. "We should probably go back downstairs. I don't want Nathan and Daniel to think we're missing when they get here."

I take another step back. Then another. Then another. He matches my every move, his grip tightening on my waist—when had it landed there?

His wry grin doesn't falter. "I told Charlotte not to bring them."

My heartbeat skips. "You…what?"

I feel my back press to the bedroom wall as he chuckles. "It's just you and me." Shock renders me incapable of deciphering thought or reason behind his behavior. I do nothing but stare. He brushes the fringe from my brows again, giving me an unfiltered view of his eyes—gleaming with dominance. "Daddy's right here."

In one breath, my bottom lip is quivering. In the next, he's sucking it into his mouth.

My eyes bulge as his tongue parts my teeth. He pushes me against the drywall so hard, the material creaks from the pressure. I can't think. I can't even breathe. All I can do is mimic. The way his hot mouth commands my own leaves me with no option but reciprocation. I attempt it, craning my neck to accommodate his towering height. But I don't get far, as large hands slide beneath my skirt to grab my ass and lift. I straddle his middle as I'm abruptly crushed between his muscular body and the barrier behind.

"That picture of you…I always knew you were hot, but *fuck*." His declaration is ruthless against my lips, fingers leaving my hips to grip the collar of my button-up. "I wasn't sure how much longer I could go without tearing this off."

With a strong pull, the top buttons give and pop. Some clattering to the ground as my shirt is ripped open to the base of my lacy white bra. I suck in a sharp breath as his hand slips beneath a cup to pull my breast free. Breaking our kiss to peer at my chest, he laughs morbidly before dipping to suck my nipple into his mouth. I cry out at the foreign sensation, bringing with it agonizing overstimulation as he pulls the bud between his teeth. Perturbed reality shifts into focus as I'm left to gape at what he's doing to my body.

"You said I'm like a daughter to you—" A scream clips my words as he bites harder.

"You are," he replaces his mouth with rough fingers that squeeze tightly before shifting to tongue my neck. "You're my baby girl."

His raw conviction overrides my senses. Drowning me in a deathly mix of astonishment, heat, and fear in its sharpest form. If what

Henry and I shared was love, and what Val and I shared was passion, this...this was *primal*. There seems to be no conscious thought in his movements, only instinct to attack and dominate what he sees as his.

"What does that make me?" He growls into my flesh, the stubble on his strong jaw scratching me. When I don't answer fast enough, a fist grips the base of my ponytail and yanks hard. Exposing more of my neck for his mouth to take as I whimper at the pain. "*Say it.*"

His teeth scrape my throat, forcing the word out of me in a pained yell. "*Daddy!*"

He groans, as if the title alone was all he needed to reach his end. But the way he grips my small form like I weigh nothing proves that he's far from done. My vision blurs with the room around us, and by the time my mind catches up, I've been thrown face-down onto the surface of his wide bed. Winded from the impact, I'm given no lungful of reprieve before a weight settles on my back in the form of his knee. My skirt flips to expose my rear before I'm rocked with the sting of a slap.

"God, this ass is fucking perfect." He tugs my panties high to uncover more skin before striking it harder.

I clench my jaw to keep from screaming. He doesn't hold back. All the force he isn't using to hold me in place goes to his vicious spanks. Hit after hit, I claw uselessly at the white covers.

Then, he stops. Sliding his fingers down the silky fabric between my thighs to press firmly against my clit. Gasping to the degree I can with his weight on my ribs inadvertently sends the message that he's found what he set out to. I choke back a whine as he starts furiously rubbing, hard enough that his arm blurs and the bed beneath us quakes. My body reacts before I can even consider if this is something I want. Pleasure surges from his rapid fingering. Pitiful moans escape before I can help it, smothered by the damp fabric against my face.

"Do you have any idea how many times I went back to that

babysitter story, imagining she was you?" He chuckles again. "Turns out, she was. How about that?"

It's too much. I grasp at the blankets to shift away and steal a moment of pause before it all breaks. But he has me pinned. All I can do is take it as my hips start to buck on their own accord. My lids screw shut as hot wetness floods my panties. A sensation that had always marked the manifestation of my desires. Only now, it sickens me.

His breaths grow heavier. "If you wanted me, all you had to do was say it. I would've ruined this little cunt years ago."

Suddenly, his rubbing ceases—the crotch of my underwear shifts. I shriek as he penetrates me with two of his thick fingers. My own lubrication allows them to slip deep after the few seconds of persuasion it takes him to force them inside. My entrance burns from the foreign pressure, but it intermixes with the rest of the fire consuming me as they start pistoning with revived intensity.

"Fuck, you're so tight." His voice is a sinister growl. "Are you gonna come for me, baby?"

When I don't respond, he feverously spanks me with his free hand.

"*Yes, Daddy!*" I manage between frantic gasps, out of fear that not referring to him as such would only cause further punishment. My teeth clench as he flexes his hand, digging an outer finger hard against my clit.

Everything gives. The orgasm rips through me so aggressively, it's almost as painful as the stretch of my entrance. The first I've ever had that wasn't brought on by my own doing. My mouth opens to scream, but it catches as my whole body locks with ferocious intensity. I lay there, wide-eyed and unmoving, counting seconds until the sharp pulsations inside me come to their inevitable end.

One. Two. Three. Four. Five...

It's over as quickly as it came on. And I'm left a limp, panting heap beneath his knee.

"That's my sexy baby…" His fingers pull from inside me, moving to stroke hair from the side of my face before tugging the white bow tied to my ponytail.

Like he's unwrapping a present, the ribbon slips from its knot. I watch with heavy eyes as it's mindlessly discarded, drifting to the floor beyond the bedside. He crushes me again when I'm abruptly flipped on my back. A mouth latching to mine before I can properly catch the breath I'd lost in his advance. Strong hips settle between my open legs. Among the weight, a large, stiff mass protrudes the fabric of his pants. Wet kisses trail down the side of my jaw, then my neck.

"Your mother made you out to be so devout." His tongue finds the silver cross of my necklace, lapping the skin around it before traveling lower. "But then, you came into my house wearing those skirts, always bending over so I'd take a second look. And, *fuck*, when I felt this tight little body for the first time…" Teeth rake across the top of my heaving breasts in a move I know will leave a mark. "I knew you were really a slut. Now, tell me. How many cocks has my little girl taken?"

My throat constricts, realizing all too quickly where this is leading as my mind races to make sense of it. He thinks I've done this before—that has to explain his urgency. It just *has* to. I swallow back apprehension long enough to put it into words, my voice small as I feel. "None."

He snickers. Actually *snickers* against my half-exposed chest. "Yeah, right."

I try moving my hands to force him to look at me. But somewhere in his efforts, my wrists had become pinned at my sides.

"I swear," my tone is nothing short of a whimper. "I've never done this before."

Finally, he gets the hint. His kisses slow to a stop before he lifts his head. Darkened eyes meet mine, shimmering with the gleam of arousal. "You're still a virgin?"

I frantically nod, relief rinsing me as his hold loosens.

Until a devious, frighteningly slow smile tugs the corner of his lips. "I guess Daddy's gonna have to change that."

My hot blood runs to ice.

His mouth resumes its ravishing of my skin, even more enthusiastically than before, as commanding hands slide down my hips. My gaze flickers rapidly around the room, envisioning the days when I used to *fantasize* about this very thing happening. All the times I'd looked at Mr. Lasker with longing, wishing that he would toss me to the bed and mercilessly take me. But here we lie, and the same burn of lust that once fueled those desires is nowhere to be found.

He isn't slowing down. If anything, my confession of being a virgin spurred him on. Why isn't he asking if this is something I want? I can't imagine doing this to a person without being absolutely sure. Let alone it being their *first time*.

"I-I don't..." The words die on my tongue as he sucks hard on the skin of my breast, leaving behind angry red patches in place of the ivory. Foregoing the filial act in my post-climax lull, I mutter, "Mr. Lasker—"

"Shh," he hushes me, crawling back to my face to stroke my cheek. It's a soothing gesture, but the fever in his movements tells me it's nothing but a courtesy. "It's alright, baby. It'll feel *so* good. I'll be gentle."

I almost laugh. There was absolutely nothing gentle about anything he had done to me thus far. Gritting my teeth as he licks along my jaw, I fist the covers beneath us. "I don't know if I'm ready."

His lips take pause, and my muscles lock as he slips a hand beneath my skirt to brush under the thin line of my panties. He removes the limb, holding a glistening finger up to my face. "Looks like you're ready to me." His brows narrow in concentration as he glides the digit along my cheek, coating it in the aftermath of my orgasm as I recoil. He chuckles deeply. "So wet for Daddy's big cock, aren't you?"

I whine at the unmoving weight of him, attempting to wriggle my hips free of his claim to no avail. If anything, the motion makes his grip on me tighten as I rub against his pressing erection.

I wanted this.

The idea—no, *fact*—rattles painfully through my mind with every combined sensation.

I wanted this.

I put it on paper. I got off to it. Now, it's happening. I need to accept it. Maybe even enjoy it? What right did I have to say no after practically begging?

I wanted this.

He and I are no different, really. Why were his fantasies any more condemnable than my own? None of it was real. It had all been in our heads.

Until now.

I wanted this.

His hands fondle my breasts before sliding up my skirt, fingers teasing the hemline of my panties. My throat dries at the thought of what'll happen once they're off.

I wanted this.

This is it. After years of dreaming, I'm going to lose my virginity right here in this bed. I feel like crying at how unceremonious it is. How he's taking what he wants like I'm some object, instead of a human being. A *scared* human being…

I'm human…A human.

Not a fantasy. Not words on paper. Not fiction.

I go rigid as fingers hook around my underwear. Realization hitting me with twice the force of his efforts.

I *wanted* this.

Wanted. I no longer do. What right did I have to say no? Every fucking right. My body isn't his for the taking; it's *mine* to dictate. And right now, I want him off.

"No…" I say quietly at first. But when he tugs at my panties regardless, I shout. "*No!*"

He stops. His hands cease as his eyes lock on mine, brows furrowed at my outburst.

"I don't want this," I say with assertion despite my inferior position. "Get off me."

He gives no reaction at first, until a deprecating huff escapes his mouth. "What?"

I shake my head, my voice gentler now that his efforts have been tainted. "I'm sorry, but I can't do this. I don't want it anymore." I fight to speak between heavy pants, looking at him with genuine remorse. Even if he *was* being overzealous, I had given him every reason to believe this was something I desired. The responsibility is on me to fix it. "Please, I'll go home and I won't come back here ever again. I'll tell my mom you don't need me to babysit any longer. We can go on like this never happened."

Everything, even time, seems to slow as I study his face. It's the same unreadable mask he wore when I first entered the room. And after a pause that's lengthy enough for me to recover the breath I'd lost since our endeavors began, his fingertips release the hem of my panties.

Inhaling deeply, I let out a quiet sigh as relief settles warmly over my skin.

But it's replaced with the icy sting of fear as he suddenly grips the material. Ripping fabric cuts through the stillness as my underwear is torn away, leaving cold air to chill my wet underside.

My eyes flare. "What are you doing—?!"

He doesn't look up. Tossing aside the garment like the hindrance it is, he slips his fingers between my thighs to part me.

He can't…

"I said *no!*" Terror rattles my voice. I shove a trembling palm into his face, but he doesn't budge. "Stop touching me!"

I cry out as a fist snares my wrist. It clenches so hard, my fingertips prickle. His free hand dips between us. Following it, the sound of an unclasping belt.

He can...And he *is*.

Panic wires me. Pushing against him is useless; his body is like iron. My feet kick, but don't land. I attempt it with such force that my shoes slip, clattering one by one across the room.

My throat burns as I scream, "*Stop!*"

"Shut up." He growls.

"*I SAID ST—!*" My demands are stifled by a large hand clamping my mouth. I suck in frenzied breaths through my nose as he hovers above, pinning me with furious eyes.

"Scream again, and I'll hand that magazine to your mother *myself.*" He says with all the malice of a threat and all the certainty of a promise.

After the longest silence of my short life, his palm lifts inch by slow inch from my mouth, testing my conviction. But my pleas don't return, as his clutch is instantaneously replaced by the smothering hand of dread. All at once, I'm facing losing my life as I know it, or my virginity by way of complete savagery. Option one would strip me of my future, my home, everything Erica made me swear to preserve.

Option two...was disposable.

I refuse to look at him. I can't bear witness to his madness in preparing to devour me. All I can do is stare upwards. My foggy focus aims at the white ceiling as I feel his belt slip free. Slowly, my limbs go limp against the bedding. In the textured material above us, the faces of everyone who warned of this look down on me. The ones who asserted that tempting my brothers would only lead to them enacting their innate desires, and whatever came of it would be my fault. I would deserve it. Through all their voices, that of my mother's overpowers.

Whores get what they deserve.

Her words fall like frigid specks of snow, landing on my flushed skin to melt in narrow rivulets—until I recognize those to be tears. Trailing from my welling lids to my roughed hair as I lay entirely still.

Mr. Lasker pushes on without restraint, working his pants low enough to expose himself. His tongue is on my neck again, his hands feeling every inch of skin he'd barbarically laid claim to. My eyes rest closed in forced acceptance. Proving the believers above him right in their taunting declarations of righteousness.

But when the darkness overtakes me, I see something else. More faces. Only these, I welcome.

Erica.

Lewis.

Val.

Henry.

Every person I care for. Every person who made *me* feel cared for. The people I would go to my grave to protect. The ones who showed me, despite my stubbornness, that I was worthy of being accepted just as I am. The ones who taught me mountains more than I've ever learned within the damned walls of Crosspoint Fellowship.

That I'm loved.

That I'm worth it.

That I'm human.

That I *bite back*.

There's a stiff jab at my inner thigh. Mr. Lasker moans against my neck. My tearful eyes shoot open.

Whore. Virgin. It doesn't matter. I don't deserve this.

Nobody deserves this.

Absolute, fiery indignation restarts my heart, and my will to go down fighting along with it. Lips graze my throat as his hand slips between us, grabbing hold of himself before I feel a hard mass slide between my wet folds. There's a pressure at my entrance that clumsily slips when I ghost his neck with gentle fingers, letting them glide over tan skin until they find his stubbly jaw. He stills, taking enough pause to look into my eyes.

In turn, my features soften as I show him my teeth. Stretching my pretty, immaculate, perfectly rote smile to say, "Fuck me, Daddy…"

The breath he loses trickles hotly over my face, feverish lust singeing my skin as he forces his mouth against mine. I fist the fabric beneath us, bracing myself as I part my lips. Permitting his tongue to dip inside for a few lingering moments before it retreats.

I suck his bottom lip between my teeth and bite him.

Hard.

His growl of pain rattles my skull in an instant. I clench my jaw shut, refusing release until the warranted damage is done. He tries pulling away to no avail, then resorts to striking me, throwing every ounce of his unimaginable strength into blow after blow to my face. Sharp knuckles crack against my cheekbone. The hits are strong, but *adrenaline* holds stronger. I don't budge. His bellows amplify to all-out screams as hot blood spills through my teeth, the metallic liquid flooding my mouth and airway. It's only when I sense the gut-wrenching tear of flesh that I finally let go. Mr. Lasker throws himself off the mattress. His back slams loudly against the bedroom wall as he covers his mouth with a hand, red pouring from between his fingers.

I shoot into a seated position with a retch, painting pristine covers in grotesque splatters of blood and severed skin. The crimson residuals spate down my chin and neck, staining my half-opened shirt. My tunneling focus shifts from the gory scene to my attacker. Mr. Lasker's eyes—a horrifying interweave of rage and agony—meet mine for a debilitating split-second.

Then, I run.

In one heartbeat, I'm bolting from the bed. The second, I'm tearing open the bedroom door. The third, I'm sprinting for the staircase.

Refusing to slow as my numb legs find their pace down each of the narrow wooden steps, only breaking at the demand of a thunderous echo from the bedroom behind.

"ROSIE—!"

The tone of Mr. Lasker's voice strikes like it'll jump out and attack me if I so much as turn back. I don't, but it shakes me enough to lose my footing. My socks offer no traction, sending me tumbling down the final third of the steps. I register every agonizing bump and slam until meeting the bottom with a hard *crack* of my skull against the entryway floor. Stars swim through my vision as I roll to my side, whimpering pitifully. But all it takes is the sound of heavy footsteps from above to quell the pain. I jump to my feet, stopping for a lost breath to secure my bag beside the front door before I'm flinging it open. Leaving it so, my socks hit the pavement of the driveway, and I *sprint*.

I don't slow my pace. I don't look back.

My lungs scream for air as I race down the sidewalk, passing house after house, but I refuse to stop. The burn of my legs is almost indecipherable among the surge of adrenaline. My heartbeat echoes loudly in my ears, drowning out everything but the incessant urge to get as far away as fast as possible.

But through the thumping of my heart and feet, the unmistakable sound of a starting engine reverberates down the road. There's a flash of recognition a moment before the bone-chilling prospect grips me. There's a chance it isn't him—that my mind was too afraid to discern the sound of Mr. Lasker's car from any other's. But it was a chance I couldn't take.

Spotting a narrow walkway bisecting two houses bordered by tall fences, I rush for it. Maintaining my frenzied pace as I disappear from the view of the street. A few trees litter the grassy footpath. I only stop when I reach the closest, putting it between myself and the now-limited view of the roadside. Sliding down the trunk until I meet the ground, I hold my backpack to my chest like it's some type of Kevlar.

Whoever's car engine speeds past the walkway. The sound dissipating as quickly as it came.

I sit there, unmoving, for minutes. Perhaps hours. Unable to tear my thoughts from anything other than what I had just narrowly escaped. I bury my face in my bag, hugging it tightly between my legs and arms. I can't cry, for fear it will alert the wrong person to my location. All I can do is sit. Sit and wait until I feel it's safe to emerge from this breakable pocket of security.

As if the world would ever feel safe again.

The walk from Mr. Lasker's house to mine is fifty minutes on a nice day. But today, it takes hours.

When I finally gathered the courage to leave the secluded walkway, I took an extra-long route home. Just in case he happened to be waiting for me on what he knew to be my typical path. Each time I registered the hum of a vehicle approaching, I didn't bother to wait and see if it belonged to him. I ran for whatever cover happened to be nearby. Bushes, trees, I'd even jumped a few gates on my trek. But every instance left me feeling like a fool when I peered onto the road and Mr. Lasker was nowhere to be found.

The time this took gave my mind ample opportunity to resume normal speed. But that didn't stop a million new fears from flashing before my eyes.

What if he's going to tell my mother?

What if he's going to the police after what I did?

Will they believe me when I tell them what happened?

Should I tell anyone what happened?

When I make it to my street, I'd long since lost momentum to run. My slow steps cast long shadows in the light of the setting sun, stretching the silhouette of a broken spirit across an achingly intimate front yard. And for the first time in as long as I can remember, I feel relieved to see my mother's house. Despite my state, I allow the familiarity of its weathered exterior and cracked driveway to satiate my dizzied mind.

But familiarity is precisely what draws my attention to the out-of-place mass at the edge of the lawn, right beneath my second-story window. Dry grass pricks the underside of my dirty socks as I approach it, stopping when my feet are inches from the loose pile of bent metal shards. My heart, which had been in a rapid hammer since escaping Mr. Lasker all those hours ago…*stops*.

Suddenly, gravity is pulling me with such force that it takes all my effort not to buckle at the knees—making the slow rise of my head to the window above nearly impossible. The frame is open, translucent curtains whipping in the breeze. My stomach clenches, and I swallow back the urge to vomit.

All over the shattered remains of my typewriter.

Chapter 33

The house is deathly quiet.

No rocking of my mother's chair. No televangelist shouting through the TV's speakers. Even the white noise of the suburb outside feels sucked away by the unearthly space. It might be the most still our home has been since the days following Erica's departure.

Which is disturbing, considering the storm of my lifetime is only a staircase away.

Each inclined step I take is slower than the last, as if my body is trying to hold itself in the life I know for as long as possible before it's destroyed—tossed away and shattered like the remains of my typewriter. Every creak in the wood. Every scraped stretch of wallpaper. Every mark of a lost adolescence. I let the prosaic details burn in, as if I'll never have the liberty of witnessing them again. Upon reaching the top, my bedroom door stands slightly ajar. Through the inches of allotted view, I see the wooden floor therein bathed in a sea of white. Any trace of my resolve wavers as I place a trembling hand on the knob, then exhausts as I push it open.

Pages litter the ground. Most lay discarded on the flooring, but others have been haphazardly thrown. Some drape over my desk. A few hang partially on the shelves. And the mattress houses an all-new layer of crinkled paper. The bed skirt has been torn off, the material of the box spring along with it—gutted was the interior of the structure, with every secret I'd spent my years working to hide.

My mother is sitting on its edge. Though she's facing me, she doesn't raise her head when I enter. Strips of frayed gray-blonde hair veil her face, wrinkled skin stained with the residue of dried tears. Her hands lay idle in the lap of her modest dress, clutching the spine of an all too familiar magazine. Only, it isn't that of the past issues I'd kept hidden away with my stories. It bears the body of a latex-clad brunette on the cover.

Roxy.

Somehow, despite the product of my wildest nightmares manifesting in front of me, I find it within myself to utter a single word. "Mom…"

Her icy blue gaze doesn't lift. She doesn't even flinch at the voice she'd spent all this time anticipating. She only swallows thickly before speaking in a tone almost as weak as she appears. "Spiritual fiction."

"*Mom*…" I repeat with a broken voice. The fact that my underwear had been torn off and discarded in Mr. Lasker's bedroom isn't the half of it. I feel utterly naked standing among the ruins of my fantasies before my judge, jury, and executioner.

"Staying out late. Assaulting that girl. Spending your time with Henry." Her sunken eyes settle closed. "I knew something had changed…I thought for weeks something had happened to you."

I can't find the conviction to respond. All of it goes into breathing, the burn in my lungs only occasionally reminding me to do so.

She sighs slowly. "But today, I open the front door and find this at my feet." The magazine in her grasp tremors. "I saw your naked body in it. Your name. That's when I came up here looking for the truth. And I realized, this didn't start with college, or the Fennicks…You've been lying as easily as you breathe for years, haven't you?"

Somebody had left that magazine on our doorstep.

Had Mr. Lasker gone through with his threat, or had it been someone else? Lynn? One of the Bible study girls she'd likely told about my profession? I can't know. But that doesn't stop the revelation from turning my limbs taut. The bag between my fingers slips, hitting the pages beneath me with a soft *thud*.

This finally draws Mom's eyes, which flare in indiscernible emotion the moment she catches the state of me. I'm standing before her with a swollen face. Patches of blood dried tightly against my skin. Love bites and teeth marks down my neck and chest—which lay exposed due to my shirt's missing buttons. All of that, with ripped and soiled socks from hours of traversing the pavement shoeless. Any *mother* would crumble at the sight of their child in such a condition.

But it isn't concern in her tone. It's disgust. "What in God's name happened to you?"

I open my mouth to speak, but the memory of what Mr. Lasker nearly did clamps my throat in the vice of sheer panic. She goes on before I can gather myself.

"You were with that girl. The one you put your mouth on. Val from *Bible study*." Mom tosses the magazine onto the bed, displaying the photos of me and the woman in question. Her brows sharpen to a glare that narrows on my body. "Did you and her do *this*?"

My lips part again, but now it's out of shock. "No…"

"I've spent the past two weeks cursing myself for not recognizing the demons in Lewis before he had the chance to influence you." Her lip twitches in rage. "But you were just as guilty, and I didn't even see it! In plain sight, you've been screwing around with some debaucherous pig—!"

"Don't you dare call her that!" I step forward, timidity forgotten in defense of my friend. "You're wrong. Val's a good person."

"I'm wrong? The same way I'm wrong about Henry Fennick?"

"You are." I hold my ground.

Her eyes widen. "My God, did *he* do this to you?"

"No!" I counter, raising my voice. "Henry wouldn't hurt me!"

"How blind can you be? I warned you that giving yourself to a sinner like him would lead you here. I'm surprised you're not in prison, or a *grave*. Where he already deserves to be!"

"*Mom, I love him!*" I shout the words as if doing so would force her to believe them.

Her face twists in anguish. More tears cascade as her head lifts heavenwards. "My husband's heart would break if he knew that both our daughters ended up whores…"

I gape at her. The utter madness of her remark makes my hair stand on end. Assuming it isn't an effect of the chilled breeze from the open window.

"Erica is no whore. And neither am I." I haven't spoken her name in front of our mother in years. And now, I say it without fear. Taking a single step forward, I supply her the absolute truth for the first time in God knows how long. "I was with Val last night, but I left this morning to babysit for Mr. Lasker." My skin crawls at the very mention of him. "He saw those photos of me, too, and threatened to tell you if I didn't give him what he wanted…He forced himself on me."

Her jaw clenches. "Did he? Or did you ask for it?"

My lip quivers. I had. At least, at first. Maybe?

But what he did to me after I told him to stop was beyond reprehensible.

"I told him no. He didn't listen." I suck in a shallow breath. "He tried to rape me, Mom."

"You're a liar."

"I had to bite him to make him stop." My words come out choked.

She stands from the bed, squaring her shoulders as if restraining herself from striking me. "Why the hell would you think I'm foolish enough to believe that? Why should I believe a single word that comes out of that disgusting mouth of yours?!"

"Because you're my *mom*!" I cry, the years of feeling like a prisoner rather than a daughter gouge me with her accusation. "Because I'm telling you someone attacked me! How can that not matter to you? How can *I* not matter to you?!"

"Oh, for God's sake, Mary-Rose!" She begins to pace, her voice rising with each vicious declaration. "I allocate my husband's money to your education, just for you to spend your days writing this demonic *filth*!" She kicks at the pile of sheets beneath her feet, sending pages scattering. "I pray every waking hour that you'll find success, and *this* is what you make of it?!" She slams her fist on the open magazine. "I tell my secular daughter to leave so she doesn't influence you, and *this* is what you turn into?!" I flinch as she steps dangerously close, pinning me with a look of pure disdain. "And you have the nerve to ask if you matter to me?"

I stare, unimpeded, into her steely eyes. After everything she's done to me, godly intentioned or otherwise, what I need right now isn't a despot, least of all, a sanctimonious disposition. What I need is a *mother*. And despite the pandemonium she more than willingly brought into my life—leading me to stand right where I am now—I'm all but forced to recognize how insignificant it is after escaping evil's claws by the skin of my teeth. After years of my mind tempting me with what it would be like to flee from the woman before me, in this moment of desperation, it conjures something even wilder. Blonde hair yet to be grayed by the timepiece of grief. Bright eyes that once beamed at her daughters. Open arms that welcomed them when they needed her most, rather than push them so cruelly apart. The person she was before Crosspoint. The woman my father fell in love with.

I look at her and I don't see Christine Ginger. I look at her and see *Mom*.

Regressing to a flicker in time when she was just that, I throw myself into the body that gave me life. Snaring my arms around her middle, I bury my soiled face against her chest. She stiffens at the contact, but I don't let it sway me.

"He hurt me, Mom..." The long-forgotten familiarity of her embrace fractures my will in an instant. Tears spate in scalding rivulets from my cheeks to her ivory dress. I wail like a child, reduced to nothing more in the wake of the hours behind me. "I was so scared! You have to believe me! I swear, I swear, *I swear* I didn't want it!"

I cling to her as if she's the only thing keeping my frail body from collapsing under this burden, but I'm barely strong enough to keep hold. Seconds pass, marked in time with my sobs. I feel myself slipping lower. Deeper. Losing my grip on this lone bind to reality. Until a hand slips around my back. Followed by another. They're unsteady at first, moving slowly through the restraint of hesitancy. But soon, the burn dissipates from my trembling legs as she bears the weight herself.

"You do matter to me." Her cheek nestles against my hair, sliding low so her voice—now softened—finds my ear. "You matter more than *anything*."

"Please don't take away my home. Everything here, it's all I have left of Dad." I beg weakly. "I miss him so much."

Her nails rake through my ponytail, catching on knots formed in my frantic escape. She speaks with slow, agonizing tenacity. "I know that. I promise you, Mary-Rose, I *know*. I couldn't understand why he would be taken from us. The longer I tried, the more it felt like I was going to die, too." Pulling away, her cold hands cup my wet face, raising it to meet her own. "I wasn't strong enough. It took all the faith in this world for me to accept that I'm not meant to understand why it happened. And when I did, I was finally freed. All I ever wanted was to give you and Erica that freedom, so you'd never end up as lost as I'd been. But...I failed you both." Unsteady fingers brush away my messy fringe, and I'm given an unobscured view of sorrow in its purest form as she whispers, "This is no one's fault but mine. Oh, Mary-Rose, I'm so sorry."

Though I don't give a response, I look back at her and find no trace of deceit.

She leans forward to plant a kiss on my forehead, then swallows dryly to compose herself. "Now, I want you to get changed while I go downstairs and make a phone call, okay? When you're done, meet me out in the car. We're going to get you help."

Her words are as fragile as I feel, but a smile stretches my lips at the relief they bring. "Thank you, Mom."

She nods curtly, the action sending a few additional tears down her cheeks as she straightens out the open collar of my button-up. "If Pastor Morgan can't meet us at the church, we'll make a house call. Whatever we have to do to get you seen tonight."

At once, the tether of hope she'd extended as a lifeline snaps.

I don't dare breathe, depleting the last of my air to shakily question, "What?"

"I'm taking you to Crosspoint." She softly insists. "I won't let my judgment damn you more than it already has. I can't give you the guidance you need, but he can."

My mouth hangs open, and through my incredulity, I find the will to move my tongue. "I don't need a pastor. I need the *police*."

"No, no, no." She hushes, her fingers lacing around the pressed cotton at the edges of my collarbone. "Don't start that. You're going, and I'm taking you."

"I won't—!" My voice falters at the idea. "He'll blame what happened on me…"

"You have to trust him, he's a man of God."

"Not after what he did to me last time. After what *you* told him to do!"

Her grip tightens to a vice. "Mary-Rose, you need help. Just like *I* needed help!"

"I'll burn in hell before I listen to that piece of shit tell me it's *my* fault I was almost raped—!"

I suck in a gasp as she tugs me by the collar with enough aggression to crack my neck. Only inches from her furious face, any trace of understanding in her features hardens to pure, implacable resentment. Except now, it isn't presenting by way of snide insults or vicious reprimands. It's staring through me with merciless eyes.

"Even if it did happen," she snarls through gritted teeth. "It was God's will to set a whore like you straight."

Everything...Every front and every suffocating mask I've spent my life hiding behind drops as I stand tall, screaming my truth in her face as loud as it's thundered inside my head since the day she buried my sister. "*THEN FUCK YOUR GOD!*"

The sound of a hand whipping through the air catches me a fraction of a second before her palm does. The slap lands with all her force on my already-contused cheekbone, pain and dizzying inertia taking me to the floor. Slowly, the sting dissipates to numbed prickles across my face. I hold myself to keep from crumpling entirely, resting my forehead against a strewn paper. The sound of a metallic drag persuades my lids open. I find the bottom of my initialed cross sweeping gently over the ground beneath, swaying with every heave of my chest. Grabbing it with a trembling fist, I pull hard enough that the chain snaps in a single tug. Discarding it with a mindless flick of my wrist, it skims my typewritten pages like a stone across idle water before clattering to a halt. With the insurmountable weight of it gone, I slowly find the strength to raise my chin.

Christine Ginger is staring at me like I'm some intruder as she clutches her own necklace. Fingertips tracing the cross like it could somehow spare her from the damned fate of having me as a daughter.

It wouldn't. Swallowing back the residing pain, I glare at her with every ounce of hatred a stolen childhood can harbor.

"I'm not a whore." I say with quiet resolution. "But I wish I were...I would rather fuck every man *and* woman in this city than end up like you."

More unshed tears glisten beneath icy blue irises, but she blinks them away before they have a chance to fall with the rest. "I want you out." She demands with so little affect, it chills me. "I don't care where you go or what you do with your filthy life. But you'll never set foot in this house again."

They might be the last words she ever speaks to her youngest daughter. But that doesn't stop her from turning to exit unburdened by hesitation.

When I'm alone, my eyes settle closed. The solitary overrides swelling anguish to paint images of years past, extending a memory that anchors me without warning. My father, taking careful steps across the creaky floor to tuck his sleepy toddler into her bed. A good-night kiss. A profession of unconditional love. A family. A home…

But as swiftly as it graced me, it's gone with the flutter of my tear-wetted lashes. My gaze ghosts over the shell of what used to be my bedroom. It settles on the open window, fixating as the minutes tick by and the final rays of orange bleed into cold darkness. Gradually, the sounds of the suburb outside tune in. Beckoning me.

It's time to go.

Christine said nothing when I left. She hadn't even looked up from the Bible in her hands when I walked my final trek from the staircase to the front door, passing the living room where she rocked slowly in her chair.

No, *good luck*. No, *goodbye*. Not even an, I *'ll pray for you*.

Nothing. As if the years of me had been erased from her memory like a slate wiped clean…For a third time.

I only took what I could fit in my backpack, as well as the collapsible suitcase I'd harbored at the top of my closet out of fear that this day would eventually come. The barest essentials. My father's cassette and copy of *Mary's Music*. My lamb and Henry's gifts. The remains of my stories, however, I had bundled. But not to carry with me into whatever life I was about to enter blindly. Instead, to leave in the garbage bin on the side of the street. Five years of my most intimate work, left to be disposed of—my *Holy Scriptures* notebook topping the collection like the headstone of a grave. I don't stop to give my childhood home a final look-over, but find myself sifting through the remains of my father's heirloom a drop beneath my bedroom window. Only feeling free to leave this place behind when I'd located the typewriter's severed, red-marked "R" key to tuck in the security of my stuffed bag.

It's past twilight as I wait on a lone bench at Candid Park. The light of a nearby payphone I'd used after arriving casts an eerie glow on the otherwise dusky location, barren of souls except mine. I shiver in the cold November night, rubbing warmth into the sleeves of my fresh cardigan. I had gladly torn off the tattered clothes I'd crawled home in and exchanged them for a new outfit. Burning the ruined articles would have been preferable, but leaving them in a heap on the wooden floor had to suffice. Maybe when Christine tosses them, she'll take a closer look at the missing buttons and blood stains and realize I hadn't been lying about what happened to me.

Yeah, right...

My thoughts are broken when the headlights of an oncoming car beam through the border of trees, then slow to a stop on the road before me. Through the shadowy windows, I spot the smiling face of my nephew from his car seat. His legs kick in excitement when he notices me, raising both hands to wave. I force a smile that falters when the driver's door opens, a blonde head peering above the car's roof. Her features are so akin to Christine's that it almost makes me sob with the reminder as to *why* I'm sitting on this park bench. But instead of disgust, Erica's face twists in horror at the sight of me—likely at the bruises and dried blood still caked to my skin. My sister rounds the bumper as I stand, any words of explanation dying on my tongue the moment I open my mouth to speak.

She doesn't press me for information. She doesn't say anything. She only pulls me into the warmest hug of my life.

All the weight I've carried for the past two days—or rather, five years—is mercifully lifted. She cradles my aching head against her shoulder, and the tears return. I let myself weep in the safety of her loving embrace, both in despair and relief.

Because despite all that had been stolen, for the first time in as long as I can remember, I *feel* at home.

Chapter 34

"Excuse me, are you the seller here?"

With a steady hand, I stock the final book on the display shelf. Admiring the sculpted body of the man adorning its cover before I glance at the patron addressing me. My eyes widen, shifting between him and the printed model a number of times before concluding that they're, in fact, two separate people.

"I am." I offer him a seductive smile as he nears, the warm lights of the bookstore casting hard shadows on the muscles of his chest—half exposed in his unbuttoned shirt. "Are you looking for anything in particular?"

He closes the distance between us, resting a sturdy arm against the shelves at my rear to trap my body between it and the handsome face peering down at me. "I was hoping you could tell me. Any suggestions?"

I'm wracked with shivers as his finger teases the collar of my pressed work shirt. "That depends. I personally enjoy romance, but a lot of readers need something a bit more…gripping."

He hums. "I like the sound of that."

I gasp as he fists my collar, tearing open the button-up so my breasts spill free. Taking one in his large hand, he weighs it with intrigue.

"Of course, there's—" I swallow back a moan as his thumb teases my nipple, stiffening the bud to send electric waves to my deep, low insides. "There's so much the genre has to offer. I just love a story that puts you inside the main character."

"Really?" The corner of his mouth pulls in a smirk as the hand palming my tit sinks low, clearing my skirt and sliding with nimble fingers up the *inside of my thigh until they reach their destination. His curious index finds me nude beneath, slipping between hot lips before teasing my awaiting entrance. "So do I…"*

My working fingers lock at the sudden sensation between my legs. It sends goosebumps prickling over my flesh despite the stifling temperature of the closet. Panic pulses through my chest and outwards as I disregard the foreign typewriter. Slowly, I reach beneath my skirt to feel out the inside of my underwear. Upon removing it, the arousal that always manifested during my erotic writing coats my fingertips, glistening in the fluorescent light.

But there's no trace of pleasure, nor a desire for release. There's only the onslaught of nausea that blurs my vision as I abruptly stand, chair scraping on dilapidated flooring in my rush to the storage room's mop sink. Twisting on the faucet, I pull a few paper towels while clumsily tugging down my panties, harshly rubbing my underside clean with the brittle material before trashing it. Rushing water envelops my hand in the deep porcelain well as I wipe away any evidence of my body's sexual reaction. Scrubbing gently at first, then rougher and rougher as the outpouring's temperature blends from cool to scalding. I only cut the water when steam spills over the edges of the sink, my raw hand burning a fierce red as droplets fall from each of my soiled fingertips. I stare at the appendage, sizzling pain numbed by the ice coursing through my veins.

It isn't nausea blurring my vision anymore. It's tears.

But eventually, the fear dissipates. Leaving me feeling equal parts foolish and exhausted as I right myself. The lone bulb above my head flickers in the windowless room, blacking out the space in a dark staccato. Though it's more than claustrophobic in the storage closet at *Marcy's Bookstore*, it's a bit more spacious now that the Christmas decorations have been cleared out and set up, which was one of my first assignments when the owner agreed to give me a part-time position.

Abandoning my minimal progress on the latest piece, I reclaim the small mailing desk to tuck the pages away in my backpack. When I'm finished, the door to the room swings open. Marcy's gray curls swoop as she tilts her head inside.

"I know you're on break, hon," she prefaces. "But we got someone by the rack wanting some direction."

Throat still dry, I offer an agreeable nod in place of an answer. Leaving my belongings in storage, I straighten the nametag pinned to my white button-up before rounding the corner to the rear of the store.

"How can I help you—?" I start, just for my greeting to become strangled.

I almost have to do a double-take, having never seen the woman before me with her hair free from its styled ponytail. But here she is, presenting as a manageress despite flaunting what must be her more casual attire—a pencil skirt stretching to her knees, with a silky, crimson colored long-sleeve that catches the overhead lights in soft shimmers. Unbound blonde locks slide smoothly over her shoulder, eyes cool as the December air shifting from the familiar magazine in her hands. She curiously scans my body from head to toe, foregoing the courtesy of a grin.

"I see why you like getting them from stores." Ruth raises the newest *Wild Thang* issue for emphasis. "It's been a long time since I've held a consumer copy."

Formalities evade me as I question, "How did you know I work here?"

"I told you, I like to keep tabs on my employees." She pauses, tapping the spine of the publication against her open palm. "That, and the sheets you mailed in for last week's story were watermarked."

Suddenly, I'm wondering if sending in my content via mail to avoid encountering R.J. had been worth it. The accessibility of a typewriter at the bookstore made it so that I could keep up with my

Wild Thang pieces when I had a fleeting break. Despite Armageddon and my trauma-induced loss of inspiration, the financial security of writing for Ruth was too essential to give up with the limited hours Marcy could spare to provide me.

Besides, the worst thing that could happen already did.

When I keep silent, she replaces the magazine to address me unimpeded. "I never got to speak with you about everything. Would you let me?"

Regardless of her negligence putting me in the position I'm now in, I can't help but admire her willingness to come here at all. It alone gives me the resolution to lower my chin in compliance.

Ten minutes later, she and I have claimed the arranged seating in the corner of the department. Despite Ruth's insistence on speaking, I had done most of it. Explaining the consequences of my photos getting published and the wrath of my religious mother. Resulting in me now residing with my estranged sister, who's graciously—albeit irresponsibly—risking her and her son's allotted housing with me being there. It's only when I near the end of my account that I realize I've divulged more to this woman about my intimate life in a single spiel than I have in all the months working for her combined.

"She cut off my dad's trust the day after I left, so I spent everything I saved from writing on what I still owed Trinity Grace for the semester. That's why Marcy gave me a job. She can only pay me for a few days a week, but it's something." I smooth nervous hands over the fabric of my navy skirt—my lack of funds leaving me with nothing but the small wardrobe I was able to pack in my departure. Even still, I grasp for a final tether of ambition as I ask, "You haven't heard from *Lone Legacy* about my book deal, have you?"

Any flame of hope at the prospect extinguishes as her eyes fall to the cushion separating us on the wall-mounted bench. "No, I haven't. And it's been long enough that…" She sighs heavily. "I'm not hopeful."

I expect the disappointment flooding my chest to overspill, but it simply intermixes with the rest of my despondency from the past three weeks. My back settles softly against the rest as I brace the weight of it.

"You'll have a place at the studio as long as you choose." Ruth continues. "And you don't need to mail in your stories anymore. I put Rodney in charge of our shoots at the new location. He won't be back in office."

My jaw tightens at the mention of him. "Are you here to make things right on his behalf?"

"No," she says softly. "I'm here to make things right on mine."

I shake my head, averting my gaze to keep my blood from heating. "I trusted you, Ruth."

"I know you did." She takes a contemplative pause. "But something tells me you still do, whether you want to admit it or not."

"And *why* would you think that?"

"Because you wouldn't be acknowledging me at all if you didn't. You wouldn't have told me about your life or your mother. And you wouldn't keep writing for us if you didn't have faith in what it can give you."

"You say that like there's no difference between faith and obligation."

Ruth raises a patronizing brow. "In this business? There isn't."

I study her in way of response, remembering too painfully how I'd seen a resemblance to my mother upon our first meeting. Though her appearance alone could deceive, it's her eyes that truly sanctify it—the same steely blue as the woman who'd brought me into this world. But Ruth's are swimming with a palpable sympathy I'd spent years trying—and ultimately failing—to provoke from Christine Ginger.

"You have every right to be angry." She continues. "I can't stop you from leaving *Wild Thang* behind if that's what you decide. But I wouldn't be doing my job if I didn't warn you about how dangerous straying off would be. Especially someone with your potential. I've been there, myself."

I catch a deprecating huff. "You know how it feels to lose your future?"

"Nobody understands the consequences of this industry better than I do." She lowers her head until the unbound hair curtaining her face shifts to allow a better view. "But I'm sure Val told you all about that the night she showed you my film, didn't she?"

My body goes stiff. Any retort catches in my throat before I can explain.

"She didn't tattle on you. When I found out she snuck you into the studio after hours, I put two and two together." Her mouth curves in a raw, yet condescending show of superiority. "Well, what'd you think?"

Already exposed, I take the invitation. "I thought it was amazing."

After an appreciative nod, her eyes drift over the rows in front of us. "You know, the male actor, he was my actual boss at the time—a video store manager from Los Angeles. I figured the power he had over me would translate well on-screen. Not that it took much convincing." She gives a half-chuckle. "It didn't go as smoothly as you might think. I kept missing my cues, calling him by his real name instead of his stage name. I was so eager to sell the role, I didn't stop to think that nerves would get to me."

"You starred in that video with your real boss?" I ask, unable to comprehend such devotion.

"I learned a lot from my start in mainstream pornography. One, if you're selling a story, some degree of authenticity will always put you above the rest. In a profession as competitive as porn, that can make all the difference. And two," her gaze returns to mine, the faintest warmth heating it. "When I'm playing a part, I'm terrible with names."

I offer a kind smile, but something etches in the back of my mind. "You never mentioned it to me, but Val said you showed it to everyone you hire so they understand your expectations."

"I didn't show it to you because you'd already exceeded them."

A feeling I'm hesitant to call pride after the events of the prior month settles over me. "I was only doing what felt good."

"Well, you're in the only industry in the world where nothing matters *except* that. Blurring the lines between fantasy and reality can be a tough move. But if you pull it off, the rewards are insurmountable." The conviction in her tone doesn't falter as she asserts, "You write like there's no difference between the two at all."

A reflexive panic seizes my lungs, but I force myself to breathe through it. "I guess I…never understood the difference."

"It's only one of the things that makes you a standout." She goes quiet, then reaches to tug open the collar of her partially unbuttoned blouse. Pulling the fabric, her faded tattoo of a scarlet lip-print becomes visible. "I got it before making my start in videos so I'd be recognizable. Give the audience a part of me to remember, instead of just being another face and body."

I look away from the mark like it's an intimate part of her I shouldn't be ogling. "I'm sorry it didn't work out like you wanted."

"I don't think it was ever about what I wanted." Her glossy lips purse. "After my video failed, I felt directionless. Pushed everyone away until I was left more isolated than I'd ever been in my life."

I keep my chin low, understanding the experiences of the woman beside me more than I ever thought possible.

Ruth goes on, "I spent too long trying to figure out why things happened the way they did, and I've come to learn that sometimes we aren't meant to understand. We just accept it, then keep working." Her head tilts my way. "Look at you."

"Me?" I question, wary of her observation.

"I told you I saw potential in you, and you've proven me right."

My shoulders slump. "Even if that's true, look what it cost me."

"I am looking." She counters. "You talk about your mother and your home as if your world's been taken. Like you aren't a fresh-faced eighteen-year-old with everything to offer."

"None of that matters, Ruth." The book deal fell through. Everything my father wanted for me is gone. And now, I'm nothing but a burden on the only family I have left. It takes everything in me to say it aloud, "It's my own fault I'm here..." My jaw trembles with the word. "Lost."

Silence swells, just to be broken by, "What if you aren't?"

My gaze lifts, and I expect to see the classic, indecipherable Ruth looking back at me.

But instead, I find a woman so focused that her words practically sting with resolve. "I know you're expecting an apology for what Rodney did. But if it hadn't happened, you wouldn't have moved forward from everything holding you back." She shrugs. "What if you aren't lost? What if...you're free?"

Instinct tries to draw me away from the idea, but the conviction in her tone gives me no choice but to consider it. Armageddon and everything preceding had left me battered beyond recovery, but in the weeks of finding my footing, there was no denying the shift in heaviness. Even if it had been transfigured into a weight of a whole different variety, Crosspoint was behind me. Christine was behind me. For the first time in as long as I can recall, the blinders of my decided future had been removed. Permitting me to stare straight ahead.

Directly at Ruth Sexton.

"Do you want to know the most important lesson I learned in my career?" She asks, supplying the answer when I give a hesitant nod. "I wasted my youth waiting for other people to make me a starlet. I don't wait for opportunities anymore. I hunt them, and I take them myself. I tried it with *Passion of the Scarleteer*, but I was too late. I tried it with *Wild Thang*, and I'm not there yet. But I have faith that's going to change someday. Faith has kept me going for two decades." She raises her chin a subtle inch. "And I think that's all you need."

I hold her stare. "An opportunity?"

"Faith." She concludes, standing from the bench to extend a hand. "But, if either is of interest, you know where to find me."

I take it, letting Ruth guide me onto steady feet. But anticipating her release leaves me astounded when she pulls me closer, sliding her arms around my small body in a solicitous cradle. I return the hug after a pause, the kind gesture sinking bone-deep the longer I stay nestled in her embrace. Something inside me mourns when she inevitably pulls away, a noticeable glint shining in her gaze as she gives me a parting look-over.

The offer burns in as she leaves me in her wake, sharp heel clicks leading her into blinding Albuquerque sunlight with the chime of Marcy's exitway bells.

Chapter 35

Pieces of strewn fabric, lace, and half-finished projects of my sister's lay on every available surface of the small apartment—aside from those occupied by Mattie's abundance of toys. It was a place that should feel like home. And yet, I still can't shake the overwhelming sense of guilt that I don't belong here. A feeling that had been gradually consuming me with each additional morning I woke up on the very couch I'm seated on now.

Taking advantage of the late-morning solitude that came with Mattie at preschool and Erica at the diner, I hold the fated issue of *Wild Thang* responsible for Armageddon between my fingers. I wasn't sure what drew me to secure it in my backpack the night I left, just to turn around and discard all my other work like the blighted relics they were. Maybe I wanted some tangible evidence of what happened to hold on to whenever I missed my old home. Maybe I was just a sucker for pain. Whatever the case, I allow my focus to linger on the spread of Val and my stolen photographs. Finding any residual passion from our night at her apartment out of reach, having lumped it in with all else I've had to mourn. Even so, it's nice to see her face after so many weeks of being without it.

I sigh, flipping the magazine closed to absent-mindedly trace my finger along the lines of Roxy's body. Then the edge of the laminated cover. All the way down to the bottom, where a tear had, at some point, rendered the lowermost right-hand corner missing. My brows furrow, unable to place when that had happened.

I jump when the front door of the ground-level apartment swings open, fearing I would need to hide to avoid being spotted by the complex's manager. But I sigh in relief upon spotting a pretty blonde in her waitress uniform.

"Lunch?" I ask, dropping the magazine into my bag.

"Figured I could finish the latest order if I hurry," Erica says between labored breaths, taking quick steps to sit beside me. She plucks a work-in-progress bra from the coffee table, minding the splayed threads and metal wiring sticking out the sides.

"More coming in than usual?"

"Holiday upswing." She explains, starting a new seam. "I'm definitely not complaining. The more things to distract me, the better."

Silence falls between us, evoking a thought I can't help but express. "Tomorrow's ten years since Dad died."

Erica stills, and I can sense her working a sanguine response for my sake. "I'm sorry you didn't get as much time with him, Rosie... It's crazy how much Mattie reminds me of him."

"You know, I don't mind watching him in the afternoons if it means you'll save on daycare?" I offer for, I'm fairly certain, the hundredth time since my arrival.

"The donations I get have gone up lately; they're enough to cover it. Besides, I'm more concerned with *you* saving up. You're welcome here for as long as you need, and you shouldn't be worrying about anyone but yourself while you stay." She winces as the needle pricks her index finger. "Marcy didn't give you the extra time you wanted?"

I shake my head, resting my elbows on my knees to watch her stitch. "I don't have another shift until next week."

Her mouth curves into a frown. "And your other job?"

Moving in with Erica came at the expense of coming clean about the reason I'd been disowned by our mother. Thankfully, she hadn't taken the news of my unorthodox profession as badly as I thought she would. At least, not compared to how she'd taken the aftermath that ensued. Every horrible, lingering detail of it.

"I don't know." I pause, searching for gentle words. "I'm having trouble with my stories since…what happened."

The air turns heavy as I wait for her input, but hear only the soft pull of weaving thread.

I raise my fingers to ghost my left cheekbone. The last of the bruises had blended back into the natural ivory of my skin only days ago, but the pain—real or conjured—continues to prickle beneath it. "It sounds ridiculous, but writing erotica was what got me through all the times I didn't think I could stand it there." I release a shaky breath. "Now, it all just seems so fake."

"Because it was fake." Her needle hovers over the red fabric between her fingers. "I know that hurts, but it's something worth accepting."

If only I had done that before it desecrated my life. "I'm such an idiot."

"You're not an idiot." She asserts. "You were misguided. Just like I was. There's a big difference between words on paper and actual sex. Actual sex is…*complicated*. It's an adult decision, which means it comes with adult consequences." Her gaze sweeps over the messy room, blue irises gleaming as they trail across Mattie's toys. "Sometimes, it can lead to the best thing that ever happened to you. But other times, it hurts." Her palm smooths over the skirt of her uniform. "You and I were never taught how complex these things are; we were just taught that it was gonna hurt us if we didn't do it the way everyone at Crosspoint said we should."

My eyes settle closed. "All I've done is prove them right."

Moments tick by before she goes on to ask, "You liked writing those stories, right?"

I catch her peering at me in my peripheral vision. "Yeah, I did."

"And your audience loved reading them, didn't they?" She questions further, to which I nod. "Fantasies and real sex might be different, but that doesn't mean you can't have both. Look at what I do," she emphatically raises the lacy materials. "Some people use lingerie for sex. But other people use it to *feel* sexy. I make it because, when I can give that to somebody, it feels—"

"Good." I finish her thought as if it were my own.

"Yeah," she agrees gently. "It feels good. Nobody else should get to dictate what you love. Or *who*. If it's real, you'll know it."

My guard down, I don't hold back the most pressing question. "And what if it's gone?"

"If it's gone…then you take it back." She answers, her features softening. "Think, when's the last time you were really sure of it?"

The truth of the matter comes as swiftly as it does painfully. "Dad loved us."

It wasn't just that. Our shared years on this earth and the legacy they left behind had shown me what it meant to feel safe. To follow my own path. To embrace the *real* me, instead of allowing her to be molded.

"That's a good start," Erica remarks. "Someday, you'll feel that way with other people. The good ones. After that, everything else comes." A smirk corrupts her kind demeanor. "Especially *you*."

I scoff, elbowing her in the ribs as we both devolve into laughter until a curt knock at the front door startles us.

I grab Erica's arm in fear. "Should I—"

"It's okay, the manager's out." She says with a little more confidence than warranted, and I swear I spot a smile on her face as she discards her project to answer it. Taking a brief look through the peephole, she chuckles.

"Who is it?" I ask, sitting tall.

Stepping back, she grabs the knob while shooting me an expectant glance. "I *may've* answered a little phone call when you were sleeping this morning."

She opens it, and I instantly rise to my feet. Cresting midday sunlight catches the blonde highlights of his hair, casting low enough to illuminate familiar blue-green eyes. Hands resting in the pockets of his denim jacket, he looks at me, face brightening for a fraction of a moment before undue tension stifles it. Like a manifestation of everything too good to allow myself to dream of these past weeks, he's here.

"Henry…" Erica drags, leaning casually on the open door.

His gaze shifts to her, and his shoulders relax. "Hey, Erica. It's been a long time."

"Years." She looks him up and down. "I think the last time I saw you, you were chasing my screaming sister down our street, trying to dump a jar of garden spiders in her hair."

Henry pauses awkwardly, cheeks flushing a faint red. "Good to see you, too."

Erica's attention diverts to me with a *tisk*. "Come on, little sis. You should've known getting mixed up with this one would bring trouble."

Now it's my turn to blush.

"Can't really argue with that." Henry quips, before his eyes return to mine. "Rosie, can we talk?"

I reflexively shift my weight onto my heels. Perhaps it's solely my desire to be close to him that pushes me to nod, then step past my older sister, who grins like a fool before closing the door behind us.

Shrouded in the serenity of the complex's courtyard, I tuck my cardigan tight to ward off the wind icing my already raw nerves. "You're not at the garage today?"

He shakes his head, speaking gently. "Have the week off."

The sheer gravity of the matter I need clarified pulls my gaze to the leaf-littered walkway. "What did Lewis tell you?"

"Everything you told him."

That my mother had discovered my profession, discarded me as her daughter, and that I was now with Erica. He hadn't deserved to take on everything else with his own hardships. Not when I was still trying to stomach the rest.

The few paces separating Henry and me feel immovable. Having spent each day since he left me in that hallway constructing the words I'd offer to make it right, I do so with a clumsy interweave of conviction and humility. "If I said I regret what I did to you more than anything I've ever done...would you believe me?"

His jaw tightens at the familiar question. There's a lingering beat of fear that I may be asking for too much following our time apart. But then, the affectionate glint in his eyes I'd barely caught upon his arrival returns. And a single held breath later, he nods.

At once, the mountains between us are reduced to three small steps that I take on tireless legs. Throwing my body into his hold like it's all I need to wake myself from the nightmare I've been living. It might be, because the reality of how much I've missed his touch drops with my face against his shoulder. His strong arms cradling me impossibly close.

"I'm sorry." I force the apology through my constricting throat. "I'm so sorry..."

"It's okay." He mutters, lips sinking to my ear. "None of that matters to me. Not anymore."

"What we have stays between us," I promise him. "I know what that means now. I'll never take it for granted again."

His nose nestles against my scalp. "Fuck, Rosie, I missed you so much."

"I missed you, too." I stifle a sob against his denim jacket, salty droplets wetting the material. The words I never got to say break with my inhibition. "I love you, Henry."

Fingers take the back of my head, pulling it fervently toward his own with the intention of a desperate kiss.

But it doesn't reach. Because the moment I sense his unprompted touch, it no longer belongs to him. My whole body locks with a fearful gasp. The silent understanding between us is shattered by the rapid hammer of my heartbeat, flooding my veins with a lethal dose of panic. I push away, snaring my fingers around his wrist so tightly that my nails bite white indentations into his skin.

Henry jolts. Confused eyes flaring as they shoot to my grip, then my face.

I release him. My focus falls to the concrete as I force deep breaths in through my nose and out through my mouth. Clasping one shaky hand with the other, I'm left cornered by the inevitable I'd been trying so desperately to prolong.

"Henry, there's something else I need to tell you," I admit between short breaths and only the slightest hint of courage. "Something… happened to me."

Winter-stripped trees flanking the courtyard's bench offer no protection from the cold wind. When it catches me in elongated silence, it sweeps a few tendrils of my fringe in its path. Breaking the only obstruction separating me from whatever was waiting beyond it. Keeping my chin dipped, I finally dare a glance at Henry beside me. The time I'd spent anticipating a response having long overstayed its welcome.

He's unmoving. Head low. Eyes narrowed on the dead grass at our feet. They move indiscernibly, as if searching for the words that could make this mark in time any less grievous. But none exist.

In lieu of them, I carefully offer a familiar one. "Henry…?"

His jaw clenches so tight, it shakes—the rest of him gradually following. Bracing his elbows on his knees, he covers his mouth with an unsteady palm. The longer strands of his hair fall to conceal his gaze. I can hear the effort it costs him to breathe, the swells of his chest growing tighter, quicker.

"Henry," I repeat, even softer than before. "Please talk to me."

"I left you alone…" He starts, voice muffled by his hand. "You needed me, and I left you alone."

"Stop." I kill the wretched implication before it dares take another breath. "You didn't do anything wrong."

He swallows hard. "What did the police say?"

Nausea hits me with twice the force it had upon sharing my account. "I never went."

His head raises a curt inch, but his eyes remain obscured as he breathlessly questions, "What?"

"You didn't see what I did to him," I say quietly. "I'm afraid."

"I know—" His indignant tone sputters out. "I-I mean, *fuck*. No, I don't know. But we shouldn't just—"

"Henry," my voice breaks with hollow resolution. "I'm telling you to let it go."

Whether a result of his tremors or not, he shakes his head. "No... I won't."

"It's not your decision," I say firmly.

"You can't tell me somebody hurt you and expect me to let it go."

"What do you want me to tell you?"

"That we can do something."

"We *can't*."

"Don't say that—!" He rights himself with the plea, finally looking me in the face as I'm granted a stark view of his.

There isn't a term bleak enough to describe the pain behind his tear-filled eyes. They flicker across my features in clear desperation, and I want nothing more than to shelter him in the fallout of my confession. Except, I'm just as helpless as I suspect he feels. All I can do is look back, as if to look through him, hoping to find any semblance of the Henry that had gifted me trust and adoration like I never knew I needed. But I find nothing but the remains of a soul persecuted in his own right. Heartbroken. Wordless...

Destroyed.

While only a few of the sobs he's suppressing break through, tears spate hotly down his reddened cheeks. He lifts a hand, then drops it just as quickly to clutch the bench in a white-knuckled grip. The reason behind his behavior hits me with a blow that would shatter my heart if it weren't already splintered. He's restraining himself from touching me.

The sight strips away my hesitancy, and every vein-sizzling rush of dread along with it. I take his face with gentle fingers, closing the distance between our lips until they meet with fragility. My focus tunnels on reminding myself who the man before me truly is. The fact that I'm safe with him. Anything that impedes the resurrection of my fear until he reciprocates. When he does, it's as natural as breathing. His mouth settles warmly against mine—a warmth that spreads to my waist as his hands delicately claim it. The trepidation polluting every beat of my heart since Armageddon drains the longer he lingers. And when we pull apart, I instinctively brace myself for its return.

But it doesn't come. Because the inches between Henry and me evoke something else in its ruin. Something stronger than fear. An incandescent vow outshining the darkness I'd been left to stagger through all alone. The promise in his emerald-speckled eyes speaks with more certainty than a thousand words.

I'm not alone.

While the affliction in his features still resides, it dims with his voice as our noses brush. "Promise me, Rosie. *Promise* we'll get you help."

My jaw clenches, then relaxes as cruel practicality finally grounds me. "Okay...I promise."

Henry sighs heavily in relief. Keeping his hold on my waist as he offers a sorrowful smile.

I return the gesture, but it falters when something prods my mind. All else I had admitted before the account of my assault. "So, you aren't mad about Val and me?"

The question doesn't seem to faze him. But whether the matter feels insignificant against everything else, or he genuinely understands, I can't say.

"No." He answers tenderly, then pauses. "Are you…bisexual?"

I truly consider what he's asking. For myself, more than anyone. The time for denying it had long since come and gone. "Yes."

There was no other explanation. My regard for Val had never stopped at admiration, despite all the effort I expended convincing myself otherwise.

Henry's eyes soften, supplying much-needed assurance. "Okay."

"I still care about Val, but she and I are only friends." I offer a necessary moment of reprieve before asking too much. "Do you trust me when I say that?"

A breath of hesitation lingers coldly between us, then vanishes with the slight pull of his lips. "Of course I do."

My chin dips in relief, but my loving gaze remains fixed on his. "Thank you, Henry."

His palm gently circles the back of my cardigan, warding off the chill. "You know something like that wouldn't make me look at you differently. Just ask Lewis."

I force a laugh through my nose. Though such warm acceptance feels like it should be commonplace, I know I can't hold it as the standard. Not in this age, anyway.

Henry goes on, "I figured I could hang around until he's done with his shift. I can't remember the last time all four of us were together."

My brow knits in confusion.

Which he fails to notice before nodding in the direction of the parking lot. "I brought the rest of his stuff. Is Erica okay with me dropping it off?"

I blink at him, my hands stiffening to clutch the hemlines of his denim jacket. "What are you talking about?"

"Lewis moved out two days ago. He said he was coming to stay with you." Henry's features harden. "He came here, didn't he?"

My eyes widen, panic of a whole new caliber gripping me as I whisper, "Oh my God…"

Chapter 36

Henry didn't bother finding a suitable place to park the Grand Safari when we arrived at Lewis's tech store. Sooner pulling to a reckless stop on the street-side before the two of us made our belligerent entrance. Despite whatever altercation we'd been anticipating, the clerk informing us that Lewis had "resigned" the day prior was more of a blow than I thought I could survive. Especially after spotting a group of young men sporting navy and white college attire among one of the aisles, shooting us pleased grins as we leave.

"Do you have Presley's number?" I ask when we're outside again, grabbing Henry's jacket in a fearful vice.

"No." He shakes his head, completely breathless. "Lewis has barely spoken the past few weeks."

My chest tightens. I place a hand over it as if the act could slow my rapid heartbeat. Then, I focus on the busy street. Locating a storefront that makes my skin prickle with hope. Maybe, there was a chance…

"Come with me," I say, weaving through traffic and taking a few swears from braking drivers as I cross the road. I don't look back to see if Henry trails, refusing to stop until I reach the paneled glass entrance of the café.

Warm air sweeps over me as I step inside, holding my breath as I scan partially full tables. A busy serving hatch behind an elongated counter. Several computers stationed along the far wall. And the single occupant at the seat farthest from the door.

My eyes flare. "Lewis!"

His head snaps my direction, and I can see shock reigning heavy even before I close the distance between us. "Rosie, what are you doing here?"

I throw my arms around him in a relieved hug before I answer, but come up short when a voice behind me questions, "What are *you* doing here?"

I release him to make room for Henry to approach.

Lewis's excuse comes out clipped as his brother arrives beside me. "I had a break from work."

"No, you didn't. We just came from there." I push back.

His chin dips slightly, and I notice that his brown hair is sitting messier than usual. Everything about him looks off. Despite the uniform polo he's wearing, the backpack at his feet is packed to the edge of bursting.

"You told Henry you were coming to stay with Erica and me," I say when he doesn't respond. "Where have you actually been?"

Still nothing. He doesn't even look up.

Henry, clearly growing impatient, claims Lewis's belongings. "Get your ass up. I'm taking you back to my place."

"No!" Lewis says with more authority than I've ever heard from him. I startle as he stands from the seat, tearing the bag from Henry's grip before starting for the café's exit. Henry and I share an incredulous glance before going after him.

"Lewis!" I shout once we're outside, running to match his brisk pace.

"Where are you going?" Henry calls, striding beside me.

"None of your business." Lewis bites out, stepping to avoid several passerbys on the narrow sidewalk.

"I'm your brother, of course it's my—"

"I'm not going back with you," Lewis tells him off. "I heard your roommates talk about me. They know why I'm there."

"What?" I breathe, looking at Henry in terror.

"Who talked about you?" He demands to know. "Tell me and I'll handle it."

"No," Lewis growls.

"You can come with me." I extend the vain offer. "Erica will have you. You know she will!"

Lewis shakes his head. "*You're* not even supposed to be there, Rosie. If they find out, she and your nephew will be homeless."

My stomach flips at the thought, but I ignore it. "What about Presley? You said he wasn't raised like we were. Maybe his parents will help?"

"I'm not putting this on him." He says, foregoing further explanation.

"A motel, then." I look desperately to Henry. "But I spent everything I saved from the magazine on paying off tuition."

"I can scrape enough to cover tonight." Henry's gaze shifts to Lewis before reaching to grab his shoulder. "Just let us help you—"

"*Stop!*" Lewis halts, whirling to push both of us away. "I don't want your help!"

I stagger, gaping at my friend after his outburst renders us deathly still.

"What the fuck is wrong with you?" Henry asks before I get the chance.

"You two!" Lewis looks to be on the verge of tears. "I'm through watching you guys ruin your lives over me."

My jaw trembles as I speak, "What are you talking about?"

Lewis pins me with more rage than I ever thought he was capable of. "You got suspended for assault after what happened with Lynn!" His glare sharpens at Henry. "And *you* went to jail all because some asshole said I was going to give the whole school AIDS!"

Henry retreats like he's been struck. "How do you know that?"

"Because I've dealt with people saying shit about me for years!" His eyes shift furiously between us. "You seriously think all this started with me seeing Presley?!"

"What we do is ours to deal with." I step forward with complete conviction. "We're not about to sit by and let you end up on the street. Not when we can do something about it."

"There's *nothing* you can do, Rosie! There's nothing any of us can do. All I want is to stop fucking up the lives of the people I care about." Lewis's resolution bleeds with each word, his pale skin flushing red. "I'm…I'm not worth it."

For a brief moment, only passing cars and rushing footsteps permeate the silence between us. Until Henry moves forward, pulling Lewis into a forceful hug. The younger of the siblings is slow to reciprocate. But eventually, his arms relax. The heavy bag in his hand drops to the concrete below. And though I can't see his face from where it rests against Henry's denim jacket, I hear sobs replace his breaths.

"Of course you are." Henry's voice breaks with the promise.

"What are we supposed to do, Henry?" Lewis questions weakly. "Rosie and I, there's nowhere left for us…"

I stand there, unmoving. Feeling my legs grow shaky with the revelation that he's right. Our devotion to protecting each other could only hold so strong in the absence of guidance. Hell, Lewis is in this mess because of me. I have to do something to fix this. I just *have* to.

"We'll figure something out," Henry offers the hollow assurance with a gentle kiss to the top of his brother's head.

My jaw clenches. The world around me fades into an indecipherable blur. But through it, my mind sharpens. The street-side comes back into focus just quickly enough for me to notice a city bus pulling to a stop on the near curbside. The door opens, a slew of people offloading while a short line waits to board. Fading seconds tempt me with the opportunity. All it takes is a final look at the scene of despair before I break. Discreetly, I tug the bus pass from my knee sock. Refusing to turn back, I cap the line and take a single step up the narrow stairs before my name stops me cold.

"Rosie?" It's Henry's voice.

I glance over my shoulder, meeting the confused gazes of the Fennick brothers as I clutch the railing. "Get Lewis somewhere safe tonight," I command the eldest. "I have someone to meet."

Hauling myself onto the bus, the closing door behind me silences their demands for an explanation before I'm crushed by the weight of providing one.

I take slow, careful footsteps down the hallway to hell. The corridor of red distorting my vision as I listen closely. No shuffling. No chatter. No sound at all. I've never heard the studio this quiet. It almost persuades me into leaving out of fear that I wasn't meant to be here at all.

But if fear were ever going to hold me back, it would've done so long before today.

Stopping when I reach the sable office entryway, I suck in a necessary breath before knocking. A voice reciprocates from the other side.

"Come in!"

Ruth, thank God.

I enter, finding her poised in the tall-backed chair, ogling a collection of documents. But her focus on such breaks with the click of the closing door, her gaze snapping to me with austerity. "Rosie, I wasn't expecting you."

I unsteadily shift my weight. "Can we talk?"

She looks me over, her styled ponytail sweeping as she nods to the chair opposite her desk. "Do you have the newest story?"

"No," I answer, following her direction to claim a seat on the threadbare leather. "I'm gonna need a few extra days on it. I just came here to ask…is there any way you could give me an advance for the next couple of issues?"

Her eyes neither dim nor brighten at the request. They simply remain impassive as she says, "I'm afraid I can't do that."

"I've been delivering on time for months now." I point out.

"I want to say yes. But it's against our policy."

"Please, I really need the money." I plead. "There's nothing I can do?"

"Not in your position. Cash advances are allocated to video performers." She explains gently. "We can't afford to pay them out without the guaranteed return they provide."

My crestfallen gaze consumes the desk between us, then drifts along the room's red walls spotted with memorabilia. The elongated display of *Wild Thang* covers runs the widest, showcasing twelve years of models flaunting licentious poses. Of all of them, I fixate on one of the most recent. The fated issue with Roxy's latex-clad body distinguishes itself like a relic among the rest. Its foredoomed contents responsible for my very circumstance. My jaw fixes hard at the memory of my salacious photos, instinct and fear working hand-in-hand to taunt me with every horrid consequence it had dropped at my feet.

But it isn't fear that drives my following request. It's complete, unwavering devotion. "What if I did one?"

Made-up features I always believed to be impervious slacken at the suggestion. To include Ruth's lips, which part long before she cautiously asks, "You want to be in a video?"

Want was irrelevant. The more important question was, "What would I be paid?"

Ruth pauses, dropping her pen atop the stack of documents before shaking her head in thought. "Um…that would depend on what you're willing to agree to—"

"Anything," I say with a fraction of the apprehension I truly feel. "*Everything.*"

She stares at me like I'm a stranger, then rests against the tall back of her chair. "Rosie, when you first met us, you mentioned you'd never had sex before."

"I haven't. R.J. said there's value in that, isn't there?"

She scoffs. "*Yes*. But I don't think you understand what it is you're agreeing to."

"I understand just fine." I lean forward slightly, repeating myself. "What would I be paid?"

"Assuming the shoot goes well, and *finishes*, we could advance you upwards of three thousand. Paid when you walk off set."

That amount would change everything for Lewis and me. "What would I have to do?"

"Well," she sighs. "You've already signed the releases. All it would take is some extra forms I can give you beforehand, and that would be it."

I nod. "How soon can we do it?"

"I suppose I could pull something together for next week. Maybe after the holidays if we can't—"

"That's too long." My lip trembles in desperation.

She looks at me, almost like she's looking through me. "If you're that pressed, considering the value of your niche compared to our other films...You could replace the actress set for tomorrow's shoot."

Tomorrow. It would have to do.

"Please..." I hold my breath, awaiting her confirmation.

Ruth leans her elbows on the desk. Then gives me the coldest, sternest look I've ever received in my life. "Are you absolutely certain this is what you want?"

No.

But it wasn't about what I wanted. It had never been, even before everything went to hell. The only thing that matters is getting Lewis and me out of that hell and into a place where we can move forward.

My thoughts tunnel as I consider the cost of such freedom. One day. A few hours. My virginity. All of which I have to offer.

All of which, disposable.

I could get Lewis and me there. I just need to say *yes*.

So, I do… "Yes."

Her chin raises slowly, but in lieu of addressing me further, she reaches for the telephone to dial a number. Bringing it to her ear, seconds pass before a voice carries over the receiver.

"Rodney James." Ruth requests.

After a brief wait, a deep southern accent greets her through the device.

"It's Ruth. There's been a change of plans. Tell our girl set for tomorrow she's cut." She explains. Though I can't make out his exact words, R.J.'s voice rises to a yell in clear displeasure at the news, no doubt demanding the reason. When the line quiets, Ruth's cold eyes flicker to mine. "We have a new star."

Chapter 37

It had been a useless effort trying to sleep.

At the very least, it meant I was fully awake when I slipped out of Erica's apartment before she or Mattie woke for the day. The last thing I wanted was to lie to her about where I was going. Sure, I'd still be left to explain my sudden income. But there were worse problems to have.

Problems, like how I was going to bear telling Henry.

It had been the only thing on my mind during the bus ride to the studio. Weighing heavily as I sit in Ruth's office in the same seat I had the day prior, going over all the liability contracts and forms to sign before she delivers me to the new sound stage. Despite my history of contractual missteps, I had little else to lose in the matter. Ruth remains quiet as I follow her commands, conducting herself as if I weren't an hour away from handing off my virginity in exchange for a security deposit and a few months' rent. Part of me is grateful; maybe she's behaving so casually to make me feel more at ease.

It doesn't work. But I appreciate it, regardless.

When I'm finished with signing, she collects the stack of papers. "I'll go make copies of these to be filed. Once I'm done, we're set to go."

I only nod in response, listening to the click of her heels leave the office as my eyes remain fixated on the desk phone. Standing to round the corner, I pick up the receiver and dial the number by memory. A few elongated ringbacks pass before a familiar voice answers.

"Hello?"

"Henry, it's Rosie."

"Rosie," my name comes out feverishly. "Where the hell did you run off to yesterday?"

Honesty, I tell myself. "I went to the magazine studio to ask my boss for an advance."

"Oh," he pauses. "Did they say yes?"

"Kind of. What happened with Lewis?"

He expels a defeated breath. "I set him up in a motel near the garage. I managed to cover it, but if we can't find somewhere soon—"

"I can take care of it." I cut him off. "After today, we'll have the money we need."

He hesitates before responding. "What do you mean they *kind* of said yes to your advance?"

"They're giving me three thousand on-site. But I have to take on a new job to earn it."

His voice slowly loses its tenderness. "What new job?"

My mouth dries. Leaving me unsure how to say it, even if the right words did exist.

"Rosie…" That's not just skepticism in his tone now. It's authority, interlaced with the faintest touch of fear. "*What* new job?"

There's no point in prolonging it.

"They only allow advances for their pornstars that do videos." I close my eyes for solitude like there aren't miles between us. "So…I'm starring in one. This morning."

For a while, it's so quiet that I begin to wonder if the line dropped.

Until his hushed voice chills me with the question I'd been bracing for all day. "Have you lost your fucking mind?"

A stab to the chest would've been preferable to that. "Henry—"

"Where's the studio?" He interrupts. "I'm coming to get you."

"No," he can't. We need this too badly. "It's my decision to make, and I've already made it. I just...I just thought you deserved to know now, instead of after."

"Rosie, tell me where you are!"

"*No!*" I declare like an obstinate child. "It's my body, I can do what I want with it. And I *want* to do this."

"No, you don't!"

"Yes, I do! You can't tell me I—"

"You think I don't know what it sounds like when you're putting up a front?" The forceful question silences me. Smothering my retorts as his frantic tone intensifies. "I watched you do it for years. For fuck's sake, Rosie, I can hear it in your voice! Just let me get you out—!"

"I'm sorry, Henry."

I hang up before the ache in my chest becomes too much. Sniffling, I compose myself only a moment before Ruth reenters the office to set a packed folder on the center of the desk.

"All done on my end." She starts. "We should leave, it's a—"

I jump as the phone rings, a familiar number appearing on the green display. As quickly as it starts, I pick up and drop the receiver.

"Sorry," I say weakly. "I needed to make a call."

Ruth tentatively continues, "I was just saying it's a good drive to the location. We need to be there early since you haven't been fitted."

I nod, the pressure increasing as I push myself to ask, "You'll stay with me when we get there, right?"

I expect a hasty assurance. But the give of disappointment rears, instead.

"Rodney will be handling your prep." She explains, showing enough decency to appear remorseful. "I called in a meeting with our distribution team after the change in plans yesterday. I'll be upstairs with them when you go on."

"Oh…" I mutter, lowering my chin.

She steps close to raise it with cold fingers. "Hey, don't be nervous. I'll be watching over the whole thing."

Finding the faintest solace in her blue eyes, I bring myself to nod in agreement before following her lead down the hallway to hell. Keeping up with her tall form until a figure—having just entered the building—stops us at the lobby's entrance.

"Rosie?"

I'd recognize that sweet voice even if the ruby lips didn't give her away.

My timid eyes meet hers for the first time since that morning at her apartment. But I find myself wordless as Val looks me over in surprise. She's dressed casually, in a pink off-shoulder sweater and jeans. Meaning she's likely here to handle Ruth's contractual duties while the manageress goes off-site for the day.

Unaware of the circumstances, Val's mouth quirks in a smile. "What are you doing here so early?"

I try to answer, but fall short enough that Ruth takes over.

"Rosie agreed to a pay advance," she says with startling normalcy. "I'm taking her to the new location."

"But advances are only for..." Val's brows draw tight before her entire face slackens.

Ruth doesn't bat an eye. "We swapped her for our girl today. The shoot starts in an hour."

A desperate hazel gaze captures mine, likely awaiting confirmation that this is some kind of joke.

There's no other explanation but the truth. "My mother found everything. Lewis and I are on our own now." My jaw trembles with the confession. "I need the money, Val."

Her pretty features twist in horror as she steps forward to take my hands. "Why didn't you tell me?"

I wasn't in the headspace to relive Armageddon, not with the hours ahead of me. So I simply settle for an, "I'm sorry."

Pain dims her voice as she asks, "What about your book deal?"

"They never wrote back," I say, bowing my head. "I can't wait any longer, either. I just need to do what's best for Lewis and me."

Her mouth hangs slightly agape, eyes flickering over my sullen features. "But it doesn't have to be *this*, Rosie. I told you I would help—"

"Val," Ruth quiets her with a flat tone. "I need to get her there in time for call."

The girl scowls in her direction, but I squeeze her warm hands to reclaim her attention.

"It's okay, Val. I'll see you after." I attempt a smile, but it comes out as a grimace as I release my grip to rejoin our boss.

"Her forms are on my desk for you to process. Lock up behind us." Ruth says, not bothering to look back.

I, however, can't help it. The last thing I see before stepping through the front doors is Val's sharp glare at Ruth fall into fixated despair on my behalf.

"There she is! The gal of the hour has arrived!"

My austere expression doesn't lift an inch when R.J. runs to greet me upon my entrance to the sound stage. Ruth had seen me off as soon as we'd arrived on-site to attend her distribution meetings in the upstairs conference quarters, leaving me to wander the bustling set. My jaw clenches with his approach, as it's the first time I've had to endure R.J. in any variety since he'd stolen the photos of Val and me and instigated Armageddon.

But…I would bite my tongue. Because today, *I'd* be catering to *his* area of expertise.

His toothy smile is wide as ever as he throws an arm over my tense shoulders and leads me farther into the vast studio. "I just knew our Virgin Mary would come around! Although, I suppose we're gonna have to find you a new nickname by the time we wrap today, won't we?"

"Let's just get this over with." I breathe deeply to calm myself. But release a nervous sigh, instead.

"Smile, little lady. You just signed up for the best job in the world. Not many people get paid to get laid." He waves a dramatic hand as we approach a segment of the venue outfitted with bulbed mirrors and costume racks. "Besides, with all your porn-on-paper expertise, it'll be just like one of your stories!"

Months ago, that might've tempted me. But my jaw tightens as Erica's talk from yesterday fights its way to the forefront of my mind. Fantasies were fantasies for a reason.

This? This is real.

R.J. sits me down at a vanity, the sound of clicking heels trailing us. "Cherie, here, will get you all prettied up before we get you in costume."

"Cherie?" My head swivels to find the curly-haired redhead at R.J.'s side. She looks just as unenthused as I do, but at least she's wearing clothes, which is more than I could say for our first encounter.

"Don't look too impressed, big mouth. Makeup's my side gig." She says, smacking gum as she yanks my stool forward and drops a heavy tub of products on the table.

"You know the look we're after. While you ladies get busy, I'm gonna check in on our cherry popper." R.J. declares with enthusiasm, slapping his palms together. "Have at it!"

I hold my glare on him as he disappears behind rows of assorted clothing and dressing screens, but it falters when Cherie grabs me by the chin to look forward. Padding my face with a powder applicator before I can settle in.

"Relax." Her bubblegum-scented breath wafts heavily as she speaks. "You're a smoke break from porking a stud for money, and you look like you're about to shit bricks."

I had spent all my prep time in disbelief that I'd be losing my virginity at all that I hadn't even stopped to question *who* would be taking it. I assume she knows as I ask, "Who am I doing the scene with?"

"Cummings." She answers, flicking some of her red curls away. "Is all that gak about this being your first fuck real?"

I would nod, but I fear she'll scratch my face off with her manicured nails if I impede her progress. "Yes."

"Damn, respect." Her glossy lips tilt into a smirk. "Most gals hand off their V-card to the first jackass who calls them pretty, then take a trip to the funny farm when he splits. May as well get paid for it, right?"

"Feels a little insensitive," I admit, my gaze falling as powder tickles my cheeks.

"So is every other job. These days, you can get nailed by a nine-to-five shift, or a nine-to-five shaft. Either way, you're getting fucked. There's no shame in sex work."

Says the woman who nearly knocked my teeth in for assuming she was a pornstar all those months ago. But even so, it isn't the *work* that feels shameful—people in this industry deserve to be respected. It's the fact that I'm having so much trouble accepting that I was about to become one of them when I never desired to. But I shut down that thought, along with any others that may dissuade my decision, while she finishes with makeup. A heap of various products and grueling applications later, she steps away to look me over.

"Hm, not bad." She remarks, turning my stool so I can view myself in the mirror.

I blink in the light of the vanity, reflecting brightly in my brown eyes. Which are, despite their natural doe-like distinction, accentuated in white liner and false lashes to appear twice as large. My cheeks are a bright, almost obnoxious pink. Only matched by the satin magenta pigment coating my lips. I look like a little girl who's raided her mother's makeup drawer.

I startle when Cherie drops a cardboard box beside the tub of cosmetics filled with miscellaneous accessories.

"Show me your teeth." She commands. I hesitate, but don't question. Parting my bright lips with a clenched jaw, I track her as she holds up an elastic band spotted by silver brackets in front of my mouth. "R.J.—!" Her nasally voice carries across the set. "We going with the fake braces or not?!"

Braces…? Was the *little girl* look intentional?

My stomach churns, then drops completely at the sound of reapproaching bootsteps. "Nah, leave 'em. They have a knack for getting snagged on things and hitting us right in the workers' comp."

Cherie shrugs, tossing the accessory back into the cardboard box before continuing to riffle through it. A heavy hand lands on my shoulder as R.J.'s face appears in the reflection beside mine.

"Our guy is getting fluffed as we speak." He chuckles, nearly batting me with his cowboy hat as he emphatically shakes his head. "What a beauty…Just think, a month or so from now, this face will be on a VHS cover every man in America hides from his Mrs., and *you're* gonna satisfy each and every one of 'em."

The prospect sounds more like a nightmare than an aspiration. "I think you're overestimating."

"Hardly." He squeezes my shoulder until I look at him, a rousing gleam in his eyes. "Baby Ruth ain't upstairs with our typical band of yes-men. When you gave the go-ahead yesterday, she called up a connection she's kept in her back pocket since our startup. You ever hear of *Vixen Pictures*?" He avidly continues when I shake my head. "They are *the* industry giant of adult video, Virgin Mary. Sell out their movies in stores nationwide. Baby Ruth's been pitching our pics to them for years."

Confusion etches lines between my styled brows. "I thought you only sold videos through the magazine?"

R.J. rubs the side of his neck with a wince. "We do. At least, since we had to cut funds after a little ethical settlement at my expense back in the '80s." He perks up again. "But as soon as you gave the green light for this shoot, Baby Ruth got in touch with her pal at *Vixen* to give an update on our fresh-faced little star. When she told them about your special niche, they had their rep on a plane from Cali in *hours*. They're so convinced it'll be a hit, they wanna peek at the footage the second we wrap. If you sell the role, we're looking at national distribution on a level *Wild Thang*'s never seen."

National distribution. The whole country will be able to walk into a video store and *purchase* my first time?

"Oh, almost forgot." R.J. retrieves something from his backmost pocket to set on the vanity—a palm-sized bottle of crimson liquid.

I study it with incredulity. "What is that?"

"Fake blood. In case your own doesn't show up well enough on cam." I fight the urge to gag as he slaps me on the back. "Don't worry, the formula's safe for your lady bits."

Out of the corner of my eye, Cherie pulls a red ribbon from the box of accessories. Keeping my hair in its ponytail, she ties it into a harrowingly familiar bow around the elastic.

"Now, uh…" R.J. kneels to my level, rubbing his lips together in hesitation—which scares me. I'd never once heard this man say anything that wasn't wildly unfiltered. If whatever working in his mind gave him pause to deliver it appropriately, it must be something pulled from the deepest circle of hell. "I just wanted to give you some pointers before you go on. What with this being your intro to, well, *everything*. First impressions are important around here."

I wince as Cherie secures the ribbon with a tight pull. "Okay?"

His fingers rhythmically drum the surface of the table. "So the sell here is your purity. But we're gonna need you to…play it up a bit. A girl's first time is sexy and all. But chances are, it's not gonna be too pleasant on your end of things." He points at me expectantly. "And *that's* the mark we need to hit. Baby Ruth wants this to look hot, but authentic. Act nervous, whimper on about how big he is, throw in some tears if you can manage. Hey, *hey*—!"

His grip snags my arm before I can go tumbling onto the concrete flooring. I grasp the edge of the vanity in one hand and slap the other over my mouth, gulping back the salty precursor to vomit. The spacious room swirls in vertigo as I attempt to set myself straight, having gone too dizzy, too fast.

R.J. snaps beside us. "Cherie, why don't you grab our star a pre-shoot remedy?" The woman responds with a snide remark I can't make out over the ringing in my ears. An incessant hum that dissipates as R.J. takes me by the shoulders. "Hey now, no reason to get yourself all worked up."

I blink hard despite the false lashes weighing down my lids, blurriness giving way to a crisper picture as my pulse resumes normal speed. "Sorry…I just…"

"First time jitters. We can do something about that." R.J. remarks as Cherie returns, dropping something in his palm with a bottle of water. "Open wide."

I hesitantly oblige, watching as he presses a small pill to the center of my tongue.

"Just a little something to take the edge off." He goes on, handing me the water as a suggestive smirk curls his lips. "We've got a saying around here. The higher you are, the closer you are to God."

Sensing the anxiety clawing its way to the surface again, I do as I'm told. Drinking down the dose of compliance with a hard swallow.

R.J. hovers over me, admiring my reflection with a proud grin. "I could always tell this is where you belonged."

Setting the bottle aside, I try to match his conviction. "Don't get used to it. This is a one-time thing."

"We'll see about that." He muses. "You know we had to disconnect our answering machine after you made your nude debut last month? It was so jammed with demands to get M.R. back in front of a camera, we could barely hold a call."

My entire body stiffens at the mention of the pictures *he'd* stolen. I bite my tongue to keep from screaming at him for all but ripping my future away. But his next statement breaks my discipline in an instant.

"I just wish you'd given them to us sooner. We would've put your tits on a coated print the day you signed on."

I raise my chin to lock him with a glare. "What do you mean *given them* to you?"

Is he serious? He can't actually be insinuating that I asked for this. And yet, that's precisely what he does.

"That feature with those sexy pictures," his southern accent drags. "Don't know why it took you so long to request it."

I stare, deconstructing his words as vital seconds pass. But not enough for me to question him further before a voice echoes across the sound stage.

"Lights up in fifteen!"

"Oh!" R.J. jumps at the call, nodding over his shoulder. "Come on, Virgin Mary, we still gotta get you dressed up." There's a glint in his eyes as they flicker over my seated form. "Or should I say, *down...*"

Chapter 38

We wasted ten minutes sifting through on-site costumes before R.J. decided that my everyday attire was accurate enough for the "innocent young girl" look.

Although, modifications were made. Including slicing six inches off the bottom of my skirt with a pair of shears so it barely concealed the curve of my hips. My white button-up had avoided similar permanent damage, but had been untucked and opened, tied over my chest in a knot to show more skin. I'd also been stripped of all underwear. And, oddly enough, instructed to keep the knee socks and Mary Janes on, which seemed counterintuitive. But the way everyone seems to tower above me as I stand like a prop at the edge of the set tells me I have no room to argue creative differences.

Whatever planned for the space in front of me had been entirely gutted since my participation was announced. Now there's nothing but a few bare walls surrounding a raised king mattress fitted with a singular white sheet, no blankets. Blinding stage lights train in all directions, illuminating the scene flatly. Opposite the bed, a line of filming equipment is manned by a handful of darkly dressed technicians. Two of them with giant headsets hold free-range cameras tethered by long cords to separate monitors. Despite the mellowing effect of the pill R.J. had prescribed me, my heart pounds when I realize that those cold, glassy lenses are about to be aimed at *me*.

Well, me and—

"Hey, Rosie."

I look left to where my co-star takes a confident stance. Having traded in his pastor uniform for a pair of loose cargo shorts and an unbuttoned top that curtains his muscular torso.

"Hi, Cummings," I say as casually as I'm able.

His dark eyes drift up and down my body. "You look good. Ready to get started?"

I cast a glance over the man I'm about to lose my virginity to, taking caution to keep from focusing too low and giving any more attention to the protruding bulge in his shorts than I would later. He's a signature pornstar, no doubt. Tall, with tanned skin, dark hair and matching stubble that outlines a strong jawline. His features are youthful, in a college boy kind of way. Part of me wants to know his real name, or how old he is, but I don't find it in me to ask. Today, he's a necessity. Tomorrow, he'd be nothing but a memory I'd spend the rest of my life trying to suppress.

I force an answer. "Think so."

The corner of his mouth dips in a frown. "So this is, like, *actually* your first time?"

I nod, hoping I'd be spared from that question from here on out.

"You gonna be okay?" He rubs the side of his exposed neck, concern etching his face. "I mean, I'm set no matter what. But that seems pretty heavy for your first shoot, don't you think?"

"I'll be fine," I say more to myself than to him, my gaze fixing on the wide mattress a few yards away.

"If you say so." He gently pats my back. "Just remember, those contracts we sign might seem set in stone, but walkaways are built in for a reason. You can stop if it's too much."

"I know. It's just…" I peek up at him through my thick lashes. "I have a boyfriend."

Cummings's expression doesn't shift, his head tilting in lieu of a shrug. "I have a girlfriend. Sex here doesn't mean anything like that. It's just work."

Just work. I repeat mentally.

Before I can say anything else, R.J. steps from the slew of technical equipment to point at me. "Virgin Mary! We're geared up, let's get you on that bed."

I bite back a final surge of fear. The cloud of weariness hovering above me with every step I've taken today follows as I enter, PAR can lights enveloping me.

Just work.

Key art had been first. The way it was explained to me, this was the imagery that would be used for marketing, VHS cover slips, and the magazine spread that would be dedicated to my new porn persona. *I'd* be making the centerfold.

The task had consisted of me modeling on the mattress in various revealing positions while photos were taken—R.J. prompting me the entire time. If I could give that animal credit for anything, he knew how to direct porn. Being especially specific about my every pose. From how many microinches my clothing was to exposing me, down to the angle of my body to best highlight curves when the camera was shooting from a low or high position. All the while, I keep a tight cap on my anxiousness.

Whatever drug he'd given me was in full effect by the time I was sprawled out on the sheet, making the lights above blur in irradiant beams. Tremors subdued and sensations dulled, my defenses fall in ruinous ash as I follow his every command, and accept his every praise. *Good girl. Sexy baby.* I move with sedated grace. Time is foregone, marked only by the *snap, snap, snap* of the camera's release. I only notice they've concluded when Cummings appears at the edge of the set, waiting for his cue as the two cameramen prop necessary filming equipment on their shoulders. My head spins as I right myself, blinking hard to focus in.

"Alright," R.J. drags, standing between the operators with his thumbs in his pockets. "*Virtuous Vixen Venerates Virginity—*" He pauses, losing his grin before giving a quick shrug. "I'll work on that. Take one."

A clapperboard strikes. The act begins.

"Arch your back a little more. Keep your eyes up." R.J. directs me, raising his hand above one of the cameras. "Flutter those lashes, give a cute little smile…Perfect."

I comply with his instructions for the opening shot. Following this, Cummings steps into view, taking a seat on the mattress beside me.

"Hi." I greet him in the tone R.J. had me practice while getting my outfit prepped, exaggerating the natural infantility of my voice.

"Hey," Cummings dons a smug smile as he flirtatiously swipes the hair from my forehead. "What's your name, beautiful?"

I stiffen, realizing I hadn't selected one. Through the fog of sedation, my gaze flickers to one of the live monitors displaying the scene in real time. At the sight of my overemphasized appearance, I claim a title fit for a familiar little girl with big brown eyes. "Mary."

Somewhere offside, R.J. hums enthusiastically.

"Mary," Cummings strokes his fingertips lightly down the side of my jaw. "I've heard a rumor about you."

"What kind of rumor?"

His thumb grazes my pink bottom lip. "That you're a virgin. Is it true?"

Apparently, I wasn't free from the question. "Mm-hmm."

"Well," his hand slips lower, teasing the collar of my shirt before following its hem to the knot. "You want me to do something about that?"

"Banter!" R.J. calls, pulling my focus for a stolen glance.

But when I'm drawn back, my eyes lift above the set's walls to fix on one of the conference windows overlooking the sound stage. Fluorescent lights illuminate the room beyond in a gray and white blur, masking figures that pass within. One of them takes a familiar form.

"Mary!" R.J. snaps.

I shiver back into character. "Um…I don't know. Can you?"

"I can." Taking my hand, he painstakingly slides it up his thigh to rest on his thick bulge.

My lips part at the feel of it, hot and alive beneath my palm despite the fabric between us. Recalling R.J.'s orders, I clumsily play along. "Is it supposed to get this big?"

"Only when I'm around sexy girls," Cummings says, never ceasing his steady touches. "Especially the sweet little pure ones."

I bat my long lashes. "But I'm so nervous. Once I give it away, there's no getting it back."

"Then I guess I'll have to make it *extra* good, won't I?" His fingers pinch the knot at the base of my chest, then tug. Exposing me as the button-up falls open. I gasp as he squeezes one of my breasts. "Fuck, you're so hot."

A beat later, his mouth is on mine. For the next few minutes, we make out in different positions by R.J.'s command. I slowly accept the hands roaming my near-nude body, and ignore the guilt that embalms me the longer they do. I try imagining they belong to Henry, but doing so only sours my mouth with every swipe of Cummings's tongue against my own.

"Alright, let's move things along," R.J. instructs.

The cameras move in closer, each poised in varied directions. One on me, one on my counterpart.

"I bet you taste as good as you feel." Cummings purrs, releasing his grip on my breasts to slide lower. But an all-new grip constricts my heart when I realize where he's going.

R.J. worsens it. "Mary, you're nervous!"

It takes me too long to realize that he isn't pointing out the obvious, but *encouraging* me to appear even more scared for the sake of the role. "I-I don't know if I'm ready."

Unbeknownst to Cummings, I truly mean it. He kisses down my stomach, then settles his shoulders beneath my thighs. "It's alright, baby. It'll feel *so* good."

Hot breath catches in my throat. The serrated memory of a voice etching the same sentiment in my head cuts through R.J.'s depressant like the band-aid it is.

"That's *perfect*." Our director praises me from beyond the set. "More of that face."

Jaw trembling, my eyes dart over the watching crew as Cummings's touch triggers a nightmarish evocation of the worst day of my life. But that doesn't stop the man between my legs from lifting one to give the camera a proper angle for tracking his movements. I swallow dryly, pulling myself together enough to play along upon the first drag of his tongue against my slit.

It isn't bad. I suppose. The unfamiliarity of a mouth down there is enough for me to arch my back in reaction. Supplying a few gasps that likely pass as pleasured, but are more derived from mediocre surprise. Maybe Cummings isn't as experienced in this department as I'd imagined a pornstar would be. Or maybe he is, and was simply doing what looked sexiest for the shot. But either way, he was missing the...*point*.

Feigned moans pour from my mouth for an uncomfortably long time. Writhing my head to and fro, I run my hands through Cummings's hair until a piercing voice halts them.

"Come!"

I go still, lifting my head awkwardly to peer at R.J. "What?"

He scoffs, emphatically waving his arms. "Climax. Orgasm. Reach the zenith. *Whatever* you call it in your stories, just do it!"

"But I'm not—" I find Cummings between my legs, still working at an impressively unsuccessful rate.

R.J. slaps a hand to the side of his face. "Fake it!"

I stare up at the lens recording my every breath. *I can do this.*

So I do. Fisting the sheet beneath me while twisting my head to the side, I let out a choked scream in my best attempt. After a warranted bout of this, the confirmation that it was good enough arrives.

"Atta girl," R.J. praises. "Now, back at it."

Cummings kisses his way back to my face, settling his weight on top of me to brush away my fringe. "How was that?"

"It was so new, but…it felt really good." I lie with an uneasy smile.

He smirks, then moves to tongue my neck. "You ready for the real thing?"

"I…" The words evade me. Against my inner thigh, I feel the jab of his hard length behind a veil of loose shorts. The induced barricade separating me from inconsolable panic cracks with every second that ticks on. Tears wet the corners of my eyes. "I don't know…"

"Brilliant!" R.J. hollers. "Keep it up!"

I sob. My bare chest heaving with each labored breath.

Cummings's teeth graze the side of my neck. "I think you do, Mary."

Twisting my head to desperately seek R.J., I open my mouth before losing any protests to hesitation. It's as if he's looking straight through me. Consuming the scene like the product it is. The product *I* am. In his hand, the freshly retrieved bottle of artificial blood shifts with every mindless tap of his fingers against the plastic. I fixate on it, then the bed beneath me. The manufactured illusion fractures into a million shards. My brain takes over, vivifying the brutality of a memory—not an act. An unmoving weight. My legs spread for the taking. Red splatters on pristine sheets. The echo of my heartbeat as I ran for my life…

Adrenaline grips me like it had in those moments forever burned into my mind's eye. Cummings's arm disappears between us, unclasping the buttons of his shorts. And I *break*.

"STOP!" I wail, thrashing to free myself. "GET OFF ME! GET OFF ME! *GET OFF ME!*"

My co-star rears backward, finally realizing that I'm no longer acting as he raises both hands to keep from touching me. His eyes are wide, filled with absolute terror at my expense. But I haven't the will to care, pulling myself upright to hug my legs. As if it could succeed in making me any smaller, I bury my face between my knees. The heat of the lights above us works to convince me that this isn't Mr. Lasker's bedroom, but not well enough to quell the fear rinsing me like the mascara-tinged rivulets down my cheeks. A few deep, unsteady breaths later, the sound of bootsteps halts beside the mattress.

"It's okay, now," R.J. says. A hand presses to my back, making me curl in tighter. "Everyone's bound to get cold feet their first shoot."

"I don't wanna do this." I shake my head, raising it enough to peer at him. "I *can't* do this."

His face is void of its typical ardor, and he gives what might be the sternest look I've ever seen on him. "Alright. But if you cut before the finish, everything's useless." He scratches the side of his neck, blowing a sigh. "Would sure be a shame to walk away from all this with nothing."

It was callous, but it was the truth. If I stopped now, Lewis and I would be entirely out of viable options. I'd already made it this far. But how could I pull through when I *clearly* don't have the strength? Swallowing hard, I wipe away a few stained tears before more take their place. But when I avert my gaze again, it isn't drawn downward into the security of my tightly drawn form.

At the behest of a seraphic coax, I raise my chin to the window overtopping the stage.

Ruth is looking down on me. She's unmoving, but the impassive look on her face is something akin to a predator stalking its prey. Indifferent that it's about to desecrate the life of an innocent creature for its own survival. Through the distance, her focused eyes watch me with expectation. I'm swept into the silence of beholding, every nerve in my body heating with the onset of providence.

Providence that commands me to utter the following words, "Okay…I'll do it."

Cummings narrows a dubious look at me. "Rosie, if you need to end this—"

A sharp *hush* cuts him off. R.J. holds a finger to his lips before cautiously raising it my direction, like I'd rear up and high tail it out of the studio if provoked again. "*Mary* has spoken."

"It's alright, Cummings," I say with no affect, surrendering my gaze to the sheet between us. "I wanted this."

R.J. snaps his fingers. "You heard her, get those clothes off."

I sit there, losing myself in the endless white of the bed as my counterpart does as he's told. Never once do I look, but when he returns to the shot and gently pushes me onto my back where we left off, he's naked. R.J. instructs the cameras to move back in. Cummings climbs atop me, kissing slowly along my jaw and neck. Over his form, I spot Ruth at the peak of my view again. Other bodies have joined her. Faceless silhouettes crowd the creator as she leans with arms extended on the window frame, a satisfied grin curving her lips.

Somewhere out of sight, R.J.'s voice reaches me. "For God's sake, Mary, you look like somebody died. Try giving us a smile."

My view of Ruth is broken when a glassy lens eclipses her. Hovering to aim directly on my face, its benumbed eye casts a dark mirror image. The opposite camera moves lower, trained at where my legs are parted to accommodate Cummings. My shortened skirt leaves nothing hidden in the position. His hand disappears between us. I take the cue. Looking into the lens as if presenting to hundreds... thousands...*millions*. My gaze locks on the human in its reflection.

No...not a human. A spectacle. A starlet. Tears pool in my brown eyes, adding one hell of an illusory gleam as I hit my mark.

Chin up.

Don't look anyone in the eye; they might see right through you.

Smile like you mean it, or they'll make you do it again.

"What the fuck—?"

Pretend.

Endure.

"Hey! You can't be in here!"

Pretend.

Endure.

I show the audience my teeth.

"This is a live set, who let you—?!"

The unfamiliar voices of crew members scatter around us, growing louder and more accusatory until they amplify to shouts. Two hands grab Cummings's shoulders, pulling him off me with enough force that the sweep of air in his absence chills my near-naked body to the bone. Both cameras retreat, and I have a full view as my co-star is thrown from the mattress.

I find the source of the outbreak, just as Henry's furious eyes shift from the chaos to mine.

Chapter 39

"Henry?!" His name leaves my mouth with a gasp as I push myself upright, too stunned to mind my state of undress.

His expression breaks from unbridled rage to sheer horror at the sight of me.

"*Fuck*—" He bites the swear, tearing the denim jacket from his torso in one breath and tucking it around my exposed body in the next. His hand finds my tear-streaked face, cradling it like I'm a glass doll one touch from shattering. "Are you okay?"

R.J.'s vicious commands snuff out any answer. "We're in the middle of a shoot! Someone get him out of here!"

From behind the wall of equipment, a few of the larger crew members rush forward. Henry doesn't give them a shot, releasing me to shove the closest away. "Get the fuck away from us!"

Before I can plead with him to stop, another figure charges from the corner of the set. Running full speed as if Henry had left them behind in his haste. My mascara-smudged eyes flare as the blur of a human takes the form of Lewis. But he isn't alone. On his heel is someone else, moving just as madly in my direction.

Her name comes out as a shaken cry, "*Val?!*"

"Rosie!" Val's frantic voice echoes as she and Lewis make it to the edge of the bed, each of them grabbing my wrists.

"You have to come with us!" Lewis demands, ignoring the nearby havoc—where his older brother threatens anyone who dares intervene.

But despite my confusion, practicality grounds me to the mattress. "You need to leave." I narrow on Lewis. "I have to finish this, for *us*!"

"No, you don't." Val takes me by the shoulders.

"Yes, I do!" I grab her arms with the intent to push them away, but my trembling deters me. "If I don't, Lewis and I—"

"*Rosie!*" She silences me, leaning close enough that I witness the remorse in her hazel eyes give way to irrepressible fury. "She lied to you."

The statement renders me stiff. For a fraction of a moment, my fearful gaze flickers to the overlooking conference window. Finding it filled with watchful silhouettes minus one. Ruth is gone.

Henry's shouts reverberate off the high walls of the venue as he shoves another crew member.

"Alright, we've gotta go." Lewis fixates on his brother, frantically tapping Val's shoulder. "Right now!"

"Come on..." She gently begs, pulling me onto unsteady legs.

Clumsily shoving my arms through the sleeves of Henry's jacket, Lewis and Val tug me away. Only releasing their grips when the three of us break into a run for the studio's lobby.

Our feet pound the concrete as I breathlessly question, "What do you mean she lied? How did you three—?"

My words are gagged when something snags the denim collar around my neck, pulling forcefully enough to wind me. Time stalls as I find myself staring up at the furious face of R.J.

He places himself between me and the distant exit. "Where the hell do you think you're going?"

"Get out of my way!" I warn. But when I attempt to shove past him, R.J. snatches my wrist in a vice, unyielding fingers tethering me to the chaos. I gasp as he yanks me close with a fierce glare.

"Do you have any idea what you're throwing away?" He growls. "This deal is gonna change everything for—"

Suddenly, his fist is torn free as I'm pushed aside by a blind force. I stagger to catch my balance, focus tunneling on the person responsible. Henry's clutching R.J. by the Western button-up, a wrath flaring in his blue-green eyes that I can only match to one single hazardous memory.

Peakshire High's parking lot.

Henry rears back, throwing every inconceivable ounce of his power into a punch to R.J.'s face. Scarred knuckles meet bone with a sickening *crack*. Ruth's indecorous counterpart is unconscious before he even hits the ground, cowboy hat careening from his heap of a body. I gape at the sight, fear seizing me when Henry steps forward with intent to strike the downed man again.

I rush to take hold of him. "Henry, don't!"

Though an intermix of inertia and fury carries him forward, it takes his gaze falling to mine before he truly ceases. The malice in his features softens as he looks me over, before lifting his chin to the line of exit. I follow his focus, where Lewis and Val are awaiting, having watched the carnage unfold.

Whether it be from the terror on his little brother's face, the desperation on mine, or the unity of both, Henry composes himself enough to slide an arm around my waist. "Let's go."

We continue forward. Heavy air of the wide stage gives way to a condensed, carpeted lobby as we make it to the building's entrance. But just a few paces shy of the glass exitway doors, a voice strikes like lightning behind us.

"*Rosie!*"

Henry nearly topples over as my feet drag to a halt. Looking to the source of the command, my skin prickles. Ruth is standing at the base of the upper quarter's staircase, her seething eyes darting between the four of us. I open my mouth to speak, but a flash of pink cuts me off.

Val squares herself protectively between me and our boss, voice amplifying to a yell as she spears the woman with a stream of Spanish profanities.

"Val—!" Ruth silences her, jaw ticking as she stalks toward us. "I have a dozen distribution heads and the assistant executive of *Vixen* upstairs. Before I humiliate myself by walking back up those steps, I would like you to tell me exactly *what* you're doing here and *how* I'm supposed to explain this to them?!"

"Go to hell!" Val snarls, marching forward in a move that draws my focus to her backmost pocket—where a folded slip of paper resides. "How could you do this to her?!"

Despite the girl's advance, Ruth holds her ground. "Rosie told you she made her decision. You getting involved is doing nothing but destroying her opportunity."

"It was only a decision she made because *you* manipulated her!" Val shouts, tugging the slip from her rear pocket to unfurl. "Or did you conveniently forget receiving this?"

When Ruth's steely irises find the page, her furious expression slackens.

"Val," I interject, drawing her attention. "Tell me what's going on."

Val's rage pacifies as she nears, handing me the letter to read. In the top corner, *Lone Legacy Press* is printed in bold lettering.

"The publisher that reached out to you?" Her voice is softer now. "They got your submission, and they loved it. They're waiting for you to respond so they can negotiate a deal."

I lock on her hazel eyes. A blinding mix of shock and relief hit me simultaneously, but neither matched my confusion.

"I found it in Ruth's desk after you left this morning. And it was postmarked two weeks ago." Val turns to scowl at the woman, ferocity reviving her tone. "She was keeping it in case you didn't agree to the video, Rosie. Because even though she'd earn more from putting you in front of a camera than she would as your manager for some book deal, she was going to get paid either way."

Ruth crosses her arms, challenging Val's heated composure. "Derailing our shoot? Going through my desk? If you think I'm ever letting you set foot in that studio again, you're mistaken."

"Oh, I'm not mistaken. I quit!" Val finishes with a confident raise of her chin.

I fixate on the letter poised in my hands. Ruth…she'd kept it from me.

Taking risky steps forward, I stop halfway between her and the three behind. "You lied about everything…for money?"

For the first time since meeting her, I witness Ruth's fortified exterior waver. Shifting her unsteady balance, she speaks with twice the authority I suspect she possesses. "Rosie, I wasn't lying when I said I saw potential in you."

"For my *writing*." My voice breaks. "Not turning me into a pornstar when that's never what I wanted."

"You're a talented writer. But I know this world, and I knew I could turn you into something great. Something that would give you real chances—"

"By losing my virginity in front of a camera?!"

"Chances nobody gave me!" She carries on despite my outcry, closing the distance between us to pin me with a glare. "For fuck's sake, Rosie. *Erotica*?! Over an opportunity like this?! Thirty years in this business and I've never seen *anyone* handed a golden ticket like I'm offering you." Her breaths grow labored as she hounds me with, "It's time for you to face the truth. I've been through it. I learned from it. I know what makes someone a standout in this industry, and you have it. I couldn't stand by and watch you turn into another wasted youth!"

I stare at her, my knees nearly giving out as realization hits me with crippling weight. "Oh my God…it was you."

She doesn't break. She hardly *blinks* at the vague accusation.

Through my working mind, the hush of my tone carries with fragility. "You stole those photos from my notebook. You told R.J. to feature me." Betrayal gouges me with such aggression, I stagger backwards. Tears fog her tall form as my mouth hangs open. "You put that magazine on my mother's doorstep. Because you knew what would happen when she found it…" I force the last of my assertion through trembling teeth. "You knew I'd be desperate."

Finally, Ruth gives some indication that my words ring true. But only by way of a tremor in her jaw so subtle, it's nearly imperceptible. She doesn't deny it. Any of it. She simply lowers her chin, holding my gaze. "It isn't too late to make the right decision."

"Right decision for who?" I demand. "It was never about me. This is nothing but a front!"

"No, it isn't." She points a finger at the floor. "This is a crossroads, Rosie. And you have two choices. You can walk back into that studio, finish what you *agreed* to, and come to terms with your true purpose." Her narrowed eyes flicker to the building's exit. "Or you can walk out those doors and spend the rest of your life regretting it."

Cold air sinks heavily against my skin as I'm left with no choice but consideration. The prospect unfolds in my head, evoking visions of a future reinforced with the promise of salvation. At the expense of blind devotion, I would be handed the success I've always desired. The chance to leave my past behind without so much as a second look…

A second look that I take.

Behind me, Lewis, Henry, and Val await with bated breath. I accept each of their stares before fixating on the most familiar of all, Lewis, who gives a slight raise of his hand—holding it palm-up as an offer of a whole different sort. *It's time to go.*

My heart constricts as I look back at Ruth, who continues to watch me with fierce expectation.

"What's your decision?" She asks, the question as condescending as it is pointless.

Because I don't have to decide. I don't have to submit myself. I don't *have* to do a God damned thing. I supply an answer because I choose to, but it doesn't come as agreement or denial. It comes as the only two words left to say.

"Bite me."

I don't stick around for a reaction. All I notice is her body lose the tension it had been holding as I turn away. Her calloused demeanor faltering enough for me to suspect that my response comes as a final blow. Which is confirmed when her desperate tone resounds through the lobby. "Rosie…"

I ignore her, taking Lewis's offered hand in mine. He gives me a sad, generous smile, as if welcoming me home.

"*Rosie!*" Ruth beckons again.

I don't look back.

Keeping Lewis's hold, the two of us move forward as Henry and Val push open the glass doors, chilled air spilling in as we step into the sunlight.

Chapter 40

Trickling water pools in my cupped hands, warming flushed skin as I rinse away any traces of soap. After drying myself with a strewn towel, I stand upright, spotting a bare-faced reflection glowing in the gentle light of the bathroom. My fringe splays messily from the commotion, and my scalp aches from ten years of the same tight ponytail. I wince as I pull the elastic free, taking the tied ribbon with it. A crumpled bow tangled with knotty strands of light-brown hair nests in my palm for a few burning moments. Before the stripe of red slips into the garbage bin at my side.

A light knock at the door preludes Val's sweet voice. "Can I come in?"

"Go ahead," I reply, brushing fingers through my loose hair as she enters.

Stopping with her grip on the knob, hazel irises drink me in. "Are the clothes good enough?"

The oversized long-sleeve and sweatpants she'd given me had been a far cry from the outfit I'd been wearing when we arrived at her apartment. I smooth over the soft fabric. "They're perfect."

Her cheeks swell with a smile before she nods at the pile on the ground. "I can toss those if you want."

As if they were contaminated, the discarded articles sear my flesh upon retrieval. A pain that subsides when I hand them off to Val. She pauses, holding the navy and white bundle to linger on me.

"What?" I ask with a half-laugh.

"Nothing," she softly remarks. "I'm just thinking how beautiful my friend is."

Blushing, my focus drifts to the mirror to find a girl I'd never had the pleasure of meeting before. One stripped of every mold and expectation. A grin curves her lips, the sparkle of fortitude gleaming in her brown eyes.

When Val leaves, I follow her to the living area of her vibrant home. Lewis is seated on the couch while Henry paces idly in front of it. Their attention lifts to me as I enter.

"You look better," Lewis says, patting the sofa beside him.

I claim the spot with a sigh. "That's the understatement of the century."

"No," Henry crosses his arms, looking at me sternly. "'You made the most reckless decision of all time,' is."

My skin heats with the warranted scold. I feel the cushions to the left of me dip as Val takes a seat of her own, drawing my focus. "How did you three even find each other?"

"After I found that letter, I was leaving to make it to the sound stage. Lewis and Henry had just pulled into the parking lot." Her gaze flickers to them. "They were trying to get to you, too."

"I recognized Val from the magazine," Lewis explains. "You've been talking her up for months. I knew we could trust her."

Guilt wells in my stomach for putting them through such frantic worry. My head lifts to Henry. "You brought Lewis to the studio?"

"Figured if I couldn't talk sense into you, he could. I got the address off that issue my roommate had." He looks away, rubbing the side of his neck. "I wasn't gonna stop until I found you. Just…to make sure you were okay."

Val raises a fond brow at him. "When I ran from the office to the lobby, you were going at the front doors with a tire iron."

He shrugs innocently. "I never said I was civil about it."

Now *that* was the real understatement of the century.

Lewis sets a palm on my leg, his gentle expression hardening. "What were you thinking, Rosie?"

"I was thinking that, if I didn't act as quickly as possible, something terrible was bound to happen to you." Despondency tightens my jaw. "For God's sake, Lewis, you were out on the street."

His shoulders tense, wary eyes falling between us.

I go on, "I was gonna do whatever I needed to take care of us both. Like we've always taken care of each other." My hand rests atop his. "And still do. I have you guys to thank for getting me out of that mess."

"No, not us," Val interjects, nodding to the folded slip of paper on the coffee table with a proud smirk. "That letter is all Rosie Ginger."

Ambition guides my touch as I retrieve the sheet, unfurling it to read over. Despite the good news, practicality dims the hope it provides. "Whatever book deal I can make will be great. But it won't be immediate." My disheartened gaze returns to Lewis. "You still need somewhere safe. Both of us do."

For a moment, he matches my concern with an uncertain silence.

"No, you don't." Our heads swivel to Val as she curtly raises her chin. "Because you two can stay here."

I stare at her. "You'd really…?"

"Of course I would." She assures, before pulling me into a hug.

Reciprocating the gesture, I whisper, "I don't know what I'd do without you, Val."

"You'll never have to know." Her ruby lips settle against my ear. "You're not on your own…I won't make that mistake twice."

Warmth envelops us further when Lewis's arms slip around me from behind. Nestled in their embrace, the bodies around me should be nothing if not a barrier between me and the hours behind, or a remedy to the afflictions I endured in their wake. But the burn of their affection runs skin-deep. Inside, my heart constricts in ice-cold thumps that render me stiff. The two at my sides don't take notice, as I avert my gaze to spare them from the desolation tainting my face—only for it to be caught by someone else.

Henry's sweet smile fades upon the unobstructed sight. Though he remains wordless, something stirs behind his exterior the longer he looks. Something that rattles my defenses, fragile as they remain. I can't let them fall so easily. Not after Armageddon. Not after today.

A thought I use as an excuse to lower my head, forcing myself behind the sanctity of an all too familiar mask.

Sleep had come easier than I thought possible. Tucked in the warmth of Henry's denim jacket, the Grand Safari's bench seat had offered ample room for slumber as we took the late afternoon move from Erica's to Val's. The claim of my belongings out of the way, I'd settled against Henry's leg with every intention of tuning out the besieging world.

But it isn't reality that stirs me lucid. It's the melody of a memory.

When my lashes flutter away the sting of exhaustion, however, the dim interior of the vehicle provides enough to discern that I'm not slow dancing in a hospital room. My suitcase lies unzipped in the floorboard, gentle chords humming through the car speakers as Henry sets aside the empty casing of my father's cassette. He looks down when he notices I've woken, a tender grin pulling his lips. I mirror the expression as he reaches to stroke the unbound hair from my face. Lifting from his thigh, I right myself to peer forward. Anticipating the gray stretch of Val's apartment complex.

Instead, I find a sunset.

My eyes widen to burn in every mile of the far-reaching view. Descending sunlight frames vast clouds sitting idle. Divided by streaks of violet, pink, and shimmering orange rays that cast lowly on the pass beneath. I blink to adjust, unconvinced that the sight before me isn't the product of a storybook, or a dream interwoven with the familiarity of my dad's favorite song. But all it takes is a final glance at Henry, and the rush of reverie he fills me with to prove that we're truly here. Cold air spills into the cab as I open the door, leaving it ajar as my stiff legs tread slowly on dirt and gravel. Only stopping when I've reached the wooden fencing marking the perimeter of the barren lookout. I stand on the lowest link, lifting myself for a better view.

The Sandia crests reduce Albuquerque to a glorious web of shimmers on the waning horizon—every trial and fortune I've weathered in its confines, fading into the coming night. With mountains between me and the years behind, I look up, admiring the vivid sky free of hindrance. Bright, isolated rays cut through the frigid air like divine spotlights. And through their warmth, I sense a curious, familiar urge to smile. One that doesn't belong to me.

But I act on it, nevertheless.

My cheeks swell, my lips splitting wide with authentic, unabridged rejoice. It doesn't falter as the sound of approaching footsteps slows to a halt beside me. Sensing the heat of his body, I turn my head to find blue-green irises reflecting the vibrant skyscape. His hands slide over the familiar denim concealing my middle, gaze lingering on my face as if the angelic sight in front of us is nothing by comparison.

"There she is..." Henry says, voice soft as the gentle wind.

It sweeps my loose hair in its pass, ruffling my fringe until nothing is concealing the way my eyes well. Henry leans close, pressing his lips to my own in a long, enduring mark of love. It vanquishes the trepidation with each lasting moment, and when we part, my smothering mask falls in tandem with a single tear. The former hits the world below to shatter into grains of dust, but the latter doesn't make it far, as Henry brushes his nose with mine before kissing the salty streak away.

Somehow, I lose *and* find myself in his embrace. Breathing in a tight lungful of thin air, I release it with the burden of expectation. Because in this moment, I'm safe. I'm freed.

I'm *me*.

Chapter 41

SIX MONTHS LATER

Early morning sunlight streams through the outstretched windows of *Marcy's*, dimming as I travel to the deepest corner of the bookstore. Pushing along a cart stacked to the brim with boxes containing new editions. My first stop: The magazine rack.

I know the placement of all of them by heart, which borders the task of restocking on mindless, if not for the extra time I'd been taking to sift through the latest dirty magazine issues as of the past couple of months. The usual bunch is fully available. *Playboy. Penthouse. Genesis. Hustler.* But *Wild Thang* is nowhere to be found.

It's been some time since Val and I dared to discuss the studio's endeavors. Though, the last time we had, she'd mentioned hearing word that it had fallen into foreclosure. The reason had never proved definite, despite rumors of Ruth's debts and R.J.'s ethical settlement. But that didn't stop the two of us from indulging in the speculation that it was an unforeseen effect of Valentina Amor and M.R.'s departures.

Having Val in thought brightens my gaze when I reach the local catalogues, seeing a familiar Latina clad in masterfully stitched undergarments on the cover of one in particular. Too proud to help myself, I set the stack of issues at the forefront of the display for all to see. The title of the publication hovering in bold lettering above Val's pretty head.

Bite Me: Women's Lingerie Catalog

Erica needed a name. And both of us happened to know a model who looks lovely in sexy underwear. Val's networking had paid off, making the startup as simple as it could be, and the investment proved worth it for all parties who'd contributed. I'd long since made back the portion I put in from my book advance. A thought that lights a spark in me as I finish stocking the rack, pushing aside the cart to finish out my morning shift.

When I retrieve my backpack from storage to make my way out, I stop before the adult section. Pulling a hardcover from my bag that I'd kept stored away for the sheer thrill of it. I hold it up to the shelf, eyeing the title's place among the stockpile of explicit literature.

Rosie Ginger's Erotic Collection

Lone Legacy Press had been more than pleased with my final submissions. Even showing encouragement when I asked to swap out M.R.'s babysitting account for Rosie Ginger's first-ever sapphic work of fiction. It was simply an advanced copy; distribution wouldn't push out for another several months. But come that time, my stories would grace the shelves of bookstores across the American Southwest just like this one.

"You were right, Dad. I was never lost." I quietly remark, trailing a finger down the chain around my neck until it finds his linked typewriter key. The red-marked "R" evokes a smile, which quickly breaks into a grimace when I drop the book back into the sanctity of my bag. "Just…promise me you'll never read this one, okay?"

I leave the bookstore after offering Marcy a warm goodbye. Satisfaction reigning brightly on my face upon stepping into the May sunlight, but I don't relish my fill quite yet.

After all, my big day was only getting started.

"Hey, Mrs. Fennick!" I greet the woman as I enter the apartment I share with her youngest son. Spotting him beside his mother, ogling several outfits laid out on the sofa.

"Hi, Rosie!" Her cheery welcome graces me, but Lewis hardly glances up.

"This one is too casual." He points to a pair of khakis matched with a polo shirt.

"No, it isn't. You're going to a birthday party." Mrs. Fennick adjusts her cat-eye glasses, inspecting the articles closer.

"*And* a ceremony." He laments, rubbing his chin in contemplation. "That's not even counting tonight."

"What's happening tonight?" His mother asks sweetly.

Lewis stiffens, eyes darting to me in the hopes I'll spare him.

I don't. Instead, I choke on a deprecating laugh while tossing my bag aside to enjoy the show. One that's sadly cut short as Mrs. Fennick finds the entryway clock.

"Oh, is that the time?" She smooths an unsteady hand over her pastel dress. "I'd better get going, your father will be home soon."

It pained me that she had to sneak around to visit her own child, but I knew the effort meant everything to Lewis. Perhaps someday, she'd be free from the same burden he'd managed to outrun.

"Alright, Mom. I'll see you soon." Lewis's shoulders rise as she presses a loud smooch to his cheek, staining it with a maroon tint.

The woman stops beside me to give my arm an affectionate squeeze. "Give Henry a big kiss for me, okay, Rosie?"

"I will," I promise as she exits. When we're alone, I raise a brow at Lewis. "You still need your mom to pick your outfits?"

"I wanted a professional opinion." He shoots back, giving me an incredulous once-over. "Are *you* wearing *that*?"

I follow his gaze. The privilege of financial stability had come with the freedom to experiment with clothing that wasn't all button-ups and navy skirts. Turns out, I was a faded, high-waisted jeans kind of girl. Having discovered what a match they made with sneakers and a fitted top, as I'm wearing now.

"What's wrong with it?" I ask playfully.

"Nothing, if you're going for the 'sexy sitcom mother' look."

I confidently brush aside some of my loose hair, styled in voluminous waves the way Val had taught me in our time living together. "I take that as a compliment."

The sound of an electronic *ding* interrupts us, drawing our focus to the bulky computer nestled in the corner of the living room.

"Another order." Lewis dons a proud smirk as the two of us approach the monitor. "They've been coming in all morning."

"I stocked the new catalogues at work; they looked great." I lean close to view the website Lewis created for *Bite Me*'s lingerie collection. Being a nerd sure pays off, as his jumping between part-time positions over the past months was nothing compared to the commissions he was bringing in from the convenience of our home. "You fax any of these to Erica yet?"

"Figured I could hand them off once we get there." He says, returning to his wardrobe selections on the sofa with an indecisive grumble.

I sigh impatiently. "You know, we have a big night ahead of us. I'll drag you out of this apartment naked if you don't choose."

"We've waited this long. Let's not get carried away with hours to go." His brow quirks at me in a hint that flushes my belly with anticipation. Then, he grabs a bundle of clothes off the cushions—the casual set.

"Love you, Lewis." I melodically call as he enters his bedroom.

"Love you more, brain whore."

"Twenty pages?" Erica's mouth hangs open as she flips through the orders.

"Oh, these are just the ones I could print." Lewis rubs the back of his neck, which burns red from our time outdoors. "I ran out of paper, but I'll fax the rest when we get more."

In the grassy courtyard of Erica's complex, balloons and party decorations litter the patch closest to her apartment. A *Happy 5th Birthday!* banner hangs from the window, flapping in the hot wind to intermix with the sound of laughing children.

Erica stacks the pages, chuckling in disbelief. "I can barely keep up with them anymore. I'm profiting more in a week than I used to in a year."

"Top brand in New Mexico, here you come," I say, watching with a grin as Mattie and his little friends play with the T-ball set Lewis and I had gifted him.

Her expression fades to a proud smile. "You know, at this rate, Mattie and I will be able to move out of here before too much longer."

"You could always find somewhere closer to us," Lewis suggests. "But if you visit all the time, steer clear of the furniture. Henry and Rosie don't know how to keep their dry humping in the bedroom."

"Watch it!" I shove him. "You shouldn't talk that way in front of Lizzy."

Erica narrows a look at me. "Who's Lizzy?"

I place a hand on my abdomen, glancing between the two. "Your niece."

My sister goes pale in the harsh sunlight, eyes flaring wide as they fall to my stomach.

Lewis, however, doesn't hold back a wise smirk. "Nice one."

I snort, doubling over to contain my hysterics. At this, Erica sighs in obvious relief.

"You should see your face." I tease her between heaving laughs, as if the concept was even a possibility. Which it wasn't...as of this afternoon, anyway.

"The point still stands," Lewis remarks. "At least Presley and I have decency."

I shrug. "Call it what you want. I know you'd rather douse your eyes with bleach than walk in to see your best friend's lips around Henry's—"

He clamps a firm hand over my mouth, pointing at me with a glare. "Finish that sentence, and I'll—*EW!*" Lewis retreats as I drag my tongue over his palm. He wipes it on his khakis. "Do you always drool this much?"

Too easy. "Ask your brother."

Erica chuffs, affectionately rolling her eyes. "You two…"

I wait for her to continue, but her gaze lands somewhere behind Lewis and me, her crossed arms going stiff as she loses any trace of joviality. My brows knit as I follow her focus, the sight leaving my body just as rigid. Chimes of nearby laughter bleed into the thumps of a heavy tempo. I only realize it belongs to my heartbeat after the empty seconds that follow leave us reactionless.

Standing there, at the edge of the complex, is Christine Ginger.

I blink a few times to make sure it's really her and not some apparition. Unconvinced by virtue of not seeing or hearing a trace of the woman since my departure from home. But any speculation that she's nothing but a cruel vision shatters when she starts toward us. Perilous flashes of Armageddon reach out to grip me, but a hand beats them to it. Whether Erica intertwines our fingers to steady me or herself, I'm unsure.

Christine stops a respectable distance from us. Her throat constricts with a swallow as she anxiously shifts her weight from foot to foot, ivory dress brushing the concrete walkway.

"Erica." The greeting comes gently, before her steely gaze shifts to me. "Rosie."

I fix my jaw to keep it from falling open—*Rosie*, not Mary-Rose.

Thankfully, Erica takes the lead. "What are you doing here?"

She interlocks shaky fingers, fidgeting with them as she speaks. "I know my grandson's birthday."

I feel Erica tense, no doubt at the label of *grandson*.

"How are the two of you doing?" Christine asks weakly.

"Good," Erica answers with no affect.

The woman pauses. "Rosie?"

For once, the sarcasm she's so used to hearing from me is nowhere to be found. "*Great.*"

"That's wonderful to hear." She says, and for a moment, I almost believe it.

It's only then that I *truly* study what's become of her. No wonder I'd almost mistaken this woman for a ghost. She seems frailer, more fragile—like a gust of wind could come by and blow her away in a single sweep.

"Momma!" Little footsteps permeate the standoff just as Mattie tugs at Erica's blouse. "Can we have more cake?"

Erica forces a smile, running fingers through his blonde hair. "Of course, baby. Give me a second?"

Christine fixates on the boy while raising a quaking hand to the cross around her neck. Her voice is so small, I barely catch it as she utters, "Is this Matthew?"

Mattie looks at the woman, then lifts his chin. "Who's that, Momma?"

Erica doesn't take her eyes off her son. "She's your grandma, Mattie."

My nephew gives no reaction. Why would he, when he's never known the meaning of the word?

"Go play with your friends," Erica tells him. "I'll be over soon."

Mattie obliges, rejoining his group of scattering classmates.

"He's beautiful." Christine watches him go before forcing her gaze back to Erica and me. "Does he…need anything? Do either of you?"

I can't hold my tongue any longer. "Why would that matter to you?"

"I just worry." She admits, tucking her lengthy cardigan tightly around her middle. "I know Erica receives donations, but if they don't cover everything—"

"I've stopped receiving them." Erica cuts her off, a hint of warranted pride in her tone. "I don't need them anymore."

"In the case that you did, your father's money is always there." Christine's eyes flicker to the front of the complex. "What's left of it, at least."

"What's left?" I ask, my blood heating for too many reasons. "It's allocated to us."

"Yes, it is." Her focus returns to Erica, her posture straightening. "The donations, were they ever put to a name?"

My sister stalls at the question. "No…"

"Good," Christine mutters, lowering her chin. "I was afraid you would refuse them if they had been."

Suddenly, the heat of New Mexico May has nothing on the cold prickle needling under my skin. I look to Erica, who appears just as stunned. She opens her mouth to speak—likely to *question*—then closes it just as curtly.

"Rosie," Christine addresses me like she hadn't rendered both of us speechless. "If you want to return to school, or use it however you see fit, your allocation is there, too."

My sister and I stare at the woman who brought us into this world, then raised us to fear it. Only now, we weren't the fearful ones. If anything in this picture of dubiety was clear, it was that.

"I hope today is special." She says, stealing a final glance at Mattie before finding the decency to retreat. "Whatever you girls decide, my door is open."

Erica and I watch, bemused, as Christine leaves us. Not a single word is uttered until she's out of sight. And even then, it doesn't fall from our lips.

"Holy fucking shit," Lewis remarks breathlessly.

It's then that I realize he'd bore witness to the entire thing. Not once had he been addressed or even looked at by Christine, who used to view him as a son. Apparently, some miracles weren't as apt to be granted as others.

Unable to construct much of a response, I voice the thought at the forefront of my mind. "What are we supposed to do?"

Erica lets out a heavy breath like she'd been holding it the entire time. "I think...we decide."

Something deep inside me—something the two of us share—attests that she isn't talking about our father's allocations.

How confounding those short minutes must've been for Christine Ginger. To have cast out your own blood for the gain of deliverance, only to look true freedom in the eyes after bearing the weight of it for too long. She may have been our mother at one point. By flesh, she still was. But she wasn't *a* mother. Perhaps someday, through trials and arduous mending of the maimed years she'd stolen from us, that could change. How could someone navigate such a responsibility? Achieve a task so impossible? Even I couldn't say.

But, for once, that wasn't my burden to shoulder.

Discussion of the matter ends there. As Erica hands out the second round of cake to Mattie's partygoers, Lewis grabs me by the arm.

"It's after one!" He exclaims, raising his watch for me to view.

"Shit—" I bite the swear.

Noticing our grievance, Erica waves us off from the serving table. "Go! Go! We're all set here."

I offer my sister a final thanks. Then supply Mattie a big hug and kiss goodbye, wishing him a parting happy birthday before Lewis and I rush off to the complex's parking lot.

An hour of traffic, boiling May heat, and shuffling through hurried bodies later, the two of us are sneaking through a vast auditorium at max capacity. The ceremony begins as we locate Val's parents, who generously saved us two seats. When we're settled down, I ignore the droning voice of the Dean giving his welcome monologue to search the sea of graduation caps, finding one topping a head of wavy black hair that frames a pretty face with bright, ruby red lips. I focus on her until she finally spots us in the crowd, hazel eyes lighting up in tandem with a wide, beautiful smile. I watch her momentarily debate maintaining decorum or waving at us in her excitement.

She waves.

And when valedictorian of her class, Valerie Ramona, walks the stage to give her speech, Lewis and I don't wait for her to get a single word in. We jump to our feet and cheer like fools.

"Just think, after this summer, you'll be ditching us for all the smarty-pants UNM Law friends you're going to make." I tease with a smirk.

"¡Embustera!" Val hushes me with a playful shove, our laughter overtopping the drive-in's powerful sound system.

After spending the remainder of the afternoon at Val's graduation party, she'd been more than enthused to join us for our planned movie night. Greer Garson and Laurence Olivier converse over rows upon rows of gathered vehicles—the one stationed behind us shaking from interior jostling. Shooting a glance at the Grand Safari from our place on the bench, the pride in my chest gives way to an uneasy tug somewhere deep.

It must show on my face well enough for Val to gently remark, "Hey, don't be scared. It's going to be wonderful."

With reluctance, I lift my gaze to hers. Finding the same compassion she'd so graciously offered over the past months. Hazel eyes that had borne witness to countless anxiety attacks, guided me through unsteady proceedings she understood with a passion, and welled with tears in my favor upon a no-contest plea.

Turns out, lying isn't so easy when you're doing it through reconstructed lips.

Footsteps punctuate our shared thought moments before the seat to my left is reclaimed.

"Did I miss anything?" Henry asks, handing me the popcorn he'd left to procure.

The cinema-lit glow on his features brightens my own. "Just me."

A grin stretches his handsome mouth as a denim-clad arm settles around me. I cuddle close, humming at the familiar scent of his jacket. Only now, *he's* the one sporting it after dark. Since I favored the article so much, he'd opted to gift me one of my own for my birthday in March. A lighter shade, fitted to my size, and topped with a red embroidered rose on the front. I trace a restless fingertip over the tight threads of such until the long-anticipated click of a car door draws me.

Clumsily, Lewis and Presley emerge from the Grand Safari. Both winded and fumbling to straighten their newly donned clothing. Too impatient to give him a moment of reprieve, I jump from the bench to snag Lewis by the hand. Pulling him far enough so my whispers reach him alone.

"How was it?" I demand, an expectant smile swelling my rosy cheeks.

Lewis, still dazed, takes enough pause to collect himself. Upon doing so, delight heats his face with a pink flush—matching the myriad of fresh love bites peeking from beneath his collar. "It was perfect."

The fact that Lewis held out this long for nobody's sake except mine was a mark of devotion even I struggled to comprehend. But regardless, I wasn't about to let him slip off without spilling all the details of his first official time.

"Come on," I deride his attempt at evasion. "I need specifics. What was the best part?"

His eyes drink me in before flickering somewhere behind. I can tell by the glint in them alone that they've settled on Presley. "He was."

Happiness and pride fill me to the brink of implosion, but it drains to a cold timidity with his following words.

"You'll see." He promises warmly, then leaves to rejoin his boyfriend with a fulfilled gait.

Expelling a rattled breath, I follow his lead to slide my hands over the shoulders of the only person in our group oblivious to tonight's significance. "Ready for a little privacy, babe?"

Henry glances up at me, brows quirking in suggestion. "After you, Angel Face."

Taking his hand, I guide him from the bench to the Grand Safari's rear door, catching a final glimpse of Val before our entry. Her gaze meets my own for a few unsteady moments, and something simmers behind her exterior that gives me enough pause to examine. If I didn't know any better, I would call it yearning. Mixed with a formidable, yet buried feeling that neither of us possessed the courage to exhume. But whatever it is, it doesn't linger. As the face of a lost love melts into that of an irreplaceable friend, admiration splits ruby lips into that perfect smile of hers.

An indistinguishable time later, my naked body lies writhing in the sanctity of the vehicle's spacious rear. Spreading my thighs wider, the head between them bobs in time with speedy licks.

"*Henry...*" I whine, tightening my grip on his blonde highlights. Hot pleasure courses as deep as his fingers, two of which slipping in and out of me in rapid thrusts. The penetration in combination with his skilled tongue threatens an impending release as I warn, "I'm close."

"Stay with me." He hushes sweetly. Using his unoccupied hand to take one of my own, he squeezes it assuringly before resuming his tonguing of my clit. Teasing it at the angle he's discovered to be the most sensitive in our months of exploration. A time of taking back what had been so cruelly stolen.

I have nobody but Henry to thank for finalizing my expanded collection of erotic stories in the wake of Armageddon. Day after day, week after week, we'd tiptoed through the minefield that was getting my mind and body to reaccept arousal. With it came fear, trepidation, and more than a few missteps that left me reeling in the fallout. On those wearing nights, he would hold me, caress me, and assure me that we would make it through together. Eventually, I was able to feel sexual longing without smoldering panic spoiling our endeavors. For a long time, I couldn't reach climax. And often found myself sick at the prospect of desiring a thing I used to live for.

But through it, I came to realize how much more there was to sex than reaching a momentary finish. And when he did gift me my first orgasm by the doing of someone I truly trusted, it didn't feel obligatory. It simply felt *right*. I learned what it meant to pleasure him, as well, and took so much joy in doing so. Joy that reduced these mountainous leaps to idle paces. Until there was only one essential step we'd yet to take.

I come undone when he sucks my clit between eager lips, his fingers digging deep as I pulse around them with rhythmic squeezes. I keep hold of his hand until the waves pass, leaving me to relax as he climbs to reach my mouth with his own. The kiss lingers with the taste of my slick arousal, which he happily shares with every stroke of his tongue along mine. The mix of sensations renders me burning for another release, but I keep the fire contained long enough to gaze up at him upon our parting.

"You okay?" He asks, brushing sweaty hair from my face.

I nod, glancing between our naked bodies at the feel of a hot drag. His erection lies stiffly against my leg, giving persistent throbs the longer my eyes consume it. An intrinsic longing nestles within me at the sight. Akin to the delight that came with bringing him to his end, just so I could watch him finish on my hand, or face, or—my favorite—in my mouth. But *this* urge runs far deeper. An indissoluble ache in my heart and loins that I knew one single act could remedy.

Henry follows my gaze, then gives a nervous chuckle. "I can hold out. Want me to give you another?"

"That sounds nice..." Years of anticipation guide my hand to the door pocket. Pulling a wrapped sheet, I offer it. "But why don't we try this?"

He stares at the condom for a long while, disbelief thinning his tone. "Really?"

"Yes," I say without a shred of doubt. Sliding the foil into his palm before running mine over the taut muscles of his chest. "I'm ready."

"Obviously, I want to. But..." His focus sweeps over the red interior of the vehicle. "Here? Just feels a little unceremonious."

"It's perfect." Brushing the longer ends of his hair back, I peer up at him with every ounce of certainty I feel. "*You're* perfect. I trust you, Henry."

The affection that softens his face threatens to end me before his body has the chance. "Good...because I love you, Rosie."

I breathlessly observe as he tears the wrapping and carefully rolls the condom over his hard length. Taking position between my spread legs, he shoots me a final glance, which I return with a single nod of assurance. Henry presses his tip to my prepared entrance. Then, he moves.

My eyes flare wide at the sensation. Inch after burning inch, I'm stretched and filled beyond anything I've ever attempted at my own hand. I wince, gritting my teeth until the deep pain of first insertion slows to its inevitable halt. When it does, I release the heavy breath I'd been storing, then look between us. Finding his hips flush against my own. Time stops as I meet his blue-green gaze. It's flooded with worry, awaiting the confirmation that I'm okay.

I give it to him in the form of a smile so beaming, a triumphant laugh escapes with it.

Henry returns the expression, then smothers my grin with a desperate kiss.

Our first time is spent with him on top of me, enriched with hushed declarations of love and wild gasps of pleasure. He guides me through the pain, and when it's gone, I realize that the feeling of him inside me is something I never want to live another day without. There's no fear. There's no shame. There's only love.

Real love.

So I savor it. Letting the euphoria of our shared passion, on its own, pull me into rapture. While it had once commanded my every impulse, I don't lose myself in the chase for release. I lose myself in Henry's eyes. Speaking louder than a thousand words ever could. They offer a promise with every perfect meet of our hips. One that casts away any doubt that he would ever, *ever* let me go. A vow that transcends flesh and the mindless thrill of orgasms.

But when I have one anyway, I don't complain.

Acknowledgements

First and flirty-most, I want to extend my deepest gratitude to every reader who took a chance on my debut novel. Whether you were in it for the humor, drama, queer awakenings, or sexy '90s bad boys, you've reached the end of Rosie's story. My dream, from blank page to finished product, has always been to deliver a book that will transport those looking to escape from our world into one that I created. And if you've made it this far, it means you've helped me achieve my dream. With every word I've written, and every word I've yet to write, I thank you.

I want to thank everyone in my inner circle brave enough to give *Bite Me* a shot before the rest of the world. Mackenzie Nicole, for being the first person to both experience Rosie's story and aid me in making it what it became, I'm honored to know such an incredible fellow author. José Alvarez, for always holding me to standards I never thought I could achieve, and assuring that Val's Spanish wasn't completely unintelligible. Brittany Gillis (aka, Princess Magnificent Pants, inspiration to all), for instructing me on proper craft terminology and single-handedly sparing me from the wrath of the crochet community. And Laura Jarek, for being my (and Henry's) biggest fan from the jump—you're right, if I were doing anything else with my life, I'd be making a mistake.

I would also like to thank Albuquerque, New Mexico, and every wonderful soul I met during my stay. Even though my time within your limits was short, I could see that you are so much more than flawed presumptions and fictitious kingpins. You are filled with history, culture, and those who are proud to call you home. From the lights of the State Fair to the top of the Sandia Mountains, I saw your beauty clear as the desert day. And now, my readers will, too.

Finally, and most of all, I want to thank my father for believing in me, especially when I didn't believe in myself. From the bottom of my heart, this wouldn't have been possible without you. Just...promise me you'll never read this one, okay?

About the Author

A.J. Louise is a storyteller and retired Sergeant in the Army National Guard residing in Southwest Missouri, where she grew up. As a lover of both cinema and literature, she prides herself on writing captivating stories that give pages in a book the glitz and splendor so often limited to the silver screen. Unbound by any single genre, her character-driven tales capture everything from the tragicomic realities of growing up, to conquering personal wars, to finding the light in life's haziest days. When she isn't telling her stories and developing characters, she's thinking about her stories and characters on a farm with cows, and her orange cat named Toast.

For more information, visit her website at **ajlouisebooks.com**.

www.ingramcontent.com/pod-product-compliance
Lightning Source LLC
LaVergne TN
LVHW091613070526
838199LV00044B/781